## PRAISE FOR THE FALL AWAY SERIES

### *Rival*

"Witty dialogue, great chemistry, and a great plot make *Rival* a book you don't want to end. Combined with the sexy Madoc Caruthers, *Rival* becomes a book you want to read again."

—#1 *New York Times* bestselling author Colleen Hoover

### *Bully*

"*Bully* was a wonderfully addictive read that kept my heart racing from start to finish. I could not put it down! 5 stars!!"

—Aestas Book Blog

"A heated and passionate novel, full of feeling and intensity that will appeal to the reader seeking an emotional rush."     —IndieReader

# Rival

A
*Fall Away*
Novel

## PENELOPE DOUGLAS

NEW AMERICAN LIBRARY

New American Library
Published by the Penguin Group
Penguin Group (USA) LLC, 375 Hudson Street,
New York, New York 10014

USA | Canada | UK | Ireland | Australia | New Zealand | India | South Africa | China
penguin.com
A Penguin Random House Company

First published by New American Library,
a division of Penguin Group (USA) LLC

First Printing, September 2014

LIBRARY OF CONGRESS CATALOGING-IN-PUBLICATION DATA:
Douglas, Penelope (Novelist)
Rival: a fall away novel/Penelope Douglas.
p. cm.—(The fall away series)
ISBN 978-0-451-47242-7 (paperback)
1. Love stories. I. Title.
PS3604.O93236R58 2014
813'.6—dc23            2014016910

Printed in the United States of America
1  3  5  7  9  10  8  6  4  2

Set in Janson Text

# RIVAL PLAYLIST

Music inspires the development of my characters and inspires my scenes. Enjoy!

| | |
|---|---|
| "Far from Home" | Five Finger Death Punch |
| "All I Want Is You" | U2 |
| "Numb" | Linkin Park |
| "Headstrong" | Trapt |
| "21 Guns" | Green Day |
| "Why Don't You Get a Job?" | The Offspring |
| "La La" | Ashlee Simpson |
| "All I Need" | Method Man |
| "What I Got" | Sublime |
| "Whore" | In This Moment |
| "Say Something" | A Great Big World |
| "Schism" | Tool |
| "Rockstar" | Nickelback |
| "You're Gonna Go Far, Kid" | The Offspring |
| "Sail" | AWOLNATION |
| "Inside the Fire" | Disturbed |
| "Team" | Lorde |
| "Silhouettes" | Smile Empty Soul |
| "Paradise City" | Guns N' Roses |

*This novel is dedicated to my husband.*
*Honey, I know life without me would be unbearable,*
*but life without you would be unbearable*
*AND boring.*


*To Hubs . . .*
*There are so many things throughout the years,*
*Things you have done that have brought me to tears.*
*You refuse to replace the empty toilet paper roll,*
*Or to load the dishwasher with your messy ice-cream bowl.*
*I pick up your socks, and you never have to vacuum,*
*And I toss your empty Coke cans, which you leave in every room.*
*But then I think of all the wonderful things that you do,*
*Like stocking the zombie weaponry with guns that are new.*
*We have machetes, daggers, water purifiers, and radios,*
*And the zombies will never get our stash of SpaghettiOs.*
*Your skill with back rubs and burgers is no small feat,*
*And I love that Zebra Cakes are your favorite treat.*
*You put up with my drama and inappropriate humor,*
*And I know you wish my* Fifty Shades *obsession was just a rumor.*
*I promise to always untie you as soon as I'm through,*
*Because, baby, there's no one in the world as loving as you.*

## ACKNOWLEDGMENTS

To my husband, who is my biggest supporter and always takes care of me. He is my partner and brightens my day with his wonderful sense of humor.

To my friends Bekke, Marilyn, Tee Tate, Ing, and Lisa—you have been constantly supportive with advice, feedback, words of encouragement, and humor. Thank you for sticking by my side.

To my agent, Jane Dystel—thank you for always being available and working so hard for me. You're the only person who asks if I'm eating or sleeping enough, and I love how you look out for me.

To my editor, Kerry Donovan—you have been great holding my hand and making me happy during this new adventure. I am so grateful to have someone easy to talk to that cares as much about the characters as I do.

To all of the bloggers, reviewers, and readers—what a crazy ride we've had together, and it's not over yet! With your love and support, I've been able to devote myself to writing and am so incredibly happy to be able to do this every day! Thank you, thank you, thank you for your positive comments, reviews, and promotion. You have honored me, and I hope that I continue to write stories you adore.

# Rival

# FALLON

There were people I liked and people I didn't like. People I loved and people I hated.

But there was only one person I loved to hate.

"Why are you doing this?" I heard a whiny female voice ask as I rounded the hall to sophomore P.E.

I immediately halted, locking eyes on a red-faced Tatum Brandt as she faced off with my douchebag stepbrother, Madoc Caruthers, and his friend Jared Trent. They stood in the hallway next to the lockers with flat expressions, looking bored, while she clutched her backpack straps for security.

"You barked at me yesterday," she continued, pinching her eyebrows together at Jared as Madoc smirked from behind him. "And then all of your friends followed along. It's been forever, Jared. When are you going to stop? Why are you doing this?"

I sucked in a long breath and completed my usual awesome combination of eye-roll-head-shake.

I really hated turning corners. I hated closed doors. I hated not seeing the path ahead.

Corner #1: *Your dad and I are getting divorced.*

Corner #2: *We're moving. Again.*

Corner #3: *I'm getting married. Again.*

Corner #952: *I don't really like you or my husband or his son, so I'm going to take fifteen vacations a year by myself!*

Okay, my mom never really said that, but I'm damn good at interpreting shit. And corners sucked.

I hung back and stuck my hands into the pockets of my skinny jeans, waiting to see what this girl would do. Would she finally grow some balls, or at least take the little ones these idiots had? I kept hoping she would step up to the challenge, and she always disappointed me.

Tatum Brandt was a wimp.

I didn't know much about her. Only that everyone called her Tate, except Madoc and Jared; she was a rocker on the outside, but played it safe on the inside; and she was pretty. Like cheerleader pretty.

Long blond hair? Totally.

Big blue eyes? Absolutely.

Long legs, full lips, and big boobs? Even at sixteen.

She was the perfect package, and if I were my stepbrother, I wouldn't have any problem sticking my tongue into her mouth. Hell, I might do it anyway.

I chewed the corner of my lip, thinking about it. Yeah, I could be a lesbian. Maybe. If I wanted.

No, never mind.

The point is . . . why Madoc and Jared tormented her rather than tried to date her was a mystery to me.

But for some reason I was interested. From the start of freshman year, they had both bullied her. They spread rumors, harassed her, and did everything they could to make her unhappy. They pushed, and she retreated time and again. It was starting to piss me off so much that I was about to go knock their heads together to defend her.

Except I barely knew her. And Tatum didn't know me at all. I stayed so far off the radar that sonar couldn't pick me up.

"Why?" Jared answered her question with a question and jutted into her space with a cocky swagger. "Because you stink, Tatum." He scrunched up his nose in mock disgust. "You smell . . . like a dog."

Tate straightened immediately, and the tears in her eyes finally spilled over.

*Kick him in the balls, bitch!*

Exhaling a furious breath, I pushed my glasses back up the bridge of my nose. It's what I did before I braced myself.

She shook her head. "You don't even remember what today is, do you?" She folded her trembling lips between her teeth and looked down at the ground.

And without even seeing her eyes, I knew what was there. Despair. Loss. Loneliness.

Without looking at him again, she turned around and walked off.

It would've been easy to hit him. To toss an insult back at him. And while I despised her weakness, I understood one thing that I hadn't before. Jared was an ass, but he was an ass who could hurt her.

She was in love with him.

Crossing my arms over my chest, I walked over to the lockers where Jared and Madoc stood staring after Tate.

Madoc spoke up behind him. "What did that mean? What's today?"

Jared shrugged off the question. "I don't know what she was talking about."

"It's April fourteenth," I piped up over Madoc's shoulder, causing him to spin around. "That mean anything to you, Shit-for-Brains?" I directed at Jared.

Madoc raised a dark blond eyebrow at me, a hint of a smile in his eyes. Jared twisted his head only enough so that I could see the side of his face.

"April fourteenth?" he whispered and then blinked long and hard. "Shit," he murmured.

And Madoc reared back a hair as Jared slammed the palm of his hand into the nearest locker door.

"What the hell?" Madoc scowled.

Jared ran his hands down his face and then shook his head. "Nothing. Never mind," he growled. "I'm going to Geometry." Stuffing his fists into his pockets, he stalked off down the hall, leaving Madoc and me.

Between my stepbrother and his friend, I respected his friend more. They were both Grade A assholes, but at least Jared didn't care what people thought of him. He stalked around like a weird cross between a jock and a goth. Popular and foreboding. Dark but extremely coveted.

Madoc, on the other hand, cared what everyone thought. Our parents. The principal. And most of the student body. He loved being loved, and he hated his association with me.

As sophomores they were already starting to wield power that was going to be out of control by the time they reached senior year.

"Wow, your friend is a loser," I teased, sliding my hands into the back pockets of my jeans.

Madoc zeroed in on me with his playful half-smile and relaxed eyes. "So are your frien—" he started, then stopped. "Oh, that's right. You don't have any friends."

"Don't need 'em," I shot back. "I travel faster on my own. I'm going places. You know that."

"Yeah, you're going places. Just stop at the dry cleaners on your way, Fallon. I need my shirts picked up." He smoothed an arrogant hand over his navy Abercrombie button-down. With his medium-wash boot-cut jeans, black Paracord bracelet, and styled dark blond hair, Madoc dressed to impress. Girls flocked to him because he looked good in clothes, could talk the ears off an elephant, and loved to play. For all intents and purposes, he was a fun guy.

And he always made me feel small.

I talked a lot of shit, but truth be told, it was more for my ears than anyone else's. Madoc was designer. I was Target. He was Godiva. I was Snickers. And as far as he was concerned, he was entitled, and I was the freeloading daughter of the gold-digging whore who had snagged his father.

Madoc thought I was dirt under his shoe. *Screw him.*

I gave his outfit a condescending once-over. "Your shirts—which are super stylish, let me remind you. The gay community would be proud."

"You could get nice things, too. My dad pays your mom enough for her services, after all."

"Nice things? Like the miniskirts you date?" I challenged. Time to educate the little shit. "Most guys, Madoc, like something different. You know why you want to see me in 'nice,' skimpy things? Because the more I show, the less I'm hiding. I scare you."

He shook his head. "Nada, little sister."

*Little* . . . I was only two months younger than him. He said shit like that to piss me off.

"I'm not your little sister." I took a step forward. "And I do have friends. And plenty of guys interested. They like how I look. I don't subscribe to you and our snotty parents' stand—"

"Wow, I'm bored," he cut me off with a sigh. "Your life doesn't interest me, Fallon. Holiday dinners and once in a while around the house. Those are the only times I want to run in to you."

I tipped my chin up, trying not to give anything away. It didn't hurt. Not his words or his opinion of me. There was no ache in my throat that dropped down into my stomach and twisted the ever-present knots tighter. What he said didn't matter. I liked who I was. No one told me how to dress, how to behave, what clubs to join . . . I made my own decisions. Madoc was a puppet. A drone.

*I'm free.*

When I said nothing, he started walking backward away from me. "The parents are out for the night. I'm having a party. Stay out of the way. Maybe hide out in the servants' quarters where you belong."

I watched him go, knowing I wouldn't listen.

I would wish that I had.

# CHAPTER 1

## MADOC

*2 years later*

"Seriously?" I exclaimed. "Could she move any slower?" I asked Jared as I sat in the backseat of his girlfriend's G8 with my hands locked on top of my head.

Tate twisted around in the driver's seat, her eyes sharp like she wanted to drive a knife right through my skull. "I'm heading around a sharp turn at nearly fifty miles an hour on an unstable dirt road!" she yelled. "This isn't even a real race. It's practice. I told you that already!" Every muscle in her face was tight as she chewed me out.

I dropped my head back and let out a sigh. Jared sat in front of me with his elbow on the door and his head in his hand.

It was Saturday afternoon, a week before Tate's first real race at our local, makeshift track—the Loop—and we'd been on Route Five for the last three hours. Every time the little twerp downshifted too soon or didn't hit the gas fast enough, Jared kept quiet—but not me.

He didn't want to hurt his girlfriend's feelings, but I didn't care. Why tiptoe around her? I wasn't trying to get in her pants.

Not anymore, anyway.

Tate and Jared had spent most of high school hating each other. Battling with words and antics in the longest-running game of foreplay I'd ever seen. Now they were all up in each other's shit like Romeo and Juliet. The porno version.

Jared turned his head but not enough to meet my eyes. "Get out," he ordered.

"What?" I blurted, my eyes widening. "But . . . but . . ." I stuttered, catching sight of Tate's triumphant smile in the rearview mirror.

"But nothing," Jared barked. "Go get your car. She can race *you*."

The zing of adrenaline shot through me at the prospect of some real excitement. Tate could definitely race a chick who had no idea what she was doing, but she still had a lot to learn and some balls to grow.

*Enter me.* I wanted to smile, but I didn't. Instead, I just rolled my eyes. "Well, that'll be boring."

"Oh, you're so funny," she mocked, gripping the steering wheel even tighter. "You make a great twelve-year-old girl when you whine."

I opened the back door. "Speaking of whining . . . want to make a bet on who'll be crying by the end of the day?"

"You will," she answered.

"Not."

She grabbed a package of travel tissues and threw them at me. "Here. Just in case."

"Oh, I see you keep a ready stock," I retorted. "Because you cry so much, right?"

She jerked around. *"Tais-toi! Je te détes—"*

"What?" I interrupted her. "What was that? I'm hot, and you love me? Jared, did you know she had feelings—"

"Stop it!" he bellowed, shutting the both of us up. "Goddamn it, you two." He threw his hands up in the air, looking between us like we were misbehaving children.

Tate and I were both silent for a moment. Then when she snorted, I couldn't help but let out a laugh, too.

"Madoc?" Jared's teeth were practically glued together. I could hear the tension in his voice. "Out. Now."

I grabbed my cell off the seat and did as I was told, only because I knew my best friend had had enough.

I'd been trying to bait Tate all day by making jokes and distracting Jared. She was finally racing a real opponent, and even though Jared and I had been working with her, we knew things went wrong out there on the track. All the time. But Tate insisted that she could handle it.

And what Tate wants, Tate gets. Jared was whipped worse than cream when it came to that girl.

I walked back down the track to the driveway leading in to it. My silver GTO sat along the side of the road, and I dug in my jeans for my keys with one hand while I ran the back of my hand across my forehead with the other.

It was early June, and everything was already so miserable. The heat wasn't bad, but the damn humidity made it worse. My mom had wanted me to come to New Orleans for the summer, and I gave her a big, fat hell-to-the-no.

Yeah, I love sweating my balls off while her new husband tries to teach me shrimping in the Gulf.

*Nope.*

I loved my mom, but the idea of having the house to myself all summer while my dad stayed at his apartment in Chicago was, no doubt, a much better prospect.

My hand tingled with a vibration, and I looked down at my phone. *Speak of the devil.*

"Hey, what's up?" I asked my dad as I came up on the side of my car.

"Madoc. Glad you answered. Are you home?" He sounded unusually concerned.

"No. I was about to head there soon, though. Why?"

My dad was hardly ever around. He kept an apartment in Chicago. since his big legal cases kept him working long hours. While often absent, he was easy to get along with.

I liked him. Didn't love him, though.

My stepmom had been AWOL for a year. Traveling, visiting friends. I hated her.

And I had a stepsister . . . somewhere.

The only person I loved at home was Addie, our housekeeper. She made sure I ate my vegetables, and she signed my permission slips for school. She was my family.

"Addie called this morning," he explained. "Fallon showed up today." My breath lodged in my throat, and I nearly dropped my phone.

*Fallon?*

Putting my palm down on the hood of my car, I put my head down and tried to stop grinding my teeth.

My stepsister was home. Why? Why now?

"So?" I spat out. "What does that have to do with me?"

"Addie packed you a bag." He ignored my question. "I talked to Jared's mom, and you're going to stay with them for a few weeks until my schedule frees up. I'll come home then and get this sorted out."

*Excuse me?* It felt like the phone would crack under my fingers as I clenched it.

"What? Why?" I yelled, breathing hard. "Why can't I stay at my own house?"

Since when did she get the run of things? So she was home. Big deal! Send her on her way then. Why did I have to be sent away?

"You know why," my dad answered, his deep tone threatening. "Don't go home, Madoc."

And he hung up.

I stayed planted where I stood, studying the reflection of the trees on the hood of my car. I had been told to go to Jared's house, where Addie would bring me clothes, and not to go home until further notice.

And why?

I shut my eyes and shook my head. I knew why.

My stepsister was home, and our parents knew everything. Everything that happened two years ago.

But it wasn't her home. It never was. It's been my home for eighteen years. She lived there for a while after our parents got married and then disappeared a couple of years ago.

I'd woken up one morning, and she was gone. No good-bye, no note, and no communication since then. The parents knew where she was but not me. I wasn't allowed to know her whereabouts.

Not that I fucking cared anyway.

But I damn well wanted to be in my own house for the summer.

Two hours later I was sitting in Jared's living room with his half brother, Jax, biding my time until their mom stopped watching us like a hawk. The more I sat, the more anxious I got to go find some distractions. Jared had a ton of liquor up in his room that I'd brought over from my house, and it was time to start my Saturday night warm-up. Jax was slouched on the couch playing video games, and Jared had left to get tattooed.

"This is not how you handle it, Jason," I heard Katherine Trent whisper-yell from the kitchen.

My eyebrows shot up. *Jason?* That was my father's name.

She crossed the doorway as she paced, talking on the phone.

She calls my dad Jason? Not weird, I guess. That's his name. It just seemed weird. Not many people got away with calling my father by his first name. It was usually "Mr. Caruthers" or "sir."

Getting up, I inched into the dining room, which sat right off the kitchen.

"This is your son," I heard her say. "You need to come home and deal with this." I stuck my hands in my pockets and leaned back against the wall right by the door leading to the kitchen. She was quiet for a while except for the sounds of dishes clattering. She must've been unloading the dishwasher.

"No," she answered. "One week. Tops. I love Madoc, but this is your family, and they need you. You're not getting off the hook. I already have two teenage boys. You know what they do when I try to impose a curfew? They laugh at me." I fought between smiling out of amusement and clenching my fists in irritation.

"I'm here," she continued. "I want to help, but he needs you!" Her whispers were futile. It was impossible to try to order my father around and be quiet about it.

I shot a look to Jax and noticed that he'd stopped his video game and was watching me with a quirked eyebrow.

Shaking his head, he joked, "I haven't obeyed a curfew in my entire life. She's cute about it, though. I love that woman."

Jax was Jared's half-brother. They had the same father but different mothers, and Jax had spent most of his life either with their sadistic dad or in foster homes. Late last fall, my father had helped Katherine get Jax out of foster care and into her home. Jared and Jax's father was in jail, and everyone wanted the brothers together.

Especially the brothers.

And now that Jared, who'd been my best friend all through high school, had found his soul mate and love of his life, he wasn't around as much as he used to be. So Jax and I had grown closer.

"Come on." I jerked my chin at him. "I'm grabbing a bottle from Jared's room, and then we're going out."

"I want to see your biggest balls," I ordered in the deepest voice I could muster. My eyes were narrowed, and I had to press my teeth together to not laugh.

Tate's back straightened, and she slowly spun around with her chin down and eyes up. It reminded me of how my mother looked at me when I had pissed in the pool as a kid.

"Wow, I haven't heard that one before." She widened her eyes at me. "Well, sir, we have some quite heavy ones, but they all take two fingers and a thumb. Are you that skilled?" She had an expression on her face like we were talking about homework, but I could see the smile playing at the corner of her mouth.

"I'm so skilled," I teased, my tongue suddenly too big for my mouth. "You'd be jealous of what I could do to that ball."

She rolled her eyes and approached the counter. Tate had been working at the bowling alley since last fall. It was almost a court-ordered requirement that she get a job. Well, not quite. It probably would've been court-ordered if Jared had pressed charges. This five-foot-seven, one-hundred-twenty-pound bit of nothing had taken a crowbar to her boyfriend's car in one of her famous violent fits. It was pretty nasty and pretty awesome. The video was on YouTube and had practically started a feminist movement. People did their own renditions of it and even put it to music. They titled it *Who's the Boss Now?*, since Jared's car was a Mustang Boss 302.

It was all a misunderstanding, though, and Tate paid for the damages. She grew up. Jared and I grew up. And we were all friends.

Of course, they were sleeping together. I got no such perks.

"Madoc, have you been drinking?" Tate put her palms on the counter and looked at me like a mom.

"What a stupid question."

*Of course I've been drinking.* It's like she didn't even know me.

Jerking her head up, she looked over to the lanes behind me, and I was afraid her big blue eyes would actually fall out of her head.

"You got Jax drunk, too!" she accused, clearly pissed now.

I twisted around to see what she was looking at, stumbling when my foot got caught in the legs of the stool next to me. I let a holler rip from my throat.

"Whooooo!" I shouted, holding up the bottle of Jack Daniel's in the air when I saw what Tate saw.

A crowd of people was gathered in front of one lane, laughing and watching Jax run and do slip and slides down a bowling path. "Hell, yeah!"

The bottle was torn out of my fingers, and I turned to see Tate stuff it under the counter, pressing her angry lips together and scowling.

"Why is the whiskey gone?!" I imitated Captain Jack Sparrow and pounded my fist on the counter.

Tate stomped down the aisle toward the door leading out to the lanes. "You're in deep shit when I get over this counter," she whisper-yelled at me.

"You love me. You know you do!" I laughed and sprinted away through the maze of tables and chairs around the concession stand to where Jax played. A couple of other guys had joined in and flew down the lanes, much to the delight of the Saturday night crowd. At this hour, there weren't too many families out and about, and the only people not entertained were the single dudes who spent their older years lamenting their beer bellies and how lucky they were to escape marriage. They just watched and shook their heads.

*"Fallon's home. Don't go home."*

I swallowed down the whiskey that kept creeping back up and

threw my head back. "Woohoo!" I bellowed, before pounding down the light-colored hardwood floor, leaping onto the lane on my belly and sliding down the alleyway.

My heart pounded, and excitement bubbled in my chest. *Holy shit!* These lanes were crazy slippery, and I just laughed, not caring that Tate was pissed at me or that Jared's fist would leave a permanent mark on my face for messing around at his girlfriend's work. All I cared about was what got me from one moment to the next.

*I can't go home.*

The crowd cheered and yelled behind me, some of them jumping up and down. The only way I could tell was because I felt the vibrations under me. And when I rolled to a stop, my legs dangling into the next lane, I just lay there, wondering. Not about Fallon. Not even about whether I was too drunk to drive home at this point.

I wondered out loud, "How the hell am I going to get up?"

These lanes were slippery. Duh. Couldn't stand up, or I'd slip. Shit.

"Madoc! Get up!" I could hear Tate's bark from somewhere near me.

*Madoc. Get up. The sun's up. You have to leave.*

"Madoc. Get. Up!" Tate shouted again.

I snapped to. "It's okay," I grunted. "I'm sorry, Tate. You know I love you, right?" I jerked to a sitting position with a hiccup. Then I looked up to see her walking on the median between the lanes.

Like a boss.

She put her hands on her hips, a stern set to her eyebrows. "Madoc, I work here."

I winced, not liking the disappointment in her voice. I always craved Tate's respect.

"Sorry, babe." I tried standing up, but I only slipped again, a deep ache settling on the side of my ass. "I already said sorry, didn't I?"

She squatted down and wrapped her arms around one of mine, hauling me up. "What's wrong with you? You never drink unless you're at a party."

I lodged one foot in the gutter and wobbled until Tate pulled me closer to her and I was able to set the other foot on the median.

"Nothing's wrong with me." I gave a half-smile. "I'm a joker, Tate. I'm . . ." I waved my hand in the air. "Just a . . . joke—a joker," I rushed to add.

She continued to hold me, but I could feel her fingers ease up underneath the hem of my short-sleeved T-shirt.

"Madoc, you're not a joke." Her eyes were serious again but softer this time.

*You don't know what I am.*

I held her eyes, wanting to tell her everything. Wanting my friend—someone—to see the real me. Jared and Jax were good friends, but guys didn't want to hear that shit, and we weren't that observant. Tate knew something was wrong, and I didn't know how to tell her. I just wanted her to know that underneath it all, I wasn't a good guy.

"I do stupid things, Tate. That's what I do. I'm good at it." I reached up slowly and tucked the few stray hairs from her ponytail behind her ear, lowering my voice to a near whisper. "My father knows it. *She* knows it." I dropped my eyes and then looked back up. "You know it, too, don't you?"

She didn't answer. Only studied me, the wheels in her head turning.

My hand fell to her cheek, and I remembered all the times that she had reminded me of Fallon. I stroked Tate's cheek with my thumb, wishing she'd yell at me. Wishing she didn't care about me. How much easier it would be to know that I didn't have anything real in my life.

I held her sweet, unknowing face and leaned in closer, smelling her barely-there perfume as I brought my lips closer.

"Madoc?" she asked, her voice confused as she watched me.

Tilting my head down, I planted a soft kiss on her forehead and then leaned back slowly.

Her eyebrows were pinched together in worry as she stared at me. "Are you okay?"

*No.*

*Well, sometimes.*

*Okay, yes. Most of the time, I guess.*

*Just not at night.*

"Wow." I took a deep breath and smiled. "I hope you know that that didn't mean anything," I joked. "I mean, I love you. Just not like that. More like a sister." I burst into laughter and hunched over, barely finishing the sentence as I closed my eyes and held onto my stomach.

"I don't get the joke," Tate scolded.

A high-pitched whistle pierced the air, and Tate and I looked up.

"What the hell's going on?" Jared's big and angry daddy voice ripped through the bowling alley, making my ears ache.

But as I turned around to face him, I accidentally stepped back onto the slippery lane.

"Oh, shit!" My breath caught as I slid, and I stupidly kept my weight on Tate, which was too much for her. Backward I fell and into my lap she stumbled. We slammed to the floor, hitting the wood hard. I'd probably bruised every damn inch of my ass, but Tate was cool. She landed on me. That was cool for me, too.

But when I looked over at my best friend standing at the start of the lane, looking at us with murder in his eyes, I pushed Tate off me in disgust.

"Dude, she slipped me whiskey and tried to date-rape me!" I pointed at Tate. "She keeps it under the counter. Go look!"

Tate growled and crawled back up to the median, her messy ponytail hanging by a prayer.

"Jax!" Jared yelled to the lane at my right where Jax was crawling back up the lane. "And you." Jared's eyes shot bullets at me. "Get in my car now."

"Ooooh, I think he wants to give you a spanking," I singsonged to Tate as she stomped down the median to her boyfriend.

"Shut up, doofus," she spat back.

# CHAPTER 2

# FALLON

"*Was that your first kiss?*" *he asks, pulling his head back to look at me. I keep my gaze down and clutch the kitchen counter behind me. This feels wrong. He's pressing my back into the countertop, and I can't move. It hurts.*

Just look at him, *I will myself.* Look up, you idiot! Tell him to back off. He doesn't see you. He's a user. He makes you feel dirty.

"*Come here.*" *He grabs for my face, and I cringe.* "*Let me show you how to use that tongue.*"

*This feels wrong.*

"Fallon?" The soft, feathery voice broke through my dream. "Fallon, are you up?"

I heard a knock.

"I'm coming in," she announced.

I opened my eyes, blinking away the fog of sleep from my brain. I couldn't move. My head felt separated from my body, and my arms and legs were molded to the bed, as if a ten-ton weight sat on my back. My brain was active, but my body was still sound asleep.

"Fallon," a voice sang out to me. "I made you poached eggs. Your favorite."

I smiled, curling my toes and clenching my fists to wake them up. "With toast to dip?" I called from underneath my pillow.

"White toast, because multigrain is for pussies," Addie dead-panned, and I remembered I'd told her those very same words about four years ago when my mom married Jason Caruthers and we came to live here.

I kicked the covers off my legs and sat up, laughing. "I missed you, girlfriend. You're one of the only people in the world I don't want to cut."

Addie, the housekeeper and someone who'd acted more like a mother to me than my own, was also one of the only people that I didn't have hang-ups about.

She walked into the room, carefully maneuvering a tray full of all the things I hadn't eaten in years: poached eggs, croissants, freshly squeezed orange juice, a fruit salad with strawberries, blueberries and yogurt. And real butter!

Okay—so I hadn't tasted it yet. But if I knew Addie, it was real.

As she set the tray over my legs, I tucked my hair behind my ears and grabbed my glasses off the bedside table.

"I thought you said you were too cool for hipster glasses," she reminded me.

I dipped a wedge of toast in egg yolk. "Turns out I had a lot of opinions back then. Shit changes, Addie." I smirked at her happily as I took a bite, salivating more as the warm saltiness of the yolk and butter hit my tongue. "But apparently not your cooking! Damn, girl. I missed this."

Addie is far from a girl in looks but more so than anyone I know in personality. She's not only a valuable housekeeper, but she proved to be the lady of the manor that Mr. Caruthers needed. She took care of things the way my mother didn't. Of course, Addie and Mr. Caruthers weren't sleeping together. She was a good twenty years older than him. But . . . she took care of everything. The house, the grounds, his social calendar outside of work. She anticipated his needs, and she was the only person he'd never fire. Seriously. She could call him a fuck-up, and he'd just roll his eyes. She made herself invaluable, and because of it, she called the shots in this house.

She also took care of Madoc. That's why I needed her.

"And I missed you," she replied, picking up my clothes from the floor.

I cut a piece of egg and put it on my toast. "Come on. Don't do that. I'm a woman now. I can clean up after myself."

I hadn't been paying my own bills, but for all intents and purposes, I'd been taking care of myself completely for two years. My mother had deposited me at boarding school, and my dad didn't micromanage. When I got sick, I dragged my ass to the doctor. When I needed clothes, I shopped. When it was laundry day, I studied next to the washing machines. No one told me which movies to see, how often to eat vegetables, or when to get my hair trimmed. I took care of it.

"You are a woman. A very beautiful one at that." She smiled, and I felt a warm hum in my chest. "A few more tattoos, but you took the piercings out, I see. I liked the ones through your septum and lip."

"Yeah, the school I went to didn't. You gotta know when to fold 'em and know when to hold 'em."

I wouldn't exactly say I was going through a phase the last time Addie had seen me, but I'd definitely loaded up on multiple forms of self-expression. I had had a piercing through my septum—a small ring—and another through the side of my lip and a stud in my tongue. I hadn't kept any of them, though. St. Joseph's, my boarding school, didn't allow "unorthodox" piercings, and they limited you to two in each ear. I also had five in my left ear—my industrial was one piercing, but it took two holes—and I had six in my right ear, counting my tragus, two in my lobe, and three going up the inside ridge of my ear. The school had ordered me to take those out, too.

But when Mom didn't answer her phone to deal with their complaints, I finally told them to "fuck off." When they called my dad, he gave them a hefty donation . . . and then told them to fuck off.

"You and Madoc have both grown up so . . ." She trailed off, and I stopped chewing. "I'm sorry," she finished, looking away from me.

If someone had tried to take my heart right then, they would have needed both hands to hold it. I swallowed the heavy lump of food in my mouth, and took a deep breath.

"Why are you sorry?" I shrugged.

I knew why.

She knew why.

Madoc and I hadn't been alone in this house after all. Everyone knew what had happened.

"You don't have to worry," she assured me, sitting on the edge of the bed. "Like I told you last night. He's not here, and he won't be back until your visit is over."

*No.*

"You think I have a problem with Madoc, Addie?" I snickered. "Madoc and I are fine. I'm fine. We took our idiotic rivalry too far, but we were kids. I want to move on." I kept my tone light, and my shoulders relaxed. Nothing in my body language was going to give me away.

"Well, Jason thinks it's unsafe. He says you're welcome to stay for as long as you like, though. Madoc won't be here."

This was why I needed Addie. I could talk her into getting Madoc home. I just couldn't be too obvious about it.

"I'll only be here for a week or so." I took a sip of my juice and set it back down. "I'm going to Northwestern in the fall, but I'll be staying with my dad in the city for the rest of the summer until school starts. Just wanted to visit before I start the next phase."

She looked at me the way moms on TV looked at their daughters. The kind of look that makes you feel like you've got a thing or two to learn, because honey, you're just a kid, and I'm smarter.

"You wanted to face him." She nodded, her blue eyes locked with mine. "To resolve things."

Resolve things? No. Face him? Yes.

"It's cool." I pushed the tray down the bed and climbed off. "I'm going for a run. Do they still keep that trail trimmed around the quarry?"

"As far as I know."

I walked across the newly decorated room to the walk-in closet where I'd thrown my duffel bag yesterday when I got here.

"Fallon? Do you usually sleep in your underwear and a T-shirt too short to cover your ass?" Addie asked with a laugh in her voice.

"Yeah, why?"

I heard nothing for a few seconds as I bent over to get my bag. "Good thing Madoc's not here after all then," she mumbled in an amused tone and left me alone.

I got dressed, looking around my bedroom in the light of day. My old room with new décor.

When I'd gotten in yesterday, Addie had walked me up to my room, but the interior was very different than the way I'd left it. My skating posters were gone, my furniture had been replaced, and my red walls were now a cream color.

Cream? Yeah, gag.

I'd had a whole wall lined with bumper stickers. It now featured some impersonal mass-produced photographs of the Eiffel Tower and French cobblestone streets.

My bedding was a light pink, and my dressers and bed were now white.

My graphing table with my drawings, my shelves with my Lego robots, and my DVDs and CDs were gone. I can't say I thought about any of that shit over the last two years, but I felt like I wanted to cry as soon as I entered the room yesterday. Maybe it was that I'd assumed they'd still be here, or maybe I was thrown off that my entire life could be thrown away so easily.

"Your mom redecorated shortly after you left," Addie had explained.

Of course she did.

I allowed myself about two seconds to lament all of the hours I'd spent skating on boards that were now in a trash dump and building with precious Legos that were now rotting in the dirt somewhere.

And then I swallowed the ache in my throat and moved on. Screw it.

My room now was mature and even a little sexy. I still liked boys' clothes and wild forms of expression, but my mom didn't suck at decorating. There were no floral motifs anywhere, and the room was designed for a grown-up. The soft pink tones of the bedding and draperies, the innocence of the romantic furniture, and the black-and-white photographs in vivid frames made me feel like a woman.

I kind of liked it.

And I still kind of wanted to kill her for throwing away all of my stuff, too.

The best part about my mom marrying Jason Caruthers was that his house sat in the Seven Hills Valley, a huge gated community—if you considered it a "community" when your nearest neighbor was a half mile down the road in either direction.

Rich shits liked their country houses, their space, and their trophy wives. Even if they used none of them. When I thought of my stepfather, Richard Gere in *Pretty Woman* always came to mind. You know the dude who reserves the penthouse suite but can't stand heights, so why the fuck did he reserve the penthouse suite?

Anyway, that was Jason Caruthers. He bought houses he didn't live in, cars he didn't use, and he married women he didn't live with. Why?

I asked myself that all the time. Maybe he was bored. Maybe he was looking for something that he never seemed to find.

Or maybe he was just a rich shit.

To be fair, my mom was the same. Patricia Fallon married my father, Ciaran Pierce, eighteen years ago. Two days later, I was born. Four years later, they divorced, and my mother took me—her meal ticket—on all of her gold-digging adventures. She married an entrepreneur who lost his business and a police captain whose work turned out not to be glamorous enough for my mother.

But through him, she met her present husband and in him my mother found exactly what she was looking for: money and prestige.

Sure, my father had it, too. In certain circles. I had never truly wanted for anything. But my father lived outside of the law—far outside of the law—and to protect his family, he kept us hidden and quiet. Not really the glamorous life my mother was looking for.

But despite her selfish decisions, I liked where she ended up. I liked it here. I always had.

The estates all sat tucked away beyond large driveways and dense little neighborhoods of trees. I had loved running—or even walking—along the quiet, secluded roads, but what I anticipated more now was the way the community connected into the Mines of Spain recreational area that featured narrow woodsy trails and deep quarries. The sandstone all around, the greenery, and the perfect blue sky overhead made this the ideal place to get lost.

Sweat poured down my neck as I pounded the shit out of the dirt under my feet. Tool's "Schism" played through my earbuds while I zoned out on the trail, and I had to remind myself to keep my eyes up. My father hated that I ran alone. He hated that I ran in quiet, unpopulated areas. I could hear his voice in my head: *Keep your head up and protection on you!*

He had ordered a crap-load of running shorts with gun holsters attached to the back, but I refused to wear them. If he wanted me to attract less attention, that was the wrong way to go about it.

*If you run in your underwear, someone will get the wrong idea,* he'd said. *And then I have to hurt people. You know I like to do that as little as possible.*

I didn't run in my underwear. But some spandex running shorts and a sports bra? Fuck it, it was hot.

So we had compromised. He had a bracelet designed that featured a small pocket knife and some pepper spray. It looked like some sick, twisted charm bracelet, but it made him feel better to know I wore it whenever I went out running.

Scanning the trail ahead of me—because I listen to my daddy—I noticed a young woman, about my age, standing between the trail and the pond, looking out over the water. I saw her lips were turned down, and she sniffled. That's when I noticed the shake to her chin. Slowing to a walk, I took a quick inventory. She was dressed like me, running shorts and sports bra, and from what I could see, she wasn't hurt. There were no other runners or hikers. She just stood there, eyes narrowed, watching the soft ripple on the water.

"Nice tunes," I yelled over the noise from the iPod strapped to her arm.

She jerked her head toward me and immediately wiped the corner of her eye. "What?" She pulled out her ear buds.

"I said 'nice tunes,'" I repeated, hearing Guns N' Roses' "Paradise City" spitting out of her ear buds.

She choked out a laugh, her flushed face brightening a little. "I love the oldies." She reached out her hand. "Hi, I'm Tate."

"Fallon." I reached out and shook her hand.

She nodded and looked away, trying to covertly wipe away the rest of the tears.

*Tate.* Wait . . . blond hair, long legs, big boobs . . .

"You're Tatum Brandt," I remembered. "Shelburne High?"

"Yeah." She draped the cord to her ear buds around her neck. "I'm sorry. I don't think I remember you."

"It's okay. I left at the end of sophomore year."

"Oh, where'd you go?" She looked me straight in the eye as we spoke.

"Boarding school out east."

Her eyebrows shot up. "Boarding school? How was that?"

"Catholic. Very Catholic."

She shook her head and smiled as if she couldn't believe what I'd told her. Or maybe she thought it was ludicrous. Didn't people ship their unwanted kids off in her world? No? Weird.

The wind blew through the trail, causing the leaves to rustle, and the breeze was a welcome comfort to my hot and wet skin.

"So are you just back for the summer before college or for good?" she asked, sitting down on the ground and looking up at me. I took that as an invitation and sat down, too.

"Just a week or so. I'm heading to Chicago for school. You?"

She looked down, losing her smile. "I was supposed to go to Columbia. Not now, though."

"Why?"

Columbia was a great school. I would've applied, but my father didn't want me so close to Boston. The farther away from him the safer, he'd said.

"My dad is having some . . . issues." I could see her damp lashes as she leaned back on her hands and continued to study the pond in front of us. "For a long time, apparently. I think it's best to stick close to home."

"It must be hard to give up Columbia," I offered.

She stuck her bottom lip out and shook her head. "Nope. I didn't think twice about it, actually. When someone you love needs you, you suck it up. I'm just upset that he didn't tell me. He's had two heart attacks, and I only found out through hospital bills I wasn't supposed to see."

She acted like it wasn't even a choice. Like it was so easy. *My dad is sick. I stay.* I was jealous of her resolve.

"Wow, I'm sorry." She smiled and sat up, dusting off her hands. "I bet you're glad you stopped to say hi."

"It's okay. Where do you think you'll go to school now?" I looked over at her and saw that she had a little tattoo on the back of her neck. Down at the curve where it met her shoulder. It wasn't that big, but I could make out flames bursting out of a black lantern.

"Well, I got into Northwestern," she offered. "It's a good option for my degree, and it's only about an hour from here. The more I think about it, the more excited I get."

I nodded. "Well, that's where I'm going."

She raised her eyebrows, surprised. "Well, well . . . you like old-school GNR, you're going to Northwestern, you've got some nice ink"—she motioned to the Out of Order tattoo I had written behind my ear at my hairline—"and you jog. Tell me you're into science, and I may have found my hetero soul mate."

"I'm majoring in Mechanical Engineering," I singsonged, hoping that was close enough.

She put her fist out to bump me and smiled. "Close enough."

Her smiles were a lot more frequent than the last time I'd seen her. She must've either gotten Thing 1 and Thing 2 to leave her alone, or she'd put them in their place.

"So," she started, standing up and brushing off her butt. "My friend is having a party tomorrow night. You should come. He has no problem with pretty girls crashing. You may have to forfeit your underwear at the door, but I'll protect you."

I stood up, too. "He sounds like a hell-raiser."

"He tries." She shrugged, but I could see the proud little smile underneath the gesture. She grabbed my phone out of my hand and punched in some numbers. "Okay, I just called myself. Now you have my number, so text if you're interested. I'll shoot you the address and time."

"Whose party is it?" I asked, taking my phone back.

"It's at Madoc Caruthers's house."

I closed my mouth and swallowed at the mention of his name.

She continued. "He requires that you wear a bikini, but if you kick him in the balls, he'll shut up." She hooded her eyes in an apology. "He's one of my best friends. It just takes some time getting used to him," she explained.

*Best friends? Huh?*

My breathing turned shallow. Madoc was supposed to be having a party tomorrow night?

She backed away, getting ready to leave. "See you tomorrow, I hope!"

And then she was gone, while I stood there, shifting my gaze left to right, searching for I-don't-know-what. Madoc was friends with Tatum Brandt?

How the hell did that happen?

*"I like that metal in your mouth. I heard a tongue piercing can be all kinds of fun for things other than kissing." He grips my hair, breathing into my mouth. "So are you really a bad girl or just playing at one? Show me."*

I'm not sure what woke me up first. The nausea rolling like

thunder through my stomach or the high that was flooding my nerves with excitement.

Nausea and excitement. Sickness and thrill. Why did I feel both at the same time?

I knew the queasiness was from the dream.

But the excitement? The thrill?

And that's when I noticed what had woken me up. The flow of air in the room had changed. It was now filtering out into the hall. My heart beat faster, and my belly tingled with butterflies. I tensed my muscles in response, because the elation flowing through them was too much.

My bedroom door was open!

I snapped my eyes open and bolted upright in bed, my heart lodging in my throat as I tried to take a breath.

A dark figure, much bigger than I remembered, stood in the doorway. I almost screamed, but I clamped my mouth shut and swallowed.

I knew who it was, and I definitely wasn't scared of him.

"Madoc," I fumed. "Get out."

# CHAPTER 3

## MADOC

I leaned against the door frame, bringing the bottle of beer to my lips.

She was right. I should get out. *Bad fucking idea to stay, dude.*

But for some reason, I just had to see for myself.

I don't why I didn't believe it. My dad had told me, and Addie confirmed it, but I just couldn't swallow the fact that Fallon Pierce was back in town after so long.

I'd nursed a nasty hangover this morning, thanks to her, and then driven home after I knew everyone would be in bed. There had been no plan to come to her room, and I had no plan to enter, but I was too damn curious. What was she like now? How had she changed? And there were some answers I needed, whether I liked it or not.

She reached over and grabbed her black-rimmed glasses off the nightstand. The moon was under cover tonight, so I couldn't see shit. Only her form.

"So you're really back." I pushed off the door frame and sauntered toward the end of the bed.

"You're not supposed to be here. Addie said you were staying with friends."

*What the fuck?*

They were right. She *was* afraid of me. But why? What the hell had I ever done to her?

I squeezed the green bottle in my hand and tried to make her out in the darkness. She wore a dark blue T-shirt with some white swirly writing I couldn't read, and her hair was all over the place. She used to have piercings, but I couldn't see anything right now.

"This is my father's house." I spoke low and straightened my back. "And someday all this shit will be mine, Fallon. That bed you sleep in, along with everything else under this roof."

"Not me, Madoc. You don't own me."

"Yeah." I brushed her off. "Been there. Done that. Got the T-shirt. Thanks."

"Get out," she ordered, her tone hard.

I took another sip of my beer. "The thing is, Fallon . . . I told you before to lock the door if you wanted me to stay out. Funny thing is . . ." I leaned in. "You. Never. Did."

In one swift movement she whipped off her covers and stood up on the bed. Charging to the end, she slapped me across the face before I even knew what was happening.

I almost laughed. *Hell, yeah.*

My body stayed in place, but my head had twisted to the side with the blow, and I closed my eyes out of reflex. The sting started as a few little needles under the surface but exploded and spread like electricity. I kept my eyes shut for a few seconds longer than necessary, savoring the rush.

With the bed elevating her, she stood about six inches higher than me, and I turned my head back to her slowly, welcoming whatever she had.

She scowled down at me. "I was sixteen years old and too stupid to keep you off me," she spat. "Little did I know that they have toothbrushes bigger than you. And I've definitely had better than you in the past two years, so count on the door being locked from now on."

Sometimes I wore smiles but didn't feel them. Sometimes I felt them and didn't wear them. I didn't want her to know how much I craved this. I bit my bottom lip.

She spun around, heading back up the bed, and I reached out and pulled her ankle out from underneath her. She crashed down onto the mattress, landing on her belly, and I quickly came down onto her back, whispering in her ear.

"Do you think I'd even touch you now? You know what I used to call you? Pussy-on-the-Premises. You were convenient when I needed to blow a load, Fallon."

She whipped her head around to look at me but couldn't twist far enough with my weight on her back.

"And don't think I ever thought it was more than that, either, Madoc. I was bored, and it was cute to see you brag about your skill. I've never laughed so hard." I could hear the smile in her voice. "But I know better now," she finished.

"Yeah?" I asked. "Spreading yourself around like your mother? You were right, Fallon. You sure are going places." I pushed off the bed and watched her flip over and sit up. It was then I noticed what she was wearing. A T-shirt and bikini underwear.

*Shit.* I blinked long and hard.

My dick jolted against my basketball shorts, and I clenched a fist, forcing control. "But," I continued, "don't overestimate yourself, baby. You can't get me kicked out of my own house. I live here. Not you."

Her chest rose and fell hard, and the anger in her eyes brought back everything I lived for two years ago. Her facial piercings were gone, and I wished she still had them, but her hair was beautiful chaos. The way it always looked at night. She still wore her sexy glasses, and I couldn't help thinking about those strong legs.

I'd been there.

And her temper? Yeah, the Irish in her was no lie.

"Madoc?"

I sucked in a breath and turned around to see Hannah standing in the doorway in her bikini.

"The Jacuzzi's ready," she said, hands on her hips.

I looked at Fallon, still sitting on the bed and her eyes going round at seeing my date.

I smiled.

"Stay," I told her in a relaxed voice. "Eat the food. Use the pool. And then get a fucking life of your own when you leave."

# CHAPTER 4

# FALLON

I knew exactly how I felt about Madoc. And I knew why I felt that way. I hated him. I hated what he did to me. But why in the hell did he hate me? I scrubbed my face, going through my morning rituals, while I thought about him. Madoc had been rude last night. Volatile. He clearly despised me. That wasn't part of the plan.

We had left things unfinished, but what was his problem? He got what he wanted, didn't he?

Why was he so angry?

I dried my face and threw on my glasses, heading downstairs as I replayed his words from last night.

*"Do you think I'd even touch you now? You know what I used to call you? Pussy-on-the-Premises. You were convenient when I needed to blow a load."*

He was never that cruel. Not even before we started—

A loud scream echoed through the long corridor heading to the stairs, and I stopped.

"Madoc, put me down!" Addie's voice rang from downstairs

somewhere. I crossed my arms over my chest, realizing I was still in my tank top with no bra, and Madoc was still in the house. But I quickly dropped them again.

He's still here. *Good.* This was where he needed to be, and now I wouldn't have to work Addie to get him back home.

I tipped my chin down, straightened my shoulders, and headed downstairs. Entering the kitchen, I saw Madoc standing behind Addie and reaching over her shoulder to dip his spoon into the batter she was mixing. His easy smile that always reached his eyes stopped me short, and I narrowed my eyes.

*Stop smiling,* I mentally ordered him. I narrowed my eyes even more so that my eyebrows were probably touching.

He flipped the spoon upside down and stuffed the chocolate-looking goo into his mouth as Addie tried to snatch it back. He twisted away, and she tried to swat him on the head, but they were both laughing.

"Don't double-dip, you little brat! I taught you better than that." She shook her big wooden spoon at him, flinging drops of batter onto her white shirt despite the apron she wore.

Madoc winked at her and walked to the refrigerator, silver spoon still hanging out of his mouth—go figure—and grabbed a Gatorade.

My gaze lingered on the huge tattoo across his back, stretching from shoulder to shoulder.

And my heart missed a beat. *Was that my name?* But I blinked and shook off the ridiculous idea. *No.* The tattoo said "Fallen." They had messed up the "e" by inking it to look like flames.

It was a good-looking tattoo, though, and I had to stop myself from dwelling on how it made him hotter. Tattoos made everyone hotter.

My mother—when I spoke to her—was known to comment on how I'm going to look at eighty with tattoos.

I'm going to look awesome.

His jeans hung low without a belt, and he didn't have a shirt on as if he just woke up and forgot to finish getting dressed. But who was I to talk? I was standing there in my sleep shorts and tank top, looking a hell of a lot more indecent. My hair was everywhere, spread around my face and down my back in knots and tangles.

He was fresh and bright, and I was wilted.

"Fallon!" Addie exclaimed, and I blinked. "You're up." She wasn't fooling anyone with the nervous edge to her voice.

Madoc faced away from me, but I noticed his arm freeze for two ticks as he took a swig of the Gatorade. He recovered quickly, though.

"Yeah," I drawled out. "It's hard to sleep with the commotion going on down here."

Madoc twisted his head to face me and eyed me over his shoulder with an arched brow. He looked annoyed.

His gaze slowly dropped, taking in my appearance or maybe just trying to make me uncomfortable, but my cheeks immediately warmed anyway. He scaled down my chest, over my stomach until he reached my bare toes, and then came right back up to meet my eyes, disgust clear in his blue depths.

The same flare to his nostrils as last night was there, but his gaze was flat. I clenched my teeth to force myself to breathe more slowly. I couldn't get upset with the way he looked down on me. I'd trained myself to not get upset.

Madoc was always calm, after all. So calm all the damn time growing up. He didn't shout or show his anger until he'd had enough. And you never knew exactly when that was going to be. That was the scary part about him.

"Fallon, Madoc surprised me this morning," Addie jumped in to explain. "But he's heading back out after breakfast, right?" she asked Madoc, prompting him with raised eyebrows.

He looked to her and back at me, mischief and pleasure evident in his expression.

He shook his head. "Nah," he said, brushing off Addie's concern as if he'd just told her he didn't want any dessert. "Fallon and I talked last night. We're cool." He looked over at me, his eyes squinting up in a smile. "I have a hell of a summer planned, and this is a big house. Right, Fallon? We'll play nice or stay out of each other's way."

He nodded as he spoke and looked to Addie with the same carefree, innocent, wide-eyed bullshit I've seen him use a million times.

This is why Madoc was going to be a great lawyer like his dad. Working people wasn't just about the words you spoke. It was about body language, tone, and timing. Keep your voice natural, your body relaxed, and distract them with a change of subject as soon as possible.

*Here it comes in three, two, one . . .*

"Come on," he nudged Addie. "It's fine."

He came up to stand behind her at the counter and reached around and placed his arm across her chest, hugging her close but with his eyes dead set on me. "Just finish my chocolate pancakes. I'm fucking starving."

"Madoc!" she whisper-yelled, scolding him but failing to hide her smile.

And that was it. He'd won.

Or so he thought.

I cleared my throat. "Yeah, Madoc's right, Addie. I have no problem with it. I told you that yesterday." I saw Madoc raise his eyebrows. I bet he thought I was going to fight him on this. "And anyway, I'm gone in a week. I only came to eat the food and use the pool."

I let the sarcasm drip slowly from my tone and kept my eyes locked to his. I'd missed playing with him more than I wanted to admit.

"Where are you going?" he asked, leaning on his elbows over the wide granite island.

"Chicago. I'm starting Northwestern in the fall. You?"

"Notre Dame," he sighed, thinning his lips with a hint of resignation to his voice.

No, not resignation exactly. Acceptance. As if he'd lost a battle.

Notre Dame was the family school. Madoc's father, aunts and uncles, and grandfather had all gone there. Madoc didn't dislike the school, but I couldn't tell if he actually liked it, either. It was hard to tell if he had any dreams of his own aside from what his father had planned for him.

"Oh, that's right!" Addie dumped the spoon into the bowl and brushed her hands on her apron. "I completely forgot to give you your graduation presents." She walked across the kitchen and grabbed two "somethings" out of a cabinet.

"Fallon, I didn't know that you'd be here, but I'd gotten you one anyway to ship to you. Here." She handed both Madoc and me what looked like lanterns. They were black plastic on the bottom with a glass capsule on the top half. The bottom featured five rows of the alphabet.

"A cryptex!" I smiled at her while Madoc looked at his like it was an alien baby.

"But . . ." He pinched his eyebrows together. "You know I just wanted to see you in a bikini," he told Addie.

"Oh, put a cork in it." She waved her hand.

"What is this?" His eyebrows were still pinched together while he studied the puzzle case.

"It's a Puzzle Pod Cryptex," Addie explained. "You have to solve the riddle that I have taped to the bottom, and dial the five-letter answer to open the pod. Then you can retrieve the present inside.

Madoc read his out loud. "'At night they come without being

fetched, and by day they are lost without being stolen. What are they?'" His eyes shot up to pin Addie. "Seriously?"

He threw back his arm, raising the cryptex high above his head, when Addie reached out and grabbed him.

"No, don't you dare!" she yelled, while he mock-scowled at her. "You're not breaking it open! Use your brain."

"You know I suck at stuff like this." But then he started dialing letters, guessing at the answer.

I read mine to myself. "What gets wetter the more it dries?"

*Please.* I snickered and dialed in "towel." The cryptex opened, and I pulled out a gift card to a skate shop I used to frequent in town.

"Thanks, Addie," I chirped, not wanting to tell her that I no longer skated.

I looked over at Madoc, who was still working his puzzle with an eyebrow arched. He was struggling, and the more he struggled the dumber he was going to feel. Walking over, I took the cryptex out of his hands, my breath catching for only a moment when my fingers brushed his.

I looked at the puzzle and spoke quietly as I dialed. "'At night they come without being fetched, and by day they are lost without being stolen.'" It clicked, and I met his soft eyes staring down at me, not the cryptex. "Stars," I said, almost in a whisper.

He wasn't breathing. The stern set to his eyes as he loomed over me reminded me of so many times I'd looked up at him, wanting things I was afraid to ask for.

But we were different now. I wanted only his pain, and judging from the girl he'd come home with last night, Madoc was still the same. A user.

I hooded my eyes, trying to appear bored, as I shoved the now-open cryptex back at him.

He took a deep breath and smiled, the intense concentration now gone. "Thank you." Then he turned to Addie. "See? We're getting along fine."

And he left through the sliding-glass doors leading to the vast patio and pool area with his gift card to the go-kart track.

I swallowed, trying to calm the windstorm in my stomach. "So that's it?" I asked Addie. "You're letting him stay, after all?"

"You said you were okay with it."

"I am," I rushed to add. "I'm just . . . I just don't want you to get in trouble with the boss."

She gave a half-smile and started pouring batter onto the griddle. "Do you know that Madoc started playing the piano again?" Her eyes stayed glued to her task.

"No," I responded, wondering about the change in subject. "His father must be thrilled."

Madoc had taken music lessons since he was five, specifically the piano. Jason Caruthers wanted his son proficient, but when Madoc turned fifteen—around the time my mom and I moved in—he realized that Daddy really just wanted him to perform. Something else for Mr. Caruthers to brag about and show off.

So Madoc had quit. He refused lessons and threatened to trash the piano if it wasn't moved out of sight. It was taken down to the basement where it sat with my half-pipe.

But I had always wondered . . .

Madoc did love to play. It was a release for him, or it seemed to be. He usually only practiced at required lessons, but he ran willingly to the piano when he was upset or really happy.

After he quit, he started doing stupid shit without that release anymore: hanging around that asswipe Jared Trent, bullying Tatum Brandt, breaking into the school to steal car parts, which no one knew about but me.

"Oh, I doubt his father knows," Addie continued. "Madoc still won't perform or take lessons. It's more of an in-the-dead-of-the-night thing when the whole house is asleep and no one can see or hear him." She stopped and looked up at me. "But I hear him. The light tinkling of the keys trails upstairs from the basement. It's very faint. Almost as if it's a ghost that can't decide whether to stay or go."

I thought of Madoc playing alone downstairs in the dead of night. What kind of songs did he play? Why did he do it?

And then I remembered the Madoc from last night. The one who'd insinuated that I was a freeloading slut.

And the rapid beat of my heart slowed to a dull thud.

"When did he start playing again?" I asked, looking out to the patio where he talked on his phone.

"Two years ago," she said softly. "The day you left."

# CHAPTER 5

# MADOC

Now I understood why Jared drowned himself in constant partying over Tate. Distractions were useful. If you had too much on your mind, then you could push your thoughts away with noise, liquor, and girls and keep moving forward at lightning speed. When my friend slowed down long enough to think, that's when he got into trouble. But eventually things worked out for them. He pushed her, and she started pushing back. He kept pushing, and she finally knocked him on his ass.

Fallon and I were a lot like them. Only I didn't love her, and she didn't love me. I was infatuated with her once—and loved that she let me take my pubescent urges out on her—but we weren't in love.

We were two people in a fucked-up family taking our cues from fucked-up parents.

And neither one of us knew how to do anything differently.

She stomped up to her room after pancakes, and I got ready for my party that was starting mid-afternoon but going 'til the next morning if I had anything to say about it.

I hoped that she'd show up, and at the same time I wanted her far away from me.

Fallon affected my body in weird ways.

*But only because she's different*, I told myself.

The last time I saw her she was sleeping on the leather couch in the theater room wearing only my T-shirt. She had twisted her lips up as she rubbed her nose in her sleep, and I remember thinking how much I couldn't stand her during the day but how much I wanted her when she put her forked tongue away at night.

Everyone at school thought she was a freak. They definitely thought she was a lesbian. And none of the guys thought she was hot.

Pretty? Sure. Even with the beanies that covered her head and the glasses that hid her eyes.

But not hot. Her piercings were scary to them, and her clothes were an embarrassment to any guy calling her his girlfriend.

Only I knew the truth. I'd seen her without the clothes—accidentally of course—and I knew what she covered up.

But that was two years ago. She wasn't sexy to me anymore.

Now she was lethal. Despite her pale Irish ancestry, her skin was golden with the most beautiful sprinkle of freckles across her nose and under her eyes. Her hair had been colored. Whereas before it was a dull, light brown, now it was about three different shades of brown with some modest chunks of blond blended in.

Her green eyes stood out more than I remembered, and it took clenching every muscle in my body this morning to look like I wasn't checking her out. Seeing her walk into the kitchen in her pj's, looking like she'd been blissfully fucked all night long, made me hot.

But what-the-fuck-ever. That ship between us sailed long ago, and there was no way she'd redeem the damage she'd done.

"No one drives." Addie pointed a finger at me as I set up my laptop and hauled my speakers outside onto the patio in preparation for the party.

I gave a halfhearted salute and shooed her away. "Go watch your reruns of *The L Word*."

She rolled her eyes before walking up the stairs to her bedroom on the third floor.

We weren't that pretentious that we kept the servants so far away from us. It was just that Addie was our only live-in, and the third floor was like an apartment in itself, complete with a kitchen, two bedrooms, two bathrooms, and a living area. It wasn't always like that, but my father had it converted for Addie when he realized he wouldn't let her go in his lifetime.

Fallon had taken off on her sport bike late this morning and had come back around one. Other than that, I hadn't seen her. And by three thirty, my house was slammed with just about everyone from my graduating class. Jax arrived early on, helping me set up and put out the food I had had delivered. I saw Jared's car parked on the side of the house, which meant Tate and he were in their room—the one I gave them so they could have "alone time" without her dad on their case.

Screw him. They're in love, and I loved them like family, so *mi casa es su casa*.

"Come on, dude. Hurry up," Jax pressed, carrying the tap for the keg while I grabbed the cups. Everyone filtered in and out of the house and in and out of the pool, enjoying the balmy afternoon.

"Jamison," I called out to Ben, who was in the pool hitting on Kendra Stevens. "Don't even think about it, man. I've already been there," I teased.

"Shut up, Madoc. You wish," she shot back, flying her hand across the water, trying to splash me.

"Hey, you were good, baby." I shrugged, following Jax to where the keg sat. "For a fat chick, you didn't sweat much."

Ben's eyes bugged out and Kendra screamed, "Madoc!" She kicked her skinny legs on the raft, spilling her drink.

I turned back to Jax, who was silently laughing so hard his face was turning red.

Pulling the seal off the keg and plugging in the nozzle, Jax poured about five bags of ice into the bucket around the keg, while I began pumping and pouring out the first few cups of foam.

"Hey, Madoc." Hannah and her friend Lexi came up to my side. "Jax." They nodded to him while he did no more than nod back.

"What's up, ladies?" I asked, taking a gulp of beer.

"Are you having a good summer, Madoc?" Hannah asked as if we hadn't just seen each other last night.

"Absolutely. You?"

"Pretty good so far," she answered and put her hands on her hips, making her chest more prominent. "How's your summer, Jax?"

"Couldn't be better," he mumbled, still loading ice.

"Oh, I think it's going to get a lot better." She trailed a hand down his back, and I saw him stiffen. Her meaning was clear. "See you around," she taunted, and she and Lexi walked off.

I laughed again under my breath and took another gulp.

Jax was getting a lot of attention at school, and with Jared off the market and me leaving for college, I was pretty confident Jax could handle the workload. It really depended on his mood, though. Sometimes he went all predator with a seek-and-destroy mentality. Other times he acted like he'd rather pull out his toenails than talk to certain girls.

"Resistance is futile, Jax." I slapped him on the back. "Don't let them scare you. Just enjoy the ride."

"Give me a break." He stood up straight, throwing the empty bag aside. "I've been having sex longer than you. I just don't like women like that." He stared off into the crowd across the pool. "They see me as a toy."

I handed him a beer. "And what's wrong with that?"

His jaw twitched, and his voice was quiet. "I just don't like it."

Jax wasn't scared of women by any means, and while I knew he'd had a hard life, I often wondered if I really knew what the hell "a hard life" was like. I'd caught on after more than a few clues that Jared and Jax's dad—who was currently in jail—had abused them physically. Jax more so, because he grew up with the man, whereas Jared had only spent one summer with him.

Jared's dark moods tended to be more noticeable and more volatile than his brother's. Jax had them, too, but we rarely saw them. He'd disappear for long hours, stay out half the night and still be up for school early the next day. The brothers both had a lot of anger, but they had different ways of dealing with it.

When you stepped on Jared's toes, you'd get punched in the gut. If you stepped on Jax's toes, he'd hack into the county database and issue a warrant for your arrest.

If you hit Jared, he'd pound you into the dirt.

No one hit Jax. He carried a knife.

"Now her on the other hand," Jax piped up, gesturing with the beer in his hand. "She looks like a librarian in a porno bookstore. Who the hell is that?"

I followed his gaze across the pool to the patio doors where Fallon had just appeared.

*Jesus Christ. What the hell?*

Fallon didn't show skin, she didn't wear makeup, and she didn't tame her hair.

So why the hell was she doing it now?

Tate walked up to her, taking her hands and smiling. Leading her over to one of the tables, she looked like she was introducing to her to Jared.

But Jared knew Fallon.

How did Tate?

# CHAPTER 6

# FALLON

"Now I'm in the twilight zone," I blurted out when Tate introduced me to her boyfriend. "You're dating *him*?" I asked her.

First the girl is friends with my stepbrother, and now she's sleeping with the other half of the Dipshit Duo.

I mean, I get it. Kind of.

Madoc has a winning personality, and he's hot. But Jared is just hot. At least Madoc has more going for him. Was she on a mission from God to reform assholes?

"Well," Tate snipped as she sat down at the table across from Jared, "she obviously hasn't slept with you if she's not a fan. That makes me feel better."

Jared slouched in the chair looking every bit like he owned the place. Dressed in knee-length black swim shorts, he ran his index finger across his lips as he studied me.

Not bothering to hide my feelings, I crossed my arms over my chest and tried not to snarl. "The last time I saw you two together, you were making her cry," I pointed out, looking at Jared and waiting.

I heard Tate snort to my right, and Jared's smile peeked out of his fingers.

"My personality has improved, Fallon. I'm not sure yours has, though. Care to start over?" He held out his hand, and I hesitated long enough to make everyone feel awkward.

But I took it.

What the hell? If the girl was happy—and she looked happy—then it was none of my business.

And they did make a good-looking couple. He still looked the same, only bigger, and she was dressed as cute as hell in red bikini bottoms and a short-sleeved black rash guard.

"Hey, man." Jared nodded behind me, and I felt pressure hitting my back. Not that someone was touching me.

"Tate," Madoc said behind me, "how do you know Fallon?"

"We met jogging yesterday. I invited her to the party. Hope you don't mind." Tate smiled at me and continued. "She never texted, though, so I didn't know for sure if she was coming. How do you guys know her? From school?"

"Fallon lives in my house," Madoc taunted me.

"Our parents are married," I explained and turned around to face Madoc. "But we're not close. Never have been."

Madoc's eyes narrowed as if he was trying to figure something out.

"I can see your bra, Fallon." He sighed and looked away, appearing bored.

I knew he could see my bra. I knew everyone could see it. It's what I wanted. I had no plans to go swimming, so I wore a black bra with elaborate straps stretching from the front of my torso to my back and down over my shoulders from my upper chest. It wasn't meant to be hidden, so I wore it with a loose, deep V-neck tank top that showed it off. Paired with my black shorts and flip-flops, I only accessorized with my earrings and glasses. I'd already gotten some appreciative looks, and I knew that that would piss off Madoc.

Whether or not he still wanted me, I knew he wouldn't want anyone else to have me.

"Does it bother you?" My lips twisted in a spiteful smile. "Tate, tell him it looks hot."

"I'd do her," she backed me up, and I heard Jared laugh behind me.

Madoc kept his eyes locked on mine in what I knew was a challenge. He wanted to play, but he also didn't want to admit it.

I leaned in to whisper to him, folding my arms across my chest. "You remember what happened the last time I showed up to one of your parties uninvited? You still think about it, don't you?"

The slow rise and fall of his chest quickened as he kept his mouth glued shut for once and pierced me with hard eyes.

"Come on, Madoc!" I shifted to my right and walked backward toward the pool. "It's a party. Don't be a pooper."

And I turned around giving him my back, not wanting to admit how much I wanted to see his face right now. With my heart in my throat, I threw my tank top over my head and let my shorts fall to the ground. I took a moment to breathe as the chatter around me ceased and partygoers stopped what they were doing to look at me in my underwear.

I was more covered than some of the other girls here. My bra was definitely made for sexiness, but it covered my breasts, and my hipster underwear was black lace. Yeah, I was more covered, yet I was the indecent one, because I wore lingerie.

My hands shook. *What am I doing?*

I didn't want to make a spectacle of myself. I wore the outfit to get his attention, not everyone else's. But it was a necessary step if I wanted him to react the same way he did two years ago when I showed up to his party. I wanted him angry and out of his mind. I wanted to trap him.

"Tate." I looked behind me, avoiding Madoc's eyes. "Get your ass in the pool. Let's talk Northwestern."

Her eyebrows shot up, and then she blinked as if unsure how to respond. "Um, okay." And she pushed out of her chair, heading for me as I dove in.

Tate and I didn't really swim. We just caroused and laughed, while once in a while someone would cannonball into the pool or some idiot would let their boyfriend throw them in. I refused to search for Madoc, but I knew he was around. I caught sight of his ridiculously preppy gray-and-black plaid board shorts and immediately averted my eyes.

Okay, so they weren't that ridiculous. Madoc made things work that others couldn't. I remembered how much I hated his attire two years ago. Safe. Conformist. From the Gap.

But I found out that they were part of a façade that he adopted. When the clothes came off, so did Madoc's mask. At night when he'd hang out in just jeans and nothing else, it was like I was seeing an entirely different guy.

Strong. Powerful. Mine.

Apparently others had seen his good side, too, if he could count Tatum Brandt as a friend. As far as I could tell, she was ambitious and levelheaded.

And although her boyfriend and Madoc's best friend could go piss up a tree as far as I was concerned, I had to admit that he seemed to have grown up. He had some nice ink, a gorgeous tree tattooed on his back, covering almost the entire area. My tattoos were smaller, but I had more. We might even have a thing or two in common now.

As much as I wanted to know Jared and Tate's story, I was more and more satisfied as the night wore on that he deserved her. He didn't say one wrong word to her, or talk to any other girls, and always touched her when they were close. An arm over her shoulder, a hand at her back, a kiss on the top of her head.

And these people were Madoc's best friends. They were people that didn't make me cringe or despise being around them.

After I'd toweled off, I put my clothes back on and poured myself a beer from the keg, while Jared and Tate joined Madoc and some blonde over at the fire pit.

The sun had set and while it wasn't chilly, there was a nice breeze coming through the trees. The party was still loud and still busy, but people were spreading out. Some went into the house to watch movies or play video games, while others filtered out onto the grounds. I was sure there were several bedrooms already occupied, as well.

"So how does Madoc have a sister?" A deep, velvety voice came up to my side.

I tipped my head up from the tap and did a double-take, my mouth falling open.

*Holy crap.*

The guy—a young one, too—was entirely too beautiful for words. Who the hell . . .

He had a smooth face, but a strong, angular jaw and high cheek-bones. His eyebrows were straight and at a slant, making his striking blue eyes stand out even more against his tanned skin. Or maybe that was his natural skin tone. He wore his dark brown hair long, but it was pulled back into a ponytail.

He had no tattoos, and he didn't need them, either. With his height and toned build, why cover any of that up? Looking like that shouldn't be legal. Hell, looking at him like I was probably wasn't legal yet, either. I hardened my eyes, hoping my glasses obscured my gawking.

"Madoc doesn't have a sister." I pursed my lips. "Who are you?"

"Jaxon Trent," he said lightly. "And don't worry, I'm not trying to hit on you. I think I'd have to get in line, what with you showing the whole world how you look in lingerie." He smiled with a twinkle in his eye. "I like your spunk. Just wanted to say hi."

"Trent? As in Jared Trent?" I took a sip of my beer and peered up at him.

"Yeah, he's my brother."

He looked so proud saying it I didn't have the heart to be sarcastic.

"I like your piercings." He motioned to my ears. "Are you the one that inspired Madoc's?"

"Madoc's what?" We started walking toward the fire pit, my flip-flops sloshing through puddles on the now drenched pool deck.

"Piercing," he answered, leaning in to whisper. "Rumor is that he has one somewhere, but we can't see it. Tate thinks it's a Prince Albert. I'm going with a Jacob's Ladder. Madoc's either all in or all out."

Madoc with a piercing? And that asshole gave me so much shit about mine. I let out a bitter laugh. "Well, I wouldn't know."

"Yeah, it's driving us all nuts," he joked as we sat down in the circle surrounding the fire.

The pit, along with the Jacuzzi, helped make the outdoor area usable all year long, even during the bitter-cold Midwest winters. It was a large copper bowl stretching about four feet in diameter, and it burned real wood. Not only did it create substantial flames, but it also generated a lot of heat.

Since the evening wasn't nearly cold enough, there was only a small amount of wood burning. The soft glow kept the area dim except for our eyes that were brightened by the dance of the flames across our faces.

Jared sat on the ground, leaning against a rock, with Tate between his legs and her back pulled up to his chest. Madoc was in a similar position; however, he sat on a chair across the fire from me with a girl on the ground between his legs.

*Figures.*

He had his hand around her neck, but not in a threatening way. His fingers lightly caressed her while his thumb moved in circles. She stared into the flames, closing her eyes every so often, clearly enjoying the attention.

I watched his fingers, mesmerized by how she was putty in his hands. He was soft and slow, gentle and attentive. Possessive. Pressure built low in my belly, and I clenched my thighs, feeling the long-forgotten burn.

And then I looked up. My chest heaved.

His eyes were on me. Pinning me with the absence of everything they usually held. The amusement was gone. The mischief had disappeared. The game was silent.

The mask was off.

In This Moment's "Whore" poured out of the speakers, and I stared into his hard eyes that were hot and urgent on my skin. My tongue moved around my closed mouth, trying to quench the dryness in my throat.

He touched her with his hands but held me with his eyes, and every time he stroked her jaw or ran his finger across her cheek, I could feel the tingle on my skin.

I closed my eyes, then opened them and blinked hard to break the contact.

"So do you still skate?"

I blinked again, registering thunder in the distance. "What did you say?" I asked, looking over at Jax. *Just breathe, Fallon.*

"The skateboard tattoo on the inside of your wrist." He gestured. "Is that your half-pipe with the severe incline in the basement?"

My half-pipe? He'd seen it?

"It's still there?" I asked, incredulous. I couldn't believe it.

He nodded. "Yeah, next to the piano."

I dropped my eyes immediately.

That was strange. With all of my other belongings tossed out with the trash, why would they keep a huge half-pipe that took up space? A lot of space. I was about to ask Jax if there were any skateboards around it, hoping against hope that maybe Madoc or one of his friends salvaged those to use for themselves, but he had started up a conversation with some guy across the fire pit.

Tate brushed my arm, and I looked to my right. "So what's with you and Madoc?" She looked like she was trying to keep her voice low, but Jared's eyes flashed to mine when he heard her question. "Seems like there's bad blood between you two," she added.

I quickly glanced at Jared again, wondering if Madoc ever told him about us, but he wasn't paying attention.

"We just never hit it off." I shrugged to Tate, keeping my voice light. "With the way these two behaved around you the last time I was in town," I joked, gesturing to Jared and Madoc, "I'm sure you understand where I'm coming from."

She grinned and twisted her head to the side, looking up at her boyfriend. "Yeah, I guess I do." And then she fixed me with a stern expression. "But I also know there's two sides to every story. You two should talk."

"We can barely stand to be in the same room together."

Madoc was still across the fire, eyes shifting between Tate and me, and there was no mistaking it. He was pissed. Maybe he wondered what we were talking about, or maybe he just didn't want me here.

Hell, I knew he didn't want me here—which was why I was here.

Clipped voices to my left caught my attention, and I dragged my gaze away from Madoc.

"I would think that if you don't have the balls to get on the track yourself, then you can shut up." The guy next to Madoc was barking at Jax, who still sat next to me.

"And race who?" Jax sneered. "You? Yeah, that'll get me off. I'll race when it's a challenge."

"I don't know what the hell you want from me, Jax, but I'm sick of—"

"You want to know what I want?" Jax interrupted, keeping his voice cocky. "I want your girlfriend to wipe off her poseur pink lip gloss and get in my car. That's what I want."

I darted my eyes to all of the snorts going off around the fire. Madoc laughed silently, shaking his head, while Jared's body shook as he buried his laughter in Tate's neck.

Tate saw my confused look and explained. "That's Liam," she whispered. "He's K.C.'s boyfriend." She pointed to the beautiful dark-haired girl sitting next to Liam, who stared at her lap, stunned. "He cheated on her last year, but they got back together. Jax hasn't said anything, but I think he . . ."

*Wants her.* I finished her thought in my head. Well, if he wants her, then why wasn't he going after her? Clearly, her winner of a boy-friend had nothing on him.

Liam's jaw turned hard as his gaze trailed between Jax and his shocked girlfriend, who looked like she wanted to crawl inside of her shell. "Is something going on between you two?" he asked her.

She pursed her lips and swallowed, averting everyone's eyes. "Of course not," she said quietly.

Everyone watched as Jax and Liam went at it, and Jared, Tate, and Madoc all either smiled, laughed, or stiffened as Jax cracked jokes or suffered an insult. I realized how much of a unit they all were, and how they all stuck together. Madoc had a smile of pride in his eyes when he looked at Jax like a brother, and he had such an ease with Tate. He had a family in them.

Well, aside from Liam and K.C., anyway. She stayed quiet, clearly embarrassed, but her quick glances at Jax didn't escape my notice, either. She looked breakable. Kind of like I was once.

But breaking was beautiful. It hurt, and it was an uphill climb back to sanity, but you came back stronger, fiercer, and more solid than you were before.

I waved my hands in front of me and shook my head at Liam, finally having enough of the idiocy. "Whoa," I interrupted whatever asinine comment he was making. "So you cheated on your girlfriend last year." I stopped and waved at K.C. "Hi, K.C. I'm Fallon, by the way." And then I shot my attention back over to Liam. "And you're worried about her cheating on you? I'd say you got a better girl than you deserve." Snorts sounded around the fire, and K.C. shifted in her seat, looking uncomfortable.

With her eyebrows narrowed, she stood up and hesitated as if she wasn't sure what move to make without instructions. My eyes dropped to her thumbnail that she kept dragging across the wrist of her other hand.

"I'm heading home." She grabbed her T-shirt and pulled it over her bikini top. "See you all later."

She walked down the stone steps to the pool deck, and I saw Jax's fists tighten when Liam got up and approached him.

He leaned down, hovering over Jax, whose forearms rested on his knees, and he did nothing more than cock his head, welcoming whatever Liam was bringing.

"Leave him alone, Liam." K.C.'s deep command surprised me, and I peered around her boyfriend to see a fire in her eyes that wasn't there before.

Liam ignored her and threatened Jax under his breath. "She's mine."

"Only until I start trying," Jax shot back.

And we all did a piss-poor job hiding our smiles as Liam marched off the patio, following K.C.

One thing I knew right then and there. I might hate Madoc, but I loved his friends.

# CHAPTER 7

# MADOC

I was going to throttle her.

Not the girl at my feet whose neck I imagined was Fallon's as I tried not to strangle it but Fallon herself.

The chick walked around my party as if this was her house, and she had friends here. She and Tate were acting like they were besties already, and Jax was smiling and chatting her up. Next thing I knew Jared was going to be talking shop about her motorbike or some shit.

What was her game? Why come home willingly after so long when she practically ran from here two years ago? She was only going to be here a week. What was she doing?

"Who is that?"

Taylor, the girl sitting between my legs, had turned around and was questioning me. She looked over at Fallon and then back at me, and I realized that I'd been staring.

*Not good.*

I flashed a smile, trying to appear cocky. "Someone who likes to watch, I guess."

Fallon had been staring, too. We'd been locked in for who knew how long, and I was hoping no one had noticed.

I did a quick sideways glance around the fire. Jared was whispering in Tate's ear, while she nuzzled into him, and everyone else was deep in conversation.

"Get lost, honey." My date, Taylor, snickered in Fallon's direction.

"You're in the middle of a party, honey." Fallon mimicked Taylor's fake sweetness. "Get a room."

Taylor made a move to get up, but I put my hands on her shoulders, gently pushing her back down.

Taylor wasn't a wallflower. She acted catty, but she had the guts to back it up, too.

"It's okay." The rumble of a laugh began in my throat, but my tone rang true. "Fallon likes to cause trouble. Don't let her draw you in."

Fallon's green eyes burned across the fire, and I waited for a reaction I thought for sure would come. She always spat something back.

"You should watch who you invite to your parties, Madoc." Taylor leaned her back into the seat of the chair, relaxing again.

"I didn't invite her," I replied. "I feel sorry for her, though. She doesn't have many friends."

Taylor laughed. "Yeah, her clothes will only get her enemies."

"Madoc, what the hell—" Tate started but got cut off.

"It's okay, Tate." Fallon sat up straight and pushed her glasses to the top of her head. The audience around the fire pit had grown as quiet as a graveyard.

Fallon continued. "We learned in school that bullies abuse others because they feel bad about themselves. They're hurting." She brought up her knees and locked her arms around them, her tone light and taunting. "We shouldn't be mad. We should pity them.

Madoc has never had to make a real decision in his entire life, which means he's never had anything real. This house, the cars, the money. It's all an illusion. It's like parading a victory when you missed the war." She took a breath and whispered slowly. "Madoc has no idea who he is."

Something gripped my heart, and it felt like it was spreading across my chest and down my arms. I let the fake amusement in my eyes seep out toward her, but I didn't feel the humor.

Fallon had always been so stubborn. Always. She spouted off and said shit that she didn't think about all in an effort to look tough.

But now it was different. More calculated. She'd thought about me. Assessed me. And anticipated my reactions.

"You're right, Fallon." I looked down at the beer in my hand, swirling the brown liquid in the cup. Letting out a condescending sigh, I took out my phone, gesturing. "But I also know that if I call my parents right now, they'll both answer. My mom would fly here on a moment's notice if I needed her, and my dad isn't hiding from wiretaps or indictments. I also have friends I wouldn't trade for any of this shit." I waved my hand, referring to the estate. "And I do have something else going for me."

I grinned as big as my face would allow and popped up, draining my beer. I didn't make eye contact with anyone, knowing they were all watching anyway.

*Don't do it.*

Tossing my cup to the side, I ran down the stone steps to the lower-level deck and circled the pool to where the music was playing near the patio doors to the house. "I can sing." The sky flashed with lightning as I got ready.

Clicking to one of my workout playlists, I opened an Offspring song—perfect for this occasion—and grabbed a water bottle to use as a microphone.

The lyrics started before the music, and I was ready. With a couple of small changes, of course. Offspring's "Why Don't You Get a Job?" gave me only a second to catch my breath, because the lyrics started before the music.

"My dad's got a wife!" I belted, standing up on the edge of the Jacuzzi. "Man, he hates that bitch!" Everyone spun around to face me.

I gripped the water bottle and when the drums started, I bobbed my head in rhythm to the beat, letting the crowd feed off my attitude.

*My attitude.* It's what I fed off of as well. It's what made people like me.

I continued the song, smiling as the crowd started singing and laughing, too. Beers sloshed as people held up their cups, dancing and hollering their approval.

A hand wrapped around my wrist, yanking me off the ledge.

"What the hell's the matter with you?" Jared asked.

I couldn't keep my amusement in check. Everyone was dancing and belting out the lyrics, clearly drunker than I was.

I snorted. "Wait." I held up a hand. "*You're* going to give me tips on how to treat a woman? Wait while I take notes."

"She's your family, dickhead. And she just ran out of here in embarrassment!"

She left?

I stepped around Jared, making for the house, but was cut off.

"I think she's had enough." His voice was softer but still firm.

I didn't know where he got off being so self-righteous. How many times had he tormented Tate—and now he was pulling the reins on me?

"Do you remember the time I wanted to help you, and you told me to keep my mouth shut?" I bared my teeth. "Time to take your own advice."

Whatever. Maybe he thought I was drunk, or maybe he was

trying to calm a situation he didn't understand, but I didn't like how he immediately went to protecting her.

Fallon didn't get to have my friends.

I threw open the sliding-glass door and charged inside, steering around people loitering in the kitchen and down the hall into the marble-tiled foyer.

Swinging myself around the thick banister, I started taking stairs two at a time.

"You're not looking for your sister, are you?" my friend Sam called behind me, and I rocked back on the step. He had door duty, checking people's keys on the way in and sobriety on the way out.

I turned around, not liking the way he'd asked that. "My stepsister," I clarified. "Yeah, I'm looking for her. Why?"

He jerked his thumb to the front door. "She just took your car."

My eyes widened. *Son of a bitch!*

"You gave her my keys?" I yelled, pounding down the stairs.

He straightened his back, pushing himself against the wall from the stool where he sat.

"She's your sister," he said as if that was explanation enough.

I held out my hand. "Give me Jared's keys," I barked.

"He and Tate keep theirs in their room. They weren't going anywhere tonight, anyway."

"Then give me Jax's!"

Sam's mouth dropped open, and he fumbled as he dug through the bowl of keys.

*Leave it alone.*

*Go to bed.*

*Or better yet, go get Taylor and go to bed.*

Sometimes I wondered if the angels talked to get me to behave or to entice the devil to come out to play.

I grabbed the keys out of Sam's hand and bolted out the door.

# CHAPTER 8

# FALLON

'd snatched Madoc's keys and run out of the house, but it wasn't until I got on the road that I realized I didn't have any fucking clue where I was going. This town had no friends for me, no family, and there was really nowhere I could run to regroup.

At least at St. Joseph's I'd found solace in the chapel. I didn't go to pray, and I barely participated in the masses even though they were required for students. But I liked the chapel. It was beautiful and quiet. Pray or not, it was a good place to think.

To plan.

No such luck right now, though. It was too dark for the quarry, and pretty soon it was going to be too wet for any outdoor space. As it was almost midnight, it was also too late for any public indoor escape, as well.

Thunder cracked nearby, echoing across the black sky, and I applied the brakes when rain started to splatter the windshield. I'd noticed the lightning and thunder at the party, which was why I'd borrowed Madoc's car. Didn't want to get pummeled with rain on my bike.

When the prince found out, it was going to take them a week to unbunch the panties up his ass. Guys didn't like their cars messed with.

And I didn't like being messed with, so I guessed we were even. I punched the stick shift into fifth gear and hit the gas.

*Slow down and get it together, Fallon.*

I already had what I needed on my mom and Mr. Caruthers. I just needed Madoc.

But I hadn't known it was going to be this hard. Seeing him. Knowing that what he said was true. I tried to act like I was stronger. I mean, after everything that had happened, I should be, right?

Tears burned my eyes, threatening to spill, but I forced down the golf ball–sized ache in my throat.

As I traveled down the deserted highway, I zoned in on the sound of the spray being kicked up by my tires and the headlights reflected off the black road. Up ahead the lights from the town glowed bright, and I spotted a familiar sign off to the side.

Iroquois Mendoza Park.

Tons of afternoons and weekends spent there flashed through my mind.

It was where I used to hang out with the few friends I did have when I attended high school here. I shook my head and almost laughed. The park had an awesome skating area.

Nostalgia pulled me into a left turn, and I drove into the park, coming to a stop right in front of one of the many bowls. Overhead lighting was usually available when events were going on in the park, but tonight everything was eerily dark. I left the car running and the headlights on to illuminate the area.

Stepping out of the car, I blinked against the light but steady fall of rain. My feet squeaked in my wet flip-flops as I walked to the edge of the deserted bowl and peered down into the smooth, shallow depth. Slipping my shoes off my feet and shivering in my now damp clothes, I sat and then slid down into the bowl, feeling the velvety cement on my toes.

A shiver ran through my body again, but I wasn't cold. The night was warm, and although the rain made the air chillier, it was a comfortable temperature. I took a step, breathing hard, feeling too damn closed in by the steep walls around me. They never used to scare me. I used to charge down the vert, relishing how my heart pumped faster as I raced at top speed toward the next incline.

This was where I used to breathe easier. But now . . .

I spun around, the low growl of an engine digging through the thick air. The peel of tires pierced the calm as a black Mustang screeched to a halt next to Madoc's GTO.

Straightening my shoulders, I tipped my chin up and prepared to face what I knew was coming.

Madoc jumped out of the car, not even caring to close the door behind him. "You stole my car?!" he shouted, peering down into the bowl.

With the headlights behind him, the area was well lit, and I tried to breathe against the flutter in my chest.

He was here. We were alone. We were angry.

*Déjà vu.*

This is what I wanted. It's what I'd planned.

But I turned my back on him, anyway.

I'd told myself time and again that I didn't care what he thought of me. I didn't want his heart, after all. It wasn't part of the equation. He didn't need to love me or respect me for this to work. I would get what I wanted without worrying about whatever was in his head. It. Did. Not. Matter.

So why couldn't I just draw him in like I'd planned? Why did I want to spit back?

"I didn't steal it. I borrowed it, princess," I shot back.

He jumped down into the bowl, his flip-flops slapping against the wet cement as he drew closer to me. "Don't touch my shit, Fallon!"

"Oh, but you got to come into my room last night and touch me? You don't get to have everything, Madoc."

He stopped a few feet from me, and I felt the walls of the bowl close in as he stared. I expected more yelling and insults, but he just stood there, looking like everything that could destroy me without even speaking a word. Looking like everything that nearly did destroy me.

He was still dressed in only his board shorts and flip-flops. No shirt. I guess he would've left the house in a hurry if he was coming after me. He'd changed so much in the years I'd been gone. Now his shoulders and arms were works of art. Madoc had always liked to work out, and it paid off. He was built like a quarterback, and he was tall. I wished I didn't feel the invisible cord pulling me to him, wanting to touch him again, but I'd be lying if I said I didn't. We always want what's bad for us.

Madoc was hot. He knew it. And he knew everyone else knew it.

But what was underneath the blond hair, boyish blue eyes, and smooth, toned body was bad. He was bad.

And someday his looks would fade, and whoever he ended up with would just have someone bad. I had to remind myself of that. There was nothing in him that I should want.

The light rain blew around his face, and he blinked away the water dripping down his cheeks. "You know what?" he sneered, looking like he was about to turn away. "I'm so over your bullshit, Fallon. I wish I knew what the hell you wanted from me." His voice got stronger. "You act like everything's fine around Addie and then you show up to my party dressed to impress down to your underwear around all of my friends, and then you bring up my party two years ago." He got in my face. "What do you want from me?" His bellow reared up from deep inside of him.

"Nothing!" I shouted, my eyes burning with anger. "I want nothing from you. Nothing ever again!"

He reared back just a little as if I'd surprised him.

"Again? Is that what this is about?" he asked. "Us fucking two years ago?"

*Fucking.* I averted my eyes.

I'd rather shove a drumstick up my nose than let him see how much that hurt. I wiped the water off my forehead and smoothed my hair over the top of my head.

"You know what?" He narrowed his eyes, speaking up before I got a chance. "You can go to hell, Fallon. I was sixteen, too. I was a virgin, same as you. You were all over me, too, and you know it. I didn't force you! You didn't have to go and complain to our parents. Jesus Christ!"

*Huh?*

By that point he was breathing hard. "They treated me like I was pressuring you or some shit!" he shouted, throwing his hand out into the air. "You told them that I was forcing you?"

"Madoc, I . . ."

*What the fuck was he talking about?* My breath, my hands, my knees—everything was shaking.

"Screw you, Fallon," he cut me off, getting angrier. "All you had to do was say something. I would've left you alone, but I thought . . ."

He trailed off, looking at the ground, looking too disgusted to speak with his pursed lips.

The air in my lungs was gone. *What the hell?*

Everything he was saying was like a slap, and I'd been knocked on my ass. What the hell was he talking about?

I inched closer. "They told you I complained?"

His head snapped up, and I saw the muscles twitching in his jaw. "Your mother told me that you hated what I was doing to you. That you had to get away from me, and that's why you disappeared overnight." Every word bled from his mouth. His cut was deep.

*Goddamn it.* I closed my eyes and shook my head. This was not happening!

If they had lied and told Madoc that I complained, then that meant he thought I wanted to leave. He thought that I went to our parents *asking* to be sent away.

I sucked the water off my bottom lip and opened my eyes, meeting Madoc's scowl.

Madoc had never wanted me gone. He thought that I ran from him.

That was unexpected.

But it didn't have to change things. If our parents lied to both of us, then I was still putting them under the knife. Maybe Madoc wasn't as malicious as I had originally thought, but he still wasn't innocent. He still treated me like a whore, and he never came for me. Never called, wrote, or looked for me. Everything I went through, I went through alone.

They were all still enemies.

"Get out of my way." I brushed past him, climbing back up the incline.

But before I reached the car, Madoc grabbed the inside of my elbow and whipped me back around. "No, no. You don't get to leave until I get an explanation."

I looked up at him, feeling the heat of his skin through my wet shirt.

"An explanation?" I shrugged. "I'm guessing it's genetic, Madoc. Penis size is inherited. Not much you can do about it."

I spun back around, heading to the GTO and my jaw aching with a smile I struggled to hold back.

Opening the car door, I jerked backward as it was slammed shut again by a force behind me.

*Shit!*

My heart pounded, and my veins rushed with liquid heat.

Before I could turn around, Madoc crowded my back, pressing my chest into the car door.

Air rushed in and out of my lungs, and I felt warm all the way up to my head.

"Tell me you hated it," he challenged, lips brushing hot on my ear. "I want to hear you say it."

*He kisses me. His mouth is wet and all over me. I can smell cigarettes everywhere now. From where his mouth and hands were. His fingers glide down my butt and squeeze.*

*"You ready to go upstairs?" he asks. "I want to see how bad you really are."*

*I shake my head. No. "I want to go back outside to the party."*

*Why did I let him kiss me?*

*I dart to his left, but he shoves his body into mine, cutting me off.*

*"But you got me all turned on. Come on, let's go have some fun." He reaches up and runs a thumb over my nipple.*

*My eyes widen, and my fists clench, about to hit him.*

*"Get away from her." I hear Madoc's voice from behind the guy looming over me.*

*"Get your own, Madoc."*

*"That's my sister." His voice is sharp. "Get away from her or get out of my house, Nate."*

*Nate backs off of me. "Fine. Didn't know she was your sister, man. Sorry."*

*He leaves, but I still feel ashamed.*

"*Madoc, I—*"

"*Shut up,*" *he barks, grabbing my hand.* "*I knew you'd show up here, trying to be the center of attention as usual. Looking for a good time just like your mother, right?*"

"*That's not what I was doing, asshole.*" *I try to pull my hand away as he hauls me up the stairs.*

"*Oh, really? You have friends here? Yeah, didn't think so.*" *We stop at my door. He lets go.* "*Go back to your room, Fallon. Play with your Legos.*"

"*You're not the boss of me, Madoc. And I'm not a slut.*" *I put my hands on my hips.* "*But if you're going to keep calling me one, then I may as well get it over with. Your friend Jared's outside, right? He's hot. Maybe he'll be my first.*"

*I walk around Madoc and go for the stairs again. He grabs me and pulls me through my bedroom door.*

"*Madoc, let go of me!*"

"*Stay away from my friends!*" *He lets go but bears down on me, crowding my space. He's so angry, but I'm not scared.*

"*Oh, like I'd really beg to be a part of your crowd.*" *I sneer.* "*A bunch of Kens and Barbies that get their reliable world news from Facebook.*"

*He advances. I'm backed up to my bumper sticker wall.*

"*You act like you're so superior,*" *he snarls,* "*but who was it macking on one of my friends downstairs? For someone that doesn't care about those people, you seemed pretty ready to open your legs for one of them!*"

*I get back in his face.* "*I do what I want, when I want. No one makes decisions for me, Madoc. Not you. Not our parents. Not my friends. I'm in control. I'm free!*"

"*Free?*" *he laughs bitterly.* "*Are you serious? Just because you have shit pierced to your face and a few tattoos? You didn't get those tattoos because you wanted them. You got them to prove that you could. It's you trying to prove something, Fallon! You're. Not. Free!*"

*I slap him hard with both of my hands, but he catches me before I can hit him a third time. He holds my wrists, and we stare at each other. Something passes through his eyes, and before I know it, his lips are on mine.*

*We both grab at each other. He pulls me hard against him, and his mouth is all over mine. This isn't like when Nate kissed me downstairs. Madoc feels real. Like nothing is planned. Everything is coming from his gut.*

*This feels right.*

*He pulls away, breathing hard, wide-eyed.*

*"Oh, my God." His eyebrows are pinched together in fear. "I'm sorry, Fallon. I don't know what I was thinking. I didn't mean—"*

*I inch back up to him, unable to meet his eyes. "Don't stop," I beg. Slowly, I reach out with my shaking hand and take him around his neck, bringing him in.*

*He jerks when my lips meet his, but after a few seconds, his arms circle my waist.*

*"I like fighting with you," he chokes out, laying me on the bed and coming down on top. "This is going to change everything."*

*I pull his T-shirt over his head. "This changes nothing," I say.*

"Say it, Fallon." He pushed into me, his lips in my hair. "Tell me how much you hated my hands on you . . . my mouth on you."

I splayed my palms against the door, remembering how my hands had been on every inch of him.

Madoc became my world two years ago. I'd wait for him at night, my heart pumping a mile a minute, knowing that he was coming. Knowing that he was going to touch me. I loved all of it. I never wanted the sun to come up.

I pushed back against his long body, the wet heat between my legs nearly making me groan.

I could barely catch my breath as I twisted my face to the side.

"You want to hear how much I wanted it?" My throat tightened on the words.

He laid his palms over my hands against the door and pressed into me harder from behind.

His lips were on my neck. "Fuck the past," he breathed. "I want to hear that you missed it."

# CHAPTER 9

# MADOC

dove down, sucking her neck into my mouth before she got a chance to answer.

"Madoc," she groaned, and her knees gave way.

I wrapped an arm around her waist, my lips still devouring her neck, and slammed her into the car.

*Damn her.*

Shit wasn't supposed to go down like this.

I threaded my fingers under her hair while I sucked on her neck, then captured her lobe, and kissed her jawline before she twisted her head toward me and I took her mouth in mine. The sweet warmth was more than I could take. My dick jerked, and when Fallon pushed her beautiful ass into me, I almost groaned.

"Fuck, Fallon," I gasped out, yanking the drenched tank top over her head and throwing it to the ground.

She dropped her head back against my shoulder, her chest rising and falling fast with her panting. Her desperate eyes pleaded with me before they squeezed shut. Her body was aching. Just like mine.

I wrapped one hand lightly around the front of her neck and ran a possessive hand across her stomach.

"I want to be inside of you." I nudged her neck, tipping her chin up to meet my eyes. "But you better not lie again."

Her face was wet, and she blinked away the rain on her eyelashes, looking so desperate that I wanted to tear her apart. All night long. I settled for kissing her, swirling the tip of my tongue against hers and pulling it into my mouth.

*Jesus, she tasted good.*

I reached down and dove into her shorts, cupping her in my hand.

"Oh, God," she whimpered.

I rubbed the wet heat between my middle finger and thumb, ready to fucking explode.

She squirmed, running her back up and down my chest as she moaned. I rubbed her clit with my two fingers and pressed my cock into her ass.

Her rain-covered body glistened with the glow from the headlights, and I could feel the pulse between her legs against my fingertips. She was needy and ready.

Unclasping her bra, I yanked it off her shoulders and unbuttoned her shorts from behind. Pulling those and her panties down her legs, I backed up to look at her.

She stood on unsteady legs and leaned against the car door, her fingers still splayed across the window.

Water droplets cascaded down her long, slender back and over her rounded ass to her thighs.

"Sit on the car, baby." I kept my voice calm even though my body was screaming. I could barely breathe.

I briefly thought that maybe we should get out of the rain, but it was still hot out, and who was I kidding? She was so beautiful like this.

Her arms fell to her sides, and she turned around, keeping her chin down and eyes on me. Walking to her right, she sat down on the hood, her feet dangling just above the ground.

I walked over as well, standing opposite her but keeping my distance.

Her breasts were bigger than I remembered, and I wanted to slow down. It'd been too long since I'd touched her, and I wanted to rediscover everything.

But there was no time. My dick was like a steel rod right now.

"Spread your legs," I said in a husky voice, a smile tugging at my lips.

Her breath caught, and I watched her breasts rise and fall with excitement. Or nervousness. Her jaw hardened as she met my challenge. Leaning back on her hands, she opened her legs wide, exposing what I wanted.

Damn this girl.

My eyes drifted down her flushed and wet body as I untied my shorts, letting them fall to the ground.

Her eyes went wide as soon as she noticed the glint of silver at my tip.

Standing between her legs, I gently pushed her back onto the hood slowly, keeping time with AWOLNATION's "Sail" streaming from the car stereo. Then, holding her at the hips, I sunk my lips into her warm, wet stomach, feasting on her soft skin, and then moved up to her nipple, sucking hard.

"Ah," she moaned and gasped, but I ignored her squirms.

Moving over, I took the other one in my mouth, sucking and biting, drawing her hard nipple out with my teeth, and damn, I loved how sweet she tasted.

Two years ago I didn't know shit. Sure, screwing around with Fallon had taught me a little, but I had still been immature and unsure of myself.

Now, I knew more, and I knew what I wanted. I wasn't afraid of taking it and taking chances.

Moving fast, I upped the pace and kissed down the length of her stomach, every inch bringing me closer to what I really wanted.

In one rushed movement, I snatched her clit between my lips and sucked it like a peach.

"Oh, my God!" She squirmed, throwing her head back, the hood bending under her movements. I couldn't see her eyes. Her face was pinched up in pleasure.

I swirled my tongue around, flicking her a few times hard.

*I hate her*, I told myself.

*I don't trust her.*

*She is going to screw me over again.*

And I didn't care about giving her pleasure.

I didn't care that she was enjoying this. I simply wanted her to come in my mouth, so she knew who owned her.

But the more she grasped at my hair and went wild under me, the more I realized I wanted to hear her call my name. I realized I wanted her to love it.

"Madoc." Her voice shook. "Madoc, now!"

I looked up and saw her looking down at me. She ran her hand down my cheek.

"Now," she begged. "Please?"

And that was what I was waiting for. Even though I didn't know it.

Standing up, I clenched my teeth, looking down at that beautiful body. That beautiful girl that hated me, and I hated her, but—

goddamn it—I loved how we hated, because it was raw and real. It didn't make any sense, but yeah—it was real.

Yanking her down to the edge of the car, I held her eyes as I drove inside of her.

"Ahhh. . . ." She squeezed her eyes shut and bared her teeth.

"Shit, Fallon." I stopped, shut my eyes, and savored the feeling.

Warm and tight around me, the heat of her spread across my thighs and up my chest. The rain did little to cool me down.

I didn't know how many guys she'd been with after me, and I didn't want to know, but I figured my piercing might take a minute to adjust to. Hovering over her, my dick inside of her, I just watched her, waiting for her eyes to open.

When they did, she looked at me and snaked her hand around my neck, bringing us both halfway in for a kiss. As I massaged her tongue with mine and nibbled on her wet lips, I started to move inside of her slowly at first, feeling every inch of her heat and savoring every little whimper she let loose in my mouth.

Breaking the kiss, I cupped her breast with one hand and steadied myself with the other hand on the hood of the car. Every muscle in my back was tense, and my shoulders were on fire. The air rushed in and out of my lungs, and I couldn't hold back anymore. I pounded into her, the volcano between my legs hot and urgent and feeling so damn good.

Her breasts bounced back and forth as I moved in and out of her harder and harder.

Her nails dug into my chest. "More, Madoc. It feels so good."

I stood up straight, pulled her back down to the edge of the hood, and hooked the back of her knees over my arms. "Tell me you missed this."

She blinked and swallowed. "Yes." She nodded, her whisper coming out shaky. "I missed it."

*Me, too.*

I entered her again and pounded into her like there was no to-morrow.

Her back arched, her tits went wild, and she moaned long and loud. "Yes . . . oh, my God!"

She tightened around my dick, her stomach shaking with shallow breaths, and her eyes squeezed shut as she came all over me.

The fire in my cock spread through my thighs and burned to the tip. I pulled out, gasping and stroking until I came all over her stomach.

My throat was dry, and my heart was trying to punch a hole through my chest. I dropped my head down between her breasts and closed my eyes, feeling her chest rise and fall under me.

No coherent thoughts formed in my head. Just words.

*Awesome.*

*Hot.*

*Damn.*

*Shit.*

I had no clue what I was supposed to do now, and her silence told me she was just as baffled as I was. I was about to get off of her when she started running her fingers through my drenched hair.

Frozen, I just lay there and let her.

And then I winced, realizing I hadn't used a condom.

*Shit. Really, dude? You have them in your glove compartment.* Why hadn't I even thought about it? I had always used them, except with Fallon once or twice when we were younger.

"I never said those things to our parents." She spoke up, breaking me out of my thoughts.

Our parents? She was bringing them up now?

"Never said what?" I kept my chin to her chest but looked up at her.

"They lied to you." She stroked my hair and looked up to the sky. "I never complained about what we were doing, Madoc. They just found out and shipped me off."

I narrowed my eyes, pushing myself up and placing both hands on either side of her head. "You're telling me you never wanted to leave me?"

# CHAPTER 10

# FALLON

*What was I doing?*

What the hell was I doing?

So the parents lied to him. Told him I wanted to leave. That hurt him. Good! That worked for me. Madoc deserved that and more, and while he wasn't on my hit list to the extreme the parents were, he was still on it.

But in my post-orgasmic bliss, I wanted to protect his heart. I wanted to keep the memory safe. I wanted to believe that he never used me.

But he did. He used me good and forgot about me.

Sleeping with him now was part of my plan. *This was all going according to plan*, I told myself. It happened sooner than I thought it would and with a lot more wanton behavior on my part, but it had been so long since I'd had sex. It was harder to resist him than I'd anticipated.

Madoc and I were crazy at sixteen. Way too young to be doing what we were doing, but we were learning together.

Now he was a man, and we both had a lot more confidence. Madoc was good. Very good. I felt guilty that I wanted more of him.

And his piercing? Holy hell.

I looked away and sat up, pushing him off me. "No, Madoc. I didn't want to leave."

He backed up, but I could feel his eyes on me. I knelt down and retrieved my soaked clothes and then turned away, using my tank top to clean off my stomach.

"How did they find out?"

"What does it matter?" I said softly. "We were too young. What we were doing was wrong. They knew it. Sending me away was for the best."

I tried wiggling back into my underwear and shorts, but they were so cold from the rain that still poured down on us. A shiver shot down my arms.

"But they lied to me." He stood there, naked. "All these years I thought—"

"We survived, Madoc," I interrupted, and avoided his eyes as I put on my bra. "I moved on, and so did you, right?"

I thought for sure it would have taken me a zillion years to pass out that night, but I fell asleep within seconds. I didn't even remember lying in bed, trying to get myself to relax. After dealing with Madoc, Addie, the party, and then the "rain," I'd closed my eyes and woken up in pretty much the same position I fell asleep in.

But as soon as I opened my eyes, I was bombarded with thought after thought, worry after worry, all charging like a storm of elephants through my head.

I sucked in a breath. *Shit. I slept with Madoc!*

*That's okay.* It was part of the plan.

*But you liked it.* No, I loved it.

*That's okay.* You haven't had sex in two years. You were horny.

*You told Madoc that the parents lied?*

Okay, so I didn't want him to believe that I would have said anything like that. I shouldn't have cared. A minor hiccup that upset nothing in the overall plan. *Relax.*

*But he'll confront his dad!* His dad will come home. . . .

*So? I want Mr. Caruthers home.* My plan would come to fruition in a few days anyway.

Everything was on schedule.

I inhaled a cool breath and exhaled a shaky one.

So why wasn't I happy?

The first year I'd spent away I was too confused—too numb—to make sense out of everything that had happened, much less get my ducks in a row. But for the past year all I'd fantasized about was seeking my revenge and seeing them hurt. Each one of them. Seeing their worlds turned upside down like mine had been.

But now my mind just kept traveling back to last night.

How Madoc's lips had felt on my neck. How he looked at every inch of my body like he was seeing me for the first time. How much his hot eyes and possessive hands had made me feel like he wanted me.

He might be a spoiled brat and a self-absorbed asshole, but he'd blown my mind.

I needed to remember that just because someone was good in bed didn't mean anything beyond that.

This was a game to Madoc—but it was a war to me.

I rolled over and sat up, swinging my legs off the edge of the bed, but then I immediately dropped my head and blew out a breath.

*Damn.*

My insides felt stretched, and the muscles below my belly were sore. I was sore everywhere.

Standing up, I tiptoed on wobbly legs across my room and cracked the door open. I heard a vacuum cleaner's *vroom* somewhere in the house and knew Addie was awake. Slipping out my door, I sprinted across the hall to the bathroom.

Madoc's bedroom had a bathroom. Not mine. I didn't rate high enough.

"You're up!" a loud voice hollered. "Awesome for me."

I twisted to my left and saw Madoc closing his bedroom door and running straight for me.

A knot lodged in my throat. What the—

He charged at me like a linebacker, swooped me up by the waist, and threw me over his shoulder.

"Madoc! Put me down!"

"Shhh . . ." He pushed us through the bathroom door, kicked it shut and planted my ass on the bathroom counter.

"Madoc—"

But I was cut off. He snatched up my lips, wrapping his strong arms around me and nearly suffocating me with how much pressure he was putting on my mouth. Every time he took a breath, I did the same, because he came back in for more within a heartbeat. His lips moved over mine, fast and urgent, needy and ready. Both of his hands pushed up under my T-shirt, kneading my breasts, and I couldn't help myself. My hands slid down his black pajama pants, grabbing his perfectly smooth ass and pulling him in between my legs.

"I'm going to apologize for my lack of coolness right now," he gasped out, trying to yank my shirt over my head, but I kept pulling it back down. "I'm hornier than a motherfucker."

"Oh, is it a morning thing?" I crossed my arms over my chest to keep my shirt down.

"Morning?" He started jabbing me in the stomach, tickling me to get my arms to release the shirt. "I've been up all fucking night torturing myself. I should never have told you to lock your door last night."

He'd walked me to my room last night, ordering me to lock my door. Apparently, he didn't always know everyone who partied at his house, and he wasn't sure who all of the people were passed out around the place. I had only seen three bodies when I'd walked through the house, but there could've been more.

"You were trying to protect me from rapists," I pointed out, biting my lip to keep myself from giggling.

"Yeah, slick move that was." He smiled down at me, jabbing me continually in the stomach. "I couldn't get at you, either."

He grabbed my face with both hands and slid his tongue into my mouth, devouring me again. Little needles sprang up over my skin, and I shivered, heat pooling between my legs like a furnace. I grabbed his face too, kissing him back.

He took that opportunity to pull the T-shirt over my head in one fell swoop like a magician that pulls out a tablecloth from underneath a fully set table.

"Madoc, no," I commanded pathetically, folding my arms over my chest. "I'm sore from last night."

He pinched his eyebrows together and arched a lip. "Sore? From me? That. Is. Awesome."

*Idiot.* I shouldn't have told him that. Now he was feeling like the man.

"Well, then . . ." He sighed and pulled me down off the counter. "You're safe. For now."

*Whatever.* I blinked slow and hard. *I'm in control. I'm in control. I'm in control.*

Everything was moving in the wrong direction. He made me smile. He made me forget. We had to slow down.

*We have to stop.*

He tipped my chin up and his mouth came down on mine. I let him kiss me, not making any effort to return it, but I still couldn't help breathing in his rich, clean scent. Damn, I loved the way he smelled.

He leaned back, smirking down at me. "It's good to have you back, Fallon." And then he walked out like he had everything he wanted in the palm of his hand.

*Damn him.*

*Damn him!*

I kicked the door shut behind him and whisper-yelled a bunch of words that I'd only ever heard my father's dockworkers spew. I didn't emerge from the bathroom for another half hour as I tried to get my head on straight again.

Things in Madoc's life were too easy. He made it too simple to fall back into the fun. His relaxed smile, his carelessness about everything, and the way he was just . . . *him!*

There were problems in this world. Problems in families. Problems in my family and his. Our history was a problem. Why did he always appear as if he didn't have a care in the world?

We'd had hot, angry sex last night after we'd insulted and upset each other. Apparently he didn't care what had led us there, only that he got his reward.

*Shit.* I scratched my head and closed my eyes as I stood in front of my floor-length mirror. I needed some alone time.

Time to think.

A nice walk. A good run, maybe.

But Madoc was like a whirlwind of activity. I'd almost forgotten.

After I dressed in some short white shorts and a Hurley T-shirt, he'd told me to march my ass back into my room and change. After flipping him off and pouring myself some cereal he'd explained that we were going to the lake with his friends, and I needed to get in a swimsuit. When I told him to go screw himself, that he didn't make decisions for me, he walked around the counter where I stood eating and stuck his hand down the back of my shorts, continuing to smile and talk to Addie with her none the wiser.

With my heart missing every other beat and sweat breaking across my forehead, I'd relented, realizing he wouldn't stop harassing me until I said yes.

Anyway, Tate was going to be there, so I looked at that as a plus. We'd also be in public, so I could count on him not to try anything.

Or so I thought.

"Where are we?" I asked as he pulled up to a small, brick one-story house. It sat in a rundown neighborhood with overgrown lawns and ugly chain-link fencing. Although the house itself appeared to be in decent shape—the porch was tidy, and the windows were clean—the brick was dulled with age and the screen door was shoddy.

"Come on." He ignored my question and climbed out of his GTO.

Following him, I slammed the door and walked a step behind him up the cement slab walkway.

"Madoc. Madoc!"

I jerked my head and stared wide-eyed as a boy, about seven, came running toward Madoc and slammed into his body. Madoc caught him in a hug.

A tightness gripped my chest, and I sucked in a breath.

Blond hair, blue eyes, and long legs. The boy looked just like him.

*No.* I shook my head. That's ridiculous. Madoc would've had to be like ten years old when this kid was born.

"My mom said if I wasn't good I couldn't go with you, but I was good," the kid shouted, smiling.

Madoc leaned back and eyed him with disgust. "Good?" he repeated. "Oh man, don't say that. Being good is like what?"

Both Madoc and the kid simultaneously stuck their fingers in their mouths and mock gagged. A smile tugged the corners of my mouth, and I had to cover it with my hand.

*Nope.* Madoc wasn't good with kids. I refused to believe it.

"That's right." He patted the kid on the back and turned to face me. "Fallon, this is my spawn."

I cocked my head and looked at him disbelievingly, still trying to get the picture of them both sticking their fingers down their throats out of my head.

"No, not my real spawn." He knew where my mind was going. "But he has potential, doesn't he?"

I put my hands on my hips and kept a pleasant tone for the kid's sake. "Madoc, what's going on?"

He opened his mouth to speak, but a woman came out through the screen door carrying a small backpack.

"Madoc," she greeted. "Hi."

"Hi, Grace."

Grace looked young, definitely under thirty, and she had a nice head of long brown hair pulled back in a neat ponytail. She wore scrubs, so I guessed she was a nurse . . . and probably a single parent from the look of things.

"Here's a change of clothes for after he swims." She handed Madoc the backpack. "There's sunscreen, a snack, and some water, too. You'll have him home by dinner?"

Madoc nodded. "We may stop at a bar, but definitely after that."

"Awesome." She smiled and shook her head at him as if she were used to his cracks. "He's so excited," she continued. "Call if you have any problems."

Madoc bent down and put an arm around the kid.

"Ohhhhh, Moooooom," they both whined as if her concerns were silly.

She rolled her eyes and held out her hand to me.

"Hi, I'm Grace. And you are?" Good mom. Making sure your kid is safe.

"Hi." I took her hand. "I'm Fallon. Madoc's . . . um . . . stepsister," I stuttered, hoping she didn't hear Madoc's snort.

Technically, I wasn't lying.

"Nice to meet you. You all have fun." She waved and walked back up the steps.

Madoc spun around, and I couldn't get over how he and the kid not only got along, but how much they looked alike. Both were dressed in long, black cargo shorts with T-shirts. But while Madoc wore black leather flip-flops, the kid wore sneakers.

"Fallon, this is Lucas." He introduced me finally. "He's my little brother. As in the program. I'm his big brother."

I exhaled. *Okay, good.* I was glad he'd explained. Because that was weird there for a while.

"Wow, they trust you with kids?" I asked, kind of serious, kind of not.

"What?" He placed his hand on his chest, appearing hurt. "I'm awesome with kids. I'll be a great dad someday. Tell her, Lucas."

Lucas looked up at me and didn't even blink. "He taught me how to tell when a woman is wearing a thong."

I burst out laughing, putting my hand over my mouth.

Madoc pulled the kid in by the neck as we walked to the car. "I told you, women are the enemy. They don't understand skills like that."

# CHAPTER 11

# MADOC

"Will Jared and Tate be there?" Lucas piped up from the backseat.

"Hey, man. Don't kick the leather," I teased, reaching behind me to stop his feet from digging into my seat. "And yes, they'll be there."

"Cool."

We sat there, bobbing our heads to the music, and I couldn't help but peek at Fallon next to me. What was she thinking? She seemed to get a kick out of Lucas but seemed really surprised to meet him.

Was it so unusual that I would spend time with a kid that didn't have a dad? Fallon always condemned me for being pretentious, self-absorbed, and whatever other words struck her on a particular day, but now I gathered that she really did believe it.

She sat there, staring out the window and completely weirded out by the situation.

Or maybe it was facing what we'd done last night in the light of day. She used to have a thing about the dark. Being alone in her room, no light, it was as if what we were doing wasn't real to her.

While she always fully participated, things changed in the daylight. She'd act like nothing happened. She'd go back to not making eye contact. She'd barely even say my name. I caught on to how she worked pretty quickly and rolled with it.

Hey, I was sixteen and had a hell of a sex life. I wasn't going to complain that she wouldn't let me touch her any other time. I was simply happy that I got what I got at that age.

But now, touching her, listening to her panting . . . everything we did last night in the rain was even better than I remembered. I used to pace my room, waiting for Addie to close up the house at night so I knew that it was safe to go to Fallon's room. I was happy and alive when I was with her. I hadn't felt that for a long time.

When Fallon left, I crumbled. Like Jared when Tate left for France for a year; I didn't lose control like he did, but I acted out.

Her mom had told me that she and my dad found out what was happening, because Fallon ratted us out. Patricia said that Fallon felt uncomfortable and pressured by me. All the confidence I'd built was ripped apart.

I didn't handle it well.

She and I might have lived in the same house, but we had never seen each other as stepsiblings. We had never even spent much time together, so I never felt like what we were doing was wrong. I loved all of it and wanted more of it. But over the past two years my hatred toward her grew.

Every girl paled in comparison, and the only time I'd felt right was when I had been with Fallon. And then last night, she tells me that she never lied to the parents. Never told them anything. I was overjoyed and pissed off at the same time. My heart pumped fire again, knowing she wanted me, but I'd spent the whole night thinking about all the time we lost—what they took from us—and I wanted shit to hit the fan.

And it would. Soon.

If I confronted my dad now, he'd come home and Fallon would be out. So if I couldn't convince her to stay longer, then I only had a few more days with her until she left for Chicago. I'd deal with my dad after that.

We parked in the lot right next to Jared's car. Grabbing Lucas's backpack, I handed that and some towels from the trunk to Fallon while I retrieved the cooler and picnic blanket.

"Tate, stop!"

I jerked my head up out of the trunk, hearing Jared's voice.

"Tate!" He stomped after his pissed-off girlfriend.

*Great.*

I'd started to think my best friends looked for reasons to fight. Seriously. It always ended in makeup sex, after all.

"Leave me alone. I mean it, Jared!" she yelled over her shoulder, and I stood shocked and pretty damn amused when she took off her black flip-flop and threw it at him.

He threw up his hands, deflecting it from his head and scowling at her, his lips tight.

"I was going to tell you," he barked. "But you're overreacting as usual."

"Ugh." She halted in the middle of the parking lot, ripped off the other shoe, and whipped it at him, damn near flinging her whole body into the movement.

"What's going on?" Fallon whispered.

I sighed, running my hand through my hair. "Foreplay."

I slammed the trunk shut and started walking for the beach, leaving my friends to it.

"Should we help?" Fallon stumbled over some rocks, looking behind her to the lot where we could still hear Jared and Tate's muffled shouting.

"Not if you want to be in the sandwich. They'll be making out in ten minutes," I promised. And that's exactly what I wanted to be doing with her right now.

I loved Lucas, but I wished I'd known that Fallon was coming back. I'd have preferred to have her alone right now. To fight. To torment. To whatever.

Hell, I'd pick a damn fight if it meant getting her naked again.

At least until I got her out of my system.

But I couldn't change the plans for the day at this point, so I set the cooler down and laid out a blanket on the small beach. Kicking off my shoes, I followed Lucas with my eyes as he ran into the water.

"Wait, aren't you going to make him wear a life jacket?" Fallon asked as she stopped to pull off her shirt.

I smiled, knowing exactly where she was coming from. There was always a pang of fear, watching him go and do things that could hurt him. Lakes were dangerous, and I had tried making him wear a life jacket the first time we came out here last summer. Yep, I tried the first time, and I never tried again. He fought me on it, and I soon found out that he knew what he was doing.

I pulled off my shirt. "His father was in the Coast Guard when they lived in Washington, and he made sure that Lucas knew how to swim. After he died, his mother brought them both back here to be near family, but he doesn't really have a lot of men in his life or chances to keep practicing. He loves it. I try to bring him as much as possible during the warmer months."

Her eyes narrowed, and she looked lost in thought as she stared out at the water.

"Come on," I nudged, walking past her.

Trudging through the chilly water, I walked forward as it covered my feet, then my calves and my thighs, and then my stomach. Kicking my feet up, I shot up and dove back down headfirst into the cool depths.

I fucking hated the lake. It's dirty and muddy. And cold! You're swimming around not being able to see what's happening underneath you.

Freaks. Me. Out.

But it's one of the only things to do in this boring-as-hell town, and I've been here too many times with too many drinks and too many girls around. There was a time when that was fun. Hanging out, getting drunk—when you had nothing better to do.

But now I was only here for Lucas, and for some reason I had wanted Fallon along today. We were probably going to get in a fight in front of the poor kid. And with Jared and Tate doing their thing by—surprise, surprise—fighting again, there would be no buffer zone if Fallon brought out her claws.

*I should've left her at home, I guess.*

I popped my head up out of the water and looked to the beach, seeing her in her bathing suit.

*Or maybe not.*

Holy hell. Son of a bitch.

My dick jerked and instantly hardened—seriously?—even in the cold water.

Her white bikini was just that. A bikini. In every possible definition of the word, it was evil and temptation in its worst form.

The bottom piece covered all the important parts, but the top part had strings that tied in the front instead of the back. All you had to do was pull. Not reach around. Not fumble as you try to find the correct string blindly. Nope. You just had to pull and everything would come spilling out.

She let her hair down out of her ponytail, and all of a sudden my hands felt too empty.

A splash of water hit me in the back, and I winced.

"You little . . . " But I caught myself and just splashed Lucas in return.

"You looked like you could use some cooling off." He laughed, throwing his arm back and swimming away.

Cooling off? Did he even know what he was talking about? *TV. That's where kids got this shit.*

Fallon still stood on the beach, hands on her hips and pacing the water's edge, dipping her toes in every once in a while. She looked half ready to either throw herself into the water or turn around and run for the parking lot.

I jerked my chin up, shouting, "Stop giving the kid a lesson in female anatomy and get in the water already."

Her gaze flashed to mine for a second, but I could feel the heat of her anger even in the chilly water. After teetering for another minute— just to piss me off—she stepped into the lake and waded out until she could dive in.

About an hour passed as we played and swam in the water. Lucas had fun, even if it took Fallon time to get over herself. At first she stayed back, floating on a raft, treading water, and keeping her distance. But when I got the raft and Lucas tipped her off of it, she'd finally loosened up.

They raced each other. She didn't let him win.

He and I dunked each other. She started smiling more.

Jared and Tate came back with two smiles they sucked at hiding.

And Fallon stayed as far away from me as she could get.

Which was fine. There was nothing I wanted from her right now anyway.

Oh, who was I kidding? I was ready to bang my head against a buoy for bringing Lucas out here when all I kept thinking about was ripping those fragile white strings loose.

"Lucas!" I growled. "Go sit on the blanket with Jared and Tate. Hydrate and eat your snack."

"Oh, man," he whined.

And I smiled, seeing him swim off as I headed over to Fallon. She sat in the purple recliner raft with her arms resting on the inflated sides. One of her feet dangled off the edge, dipping into the smooth surface of the water.

"So." I squinted up at her, resting my hand on the raft for support. "Why are you home, Fallon?"

The corner of her mouth curled, looking like there was a secret trying to escape. "This isn't my home."

I'd been so dumbstruck by the fact that she was home that I hadn't really thought about why until last night. Her mother was abroad. Italy or Spain or something. Spending my father's money on Gucci and gigolos. And Fallon had no friends here that she kept in touch with that I knew of. She barely had a relationship with my father, who wasn't at home, either, so the question begged to be asked. "Then why are you at the home of your estranged mother's husband where you don't want to be?"

Her tease of a smile curled more. "And where I'm not wanted?"

I leaned my head back into the water, closing my eyes as images of last night raced through my brain. "Oh, you're wanted," I taunted.

She snickered. "That's not how you made it sound when you came into my room the other night."

I snapped my mouth closed.

Yeah, that shut me up. I was kind of a dick the other night.

Okay, a huge dick.

I slicked back my hair and bounded up onto the end of the raft, peering over at her as she steadied herself from the jolt.

"Well, in all fairness, I did think you had lied about me. I had a right to be pissed, Fallon. You never called or came home again. What was I supposed to think?"

She didn't answer. Just sat there, hiding behind her sunglasses. Her eyes had always looked dark and lost to me, like she was searching for something but wouldn't know it if she found it.

I repeated my question. "So why are you home?"

She inhaled a heavy breath and finally looked at me straight. "Closure," she said. "I left without really saying good-bye to this place. I needed that before I started my new life in Chicago."

Closure. Is that what I needed, too?

"They found you in the theater room, didn't they?" I asked her.

She gave a half-hearted smile. "Wearing your T-shirt, and you'd left your jeans on the floor," she finished, raising her eyes at me expectantly.

"You were asleep," I explained. "I didn't want to wake you."

Her eyes were still waiting for more.

"I covered you up?" I offered, drowning like a rat.

I'd figured out that much. After our first time together, we'd found ourselves going at it every couple of days and then very quickly it became every single night for about a week. Fallon never wanted to leave her room when we were together. On her turf, in the dark, and we didn't talk about it outside of those boundaries. Those were the nonverbal rules I'd ascertained after our first couple times together.

But I had my ways. I was finally able to coerce her out of her bedroom and downstairs to the theater room. We'd watched a movie but ended up all over each other like I knew we would. She'd put on my T-shirt and then fallen asleep.

Looking back now, we were stupid to think we wouldn't get caught. If they hadn't found her, then Addie or someone would've noticed sooner or later that we were always tired. Since we were spending half our nights together, we got very little sleep.

Fallon's low voice seemed almost sad and too forgiving. "It's over. In the past, Madoc."

Eyes hooded, I looked over at her. "It's not over, and you know it."

"Last night was a fluke. We were angry."

Darting out my hand before she could move, I grabbed her ankle and pulled her down into the water with me.

"Madoc!" she yelped before submerging completely in the water. She flailed her arms and shot back up through the water's surface, sputtering. "Such an asshole," she coughed.

I pulled the raft in front of us, shielding us from view of the beach.

"A fluke, huh?" I leaned into her, whispering.

She held onto the raft, and flecks of gold danced on her face and in her hair from the sun on the water. I waited for her to look at me. Or move away. Or just breathe.

But she didn't. She stared at my chest, waiting. For what, I didn't know.

Reaching out, I ran the back of my hand across her stomach and then grabbed her waist, pulling her in closer to me.

But she pushed away, sucking in a sudden breath.

"Your . . . little brother is over there."

"And if he weren't?" I cocked my head to the side and breathed into her.

She finally looked up, her eyes turning to steel. I leaned over and whispered in her ear. "Lock your door tonight, Fallon."

And I swam off toward the shore, diving deep into the chilly water not warmed by the sun.

No reason to give a seven-year-old a lesson on the male anatomy, either.

# CHAPTER 12

# FALLON

Enough was enough. I couldn't let him continue to affect me so much. True, Madoc had grown up. No buts about it. He was smart, fun, and more good-looking than ever. He seemed to care about his friends, and someday, he might even make a good husband and father.

I just wasn't the right girl for him, and he certainly wasn't for me. He'd had me once and forgotten me. Now, I wanted to leave this house of my own free will with my head held high. I wouldn't be a rat in a cage, dressed to my mother's approval or a toy for Madoc to play with when he felt like it. I would never want to be like her and end up with her life. Jason Caruthers cheated on his wife—constantly. Although my mother also cheated. I'd found that out—not that I had doubted it anyway—through my preparations.

Their marriage was empty and superficial, and Madoc had grown up with an innate entitlement. He knew he could do what he wanted, when he wanted, and if a girl didn't like it, another one would come along to replace her.

I wouldn't be one of the numbers.

I trudged out of the water, shivering as the air hit my wet skin. Tate leaned back on her hands, legs bent and her bikini slightly more modest than mine. I would've worn a one-piece if I'd known a kid was going to be here. Jared lay on his back next to her with a hand on her thigh and his eyes closed. Lucas was eating an apple and peanut butter sandwich crackers.

"So what's up now?" Madoc asked Jared and Tate as he grabbed a towel and threw it at me. I reached up just in time to stop it from hitting me in the face.

Jared sighed as in "Here we go." "I asked her to move in with me," he admitted, and my eyebrows shot up.

Madoc snorted. "And she threw shoes at you? Sounds like a marriage to me."

"In Chicago," Tate clarified with a sharp, scolding tone. "He asked me to move in with him in Chicago. I told him that I want to be around for my dad more, so I'm going to Northwestern instead of Columbia. He then tells me that he didn't want to go to New York anyway and wanted to stay in the area to be close to Jax."

Madoc busied himself taking out waters from the cooler. "So that's good. It's a win-win. What's the problem?"

"The problem is," I chimed in for Tate and turned toward Madoc, "that he wasn't communicating with her. He already had his own plans that he wasn't involving her in."

"So did she," he argued back.

"But he sounds like he never wanted to go to New York." My voice got louder, and I could feel Tate's and Jared's eyes on me. "Now she feels like she pressured him or was making him do something he didn't want to do."

Madoc rolled his eyes. "Cover your ears, Lucas."

Lucas obeyed, and Madoc looked around the circle, meeting everyone's eyes.

"Look, I'm sorry, Tate, but you've been living in fucking rainbow-sprinkle-cupcake land if you actually thought that Jared Trent was going to move to New York City. People don't drive there. How's he supposed to stretch his legs? Do you even know how much it would cost to park a car there?"

Jared's eyes were still closed, but his chest shook with silent laughter that he was smart enough to keep to himself.

Tate's jaw hung open, and not in a wow-that-really-made-sense kind of way. It was more of a what-an-asshole-I'm-going-to-dropkick-him kind of way. I couldn't tell for sure, but Madoc probably felt the heat of her fire behind her sunglasses.

I held up my hand. "So you're saying that his car is more important than her?" I yelled at Madoc.

He blew out a sigh and walked behind me, standing at my back and covering my mouth with his hand.

I could hear the smile in his voice as he spoke to Jared and Tate. "So you'll both be in Chicago. I'll only be an hour and a half away at Notre Dame. Win-win."

Around four o'clock, Jared and Tate left to go break the news to her father about her change in college plans, and Madoc and I took Lucas home in time for dinner.

Madoc drove the twists and turns of the quiet roads leading to our—his—house, and neither of us broke the silence. The tension was thicker than wet clay, and I didn't know what was on his mind. He was usually such a chatterbox. Now, he looked almost stoic as he zoned out on the road and sped over the black highway. Trees loomed on both sides, making me feel like we were in a cave.

"Fallon," he started, and I looked to him. "We're not sixteeen anymore."

I stared at him, not sure what that meant.

"I know."

He yanked down on the stick shift, sending us into sixth gear. Between looking out the window and the front windshield and not meeting my eyes, he looked uncomfortable as hell. "I think we can get along better if we grow up. You can stay the summer if you want."

What? Was he serious? When the punch line didn't come, I just averted my gaze out the window.

*He doesn't want me to stay*, I thought to myself. Or maybe he did.

"Yeah, Pussy-on-the-Premises, right?" I felt the flutters in my stomach dull as I realized why he probably wanted me to stay.

He shook his head. "I didn't mean that."

Yeah, right. Why else would he want me around? We may have cleared up some miscommunication, but he still saw me as damaged goods. Not good enough, just like my mother said.

And I didn't much like him, either. Even if he really did want me to stay, would I want to suffer his company all summer?

"If I wanted pussy, I could get it, Fallon." He blew me off. "But what can I say? I kind of like having you around, I guess. And I know you like me, too. As much as you try to hide it, I still turn you on. So stop acting like you don't like me."

I ground my teeth together as he pushed the button on the remote on his visor, opening the gate to his community.

Was he serious? Did he not realize that just because two people have fun in the bedroom doesn't mean anything? People go to bars, know each other for an hour, and go home together! One has nothing to do with the other.

"You know what I really don't like?" I huffed, climbing out of his GTO as he parked in front of the house. "I hate your car! It sits too low, they're too many blind spots, and it looks like a Chevy Cavalier which would've cost you half the money as this waste of metal!"

I ran into the house, hearing his laugh behind me. "You seemed to love it last night when you were screaming my name!"

Who was I kidding? I'd have better success trying to jam a tree branch up my ass than convince myself I didn't want him. But who cares, right? Yeah, I want him. Sure. Who wouldn't? I could enjoy this. *Just one more time.* I just have to be the one in control, that's all.

Jumping in the shower, washing, and jumping back out took me less than two minutes. My hands were shaking a bit, and I was blinking a lot—something I do when I'm trying not to think. I dressed in black lace panties and a pale pink vintage satin bra. Actually, it was only a bra in the sense that it covered my breasts, but there was no support. It was loose like a slip that had been cut off right under the boob area.

Madoc was going to love it. Not only was it sexy, but it was user-friendly lingerie. He didn't need to remove it to get his hands where he wanted them.

Letting my hair out of the ponytail, I fluffed it, leaving it a little tangled—Madoc seemed to like it that way—and applied a little mascara and color to my lips. Before heading to the door, I snatched my black-framed glasses off the bedside table. The hall was dark as I jogged the few feet across the hall to Madoc's room. Slipping inside, I heard the water in his shower running, and smiled as I headed to his bed.

Good. I wanted to be here before he got out. For once, *I* wanted to surprise *him*.

I sat on the end, clenching my teeth to keep my smile from escaping. Heat raced through my veins, and my toes curled into the beige carpet as I put both of my palms down on the bed next to my hips.

*How should I do this?* I bent my legs a number of different ways, tried a slew of different poses, but everything felt unnatural. Legs spread, not spread. Leaning back on my hands, lying down on my side. It was all stupid. Madoc was going to laugh.

Okay, maybe not, but still . . .

Everything tonight was my way, I reminded myself. I didn't want to let him dominate me.

I decided to leave my feet flat on the ground, legs together, with my hands folded in my lap.

The water shut off, and I tried to force my heartbeat into a calmer pace.

Madoc walked out, black towel around his waist, and immediately locked eyes with me.

His eyes went round, and his mouth snapped shut. He looked intense and a little angry.

I was afraid for a moment, afraid I'd overstepped my bounds by coming in here after him even though he'd invaded my space numerous times, but then I looked down. The bulge under his towel was growing. I fisted my fingers and tried not to feel pride, but it was impossible.

My confidence boosted me up like a pair of six-inch heels.

"You're mad," I taunted, leaning back on my hands. "I changed the game."

He inched closer to me, his steps like a beast of prey. "Not mad, really. Just surprised."

"But you've had other girls in this bed, haven't you?" I asked. "Why not me?"

I hadn't really thought about it until the moment I asked the question, but it was true. Madoc had slept with other girls in this bed, in this room. Probably.

But never me.

"Is that what you want?" His voice, sultry and sexy, played with me.

But I faltered.

Did I want that?

"You didn't love girls in this bed," I assumed. "You fucked them."

They were in, and then they were out, only to be replaced with another one.

I could talk myself up one hill only to find that I was still at the foot of mountain.

I did not want to be used, forgotten, and nameless.

He was right. *What the hell am I doing?* I looked everywhere but at his eyes, not sure where the answers were or even what the hell my questions were anymore.

Madoc and I could screw tonight. I could walk out of here instead of being kicked out . . . but what would Madoc have really lost?

Nothing. Having sex with him and then taking it away didn't hurt him at all.

I blinked long and hard, finally seeing how stupid I'd been. So I stood up, tears stinging my eyes, and I swallowed the lump in my throat. "No, I guess I don't want that after all," I whispered and walked past him out the door.

"Fallon?" I heard him call, confusion lacing his voice.

But I was gone.

Running across the darkened hallway, I dove in my own room, slammed my door shut, and locked it. I collapsed against the door, breathing hard, and closing my eyes so the tears wouldn't come.

I hadn't cried in years. I was always able to stop it, to swallow it.

*You can do this*, I told myself. *Just do it. Before you do anything else stupid.*

My phone sat on my bedside table, and I opened my last text.

**Will post when you're ready.**

That text was three days ago when I arrived. My weak fingers tapped out my response.

"Fallon?" Madoc knocked on the door, and I stopped typing.

"Just leave me alone," I ordered, talking to the closed door.

"No."

*Excuse me?* I raised my voice to respond to him. "You told me to lock the door to keep you out, dickhead. That's what I'm doing."

"I came up with that line when I was sixteen and had toothpicks for arms!" His muffled voice got louder. "I have muscles now," he continued, "and this door is going to be firewood in five seconds if you don't open up!"

I raced over and yanked the door open. "Don't you dare!"

"What's your problem?" He pushed past me into the room, turning around to face me. "We had a fun day. And I had an even better night planned, beginning with the Jacuzzi."

*Of course he did.*

I slammed the door shut behind him, shaking my head and letting out a bitter laugh. "I told you to leave me alone. Why can't you just do that?" My tone stayed flat, but the muscles in my arms and legs were rigid as I walked past him.

He hooked my elbow, bringing us face-to-face.

"You come into my room, dressed like that." He gestured up and down my body. "And then you run out, expecting me to not wonder what the hell is going through your head?"

"What does it matter? You don't care. Not about anyone but yourself, anyway."

I pulled my arm away and walked over to the side of the bed, putting a safer distance between us.

His eyebrows were pinched together in confusion, like he didn't understand what I was getting at. Why would he? I'd done a complete about-face from earlier, letting him seduce me, and then I'd changed the game and tried to seduce him to prove that I could. Crashed and burned at that—and now I was pushing him away. He was confused, and he should be. I sure was. I had thought I knew exactly what I wanted to have happen when I came back here.

"Where the hell is this coming from? Is this about the other-girls-in-my-bed question?" he asked, inching toward me.

A small, quiet sigh escaped me, and with it, my plan. "It doesn't matter."

"I could ask you about other guys, but I don't." His expression was angry. "You want to know why? Because I would care. Do you really want to know how many girls I've had in my bed? How many girls I've slept with?"

*He would care?*

"No, I don't want to know. We're not in a relationship," I bit back.

Madoc stood immobile, his face hardening a bit and his chin lifting a little, but other than that his body was like stone. I didn't know if he was angry, hurt, confused, or annoyed. But I knew he was thinking. I watched his large frame, his black pajama pants hanging low on his hips, walk across my bedroom, take my wide gray cushioned chair, and carry it to sit in front of my floor-length mirror.

"Come here," he commanded, and I curled my toes, staying planted where I was.

When I didn't budge, he softened his voice.

"Please?" he asked.

He planted himself in the chair and looked at me through the mirror, waiting.

He leaned back, slouching, with his legs about a foot apart. His chest glowed smooth in the barely lit room, and I had to lick my lips, because I was so thirsty all of a sudden.

*This is ridiculous!* I planted my hands on my hips, trying to look away but always reverting back to his gaze.

*Okay, screw it.*

I dropped my hands and walked over slowly, trying to look bored. Madoc took my wrist and led me around the front of the chair, yanking me down into his lap.

"Hey!" I argued, trying to stand up again, but his hands held my waist.

"Trust me."

I huffed, but I stopped, if only to see where this was going.

"What do you want?" I snarled, inching my ass up his body, because straddling his thigh was . . . yeah.

"Look." He tipped his chin up. "Look in the mirror. What do you see?"

"What do you mean?"

*What the hell?*

"Open your eyes!" he barked, and all of the hairs on my body shot up.

*Shit.* Yeah, you could never tell when Madoc was going to go from easy to scary, but it was always sudden.

Reaching around, he twisted my chin toward the mirror, and I sucked in a breath. "What do you see?!" he shouted.

"You and me!" I blurted out. "Madoc and Fallon!"

My heart was racing.

I looked at him through the mirror. I sat on one side of his lap, so he could see from the other side, and we stared at each other, my chest rising and falling more urgently.

"That's not what I see," he said in a low voice. "Those names mean nothing to me. They're simple and empty. When I'm with you, I don't see the daughter of a gold-digging bitch and an Irish drug lord or the son of a crooked lawyer and a vegan Barbie."

I almost wanted to laugh. Madoc had an ironic way of looking at the world.

But he wasn't smiling. He was scowling. He was dead serious, and I knew from experience that his genuine moments were few and far between.

He reached up, threading one hand into my hair while the other hand rested on the chair.

"I see everything I want for as long as I can have it," he continued. "I see a woman that wears the cutest little scowl like she's two years old and was just told she couldn't have candy. I see a guy that went and got an *apadravya* piercing, because he wanted to live in her world for even a little while."

I closed my eyes. *Don't do this to me, Madoc.*

"I see a beautiful woman with a knockout body and the guy she drives insane with wanting her."

His hand moved to my neck, stroking up and down.

"I see a thousand nights of kitchen counters, showers, pools, and couches where he's going to fuck her until she screams." He lowered his voice to a whisper. "I see her eyes and how they look when she comes."

My nipples hardened, and I had to start sucking in air. Opening my eyes, I could see his blue ones, shining like crystals, watching me.

"I see the guy that went so crazy when she left that he tore all of the shit off his walls, thinking she hated him."

My face cracked, and my eyes watered; the lump in my throat had grown too big for me to swallow around.

"Madoc—"

"I see," he cut me off, trailing his hand over my stomach and into my lacy top, "the body he sucked rain off of last night and he wants in his mouth right now, because, baby, you are torturing him."

He leaned in, kissing my upper arm in soft, sensual kisses, trailing over to my back. He flipped my hair over my shoulder, digging his lips into my spine and going up as I dropped my head back onto his shoulder.

"Madoc . . ." I gasped, tingles spreading down my back.

His lips . . . oh, my God, his lips.

His hands were both under my slip-bra, kneading and squeezing as I started rolling my hips into him.

"Goddamn, look at you." His breathless voice made my sex clench.

I opened my eyes, seeing what he saw.

A young woman in lingerie, sitting on a man's lap backward with his hands up her shirt. Our eyes met, and the heat made me want to tear him apart with my teeth. I wanted him.

*Fuck, I wanted him.*

Snuggling my head into his, I kept my eyes on him in the mirror as I reached down and slipped my hand inside my panties. His eyes became as sharp as needles as he watched me. I spread my legs and gently ran my fingers up and down my heat, watching him watching me.

He leaned back, continuing to stroke my back with one hand while he just took me in.

Having his eyes on me, having him so interested, was doing things to my body I didn't expect. Madoc always used to be in a hurry, and then last night was pedal to the metal.

But now he looked like he owned the room. He looked like I was his and he wasn't rushing to have me before the sun came up.

Standing up, I slid my hands down the sides of my panties and slipped them off, letting them slide down my legs. His hands fisted where they hung off the armrests, and I saw him harden through his pants. His body needed me, and the pulse on my clit throbbed. One time. Two times. Three.

*Damn.* Everything about Madoc was intense and made me feel good.

"I . . ." I wanted to tell him that I didn't hate him. That I thought about him. That I was sorry. But the words won't come. "Madoc, I . . ." I let out a breath. "I want you here."

And I sat down in his lap backward, facing the mirror. "I want you like this."

A small smile tugged at the corner of his mouth, and then I gasped as he put a hand on the front of my neck and pulled me back to him.

Our lips came together, moving over each other. Then I reached around and slid my fingers into his soft, short hair, kissing him as if it was the only thing I ever needed to survive. His hand slid down my stomach, and I spread both of my legs to rest on the outside of his thighs.

"Madoc," I whispered, pleading. "I'm burning already."

I took his hand and led it between my thighs, sucking in a breath when his fingers slid inside of me.

*Oh, God, yes.*

His fingers moved, my wetness easing him in and out, but the fire in my belly had me so hungry I started rubbing into his hand.

"Madoc."

"I love it when you say my name." His head fell back, and his chest rose more quickly. He looked like he was enjoying this although I wasn't touching him. He just liked touching me that much?

My hips rocked into his hand, and for the first time in two years, I wanted things. I wanted this. I wanted him. I wanted it all again.

But I knew I couldn't have it. I knew this was it for us.

This was the last time he'd make love to me. The last time I'd kiss him.

The last time he'd want me.

And I wanted to bury my face in my hands and scream that I

didn't have to do this. I didn't have to walk away, but there was just too much between us to get past.

Instead I stood up and turned around, straddling his lap and facing him.

Running my fingers down the side of his face, I kept my voice quiet for fear I wouldn't be able to hold back the tears. "I want to see you." My throat ached so hard I could barely whisper. "I want to kiss you when you come."

I leaned up on my knees, giving him room to push his pants down. Before he kicked them off, I reached into his pocket for the condom.

He smiled. "How'd you know that was in there?"

"Because you're a confident son of a bitch," I whispered huskily, not sounding sarcastic in the least.

I shoved the condom into his hand before wrapping my hungry arms around his neck and kissing him hard. His lips worked mine, and we didn't lose the connection when he worked behind my back to get the condom on. Rocking my hips, I rubbed against his thick hardness, feeling the burn get heavier and heavier as the pulse in my clit pounded harder and harder.

"Now, Fallon," he breathed out, letting his head fall back on the chair. I hesitated, hearing my name. He used to call me "baby."

"Say my name again." I sat down on his cock, and we both closed our eyes with the sensation.

I was filled.

"Fallon," he gasped.

"Who's kissing you right now?" I trailed soft kisses along his jaw, slowly sucking and biting until he moaned.

"Jesus," he groaned.

"Not Jesus."

He laughed. "Fallon." And he put his head up and looked straight at me as I slowly moved up and down his length.

Up so slowly, watching his eyes as he watched my body move on him.

And back down, taking him in, amazed how his lids would close with the sensation. I'd never done this before. I was never on top, and he felt so good like this.

I mean, he always felt good, but the angle of him in the chair got him so deep.

I could feel him rubbing the walls of my womb. That piercing made me want to slow down and speed up, but it also made me never want to stop.

"Who's riding you?" I held his face, my thumbs on his cheeks and fingers at the back of his neck.

"Fallon." It seeped out of his mouth like a bullet in slow motion. My breath caught in my throat as he wrapped his arms around my waist and shot up, guiding my legs around his body. Air rushed in and out of my lips as he just stood there, his mouth touching mine. "You don't get to win this game, Fallon. Though I like how you play."

He slammed me up against the mirror, sinking his mouth into mine before letting my legs fall. God, his kiss stole my breath, but I didn't care that I couldn't breathe.

As soon as my feet touched the ground, he spun me around and cupped both of my breasts, burying his mouth in my neck.

I watched him in the mirror, and I no longer gave a damn about owning him or dominating him.

Although I wanted to control this, it was clear I wasn't in control now. Until he said, "Why do you drive me so crazy, Fallon?" His breath was ragged, and his hands and lips moved rough and fast. "Why does it have to be you?"

And that's when I realized he wasn't trying to dominate me. He was desperate.

I was in control.

"Madoc," I whispered, turning my head and melting my lips into his.

Breaking away, I widened my legs and leaned forward into the mirror. "Please, I need you." I could feel the heat of him on the inside of my leg.

Madoc positioned himself and slid into me. I bit my lip at the sweet pain of his depth.

"So good." It was barely a whisper as I felt the rest of my insides fall apart around his thick length inside of me.

And then he closed his eyes and laid his head back, his voice shaky. "You're going to ruin me, Fallon."

*No more than you ruined me.*

# CHAPTER 13

# FALLON

*I* try to pull my hand free from her grasp. "Mom, no! Please!"

My chest is about to explode. I want to scream and hurt her. Tears spill down my face in a constant stream.

"You will do this, Fallon," she shouts, yanking me further. "Stop whining, and do what you're told!"

My feet stumble across the ground as she pulls me closer to the door that I don't want to enter.

"I can't do this! Please, I'm begging you. Please!"

She stops and faces me. "What do you think is going to happen, Fallon? You think he's going to marry you? He's not even going to stay with you. If you don't do this, your life will be over. Everything I've worked so hard for will be over."

Part of me knows it is hopeless. I put my hands on my stomach, feeling the nausea roll.

Six weeks. It had been six weeks since I'd seen him and eight weeks since I'd gotten pregnant. Or so the doctor had said.

Did Madoc miss me? Was he thinking about me? I wish I could go back *and be nicer to him. When he'd tried to kiss me in the gym after school, I shouldn't have pulled away. I miss him, and I hate that I miss him.*

*I didn't mean to love him.*

*I shake my head. "I won't do it."*

*The clinic's shadow looms over us as I wipe at my tears.*

*"Why do you want it so much?" she snarls.*

*My heart still beats fast, but I keep my temper in check. "Because it's mine. It's Madoc's and mine. I need to talk to him."*

*"He's already moved on to someone else." She takes out her phone and shows me the screen. My stomach hollows out at the sight, and I cringe at the pain of trying to hold back the tears.*

*He'd posted photos on Facebook of a party at his house. He had his arm around another girl.*

*"Did you really think he loved you?"*

*"I need to talk to him."*

*She sticks her phone back in her Prada bag and fists her manicured hand at her side. "Did he ever tell his friends about you? Did you ever go on a date with him, Fallon? It wasn't love for him! He used you, Fallon!"*

*"You're lying!" I advance in her space, the agony painful in my tense muscles. "He loves me. I know he does."*

*I'd been so mean to him for so long, but I know he wants me. He never looked at other girls around me. And I can't stand being without him.*

*She throws a hand in the air. "Well, congratulations and welcome to the Land of Every Female Is an Idiot!" she shouts. "We've all been here at least once. 'He smiled at me. He really loves me. He opened the door for me. He really loves me.'" She looks straight at me. "Let me tell you what I've learned about women and men. Women overanalyze everything, and men think only about themselves. Madoc never went public with you. He doesn't want you!"*

I blinked awake, the vibrations from my phone rousing me. The room was dark, and I glanced over at the clock to see that it was only midnight. The dream was still fresh, and I noticed sweat around my hairline. I rubbed my eyes with the heels of my hands and pushed the images away.

Leaning over the side of the bed, I grabbed my cell off the floor. I remembered it had gotten knocked down with Madoc earlier.

Madoc.

I twisted my head to the side to see he was asleep next to me. He looked so peaceful, and I lay back down to look at him.

He rested on his stomach, and the sheet was pulled down to his waist. His hair had been wet after his shower, and after all of our activity, it had dried in a mess. It stuck up in twenty different directions and made him look younger. Or maybe just more carefree than he already was. His arms hugged the pillow under his head, and I envied his slow, even breathing.

The tattoo on his back had thrown me for a loop whenever I'd caught sight of it during the past two days. I would always immediately think it was my name. I wondered what the word "Fallen" meant, but I also knew I would never ask.

My phone buzzed in my hand, and I took a deep breath, opening up the message.

My father had called twice and texted. My mother had also called and left messages. I deleted those without even listening. I knew it would be a rant about why I'd come here or more bullshit I didn't want to hear.

Opening my father's text, I saw the two messages.

Fallon?

Do you want me to release this?

Looking over at Madoc, I knew my plan had changed. I typed out my response.

**No. Send it to Caruthers instead.**

**You sure?** he shot back.

No, I wasn't. I didn't want to do this anymore, but it was the only way I'd feel any closure. Madoc and I didn't have a future. It wasn't love, and I wasn't going to deceive myself for even a minute longer.

**Now.**

Opening a new text, I sent one to Madoc's father.

**Check your e-mail. I'll meet you in your office. You have two hours.**

Guys like him slept with their phones, but I knew he was probably still awake screwing his mistress.

He texted back within minutes. **On my way.**

"Katherine Trent."

I dumped a folder onto Jason Caruthers's desk and plopped myself down in the seat across from him.

He narrowed his eyes, looking hesitant, and opened the folder. His lips tightened as he sifted through the documents, receipts, and photographs. "Why have you done this?" he asked, closing the folder with a cool calmness like he already had me handled.

I looked at Jason, looking so much like his son will in thirty years, and I hated them all over again. With his short-cropped blond hair styled better than most guys twenty years younger than him and a crisp black suit, Mr. Caruthers was still a good-looking man. No wonder my mom jumped on him even before she was divorced from her last husband. He was rich, handsome, and influential. The perfect package to a gold digger.

Although I couldn't say he was ever cruel to me, his presence intimidated me. Just like Madoc. In my skinny jeans and Green Day T-shirt, I didn't have the armor to withstand him.

Or so he thought.

"Why do you think?" I bit back.

"Money."

"I don't need your money." My words were clipped, and I wanted to burn shit when I was around this guy. "I'd take my father's dirty cash before I'd take anything from you."

"Then what do you want?" he asked, getting up and going to the bar to pour himself a drink of something brown.

I sat up straight and looked out the window behind his desk, knowing he could hear me. "Getting up while someone is speaking is rude."

I felt him still and waited only a moment before he was back in front of me, sitting down at his desk.

"I was going to leak what you saw in the e-mail. Paying off judges—"

"One judge—" he chimed in.

"And the affair that you've had going on for quite some time with Ms. Trent," I continued. "You've been carrying on with her through two marriages."

I couldn't believe it when I'd found out. As I dug into his affairs, it wasn't a surprise that he'd been sleeping with other women. Hell, both he and my mother started to wander fairly quickly after their marriage. Madoc and I both knew. Even though he and I didn't talk much back then, I knew he saw that their marriage was a sham, just like I did. We knew the four of us were never any kind of family. Which was why we never felt solidarity.

Until the week things changed and we started sleeping together.

"Why didn't you leak the story?" he asked.

*Good fucking question.*

I kept my arms resting on the chair and maintained eye contact. Caruthers could sense weakness easily. It was part of his job.

"Because as it turns out, I'm not a bad person," I told him. "It would hurt people that don't really deserve it, and I'm not willing to do that. Yet."

"Thank you." He looked honestly relieved, and fuck him.

"I didn't do it for you."

He folded his hands on his table. "Where is my son?"

"Asleep." I smirked. "In my bed."

Men like Jason Caruthers rarely shout, but I knew he was angry. He had that whole close-your-eyes-and-breathe-out-slowly thing going on.

"So what do you want from me, Fallon?" he finally asked.

"I want you to divorce my mother."

His eyes widened, but I continued. "Make sure she's taken care of, of course. I don't love her, but I don't want her on the streets, either. She gets a house and some payoff cash."

He laughed bitterly, shaking his head.

"You don't think I've been trying to divorce her, Fallon? Your mother is fighting the inevitable. She doesn't want a divorce, and the attention of a long, messy legal battle would be right up her alley. Believe me, I can divorce her and not lose much doing it, either. But not without a media circus."

*Poor guy.*

"That's none of my concern. I don't care how you go about it or how it hurts you. If you want quick and easy, then I suggest you open your wallet wider."

He pressed his lips together, and I could tell he was thinking. I wasn't worried. A lawyer like him can't beat his wife in court? *Please.*

He cared about his reputation and nothing more. He was right. My mother would do anything to get attention, and she'd drag him through the mud. But she had a price.

Everyone does.

"What else?" He raised his eyebrows, clearly not liking the terms so far.

"One of my father's associates, Ted O'Rourke, is up for parole in September. See that it gets approved."

"Fallon." He shook his head at me again. "I defend the bad guys. I have no pull with the parole board."

*Who was he kidding?*

I leaned in, placing my hand on his desk. "Enough with the helpless act. Don't make me ask twice."

"I'll look into it." He cocked his head at me. "What else?"

"Nothing." I gave a closemouthed smile.

"That's it. Your mother and Ted O'Rourke. Nothing for yourself?"

Standing up, I tucked a few strands of hair behind my ear and dropped my arms to my side. Putting my hands in my pockets would also be a sign of weakness.

"This was never about me, Jason, but you made it about me, didn't you? That's why you freaked when you caught Madoc and me together. You knew who my father was and what my mother was like by then, and you assumed the worst about me. You didn't want your only son playing in the dirt."

He pinched the bridge of his nose. "Fallon, you were only kids. It was too much, too fast. I always liked you."

"I don't like you," I shot back. "The guilt, the sadness, the abandonment by adults that were supposed to stand by me at the very least, and everything that happened afterward was stuff I should never have gone through. Especially alone."

He narrowed his eyes in confusion. "What stuff afterward?"

I lost my scowl. *Didn't he know?*

Of course. Why would I have thought my mother would have told him?

I shook my head, ignoring his question. Who cared? It's not like he would have protected me anyway.

"Those are the pictures I have of Katherine Trent. I kept nothing digital."

He blinked. "You're just letting me have them now? That's not how blackmail works."

"This isn't blackmail," I sneered. "I'm not like you. But I know a lot of bad people, and that's why I know that you'll do what I'm asking. If you keep your word, I'll say nothing."

Yeah, he knew who my father was and the kind of people I knew through him. I would never have used them to hurt anyone, but he didn't know that.

He looked up and asked, "How do I know to trust you? I don't want Katherine's name dragged through the dirt."

"I've never lied to you," I pointed out and turned to walk away.

"Fallon?" he called, and I turned back to face him. "I've known for a long time where my talents lie. And my faults." He stood, sticking his hands in his pockets. "I've neglected my wives, my son, and I never took much interest in anything outside of the courtroom." His sigh was weary. "But no matter what you think, I do love my son."

"I believe you do."

"Was it so bad?" His eyes narrowed, studying me. "Being separated from him? I mean after all this time, can't you see that it was for the best? Did it really hurt so much?"

*Hurt.* My jaw tightened, and my eyes burned. *Did he ever love anything enough to be hurt?*

My voice was almost a whisper. "I thought it did. At first. It hurt when I was ripped away from him without a good-bye. It hurt that I couldn't see or talk to him. It hurt when my mother didn't call me or invite me home for holidays. And it hurt when I snuck back here after a few months and found Madoc with someone else." I straightened my shoulders and looked him dead in the eyes. "But what really hurt was being forced by my mother into that clinic, into that room, and being all alone while that machine stole his baby out of my body."

His eyes widened, and I knew without a doubt that he hadn't known.

I nodded, my voice raspy. "Yeah, that's the part that really sucked."

I turned, walked out, and tried not think about the heartbroken look on Jason Caruthers's face before he buried it in his hands.

# CHAPTER 14

# MADOC

"Madoc!"

I opened my eyes, blinking away the sleep, and shot up in bed when I saw Addie staring down at me.

"Addie. What the hell?" I adjusted the sheets to make sure I was covered.

This was fucking awkward.

Like she didn't know what was going on, anyway. I was naked in Fallon's bed for Christ's sake, but still. Addie hadn't seen me naked since, well . . . last New Year's when I got drunk and jumped in the freezing-ass pool on a dare from Tate.

"Where's Fallon?" I asked, looking around.

"Honey, I don't know what's going on, but Fallon is gone, and your father is downstairs. He wants to talk to you now." She nodded and gave me the crazy eyes which meant that I needed to get my ass up.

*Shit.* I threw off the covers, and I heard a *tsk* behind me as I'm sure Addie didn't appreciate me stalking across the room buck naked.

"Where did Fallon go?" I shouted as I crossed the hallway into my room.

"I have no idea. She was gone when I got up."

*No. No. No.* I squeezed my eyes shut and shook my head as I threw on some boxer briefs, a pair of jeans, and a T-shirt. Grabbing my socks and keys, I had no intention of dealing with my father for long.

I was going to find her and drag her back by her hair if I had to. What the fuck?

Running downstairs, I grabbed my shoes where I had dumped them near the stairs and walked into my father's office.

"Where's Fallon?" I demanded, plopping down in the chair opposite his desk and putting my socks and shoes on.

My father was sitting on the edge of his desk with a drink in his hand, and I did a double-take. Now I was actually a little worried. My father was controlled and responsible. If he was drinking in the morning, then . . . I don't even know. I've never seen him drink in the morning. I just knew it was odd, and my father lives by his routine.

"She's gone," he answered.

"Where?"

"I wouldn't know. She left of her own accord, Madoc. And you're not going anywhere. We've got to talk."

I laughed bitterly and finished tying my shoes. "Say what you have to say, and make it quick."

"You can't have a relationship with Fallon. It's just not possible."

His bluntness threw me for a loop. I guess he knew we'd started up again. Did I want a relationship with her?

I stood up, ready to leave. "You've had two failed marriages. You don't get to give me advice about this kind of stuff."

He reached behind him and snatched a folder off his desk, shoving it into my chest. "Take a look."

I sighed but opened the folder anyway.

*Jesus.*

My heartbeat echoed in my ears as I sifted through picture after picture of my father and Jared's mom, Katherine. Photos of them entering his apartment together, hugging and kissing in front of his window, him helping her out of cars . . .

"You're having an affair with Jared's mom?"

He nodded and headed around his desk to sit down. "Off and on for eighteen years now. There's nothing you can tell me about wanting something you can't have that I don't understand, Madoc. Katherine and I have had a lot of history, a lot of struggles, and bad timing. But we love each other, and I'm going to marry her as soon as possible."

"Are you serious?" I gasped and laughed at the same time. "What the fuck?"

I couldn't believe what I was hearing. Hey, I'm having an affair with your best friend's mom. Hey, we're getting married. And he talked about it as if he were commenting on the weather. That's my fucking father for you. He does what he wants, and you roll with it, or you don't. He was just like . . .

"Wait." My gut knotted up. "Eighteen years? You're not Jared's dad, are you?"

He looked at me like I was insane. "Of course not. She'd just had Jared when we met." Rubbing his hands over his face, he changed the subject. "I got this envelope from Fallon. Along with this and one of my business dealings, because for all intents and purposes, she's blackmailing me, Madoc."

The file folder crumpled in my fist. "You're lying."

"I'm not." He consoled me with his flat voice. "This is all so much more complicated than you realize, but I want you to know that although Fallon came back here with ulterior motives, I don't think she wanted to hurt you. She could've gone to the media with what she has on me. It would've hurt this family."

I stared at the pictures, my breath getting shallower, faster, and my face warming with anger.

"She's very angry," he continued softly as if thinking out loud. "But she didn't go to the media, Madoc. She didn't want to cause you any pain."

"Stop trying to protect me," I bit out, sitting down in the chair again.

If she came back to blackmail my dad, then everything else was a lie, too.

"So what does she have on you?" I asked. "Besides this?" I held up the folder.

He hooded his eyes and spoke hesitantly. "It was a payoff I negotiated. It was illegal and I could lose my license, to say the least. But it wasn't a decision I made lightly, and I would do it again." He looked straight at me. "Nonetheless, Fallon's not asking for much. And I didn't tell you any of this to hurt you. I told you so you could move forward. I didn't force Fallon to leave. She texted me last night."

He tossed me his phone, so I could see his messages. Sure enough, the first text was from Fallon.

"She's not right for you." His voice was like a distant echo as I stared at the words on his screen. "Her father, for starters . . ." He trailed off.

And then I lost him. My stomach sank, I dropped the phone on the floor, and then laid my elbows on my knees, burying my face in my hands.

I remembered this feeling. It's what I felt years ago when they'd told me she was gone all of a sudden. When I saw her empty bed where we lost our virginity together. And when I couldn't sleep, and I'd storm into the basement to play the piano.

I didn't want this again. I'd never wanted to feel that again. I inhaled a deep breath until my lungs ached so badly I thought they would burst.

"Stop talking," I cut him off from whatever he was talking about. "Just stop talking. Eighteen years?" I asked. "That means that you were seeing Katherine Trent when you were married to my mother."

His gaze dropped to his desk, and then back up to me. He said nothing, but I saw the guilt in his eyes.

*For Christ's sake. What the hell was the matter with him?*

"Madoc," he spoke low. "I'm sending you to Notre Dame early," he told me in a resigned voice.

*What?*

He must've seen the confused scowl on my face, because he explained. "Things are going to get sticky here. With the divorce, Patricia will have no choice but to come home. You'll stay at the house in South Bend until the dorms open up."

"Hell, no!" I shook my head, standing back up.

As usual, my father stayed calm, not moving. "Fine, then go see your mother in New Orleans for the rest of the summer. You will not stay here. I want you to get perspective, and you need space."

I ran my hand through my hair. *What the hell was happening?* I didn't want to go to Indiana for the rest of the summer. I barely knew anyone, other than some faculty my father had introduced me to here and there on our trips to sporting and alumni events.

I wasn't going. No fucking way!

And I wasn't going to New Orleans, either. My friends were here.

"Madoc." He shook his head at me like he could read my thoughts and was telling me no. "You will go, you will find a job or some volunteer work to pass your time, because right now I'm trying to protect you from yourself. I will pull my support, the tuition, your car, until you see the light. Distance is what you need right now. Do it, or you're going to force my hand."

In the span of a few short hours, I'd gone from disgustingly happy and excited about life to looking for a fight.

Fallon hadn't even taken anything she'd brought with her except the clothes on her back.

It was all a lie, but then what did I expect? We screwed. It's not like we talked about shit or had a date or had anything in common. There were other women to give me what she did.

But everything felt wrong again. Just like before. The clouds hung too low, the house was too empty, and I wasn't hungry. Not for food, not for a good time, not for anything except a fight.

I didn't care why I was mad. Hell, I wasn't even sure why I was mad. I just knew I had to take it out on someone.

I jumped in my car and sped over to Jared's house, knowing I wouldn't get pulled over. Cops never pulled me over. A perk of being my father's son. My sweaty palms strangled the steering wheel as I jacked up Linkin Park's "Numb" and hauled ass. My tires screeched to a halt in front of his house, and I jumped out of the car, not caring that Tate and her dad were under the hood of his car with him.

"Your mom is messing around with my dad?" I shouted.

All three of them spun around to face me.

"Dude, what?" Jared looked confused, wiping his hands on a shop cloth.

I stalked across the lawn, sticking my keys in my pocket while Jared met me halfway. "Your slut of a mother has been sleeping with my dad for years," I snarled. "He's been giving her money, and they're like getting married and shit!"

Jared's eyes flared, and he knew I was looking for a fight. Mr. Brandt and Tate looked at me with wide eyes and open mouths.

Tate looked down, talking more to herself. "I guess it makes sense. She's been seeing someone and keeping it hush-hush." She let out a nervous laugh. "Wow."

I sneered at her. "Yeah, it's awesome," I shot back sarcastically. "My mother crying when my dad didn't come home at night. Me trying to figure out why my dad worked so much instead of making it to my soccer games." I raised my hands and got in Jared's face. "When what to my wondering eyes should appear but another gold-digging whore ready to make her career."

Jared didn't wait another second. His punch slammed me square in the jaw, and I laughed as I stumbled backward.

"Come on!" I urged him forward, the heat in his eyes full of fire.

He rushed me, and we fell to the ground, scrambling over each other. He hovered over me, his fist missing my jaw. I growled and threw him over, swinging my fist into his face and bringing in my other fist across his jaw.

"Stop!" I heard Tate yell. "Jax! Do something!"

*Jax?* Oh yeah. He lived here.

"Why?" I heard him ask.

Jared's hands wrapped around my neck, and he locked his arms as straight as steel bars, holding me as far away from him as he could.

"Asshole!" I coughed.

He barely unclenched his teeth. "Fucking dickhead."

Freezing water splashed my back, splashing around my arms and hitting Jared in the face.

"What the . . . ?" I barked.

The stream of water hit me in the face, and Jared released my neck to shield his head from the cold attack while I rolled off of him. We wiped the water out of our eyes and sat up, glaring at the hose-man until we noticed it was Mr. Brandt. And he looked pissed. His khaki shorts were splattered with water, and he had grease stains on his White Sox T-shirt.

"Your parents are seeing each other." He spoke low, a hundred-pound weight in every word. "Worst case scenario they break up. Best-case scenario, you're stepbrothers."

"So?" I blurted without the good sense to shut up.

He threw down the hose and yelled, "So what are you fighting about?"

I swallowed, my mouth gone dry.

*Yeah, I forgot about that part.* Jared and Jax were already my brothers as far as I was concerned, but having our families connected like that might be pretty cool.

Unless the marriage didn't work out. Which with my father's history was damn well possible.

But on the other hand, his marriages probably failed because of his affair with Jared's mom. Now that they could be together, it might be forever.

"I don't know," I mumbled.

Standing up, I couldn't look at any of them, but I knew they were all looking at me. Why the hell did I attack my best friend? I had called his mother a slut, for crying out loud.

All of Jared's shit while Tate was in France came back. He'd missed her. He'd loved her, even though he hadn't known it then. And he had been withering away without her. He fought. He drank. He screwed.

And none of it made him feel any better.

So why was I screwing up my life for a chick I didn't even love? Who didn't even deserve my attention?

I could understand Jared losing control of himself for Tate. She was a good girl, and she fought for him. And when that didn't work, she fought against him. She never stopped showing him that she was there.

But Fallon wasn't Tate. She wasn't even in the same league.

All of this was so stupid. I had no reason to go off the rails just because she popped back into town and fucked with me again.

Holding out my hand, I was relieved when Jared took it. I helped him up, hoping he took that as an apology. Jared and I didn't need to get all girly. He knew I fucked up, and he knew that I knew it.

"Oh, look." I smirked. "Fixing your car again? That's a Ford for you."

And I walked to my GTO, hearing Tate's snort behind me.

## CHAPTER 15

---

# FALLON

My father's house had been fairly empty when I arrived two weeks ago. That was exactly what I'd been looking for. While some people craved distraction and noise, I craved quiet country roads and no one talking to me. The seventy-five-hundred-square-foot brick estate sat in a private cul-de-sac and was another example of a rich shit spending his money on something he rarely used.

Okay, my dad wasn't really a rich shit. Well, kind of. But I still loved him.

The house went for three million dollars, and when I questioned him about why he got a house when he could have gotten an apartment in the city, he gave me a geography lesson on why America is so well positioned from the rest of the world.

"Before the invention of rockets and nuclear weapons that could fly long distances," he'd said, "it was very hard for any nation to attack this country. We're strategically positioned between two oceans with friendly allies to the north and south. And let's face it"—he lowered his voice to a whisper—"even if they weren't friendly, we're not really scared of Canada or Mexico anyway. Everywhere else, you have possible enemies surrounding you. Europe is a war strategist's nightmare. Enemies can invade at any time, or threaten your buffer states. To attack America, one would have to sail over an ocean or fly a long distance. That's why the Japanese attacked Pearl Harbor. They wouldn't have had the fuel to get to the mainland. So . . ." He set the Shirley Temple he'd made down in front of me. "I pay to put a nice big buffer of land around my family and me, so I can see my enemies coming before they're at my door."

By that point I knew what my father did for a living, and while I knew it was wrong, I never hated him for it. I hated that he made me stay with my mother so much, and I hated that there were long periods when I didn't see him, but he trusted me and always spoke to me like an adult. He always used big words and never held my hand crossing streets. He taught me things and expected the best from me.

To my thinking, when someone gave out their compliments and good opinions rarely, they meant more. My father was the only person on the planet whose respect and regard I cared about protecting.

"So did you get what you want?" He strolled into the kitchen as I sat at the granite-top island working on my laptop.

No "hi" or "how are you," but I was used to it. I hadn't seen him in a month, and he'd just arrived in town today.

"Yes, I did," I replied, not looking up from my work as he went to the refrigerator.

"And your mother?" He plucked a frosted glass out of the freezer and went to the Guinness tap.

"Still AWOL. But she'll show up soon enough to contest the divorce, I'm sure."

I didn't know why he was asking me about this. I had sent him an e-mail, letting him know everything was on schedule. He'd never been totally on board with my plan for a little revenge against those who had betrayed me, but he'd let me make my own choices and done what he could to help.

"You'll get caught in the cross fire," he pointed out.

I wiggled my fingers against the keys, forgetting what I had been writing. "Of course."

"Madoc?" he pressed, and I let out a silent breath, aggravated that he was asking so many questions.

I knew what he wanted to know, though.

"I changed my mind," I explained. "I didn't want him hit with this, after all."

"Good." He surprised me, and I looked up, meeting his eyes. "He was just a kid, too, I guess," he offered.

I had returned to Shelburne Falls with the intention of releasing the media package once I'd proved that I had moved past Madoc, that he no longer had my heart or my head. Nothing went according to plan, though. Instead of humiliating Madoc, his father, and my mother, I'd taken the path of least resistance.

I didn't want Madoc hurt, because he didn't deserve it. I had been hurt at sixteen when I'd stolen one of my dad's cars and driven back to Shelburne Falls only to find Madoc with someone else. But as adult as our actions were back then, we were only kids. I couldn't hate Madoc for making mistakes any more than I could blame our unborn child for being created.

Madoc never loved me, but I knew he never wanted to hurt me, either.

So I changed the plan. I got what I wanted, but I did it quietly without any embarrassment to him or his dad.

I lowered my hands to my lap and picked at my cuticles. Nervous habit. I knew my dad didn't like it. He and Mr. Caruthers were alike in many ways.

I lightened my voice. "Ted should make parole."

"Fallon." He shook his head in aggravation. "I told you not to involve yourself with that."

"He's your uncle. Which means he's my family."

"That's not—"

"When someone you love needs you," I interrupted, "you suck it up."

I smiled at Tate's words coming out of my mouth. I wished I'd gotten to know her more.

I returned my gaze to the computer and started typing again, signaling that the conversation was over. He stood there for several seconds, taking sips of his beer every so often and watching me. I refused to look at him or let him see my shaking fingers. There were things I would never tell my father, no matter how much I loved him.

He wouldn't know that I'd lost five pounds in the past two weeks or that I'd had dreams every night that made me never want to wake up.

I clenched my teeth and blinked away the burn in my eyes, typing nonsense just so I could look like I had my shit together in front of my dad.

"*Nothing that happens on the surface of the sea can alter the calm of its depths,*" my father would say, quoting Andrew Harvey.

But the depths weren't calm. A black hole had opened up in the center of my stomach from seeing Madoc again and it was sucking me in little by little. The sky got blacker every day, and my heart beat slower and slower.

"*You're going to ruin me, Fallon.*"

I punched the keys harder. I had no idea what I was writing for the summer course I'd picked up to keep busy.

My father walked toward the doorway but stopped to look at me before leaving. "Do you feel better now?"

I swallowed the ache. At least I tried to. But I tipped my chin up anyway and looked at him head-on. "I never expected to feel better. I just wanted them to feel worse."

He stood there in silence for a moment and then walked out.

A week later, I came out of the shower to see that I had missed calls from my mother and Tate.

I clenched the phone in my hand, wanting to talk to one of them but knowing I shouldn't and knowing I should talk to the other but not wanting to. Neither had left messages, but Tate had texted after the call.

**Need a roommate at NW?**

My eyes narrowed, but I smiled a little despite myself. Without hesitation I called her back.

"Hey, there you are," she answered, laughter in her voice.

"What's this about a roommate?" I lay back on my bed, my wet hair splayed across the sheets.

"Well," she started, "my dad finally accepted that I really want to go to Northwestern—and I do. I just didn't tell him that I'd changed my plans because of him. Anyway, he won't let me live with Jared. He's insisting on the full college experience and wants me in the dorms the first year."

"You listen to your daddy. That's cute," I teased, although I envied her having such an involved parent.

She snorted. "People don't deliberately piss off my father. Especially Jared."

My face fell immediately at the mention of her boyfriend. Madoc aside, I had threatened Jason Caruthers with exposing Jared's mom. I wondered if he knew. It didn't sound like Tate did. I didn't think she would have forgiven me easily for that—and I was surprised to feel a sudden pang of guilt at having betrayed her friendship.

"So," she continued, mischief in her voice. "Are you in the dorms this year?"

"Yeah, and I happen to have a double I'm using as a single."

It was perfect actually. Tate and I got along, and for some reason, I was looking forward to school starting now.

"A single? You don't want to be in a single. It's soooo lonely," she drawled out with exaggeration.

I laughed.

But I was still unsure. Tate meant Jared. And Jared meant Madoc. I couldn't be around him.

He wouldn't want to be around me.

"Tate, I don't know. I mean, I'd love to have you as a roomie—but to be honest, Madoc and I don't get along. I just don't think it's the best situation for us to run into each other."

"Madoc?" She sounded confused. "Madoc would only be around Jared's apartment if he ever came to Chicago for visits, which I'm not sure is going to happen. Madoc's off the radar these days."

I sat up. "What do you mean?"

"He got sent to Notre Dame early. His dad has a house there, I guess, so Madoc went there until school starts and the dorms open up next month." She hesitated, and another wave of guilt racked me.

*He was gone.*

And he was probably sent away from home because of me.

She continued. "It's probably for the best. With Madoc's dad and Jared's mom getting together, Madoc was pretty pissed. He and Jared got in a fight, and no one has talked to him in weeks. We're all just giving him some space."

*Shit.*

*What about Lucas? Has Madoc come home to spend time with his little brother at all?*

My face fell, and I felt like shit all over again. This was my fault. Maybe I should have felt like it was poetic justice for Madoc to be sent away like I was, but I didn't want him alone. And I hated that he'd had to leave his little brother.

"So?" she prompted. "What do you think?"

What did I think? I wanted to say yes, but I knew I should be distancing myself from anyone Madoc-related.

I sighed, trying to hide the nervousness in my voice. "I say we're going to have a kick-ass year, roomie."

"Hell, yeah!" she screamed and then jacked up her God-awful metal music in the background.

I pulled the phone away from my ear and winced.

*Wow.*

# CHAPTER 16

# MADOC

My hands dug deep into her bottom, squeezing the firm flesh as I buried my face in her neck. I didn't look at her. If I didn't, I could almost imagine that . . .

"Mr. Caruthers, stop. Not here." She squirmed against my body and giggled as she tried pushing me away.

"I told you not to call me that," I whispered to her.

"Fine," she conceded. "Madoc, then. Let's go to your room."

"But this is more fun."

Brianna—or Brenna?—had her legs wrapped around my waist, and I had her pinned to the wall next to my bedroom in my father's South Bend house. She came once a week, cleaned and did laundry, and I didn't wait long before making my move. I wasn't sure how old she was, but she was at least twenty-four or twenty-five, and pretty as hell.

Blond hair, blue eyes, and always wearing good-girl clothes like capris and fitted polos. Definitely far from where I had strayed before.

"We need condoms," she pointed out.

I let out a sigh as I let her down and pulled her behind me into my room.

Other than Brenna, my life here was more boring than a tractor pull. Classes hadn't started yet, I hadn't made any friends since students weren't on campus yet, and the town was dead without the college crowd. Yep, like it or not, this girl was the highlight of my week. Her tits were bigger than my head, and when she left I was smiling again.

At least for a little while.

Unbuttoning my jeans, I watched as she stripped out of her clothes and dug a condom out of the nightstand. Sauntering over to me in her white lace bra and panties, she reached into my black boxer briefs and rubbed my hard-on.

She looked at me, licking her lips and grinning. My breath shook, and I looked away. I didn't know what it was, but I couldn't look at her. I never could. I didn't even remember her name half the time.

I didn't want her to be real.

Gripping her hair at the back of her head, I pulled her in for a kiss. Our teeth rubbed together, and I heard her moan. From the hard kiss or pleasure, I didn't know, and I really didn't care.

"I want it now," she panted, rubbing me harder.

My jaw steeled, and I broke the kiss, grabbing her by the elbow and hauling her over to the bed.

"You don't order me. You don't own me. You got that?" I bit out.

A flash of excitement crossed her eyes like lightning. "Yes, sir."

I stuck my fingers underneath the hem of my briefs and yanked them down my legs, kicking them to the side. Gripping the back of her neck, I brought her down with me as I lay down. "Go down."

Cool oxygen poured into my lungs, and my heart pumped faster.
*Quick-quick.*
*Quick-quick.*

*Quick-quick.*

Her mouth descended between my legs, and I squeezed my eyes shut, reveling in the pleasure of how eager she was. She licked and sucked, taking all of me in as her hair warmed my thighs.

*"I want to see you. I want to kiss you when you come."*

I tried to shut that voice out of my mind, instead putting my hands on Brenna's head and pushing her down further on my cock.

"Keep going, baby," I grunted, urging her on. "That feels good."

Her head bobbed up and down as she sucked harder, and I arched my hips up into her mouth.

*"Who's kissing you right now? Who's riding you?"*

"More. Harder," I ordered, but despite my best intentions the blond hair I gripped turned a light brown and smoky green eyes stared up me. "God, that's good, baby."

And whether I liked it or not, I retreated into my head where Fallon lived and let the fantasy take over. I didn't want to think about that bitch. I didn't want to want her, but I did.

Fallon was here, with her mouth on me right now, and I hated her. I fucking hated her, and I was going to fuck her with that hate until I came.

The nerves in my legs burned, leading in to my groin and everything pooled between my legs. I punched my hips up into her, going deeper and harder, while her tongue rubbed against my underside.

She took her mouth off me and then licked me up and down, before wrapping her hand around the shaft, stroking as she sucked the head.

*"Madoc, please."*

"Fuck." I jerked, arching my back and pulling my head off the bed.

I came in her mouth, gripping her hair at her neck and sucking air through my teeth. She worked me until I was done, and I collapsed back on the bed, letting her go.

My body always felt more relaxed.

Afterward.

But my head was in even more knots.

Fallon. It always returned to Fallon. I couldn't get off anymore unless I thought of her.

I wanted to look down and see ears full of piercings and the random little tattoos she had all over her body. I wanted to see the sexy green eyes in black eyeliner looking up and killing me with everything inside of her that she tried to hide.

Why? Why did I want her so much when she kept leaving?

"Who's Fallon?" I heard a voice tap into my head from somewhere. I blinked and asked, "What?"

"Fallon. You said that name while I was . . ." She trailed off. *Shit.*

"It's no one. You probably misheard."

*Son of a bitch! Shit. Seriously, dude?*

Brenna sat up. "You yelled it when you were coming. Are you into guys? Fallon is a guy's name, isn't it?" She looked at me out of the corner of her eye, teasing me with a grin.

"It's not a fucking guy," I growled and then looked straight at her. "It's my sister, actually."

She laughed it off until she noticed that I wasn't laughing. Then she shut the hell up.

"Um, okay." She scooted off the bed, looking like she wanted to run. "That's not weird."

She dressed quietly and quickly, saying nothing before she walked out. The rumble in my chest broke loose, and I laughed miserably as I slid back under the covers.

"Hey!" I jerked up in bed. "What the hell?" I asked, because I had no idea why my ass was stinging.

"Get up!"

I rubbed the sleep from my eyes and peered up at my mother at the end of the bed. She grabbed the sheet and yanked it off of me. Thank God I had my basketball shorts on.

Her pink lips were pressed tight in disapproval, and her hands sat on her hips.

"Did you just slap me on the ass?" I pissed and moaned, falling back onto the bed and throwing my arm over my eyes.

"Get up!" she barked again.

Normally, I enjoyed seeing my mom. She was a lot of fun, and she was a pretty decent parent actually. She and my father each remarried fairly quickly, and I hated that she had moved away. Her new husband lived in New Orleans. But asking a kid to leave his home and everything he'd known was too much. I stayed with my father and his new wife.

Bright idea, that was.

I sighed. "I was sleeping. Why are you even here?" My exasperated tone told her everything.

I just wanted to be left alone.

"Your father called and told me what happened."

"Nothing happened," I lied, keeping my bored expression focused on the ceiling. Headlights from a car outside flashed across the ceiling in the dimly lit room, and I knew that I'd slept all day.

I heard my mother's heels *clunk, clunk, clunk* across the wooden floor. "Get up!" she urged again, and the next thing I knew she was swatting me with a magazine.

I brought up my arms and legs to shield me. "Damn, woman!"

She fired the magazine across the room, tucked her long blond hair behind her ear and stomped toward my closet.

"And I fired Brittany," she bit out over her shoulder.

"Who's Brittany?"

"The housekeeper you're bedding. Now get up and shower." She threw clean jeans and a T-shirt at me and walked out of the room.

I shook my head at nothing, amazed with the women in my life. Complete ballbusters.

I flipped over, burying my face in my pillow.

"Now!" She thundered from somewhere downstairs, and I punched my pillow in aggravation.

But I got up. If I didn't, she'd be in with a bucket of cold water next.

After I'd showered and dressed, she took me to a quiet Italian place that was big on candles and Frank Sinatra. I ordered one of their pizzas, and my mother nibbled some pasta with olive oil.

"Why did Dad call you?" I asked, sitting back in the chair with my hands locked behind my head.

"Because he hasn't seen any transactions on his credit card other than to the gas station. You've probably consumed nothing except Doritos and Fanta for weeks now. And he knew you'd rather see me than him, so . . ."

That was about right. I didn't like to eat alone, so I snacked, and I was too pissed off right now to be sociable. Gas station food it was, then.

And I damn well didn't want to see anyone, but my mom was preferable to my dad.

"Did he tell you . . ."—I lowered my voice—"that he's getting married?" I didn't want to upset my mom in case she didn't know, so I tried to keep my tone gentle. I'd also heard that his current wife was suing for our house—my house—and it made me sick.

"Yes, he told me." She nodded, taking a sip of her white wine. "And I'm happy for him, Madoc."

"Happy?" I sneered. "How can you be happy? He cheated on you with her. It's been going on for years."

Her eyes dropped for a split second, and she placed her hands in the lap of her white pencil skirt. I took in a breath but immediately felt like dropping the argument. I was a dick.

"I'm happy, Madoc." She straightened her shoulders and looked at me. "It still hurts that he could do that to me, but I have a wonderful husband, a healthy and smart son, and a life that I love. Why am I going to waste my time being mad at your dad when I wouldn't change anything in my life?" She offered a small but genuine smile. "And believe it or not, your father loves Katherine. She and I will never go on shopping trips," she joked, "but he loves her, which is okay with me. It's time to move on."

Did she think I wasn't doing that? I may not be firing on all cylinders at the moment, and I may be missing my friends like crazy, but my father was right. Distance and perspective. I was working on it.

She picked up her fork, digging into her meal again. "He also told me what happened with Fallon."

"Let's not talk about her." I picked up a piece of pizza and stuffed a bite into my mouth.

"You deleted your Facebook and Twitter accounts," she scolded, "and you're holed up in an empty house. Why don't you just come and spend the last six weeks of summer with me?"

"Because I'm fine," I burst out, my mouth full. "I am. I'm getting an early start here, making friends, and I'm planning to take a look at the soccer team at Notre Dame."

"Madoc—" she tried, but I interrupted.

"I'm fine," I maintained, my voice even. "Everything's fine."

And I continued to tell her that every day when she regularly texted me to check in, every time she called, and every time she made Addie come and check on me.

For the rest of the summer, I was fine.

# OCTOBER

# CHAPTER 17

# FALLON

My alarm went off, and Sublime's "What I Got" played on my radio. I pulled my comforter back up, having kicked it off during the night. The morning chill was getting worse every day, and I couldn't believe that it was already October. Tate and I had moved into the dorm a little over a month ago, and time had flown by as we settled in and started our heavy class loads.

Neither of us had a job, but school kept us rocking around the clock. When I wasn't in my room or at class, I was in the library. When Tate wasn't in our room or the library, she was at Jared's apartment in the city.

At first she tried only staying there on the weekends—respecting her father's wishes and all—but now it had become more frequent. They couldn't stay away from each other. Most weekends they traveled back to Shelburne Falls to visit her dad and for them both to race at the Loop—whatever that was. I never went, though. No way.

While it was lonely around the dorm when she went home—I still hadn't really made any friends—I couldn't begrudge them the time they spent together. They were in love. Plus, over the past couple of months, I'd grown to like Jared a lot. He put on a macho act, but that was all it was. An act.

Tate and I studied together and went out once in a while. Since Jared attended the University of Chicago, he didn't hang around our campus much. They often invited me along on their dates, but I had no interest in being a third wheel.

The heavy wooden dorm room door clicked open.

"Fallon, are you awake?" I heard Tate call.

I sat up, leaning back on my elbows. "Yes?" I replied as more of a question, blinking against the morning light. "What time is it?"

Reaching over, I turned my alarm clock to see it was only six in the morning. Tate threw her backpack on her bed and started yanking stuff out of drawers. She was still in the same clothes from last night. Usually when she spent the night at Jared's, she came home freshly showered and dressed, ready for class. Right now, she looked rushed.

"What classes do you have today?" she asked, not looking at me as she darted around our room.

I swallowed the dryness from my mouth. "Um . . . Calc III and Sex and Scandal in Early Modern England."

"Nice," she teased in a deep voice.

"The last one is a gen. ed.," I explained, embarrassed. "Why? What's up?"

"Do you feel like skipping?" She stuffed clothes into her backpack and then turned to look at me. "Jax showed up at Jared's dorm this morning. No one's heard from Madoc. He's not returning calls, texts, IMs . . ." She trailed off, hands on her hips.

"You haven't talked to him at all lately?" I looked away, not wanting her to see the worry I was sure was on my face.

"Yeah, Jared and I let it go at first, because we thought Madoc needed his space, and we've all been so busy. But if Jax is worried, then it's definitely past time to check it out." She stopped, finally taking a breath.

She came over, tapping my leg and smiling. "So let's go on a road trip!" she said before darting over to our sink area to retrieve her toiletries.

*Go to Notre Dame?* My heart started talking a mile a minute with its *thud-thud-pound-crash* rhythm.

I shook my head and lay back down, my voice quiet. "Nah, I don't think so, Tate. You guys have fun."

"What? What are you going to do all weekend?" She popped her head around the corner. "You should come with us, Fallon. You're his family."

She talked to me like a mom, pointing out that I should care about Madoc when she thought I didn't. The truth was I did care about him even though I shouldn't.

And I did not need the reminder that our parents were still married to each other. My mother had been fighting the divorce, and to make matters worse, she was trying to take Madoc's house. Caruthers's affair came out in the media, and during a moment of weakness, I actually felt bad for the guy. I e-mailed him the photos, hotel receipts, and contact information that would give him the proof he needed that my mother had not been a loyal wife, either. Strangely, he didn't use any of it.

Maybe he didn't want my help, or maybe the proof of my mother's infidelity would only bring more attention he didn't want. I couldn't help but have a tiny bit more respect for him for not dragging her name through the dirt.

"I'm not really his family, Tate. It was never like that with us." I ran the tongue ring I'd put back in between my teeth, thinking. "And he's fine, you know? If he were dead, the credit card transactions would've stopped. In which case his father would be on top of it. He's fine."

She walked back around the corner, her eyebrows narrowed in resolve, and tossed her toiletries on her bed.

Heading over to me, she hovered. "He could be drunk twenty-four/seven or on drugs." Her tone was calm but threatening. "He could be depressed or suicidal. Now get your ass packed. I don't want to talk about this again. We leave in one hour."

Tate and I drove in her G8, while Jax and Jared led the way in the Boss to Indiana on I-90. The drive was short—only about an hour and a half—but with the way these people drove it only took a little over an hour. With barely any time on the road, I didn't have nearly enough highway to get my hands to stop shaking or my mouth to stop going dry.

*What the hell am I doing?* I almost buried my face in my hands.

Madoc wouldn't want me there. Knowing him, he was probably knee-deep in sorority princesses and keg parties. He was going to insult me, create a scene, or worse—I'd see him broken and losing control. Did I really have that kind of power over him, though?

Of course not.

I blew out a breath and pulled the tip of my cap over my eyes, leaning back in the seat.

It was foolish to even think Madoc would be upset about me leaving him without a good-bye. It's not like we had a relationship. No, if he was off the reservation, it was because his plans for the summer had been ruined. And yes—he was going to blame me for that. As he should.

I threw my baseball cap into the backseat and fluffed my hair.

*To hell with it.*

I shouldn't be in this car, but it was too late now. I could act like I was hiding and embarrassed or look like I belonged there. He got bamboozled. Well, so did I.

Taking out my brush, I teased my hair to make it messier and touched up my makeup in the mirror. My black eye shadow still looked good, but I needed more mascara and some clear lip gloss.

Addie once gave me great advice about makeup. It's not supposed to make you pretty. It's supposed to make you prettier. Translation: less is more. I added to my eyes to make them pop, because they were my best feature. But I usually left the rest alone.

My blue nail polish was chipped, and my jeans were holey. But from the waist up in my short-sleeved black T-shirt, I looked okay.

"We got his address from Addie," Tate said as we pulled up in front of a two-story house near campus. "I guess he decided against the dorms and moved in with some friends."

I peered through Tate's window as she parked across the street. This wasn't Madoc's father's house. I'd been there once. This house, although large, was still smaller and the white paint was fresh, whereas the Caruthers's house was made of brick. This must have been a rental for college students.

Jared and Jax climbed out of the car, and I followed Tate, gripping the door and debating about just staying with the car.

*Damn! Damn! Damn!* I started bobbing on my toes, and I slammed the door with too much force.

"What do we say? 'Surprise'?" Tate asked Jared, grabbing his hand.

"I don't care what you say. I'm gonna break his nose." Jared stuck his other hand in his hoodie, steam damn near coming from his nose. "This is ridiculous making us all worry like this," he mumbled.

Jared walked up the steps and pounded on the forest green wooden door, alternating between his fist and the knocker. Jax and Tate flanked him, and I stayed back. Way back.

With my hands in my pockets.

Eyes averted.

And my guilt tucked firmly up my ass.

"Can I help you?"

I spun around to see a young woman, about my age, coming up the walkway behind us.

She was dressed in a short, cute jean skirt and a Fighting Irish T-shirt. Her face sparkled in the sun with gold and navy glitter from the huge "N" and "D" painted on her cheeks.

"Yeah," Tate spoke up. "We're here to see Madoc. Do you know him?"

She broke out in a bright, white smile. "I'm sure he's already at the game."

"The game?" Jax asked.

I couldn't dislodge the bowling ball from my throat. Who was this girl?

"Yeah, the soccer game," she offered, walking past us up the steps. "The team's been gone since early this morning. I came back for chairs for the after-party. Best get them now. Everyone will be too drunk later," she laughed.

She hauled up three collapsible lawn chairs from the porch and hooked the handles over her shoulders.

"Madoc's on a *soccer* team?"

I almost laughed at Jared's question. He sounded like he wanted to vomit.

The girl stopped and cocked her head to the side, looking at him like she wasn't sure what to say. After all, if we were his friends, we would've known that he played soccer, right?

"Call Madoc, would you?" Jax approached her, using a smooth voice as he shrugged. "Our phones are dead."

She pinched her eyebrows together, knowing that he was lying. "Um, okay."

Taking her cell from the back of her skirt pocket, she dialed and tilted her head to get the phone between her blond hair and her ear.

"Hey, babe," she greeted, and my heart felt like someone had dug away the bottom and was letting the blood seep out.

*Shit. Shit. Shit.*

"Get Madoc, will you?" she asked, and I blinked. "He has friends at the house that want to talk to him for a minute."

I let out a breath, but I wasn't sure what the hell was wrong with me. That wasn't his girlfriend. But why the hell did I care if he had a girlfriend? I just hadn't thought about it. I hadn't even entertained the idea that he'd moved on. Of course he would. I guess I thought I'd never have to see or hear of it.

I watched, seeing her smile as she shook her head.

"Well, tell his girlfriend to unwrap herself from him then," she ordered, and my eyes flared. "His friends here seem . . . intense." She smirked at Jared, obviously teasing him, but my chest had gone and plummeted all over again.

*What the fuck?*

Jax came up to the girl and took the phone she offered. "Madoc, it's Jax," he said in a serious tone. "I'm at your house. Tate and I want confirmation you're not drunk, high, or suicidal. Jared's here, but he could care less. We'll meet you after your game, or I'll give Tate a crowbar and set her to work on your car."

He hung up and tossed the phone back to the girl with the abnormally raised eyebrows.

I spun around and headed down the walkway, taking a right on the sidewalk.

*To hell with this.*

What a stupid idea. Why did I come here?

"Fallon, wait!" Tate called behind me, but I dug into the pavement harder, quickening my steps.

She grabbed my arm and tried to turn me around, but I kept going.

"Where are you going?" she shouted.

"Back to Chicago! He's fine. Screwing around as usual."

The late-morning breeze rustled the leaves overhead and blew my hair into my face as I walked.

*Damn him.* I couldn't believe this. I actually came thinking he was hurt or in trouble.

"Fallon." Tate jogged right in front of me and blocked my way. "I'm confused. What's going on?"

"He's fine!" I pointed out, holding out my palm in the air. "Obviously! You were stupid to worry. I told you."

He's on a soccer team. No. He's on the Notre Dame soccer team. And he has a girlfriend! Who has her pretty little preppy self wrapped around him right at this moment.

*I'm so stupid.*

I veered around Tate and kept walking.

"Stop!" she growled in a deep voice. "How are you going to get back home?"

My steps slowed, and I looked around the neighborhood, searching my brain.

*Yeah, I forgot that part.* I wasn't walking back to Chicago.

"Fallon, what's with you and Madoc?" Tate came around to face me again, her arms crossed over her chest. "Is there something going on between you two?"

"Please." I tried to laugh it off, but it came out like a croak.

*Smooth, Fallon.*

"There is, isn't there?" She smiled knowingly. "That's what all that commotion was about when you took off with his car that night. And you're the reason he split so early in the summer."

I averted my eyes, checking out the super-interesting cracks in the sidewalk. Tate was a friend now. A good friend. And I couldn't lie to her.

But I couldn't bring myself to talk about it, either.

"Oh, my God!" she blurted out, obviously taking my silence as a confirmation. "Seriously?"

"Oh, shut up."

She crossed her arms over her chest and pursed her lips. "So is it hot?" she prompted.

I rolled my eyes, avoiding the question.

The voice in my dreams crept back into my head. *"Sit on the car. . . . Spread your legs."*

Tate must've seen the longing in my eyes, because she burst out, "I knew it!"

"Yeah, well," I jumped in, "it's not true love, Tate."

For him, anyway.

# CHAPTER 18

# MADOC

"Come on, let's get this over with." I waved Jared and Jax in to take the punch they wanted to hand out.

I'd just walked out of the locker room after showering and dressing post-game to find them waiting with Tate. I clutched the backpack I had slung over my shoulder and waited. In all honesty, I'd expected them sooner, like a month ago.

Tate walked up to me slowly, and I leaned down to pick her up in a hug.

Bad idea.

Her fist swung out and pounded me right in the arm, making me stumble backward.

"Damn it, Tate." I winced, hearing Jax laughing in the background.

At least she avoided my nose this time.

"You're a jerk," she scolded. "Here we're thinking you're in bad shape, and you're just fine! Playing soccer and partying. What's the matter with you?"

Still wincing, I rubbed my arm and dropped my backpack. "Nothing. I know I've been out of touch, but you shouldn't have worried. You're just mad because you missed my hot ass, huh?"

She huffed, and I laughed a little. They cared. Enough to show up at my school and ambush me outside my soccer game. As pissed off as they looked, it made me happy that they'd come.

In truth, I'd known they would. And for some reason, I just couldn't reach out myself. I didn't want to hear about how much fun they were having at home this summer. I didn't want to take the chance of hearing any gossip or news about my father's divorce.

I missed my friends, and I knew I'd miss them more if I stayed in contact.

That's how it had to be. Until now.

Jared stepped forward, and Tate placed a casual hand around his waist, bunching up his gray T-shirt.

"Damn right, we shouldn't have worried, asshole," he growled in a low voice. "Fallon was right."

I straightened, my neck heating up. "What are you talking about?"

I hadn't said her name out loud in months. I'd thought about her, though, even though I didn't want to.

"She came with us today." Tate looked too happy to deliver that blow but then tightened her lips. "But she split when it was obvious that you were fine."

*Wait, what?*

"Why is she with you?" I shook my head, disbelieving.

"Because Tate and Fallon are roommates," Jared chimed in, losing patience. "What's the big deal?"

"What?" I blurted. "She lives with you?"

"Yeah." Tate let out a bitter laugh. "You two don't keep in touch much, do you?"

I nodded sarcastically, bending down to pick up my bag. "That's awesome. She's living with one of my best friends and hanging out with the other two."

"Well, she's been a better friend than you lately," Jared gritted out. "I can't believe we had to chase you down like this."

"Yeah, we better get a good time out of this tonight," Jax chimed in, shoving his hands into the front pocket of his hoodie.

I barely heard them, the anger pouring in and out of my lungs faster by the second.

I looked at Tate. "Where is Fallon?" I asked.

"She said she was going to walk around until we were ready to leave." She took out her phone and began texting. "We thought we'd stay the night, but I have a race in Shelburne Falls tomorrow night, so we weren't staying the whole weekend. But . . ." She looked up. "You seem happy as a clam without us here, so I guess we'll head back tonight."

*No.*

"You're not leaving. I've been a jerk, and I can't explain right now, but . . ." I nodded. "I want you guys here."

Tate sighed, looking at her phone. "She's at the Grotto."

I blew out a huge-ass breath and tossed Jared my dad's house key. "You remember where my dad's house is at, right?" He'd tagged along one weekend when Tate was in France two years ago.

"You all go there," I said, walking toward my car. "I'll go get Fallon."


The Grotto was a landmark at Notre Dame and a reproduction of a French shrine where the Virgin Mary appeared to Saint Bernadette in the 1800s. For believers and nonbelievers, it was a beautiful spot on campus where people went to pray, meditate, think, or just be quiet for a while.

I couldn't claim to be churchgoing guy, but even I lit candles there before games and tests.

Just in case.

It's also where my father proposed to my mother more than twenty years ago. And look how that turned out.

I didn't know what I would say to Fallon, and I wasn't even sure what I wanted from this. Did I want her to leave? *No.* Should I want her to leave? *Yes.*

She deserved every fucking cold shoulder in the world. What nerve she had showing up here. Blackmailing my father; nearly throwing Jared's mom under the bus; and jerking me up, down, and all around for her own pleasure.

Sure, I'd spun out for a few weeks after getting to South Bend, but then I'd zoned in on soccer and my friends. I was fine.

And yeah, I'd gone AWOL on my best friends. And sure, I'd barely laughed since being here, but I was still handsome like nobody's business.

That worked for me.

Walking through the clean-cut lawns, veering down sidewalks under the canopy of nearly bare trees, I spotted the Grotto tucked back into a rock wall.

And Fallon was there.

Not sitting and sulking like I thought she'd be. Or wanted her to be.

No, she was standing in front of the shrine, hands in her back pockets, staring at the sea of candles flickering in the light wind. The Virgin Mary sat perched in her cove above to the right, and I shook my head, smiling at the irony.

People came here to pray. A few individuals were kneeling before the fence separating them from the shrine right now.

I couldn't yell at her here. Damn.

Sitting down on the bench behind her, I threw my arms over the back and waited for her to turn around.

Her light brown hair blew across her shoulders, and her small hands cupped her ass in her jeans pockets. I closed my damn mouth and swallowed.

"You know," she started, turning her face to the side, "it's inappropriate for you to stare at my ass here."

The couple praying looked over at her and then to me and back down to their hands.

*Yeah, pray for us.*

"But it's the only nice thing about you, little sister."

The couple's gasp made me want to laugh, and they got up, the woman glaring at me as they walked off. I tightened my jaw, not wanting to admit that this was the first time I'd genuinely laughed in a while.

Fallon's back straightened, and she turned around slowly, her patient eyes marking me, but I nudged my way in before she got started.

"So what did you think?" I asked. "That I was slowly circling the drain of despair without you?"

She hooded her eyes, embarrassment warming her cheeks. "I shouldn't have come. Tate was sure you were snorting coke off a hooker's ass on a daily basis. She bullied me."

She'd be the expert. I laughed to myself, but then I tensed up.

She talked about Tate like they were friends. Like they had a whole relationship, and I wasn't aware of it.

Hell, I wasn't. I dropped the ball, and Fallon picked up what I had let go.

Fallon watched me, and I realized she wasn't wearing her glasses. She usually wore them in public and only took them off in the bedroom. They were just reading glasses, so she didn't need them all of the time, but it was like a fashion statement or something.

Now, they were gone. Her eyes were unshielded, and she was beautiful. Always beautiful. Just different now.

"Why would I be off the rails?" I challenged as she approached me. "I'm very happy. Great team, interesting classes, a good girl to spend my nights with . . ."

That was sort of the truth. I loved playing for the team. My classes sucked, though. I was bored as hell, not sure what I was doing half the time, and I didn't have a girlfriend. I didn't want one. Friends with benefits was the arrangement Ashtyn and I had. She was a freshman, same as me, and played tennis for the school.

"Yeah, you have it good, Madoc. I'm glad." She nodded. "Really, I am."

"Yeah, right."

"Believe it or not." She came to sit down beside me, still keeping a distance. "I do want to see you happy."

I stared at her mouth and the glint of silver I saw from her tongue. She'd put her tongue ring back in.

The muscles on the inside of my leg twitched because I wanted to touch her. I wanted to feel her tongue. I wanted to feel the ball on it dragging across my skin.

*Fuck.*

I looked away before responding. "Well, I am. Things are easy here. No bullshit, no drama."

"Good," she replied instantly. "I'm sorry they worried."

Signal the end of the conversation. The mood was dead, and I was angrier than a motherfucker. I was pissed off and elated at the same time.

There was shit we weren't saying, and fights we weren't having. She thought she could nip this in the bud with a tidy little bow and walk away, but I wasn't done.

*Who the fuck was Fallon, anyway?*

I wanted to come at her. Again and again until she came undone. I wanted her screaming and crying. I wanted to chip away this tough little act until she was red with anger and sobbing miserably.

I wanted her broken.

And then I wanted her shivering and grabbing for me in need.

I stood up and stretched my arms out behind me.

"So I offered everyone my dad's house for the night. There are some bars to hit with the team, and I want to spend some time with Jared, Tate, and Jax—"

"Well, have fun," she cut me off.

My stomach knotted. "You're not staying?"

"No, we brought two cars. I'll take Tate's back tonight. I was just waiting to see what everyone else was doing before I headed out."

I rubbed my jaw, trying to figure out how to keep her here without looking like I wanted her here.

"So stubborn," I mumbled.

Her eyes shot up to mine. "What do you mean?"

Yeah, what did I mean?

I dug my keys out of my pocket and spoke without looking at her.

"Good-bye, Fallon." My tone was curt.

Walking past her, I picked my cell out of my other pocket and dialed Jax.

"What?" he answered.

"Pull the plug on Tate's throttle body," I ordered.

"Why?"

"Because if you don't, I'm going to tell everyone where you disappear to on your long nights out." My threat wasn't empty. I probably should've told Jared when I'd found out last spring.

"I knew I shouldn't have told you," he grumbled.

I sneered. Although he couldn't see it, he could hear it. "You didn't. You showed me. And now I have those nightmares to contend with. I think I need to talk to someone about it," I hinted. "I think I need talk to a lot of people."

"All right!" he hissed. "Damn! It's not like Tate's not going to figure out how to fix it in two seconds anyway."

"Well, you just make sure she doesn't look under the hood then."

# CHAPTER 19

# FALLON

At St. Joe's, I read Dante's *Inferno*. He stated that the seventh circle of hell was reserved for the violent. The inner ring of the circle housed the violent against God, the middle ring housed the suicides, and the outer ring was for the violent against people and property.

That was my ring.

Because I not only wanted to have a little tantrum with a baseball bat and this stupid karaoke machine, but I was going to fuck someone up as well.

After discovering that Tate's car was out of commission until we could get to an open auto body shop tomorrow, I'd resigned myself to having to stay in South Bend for the night.

And to make matters worse, Tate and Jax seemed to be on a mission to make sure I followed them all out to a bar.

Madoc didn't want me along. He'd joked that I'd fit in better at one of the community college parties.

So . . . I flipped him off, went upstairs to my room, and shredded the shit out of the back of my DC skating T-shirt and applied a hell of a lot more makeup than I'd wanted.

*To hell with him.* He didn't think I'd fit in.

*Baby, I always fit in.*

My jeans were tight, my T-shirt showed off my back with the twenty or so slits running across it, and my hair and makeup broad casted that I was damn well looking for a good time.

Tate thought I looked good, too. She had me do the same thing to her T-shirt, and then Jared hauled her upstairs to change. They didn't come back for half an hour, and Tate was still wearing the same shirt.

"Hey, you go to school here?" a guy shouted in my ear while I waited at the bar. I cringed and looked over at him, doing a double-take.

His espresso-colored hair was a little longer around the ears and fell on his forehead, and his blue eyes popped underneath his dark eyebrows. He was cute. Really cute.

He was dressed pretty casually—dark-wash jeans and some kind of beer T-shirt—but he wasn't hard on the eyes. And he definitely was dressed better than Madoc, who looked like an Abercrombie ad. This guy wasn't as built—he was lean, but toned—but he had a wide eye-catching smile.

"No," I shouted back over the music. "I go to Northwestern. You?"

"Yeah, I'm a senior here. What brings you to Notre Dame?"

"Visiting," I answered, handing the bartender a few bucks and taking my Coke. "You?"

"Bud," he ordered to the bartender and then looked at me. "Environmental Engineering."

Cute, engineer, and orders no-frills beer. Definitely my type. Not that I drank Budweiser or any alcohol very much. I could've if I'd wanted to. They weren't carding at the bar, since IDs were checked at the door and Madoc had worked his magic to get us in, but I still opted to stay sober.

"Very cool." I fist-bumped him and smiled. "Well, I'm heading back to my friends. Have a good night."

He nodded, looking like he wanted to say something, but stayed at the bar to wait for his drink.

Heading through the dense cluster of people waiting to place their orders, I made my way back to the two tables we had put together near the wall of windows and sat back down.

I noticed the extra body at our table right away. A girl was sitting next to Madoc, and my eyes narrowed at his hand on her leg.

Her long dark hair hung in big curls down over her breasts, and she had tanned, toned arms that looked great in a loose green tank top that showed off the black lace bra underneath. She was definitely dressed in a slutty-sexy way, yet it was completely expensive and stylish.

Whereas I just probably looked slutty.

She was drinking Amstel Light. *Of course.*

Madoc glanced at me for a split second but then turned his attention to Jared, who sat at my side. "So how are you liking ROTC?" he asked.

"It's good," Jared spoke up. "I have to go to two separate campuses for all of my classes, but it's keeping me out of trouble."

Tate, leaning into him on his other side, patted his leg. "Yep. Say it, baby. 'Tate, your dad was right.'"

Jared jabbed her in the ribs, and she started giggling, pushing him away. "Stop."

"You know you're going to be apart? Like a lot." Madoc's tone was far from friendly, and his expression was stern. "And his sexy ass is going to be in the jungle or on a ship for six months out of the year away from you. You okay with that?" he spoke to Tate.

*What the hell?* Why was he raining on their parade? I had never been a fan of Jared's, but he'd damn well earned my trust over the past couple of months. He and Tate were doing great.

Tate sobered, evening out her smile. "Of course." She nodded. "I'll miss him, but I trust him." And then she smirked at Jared. "You won't touch any of those guys, will you?"

"Not unless he gets really horny," Jax joked.

"I'll get you a vibrator, Tate," Madoc offered. "Or I could just come over. You know, to check on you when he's away."

A splinter of jealousy dug into my heart, but then I saw Jared flip him off out of the corner of my eye. I guess it was pretty regular practice for Madoc to joke like that.

"Yeah, thanks," Tate mumbled. "I'll take the vibrator, I think."

I set my drink down and looked behind me to the side at the newest idiot entertaining the crowd with bad disco karaoke.

Oh, wait. All disco was bad. Why was it that everyone who sings either goes for disco or country?

I should get up there and . . . nope. *Never mind.* I blinked away that idiot thought and turned back to the table.

And found Madoc staring at me. He still had his hand on the girl's leg, but he'd stopped rubbing. I couldn't tell if he was drunk or not. Usually he didn't sport such serious expressions, but he hadn't been up to the bar more than once.

The girl to his right had been chatting with Jax, but I wasn't even sure if Madoc had introduced her. I hadn't gotten a name, but that must have been the girl he was talking about spending his nights with.

Within seconds, though, she turned back to Madoc and whispered something in his ear.

I slouched a little lower in my seat, avoiding his eyes.

"Hey, Madoc. How's it going?" A chair appeared at my other

side, and I looked up to see the guy from the bar sitting down next to me.

He gave a half-smile, holding eye contact for a little longer than me.

Madoc's voice was slow and deep. "Aidan," he greeted. Only it didn't sound like a greeting. More like a threat.

"Tell me everything you can about this pretty girl." Aidan spoke to Madoc but motioned to me.

*Really?*

I rolled my eyes and straightened up. "Madoc doesn't know me. Not really." I offered my hand to Aidan.

"Aidan, Fallon. Fallon, Aidan." Madoc introduced us, ignoring my insult.

He shook my hand, and I smiled back, still not interested but not wanting Madoc to see that, either.

"Glad to officially meet you," Aidan said, his blue eyes piercing.

"Her mother likes young guys," Madoc chimed in again. "And her father kills people for a living."

I closed my eyes and exhaled a hot breath through my nose.

*What a dick.*

My lips twisted up at Madoc's exaggerated information.

Okay, not really exaggerated. My mother liked young guys, but my father didn't set out to kill anyone. If you crossed him, you knew what to expect.

But still . . .

Aidan breathed out a laugh. "Nice."

He obviously thought Madoc was joking.

"Fallon's also pretty easy," Madoc said in a husky voice. I glared at him, fire burning my eyes, while Aidan cleared his throat.

*I'm going to kill him!*

"Easy on the eyes, that is," he specified.

I stood up, grabbing one of the unemptied shot glasses on the table. "Oh, Madoc. You didn't tell him the best part. I can sing."

And I downed the shot, not realizing it was tequila until it hit my throat. Slamming the glass down on the table, I spun around and dived into the dance crowd, waiting until I was out of sight before I coughed out the burn from the noxious shit I just drank.

"You wanna sing?" the burly rocker dude who ran the karaoke show asked as I stepped up to the side of the stage.

"Yeah. Do you have Ashlee Simpson's 'La La'?" I swallowed the taste of the liquor over and over again but couldn't get rid of it on my tongue. One nice thing though was that I already felt it coursing through my limbs and giving me delicious chills all over my body.

"Sure." The guy nodded without looking at me as he worked the machine. "Step on up."

Doing as he said, I lifted my chin, took the mic with one hand, and stuck the other in the back pocket of my jeans. Whistles erupted around the room, and I turned to the table where my friends and enemy sat, seeing Jared and Tate turned around in their seats, smiling. Jax watched me, too, even though he had a waitress desperately trying to get his attention by bending down at his side to talk to him. I could see her cleavage from here.

Aidan had stayed at the table but stood up for a better view, and Madoc . . . well, Madoc was the red-hot blood in my veins. His fucking mouth was plastered on the girl next to him, eyes closed, and I may as well not even have existed.

I ground my teeth together and tensed the muscles in my legs, staying pissed. I saw Tate look between Madoc and me and then stand up as the music started.

"Here you go!" rocker dude shouted.

I bounced the heel of my right foot up and down, finding rhythm with the fast-paced pop tune. Closing my eyes, I smiled, relishing in the thrill of getting lost. Bending my knees, I shimmied my body lower and back on up, bobbing my head in time to the music.

"You can dress me up in diamonds," I sang, unable to contain the delicious fire racing through my body. Letting the lyrics pour out of me, I didn't even need to look at the monitors. Too many times growing up I'd belted out the words to this song.

My voice low and chin tipped down as I sang the words, playing the crowd with my eyes, I looked over and smiled in surprise, seeing Tate jumping up on the stage with another microphone.

She pumped her fist in the air as we both shouted, "Ya make me wanna la la!"

The whole crowd of guys and girls went wild, jumping up and down and singing with us as I laughed and sang at the same time.

I completely lost sight of our table once the crowd got going, which was probably a good thing. I wasn't so angry anymore, and I was thankful Tate got up there with me. It felt good to have someone on my side.

And even though I couldn't see Madoc, I hoped he was watching. If his eyes were on me, then his lips weren't on her.

*"I see everything I want for as long as I can have it."*

He seemed so different now compared to the man who had spoken those words to me in June.

His cold demeanor was distant and silent, and I wasn't sure if I came up here to prove something or to draw him out.

"La la la, la la la," Tate and I kept singing, ending the song.

I bowed my head and then threw it back, swinging all of my hair out of my face. Tate hooked an arm around my neck and whispered, "He didn't take his eyes off of you the whole time."

My heart started pounding harder, and I wasn't sure if it was that or the crowd's cheers that were vibrating through my arms and legs.

I knew she was talking about Madoc, but I acted dumb anyway. "Aidan?" I asked.

She smirked at me knowingly. "No, you idiot. You know who I'm talking about."

I refused to look over at the table, so I led the way off stage and wiped my fingers across my damp forehead.

Aidan emerged from the crowd on the dance floor and placed a hand on my hip. I stiffened as he leaned in to speak in my ear. "That was great! You're a good singer."

I offered a small smile and looked up when the surrounding speakers began playing regular music. The DJ announced a break, and couples wrapped their arms around each other and started dancing to the slow song.

"Would you like to dance?" Aidan shouted in my ear.

I looked around for Tate, who seemed to have disappeared, and I couldn't see anything through the crowd. I decided this was a good way out, though. Not that there was anything wrong with Aidan, but I was done for the night.

"Sure," I shouted back. "One before I head out."

He grabbed my hand and led me into the middle of the mix, turning around to wrap his hands around my waist. He pulled me in, and I held his shoulders as we swayed to Green Day's "21 Guns."

"How do you know Madoc?" I asked.

"We're on the team together." His thumb was rubbing strokes on my back. "Although, he's on the fast track. He'll probably be captain next year," he said, not looking particularly pleased.

*Captain by sophomore year?*

"He's that good?" I asked. I'd never seen Madoc play soccer.

"No, he's just that connected," he shot back. "Madoc doesn't have to earn a whole lot on his own."

My hard eyes fell, and I was a little pissed.

I could say Madoc was an entitled little prince with the hard path of life freshly paved for him, but for some reason, I felt the need to defend him.

I'd been there when he'd quit piano and started studying cars instead. He worked hard, read a lot, and tinkered for hours to learn his way around a garage. Madoc put in the muscle when he cared and pushed things away when he didn't.

His name may have gotten him on the team, but he wouldn't play if he didn't want to. And he wouldn't play if he didn't know he was an asset.

Aidan's fingers were slipping in and out of the rips in my shirt, caressing my skin as he pressed himself into me more closely.

"I should probably get go—" I started to tell him good-bye but suddenly felt like I was backed up against a wall.

Aidan looked directly behind me.

"Take a hike, Aidan." I blinked, hearing Madoc's voice as he came around to the side.

Turning around, I looked up at him and noticed his blue eyes shooting bullets at Aidan.

*Oh, no.* This was a zero to sixty moment with Madoc, but we had skipped the zero part.

Aidan took his hands off my waist. "Hey, man—"

But Madoc inched into our space. "Touch her again, and I'll chop off your hand." He said it so matter-of-factly.

My breathing turned shallow, but my temper rose.

*No, no, no . . .*

Aidan rolled his eyes and backed off, probably figuring it wasn't worth the fight. Madoc looked ready to draw blood.

I bared my teeth, shaking my damn head that felt like my brain was expanding and pressing against my skull. I was ready to explode.

"Madoc." I clenched my teeth.

"Just shut up," he ordered, breathless. "Just shut up, and dance with me."

*Huh? Dance with him?*

No hauling me out of here, screaming at me for one reason or another? No barking in my face and ordering me home?

I stood there trying to figure out what the hell was going on and barely noticed him pulling me in. Madoc's strong hands gripped my waist, holding me tight but barely touching me otherwise. His chest was right in front of my eyes, and I slowly looked up at him.

*Damn.*

When he stared down at me, everything was still except for our feet that moved to the music. It was like he was searching my eyes for something.

Everything about him, the shade of his eyes, the muscles I felt under his shirt, the way I already knew how his body moved when it loved, everything about him drew me in.

I sucked in a breath, wishing he'd stop touching me and wishing I could pull away. In another minute I would. In another minute I'd be satisfied with the warmth I hadn't felt in months or the heartbeat I could feel again.

In one more minute I would let him go.

I closed my eyes. Just. One. More. Minute.

I dug my fingers into his shoulders when his possessive hands threaded into the open back of my shirt and claimed my skin.

Not like Aidan's light strokes. Madoc splayed his whole hand, touching me with everything he had.

I let my forehead fall into his chest, inhaling his cologne. Butterflies swarmed in my stomach, and I smiled as the flutter descended lower. It felt so good.

Looking at him, I tried to keep the shakiness out of my voice.

"You have someone here with you, Madoc," I said quietly. "Why are you dancing with me?"

He brought one hand up, holding the side of my face with a firm hand and kneading his fingers into the back of my neck. "You ask too many fucking questions," he spat out, an angry tone to his voice.

And jerking my body into his, he slammed his mouth down on mine.

*Madoc?* I didn't say his name out loud. I think I may have groaned it, but otherwise I instantly stilled.

And then I was his.

A shudder ran through me, and I felt the dampness between my legs immediately. His heat on my lips made me hungry.

He sucked in a breath and whispered, "Because I like the way you taste, okay?"

His mouth took mine once more, covering it with heat and command like he knew exactly how my body worked and what it needed.

*Hell, yes.*

I pushed into him, kissing him back as his arm wrapped around my waist and pulled me up into his mouth.

Hard.

I threaded my fingers across the back of his neck and moved my tongue into his mouth, massaging and tasting him. It was just us. Just this.

His lips moved across mine, going in deep, his tongue working mine, flicking out again and again to rub over my ring. He devoured me. He drew my bottom lip between his teeth, and a moan escaped me as I squeezed my eyes against the sweet pain.

Not that it hurt at all. Just kissing him, touching him, inhaling him was too much. It was like an overload on my body, and the pleasure made me want to cry out. His fingers dug into my back, and I could feel his erection through his jeans.

*God, what are we doing?* We were on a crowded dance floor. He had a girl with him! Jared, Tate, and Jax were probably either trying not to watch or had left already. Opening my eyes for a second, I noticed that no one was watching us though. The couples around us were focused on themselves.

"Madoc," I barely spoke, my voice almost like a cry.

He pulled his face away, cupping my cheeks and keeping us nose to nose. We were both panting.

"I want to be inside you," he groaned, and I thought back to our night at the skate park in the rain. "But . . ." He straightened up and dropped his hands, "I'm not going to."

His voice was flat, void of any of the heat that was there just a minute ago.

And he walked away.

# CHAPTER 20

# MADOC

I almost abandoned my whole plan the minute I held her in my arms, the second I touched her lips, the instant she moaned my name.

But there was no way in hell I was going to watch her walk again. No, not this time. I'd be the one to leave.

And the corner of my mouth turned up as I made my way through the crowd. She was as stiff as an ice cube when I took her from Aidan, and then she'd melted like liquid in my arms. Now she was a puddle all over the dance floor.

*I am the man.*

Who cares that she looked like sex standing up on that stage? Or that I'd been a little jealous when Aidan started dancing with her? Or ready to kill him when I caught sight of his hand inside the back of her shirt?

*Fuck him, and fuck her.*

"Fuck you!" Ashtyn screamed at me as I came back to the table. I saw her rear her hand back, and I ducked out of the way just before her hand would've landed across my cheek.

"Seriously?" I held up my hands, laughing. "Calm down. It was just a joke."

I guessed she'd seen the kiss.

"You're an asshole!" she shouted and stomped out of the bar.

People around us chuckled, including Jax, while Jared shook his head and Tate scowled.

"Oh, please," I begged sarcastically. "You missed me, and you know it."

Tate rolled her eyes and stood up, straightening her shirt. "I thought I did." Looking around, she sighed. "You boys play nice. I'm going to go dig Fallon out of the bathroom."

I didn't know how Tate saw her head to the back of the bar through the clusters of people, but she was up and gone in no time, pushing through dancers, in search of her friend. Taking a seat, I downed the rest of my beer and lurched forward when Jax slapped me on the back.

"You're not going after either one of them?" he asked, locking his fingers behind his head and leaning on the back legs of the chair.

"Tate and Fallon?" I peered over at him. "I think they can take care of each other."

"No, I meant Fallon or Ashtyn. Isn't Ashtyn your girlfriend?"

*Girlfriend.* The word made me want to dunk my head in mud and not come up for air until I was dead.

"No." I looked back to the dance floor. "When do I have girlfriends?"

I locked eyes with Jared across the table, and he didn't speak. He said enough with his eyes, though.

He knew something was going on, and he knew I was off the rails. But like a good friend, he didn't feel the need to state the obvious.

Just knowing he was there, and that he got it, helped.

I caught sight of Tate's red T-shirt coming out of the crowd, and I sat up straight when I noticed that she was alone.

"Well," she sighed, putting her hands on her hips, "I guess we can head out. I'm done for the night."

She smiled down at Jared, a look going on between them that said *they* weren't done for the night. But I was confused.

"Where's Fallon?" I asked.

Tate busied herself, slinging her purse across her chest, barely meeting my eyes. "Oh, Fallon? Yeah, she's . . . I guess . . . heading out to another bar with that guy that was sitting here before. What was his name? Aidan?"

Anger radiated out of my pores, and my eyebrows pinched together painfully.

"What?" *What the fuck?*

Tate finally looked my way and fixed her lips into a thin line, looking like it was no big deal. "Yeah." She shrugged. "I went to grab her from the bathroom, and she was chatting with him in the hall. They headed out the back way."

I pushed out of my seat, glaring at Tate.

*She left with him?* Hell, no.

Without so much as a good-bye, I headed out of the bar and through the door. Coming out to the sidewalk, I stopped and twisted my head to the left and right.

Where the hell was she?

Oxygen flooded in and out of my lungs in heavy breaths.

To the left was nothing but darkness. To the right was the strip of college bars where he would've taken her.

I turned left first. Aidan wasn't a creeper. I had no reason to suspect that he'd lure her somewhere quiet and try anything, but it felt like the better option to make sure before I searched the populated and somewhat safer public bars.

I pounded the pavement, the town getting quieter the farther I walked.

*Son of a bitch.*

I was going to find her, punch him, and then fix Tate's car, so Fallon could get the hell out of town. Tonight.

I messed with her on the dance floor, kissed her almost beyond my own control, and then thought she'd stay invisible and quiet?

Why didn't I just let her leave this afternoon like she wanted?

In the three or so months since I'd last seen her, I'd been doing fine. Sure I wasn't happy, but like before, I got over the separation and moved on with my life. However dull it was.

Now, she had me chasing her down and in knots.

I was Madoc Caruthers. I don't get mad, and I don't chase women that don't want to be chased.

But I couldn't let her go with him. That wasn't happening.

The sharp glow from the streetlights illuminated the whole area, and so far I'd seen no one resembling Fallon. A few couples here and there. Some drunk students stumbling around together.

Stopping at a corner I looked left again and let out a breath, finally spotting her. Her legs moved briskly, and she disappeared under the shadow of trees, shielding the moon's light. But I knew it was her. That damned ripped shirt.

Digging in my heels, I walked as fire and anger urged my legs forward. I wanted to run. To race up behind her, throw her over my shoulder, and take her home.

My voice was deep and bitter as I shouted. "Where are you going?"

She spun around, stopping and scowling at me. "You followed me?" she accused.

I ignored the question. "Where are you going?" I asked again.

Her lips twisted up, enough to know she was done with me for the night and was not cooperating.

But then . . . she turned her lips up in a sinister smile and looked me up and down.

"For someone that hates me," she started as she looked at me with heat in her eyes, "you are awfully concerned about my comings and goings." She dragged a delicate hand down her neck, over her breast, continuing down to rest on the inside of her turned-out thigh.

*Holy shit.*

My eyes had a mind of their own. They just followed.

She smirked as if she'd just won, and I blinked, trying to drag my gaze away from where her hand rested. Turning back around, she walked even faster as she continued down the sidewalk toward wherever she was going.

That's when it occurred to me that she was alone.

"Where's Aidan?" I shouted, but she ignored me, steering into the dim park.

Running after her this time, I tore off my light blue button-down and threw it across her arm.

"For Christ's sake, Fallon, it's cold and dark. Take the shirt." I shook it at her, but took it away when she continued to ignore me.

I stuck my tongue between my teeth to keep from grinding them. "You can't walk through a park alone," I barked. "Where's Aidan?"

"Why would I know where Aidan is?"

"Because . . ." I trailed off, blinking long and hard.

*Fuckin' Tate.*

Realizing I'd been set up, and even more aggravated that Tate allowed Fallon to walk through town by herself in the dark, I exhaled deeply through my nose.

Of course, Tate probably assumed I'd run after Fallon, anyway.

"Well, looks like I got played. I was under the impression you left a bar with a complete stranger."

"Yeah, that would be so like me, wouldn't it?" The resentment in her comeback was thick.

"Yeah, well, you looked comfortable with him on the dance floor." I struggled to maintain pace and still look cool. She was almost speed-walking.

"Yeah, just like you with the brunette?" she said over her shoulder. "Am I complaining, Madoc? Nope, because I don't care."

*Bitch.*

"Hey." I brushed off the sting of her words with a casual smile. "I moved on. It wasn't hard. Just like you did in Chicago, I'm sure." I swerved in her path and cut her off, staring down at her as she tightened every muscle in her face. "With as easily as you open your legs for me," I continued, "I'm sure you're having a great time in college."

Her eyes flared, and she slammed her hands into my chest, but I barely stumbled. "Ugh!" she growled. Her green jewels fired in anger, and her hair fanned around her face in a wild storm.

"Come on," I challenged, breaking into a laugh. "You know I like it when you fight me. It gets you hot, and I get laid."

Her fingers balled up, and I saw her hand coming before she probably even knew what she was doing. Her tight fist landed right across my jaw, hitting the corner of my mouth, and I didn't even try to stop it. I loved Fallon's fight. I always did.

The sharp ache in my face spread across my chin, and I pursed my lips, sucking and swallowing the blood from the cut on the inside of my mouth.

Her fists didn't stop, though. Landing with two hard thuds right on my chest, I grabbed her wrists, trying to still her.

"I hate you!" she screamed, but the flutters in my stomach turned to amusement that I couldn't hold back.

I burst out laughing, and she went wild.

Her arms flailed, and she tried pulling away and kicking at me, until finally I let her body crash into mine, dragging us to the ground. She landed on top of me, but I quickly rolled us over, straddling her.

She didn't cry out, thank goodness, only wiggled and shot me with bullets from her eyes. God help me if a police officer stumbled this way, though. This "banter" was something most people wouldn't understand. I wasn't going to hurt her. I just wanted her attention.

Pinning her arms to the ground at the sides of her head, I leaned in, whispering in her ear.

"What did I say wrong?" I teased, feeling the fast rise and fall of her breasts against my chest. "You're not having fun at college, or you're mad that I called it? Don't be ashamed for spreading yourself around, Fallon. It's genetic. You're your mother's daughter, after all."

"Ugh!" She reared up, trying to throw me off, but I pressed down.

"Come on!" I challenged, seeing the tears I wanted in her eyes. "Come on. Admit it!"

Her face, hot with fierce defiance, looked about ready to explode.

And then she screamed, "I've never been with anyone but you, asshole!"

And I stopped. Everything stopped.

The air left me. My face fell. I didn't care that my heart pounded like a baseball bat across my chest.

*What the hell did she just say?*

I narrowed my eyes, studying her. She sucked in air through her teeth, glaring at me like she wanted to tear me apart.

"No one," she growled. "Now get off me before I scream."

I couldn't believe it.

"In the two years that we were apart, there was no one else?" I questioned, still hovering over her.

"There will be." Her threatening whisper sounded scarier than her shouts. "I'm going to make you a distant memory."

I narrowed my eyes at her challenge, and whether I understood it or not, my dick started to swell, as well. Maybe it was the position we were in, the heat of battle, or the need to break her down, but I wanted to touch her hard.

I saw the silver glint of her tongue ring through her teeth, and I instinctively ran my tongue across the back of my bottom teeth, remembering the feel of that in my mouth on the dance floor.

Her breathing was slowing, and she licked her lips, not wavering under my gaze.

I kept my voice low and soft, trying to reach her. "You act like you have no heart, like you just swallow your conscience with all of the pain you cause. But I see through it, Fallon. The truth is, you want me like nobody's business." She closed her mouth and swallowed. "You've always wanted me. You know why? Because I don't try to kill your demons. I run with them."

Her chest started rising and falling faster again, and her eyes faltered.

"And I never stopped wanting you," I added before crashing my mouth down on hers.

She moaned into my throat, and I was like a man at a feast. I couldn't kiss her fast enough. The more my lips moved over hers, the deeper the hunger in my stomach.

*More, more, more.* My whole body was on fire.

How did she always do this to me?

I straightened out my legs, flattening my body against hers, and moved my hands off her wrists and to the ground. I was about ready to do fucking cartwheels when she didn't hit me but instead took my face in her hands to deepen the kiss.

Her hot, slick mouth connected with mine, and I kept my lips open over hers to play with her tongue. Every time the tongue ring brushed over a part of my mouth, my dick jerked with the rush of blood.

"Goddamn, Fallon. Your fucking tongue," I gasped before diving in for more. The ball in her mouth turned me on to the point where I'd probably be okay just kissing her for the rest of the damn night.

But . . . hearing that she'd only ever been with me made me feel a ton of different things I couldn't analyze right now.

All I knew was that I wanted to be her first with everything now. I wasn't worrying about her comparing me to other guys. I was only worried about living up to her fantasies.

Which, strangely, was a taller order. I wanted to give her everything.

Moving to lie on the ground at her side, I didn't break the kiss as I ran my hand down her body and slipped it inside her jeans.

"Jesus." I pulled back, opening my eyes and looking down at her. She wasn't wearing underwear. Just her jeans.

My hand reached lower, finding what I wanted between her legs, and a smile tugged at my lips. My fingers found her center, and I could already feel the wetness at her opening. She arched her head back and panted.

"Do you know how much you turn me on?" My question sounded more like an accusation. "So wet and perfect."

*Mine.*

Sliding two fingers inside of her, I nearly fucking lost it. The heat. The wetness around my fingers. "I want inside this," I told her, pumping my fingers faster.

"Madoc, please," she pleaded, and I dipped down to trail my tongue along the ridge of her ear. She shuddered and leaned her head into me.

"Not yet. I want to give you another *first*."

Pushing myself up on one knee to hover over her again, I took my hand out of her jeans and reached up, pushing the hem of her shirt up below her breasts. Taking the skin of her stomach in my mouth, I teased it with little kisses, trailing a line down to the top of her jeans.

"Madoc, you can't." She took my head in her hands, lifting her head up. "Someone will see us."

"I don't give a damn."

I unbuttoned and unzipped her low-rise jeans and had barely yanked them down to her knees before I dove down to taste her.

It was the beginning of October and already cold as hell, but I was burning up.

Her body was so hot, and I looked up at her as my tongue swirled her clit. I breathed out a laugh, seeing her peek out of her hands.

She was embarrassed, and I was fucking ecstatic. I might be the only one that'd been inside of her, but that didn't mean that no one else hadn't done this to her. Now I knew no one else had.

My dick, my mouth, my tongue. She was mine.

I pressed my tongue down on her swollen nub and moved in circles, and soon her hands were off her flushed face and grabbing at my hair.

Her legs started shifting, the left and then the right, and I realized that she was trying to kick her jeans all of the way off.

*That a girl.*

I shot up and grabbed the hem at her ankles and yanked on the jeans, tossing them I-didn't-know-where.

"Son of a bitch," I groaned under my breath, looking down at her, T-shirt pulled up and naked all the rest of the way down.

I dropped back down between her legs, and she fisted my hair as I licked her length long and gentle and then swirled my tongue around her clit.

"Madoc," she panted, grinding herself into my tongue. "That's so good. Make me come. Please."

My whole damn body was tense, and I was on fire from the waist down. My dick rubbed against my jeans, and I could feel the sweat trail down the middle of my back under my T-shirt.

I couldn't take much more of this.

Not the wanting her, but the needing her. It was like a fire in my belly having her again, and I pushed the notion away that she didn't need me, too. She could admit it or hide it, but it rolled off of her like lightning.

Putting my whole mouth on her, I ate her out, causing her to moan more. I sucked and nibbled her, licked and plunged inside of her.

"Oh, God, Madoc." She threw her head back, her fast breaths going a mile a minute as her body shook. I gripped her hips, and she damn-near pulled out my hair as she came.

And I didn't nurse her back down to Earth as she shuddered.

Leaning back and sitting on my heels, I dug a condom out of my wallet. Before she'd even opened her eyes, I'd torn open the package, rolled on the rubber, and crowned her entrance. I wanted inside of her before her orgasm finished. Leaning over her and panting just as hard as she was, I reached behind my head and grabbed my black T-shirt, pulling it off and flinging it to the side. I supported myself with one hand on the ground and one hand on my cock, hard and ready for her. She pushed off the ground, wrapping her arms around my neck and kissing me hard.

I rubbed the tip of my cock over her clit, and she quivered against my lips.

"Lie back," I gritted through my teeth. "I need you now."

As soon she fell back to the ground, she spread her legs wider, and I worked the tip inside of her. Grabbing her hip to steady her, I plunged inside completely.

"Ah!" she moaned, and I closed my eyes, letting out a low grunt.

I wrapped my arm under her knee and grabbed her thigh with my hand, pulling her down on me as far as she could go.

"Madoc." Her whisper was wanton. She was lost, craving more and more. She grabbed my ass inside the back of my jeans, and I winced as her nails dug in. I loved that.

"That's it," I breathed, moving in and out of her in a quick rhythm. "Touch me, Fallon."

Her fingers grappled with my ass and then trailed up my back and brought my head down to meet her lips. She was wild. Her tongue licked my neck, sucked on my ear, and dove into my mouth with full force.

"Go faster, Madoc," she whispered in my ear. "Come hard."

Pulling back, I continued to support myself with one hand on the ground and one hand on her tit, pounding into her as she squeezed my hips tight with each thrust.

Her hair fanned out across the cold grass, and I watched, mesmerized, as her body pushed back and forth on the ground as I entered her each time.

I was consumed with Fallon, and while I knew I'd survive without her, I didn't want to. I wanted her in my bed, in my lap, at my dinner table, and on my arm every goddamn day from now on.

This was my girl, and I finally understood why Jared needed Tate so much. Why he hurt her when he thought he couldn't love her.

He just wanted her.

Fallon looked up at me, folding her bottom lip between her teeth, and I saw her eyes tense. She tightened around my cock, and I knew she was about to come.

"Stay with me," I urged, keeping my eyes on her.

With every thrust, a whimpered breath came out of her, her emerald eyes pleading with me. I bit down, steeling my jaw.

She finally squeezed her eyes shut and cried out, and I let it go, too. Her muscles clenched around me, spasming, and I slammed into her twice more before spilling and collapsing.

I lay there with my head on her shoulder, our ragged breaths the only sound in the otherwise silent park.

*Shit.*

I didn't even want to look around to see if we'd been caught. She'd been loud, and I felt my skin warm as my heartbeat picked up.

She twisted her head toward me, and I leaned up, inches from her mouth. Her lips parted, and her eyes begged as she just stared at me, both pain and pleasure in her eyes.

Taking the invitation, I kissed her, wrapping my arms around the top of her head on the ground and enveloping her with my body.

The full force of her lips pushed back against mine, deepening the kiss.

"Madoc," she quivered against my mouth. "I—"

"Shhh," I urged, taking her mouth again.

There were things we needed to say. But not tonight.

That night I crashed on the couch in my father's house, not wanting to push Fallon too far, too fast. Our midnight romp in the park was enough to scare her off, and I was pissed that I felt the need to walk on eggshells around her.

I had never cared about any other girl like this, and I didn't know if that was just me, or if it was Fallon. She and I started so young; maybe she'd ruined me for other women. I didn't know. And I wasn't in the mood to think about whether or not I loved her.

I settled on the fact that I was simply not done with her.

So, I backed off, not insisting that we share a bed, and opted to let her get some rest.

Tate and Jared were already home by the time Fallon and I

walked in. I didn't see them, but I could definitely make out certain little noises coming from their room that told me they weren't asleep.

I planted a long kiss on Fallon's lips before saying good night.

But the next morning, it was Jared shaking me awake.

"Hey, we're heading out soon," he alerted me.

I brought the heel of my hands up to rub my eyes. "Is everyone up?" I asked, sitting up. He threw two duffel bags into the foyer next to the door. "Yeah, but Fallon's already gone."

I threw my legs over the edge of the couch with my elbows on my knees.

"What?" I blurted out, looking at him like he better be lying.

"I guess she woke Jax up early to fix the car." He gave me a knowing look. "Obviously, that didn't take long, since he only had to plug back in the throttle body, so she's already been gone an hour." He stopped and stared, chewing on his gum and waiting for me to say something.

"Un-fucking-believable!" I shouted, picking up a vase from the coffee table and hurling it across the room where it shattered against the wall.

I slammed myself back against the brown leather couch, running my hands over my face in exasperation.

*What the fuck?*

"What's up?" I heard Jax come around the corner and ask. I laid my head back, closing my eyes and locking my hands on top of my head.

"Nothing," Jared answered. "Let me handle this."

I didn't hear Jax leave, but when I dropped my hands and opened my eyes he was gone. Jared walked around the coffee table and sat down in the brown leather chair that matched the sofa.

"She went back to Shelburne Falls for the rest of the weekend. Her mom texted saying she needed her there or something," Jax said. The anger inside of me created a fog in my head too thick to think.

Jared dug in his hoodie and seemed to be removing one of his keys. "We're heading back now," he said as he worked. "We'll visit the parents, and Tate's got a race tonight. You should come."

I shook my head, not even looking at him.

*Was he nuts?*

He held a key out to me. "To Tate's house," he explained. "Fallon is staying there tonight. Mr. Brandt is leaving town on business early this evening, and I'll keep Tate in our room at your house. You go sort this out."

I shook my head. "No way. I'm done."

What the hell did Fallon ever really do for me anyway? This was the last straw. If she couldn't open up and act fucking normal, then she wasn't worth it.

Jared stood up and threw the key on my T-shirt-clad chest. "Just go," he ordered. "Sort this shit out. I want my friend back."

"No," I maintained. "I'm not chasing after her again."

"I told the whole school about my teddy bear to get Tate back." He scowled down at me. "Chase. Harder."

But I couldn't.

Fallon knew I wanted her. She had to know that I cared about her. But I didn't trust her. She was playing me, and I didn't know why.

When she was ready to talk, she'd find me.

# CHAPTER 21

# FALLON

"*Daddy?*" *I look up from the hospital bed where I'd just been asleep. He stands over me in his cream-colored cable sweater and brown leather jacket, smelling of coffee and Ralph Lauren.*

*His eyes, pained and exhausted, scan over my body.* "*Look what you've done to yourself.*"

*My face scrunches up, and my eyes start to tear.* "*Daddy, I'm sorry.*" *A sob catches in my throat, and I look for him to hold me.*

*I need him. He's all I have.*

*The emptiness. The loneliness. I'm all alone now. I have no one. My mom is gone. She won't call me. The baby is gone. My hands instinctively go to my stomach, and I only feel a dull throb in the pit instead of love.*

*My eyes burn, and I look away, starting to cry in the quiet and darkened room.*

*This isn't my life. It's not how it was supposed to be. I wasn't supposed to love him. I wasn't supposed to break.*

*But after the abortion, everything sunk into the mud, and I couldn't walk anymore. I couldn't eat. The pain in my chest only grew, and I was constantly exhausted from the worry and heartache. Where was he? Was he trying to reach me? Did he think about me?*

*I hadn't realized until I was torn from him how much I loved him.*

*My mom said it was infatuation. A crush. That I'd get over it. But every day the frustration and sorrow deepened. I was failing in school. I had no friends.*

*I finally snuck back to Shelburne Falls only to find Madoc had definitely moved on like my mom said. He wasn't dwelling on me one bit. The only thing on his mind was the girl with her head between his legs. Backing away, I had run out of the house and jumped back in my father's car that I had stolen. Now, here I was, three days later with lacerations on my arms and a sharp ache in my chest.*

*I suck in a breath and stiffen as my father rips the blanket and sheet off of me, sending them flying to the floor.*

*"Daddy, what are you doing?" I cry, noticing his fierce green eyes.*

*He yanks me from the bed, squeezing my upper arm so hard that the skin stings.*

*"Ow, Daddy!" I wail, limping across the floor as he drags me into the bathroom. My arm feels stretched, like any minute he'll yank it from the socket.*

*What is he doing?*

*I watch as he plugs up the bathroom sink and begins filling it with water. The fingers of his other hand dig into the flesh of my arm, and I begin hyperventilating.*

*He pulls my arm hard, yanking me closer as he yells. "Who are you?"*

*Tears spill over, and I sob, "Your daughter."*

*"Wrong answer." And he grabs the back of my neck and forces my face into the filled sink.*

*No!*

*I gasp and suck in unwanted water as my head is forced under. I slam both hands on each side of the sink to push back against his hand, but he's too strong. I shake my head, my slippery hands sliding out from under me as I struggle against him.*

*The water is in my nose, and I squeeze my eyes shut against the burn.*

*Suddenly, I'm yanked up out of the water.*

*"Daddy, stop it!" I cough and sputter, water dripping from my ratty tendrils and chin.*

*His voice thunders around me. "You want to die, Fallon?" He jerks my head in his anger. "That's why you did this, right?"*

*"No . . ." I rush out before he slams my head back into the water, cutting off my air supply. I barely have time to think or prepare myself. My mind turns black as I wail into the shallow depth.*

*My father won't kill me, I tell myself. But I'm hurting. The insides of my forearms sting, and I think my cuts are bleeding again.*

*He yanks me back up, and I reach behind myself and grab at his hand at the back of my head as I sob.*

*"Who are you?" he bellows again.*

*"Your daughter!" My body shakes with fear. "Daddy, stop it! I'm your daughter!"*

*I'm crying and shivering, the front of my nightgown dripping water down my legs.*

*He growls close to my ear. "You're not my daughter. My daughter doesn't give up. There were no skid marks on the street, Fallon. You crashed into the tree on purpose!"*

*I shake my head against his grasp. No. No, I didn't. I didn't hit it on purpose.*

*My mouth fills with thick saliva, and my eyes squeeze shut, remembering leaving Madoc's house and hiding out at my father's place near Chicago. I'd taken one of his cars and . . . no, I didn't try to hit the tree.*

*My body shook, and my throat filled with pain.*

*I'd just let go of the wheel.*

*Oh, my God.*

*I steal air as fast as I can and whimper as I cry. What the hell has happened to me?*

*I stumble as my father throws my back into the wall next to the sink. Before I even have a chance to straighten myself, his hand comes across my face with a loud slap, and I wince at the sting traveling down my neck.*

*"Stop it!" I rage against the blur in my eyes.*

*He grabs me by the shoulders and pins me against the wall again and I cry out.*

*"Make me," he challenges.*

*My fists slam against his chest, and I heave my whole body into the push. "Stop it!"*

*He steps back to steady himself but comes up again and grabs my head between his hands.*

*"Don't you think that it gutted me when your mother took you away?" he asks, his eyes heartbroken. "I punched every wall in the goddamn house, Fallon. But I swallowed it down. Because that's what we do. We swallow every brick of shit this world feeds us until the wall inside of us is so strong that nothing breaks it." He lowers his labored voice, sounding stronger. "And that's what I did. I let her take you, because I knew that cunt would make you strong."*

*I clench my teeth, trying to stop my tears as I look at him. I love my father, but I can't love him for letting my mother take me away. I guess in his head he thought it was a way of hiding me from his enemies. Did living with my mother make me strong? Of course not. Look at me, blubbering and ruined. I'm not strong.*

*"You don't get to give up. You don't get to quit!" he yells. "There will be other loves and other babies," he growls, shaking my head between his hands and leveling me with his hard stare. "Now. Swallow. The. Pain!" he rages all around me. "Swallow it!"*

*His roar shatters my insides, and I stop crying, staring at him wide-eyed.*

*He holds my head tightly, forcing me to keep my eyes on him, and I focus, looking for something to grab on to. Anything. I concentrate on the tiniest point I can find, the center of his black pupils.*

*I don't blink. I don't budge.*

*The center of his eye is so dark, and I try to imagine that it feels like cruising through space at warp speed. In my world there is no one but him. The gold surrounding the black flickers, and I wonder why I didn't inherit that in my green eyes. The white in his irises looks like lightning, and the ring of emerald, before you get to the white of the eyeballs, seems to ripple like water.*

*Before I know it our breathing is syncing up, and he's setting the rhythm I follow.*

*Inhale, exhale.*

*Inhale, exhale.*

*Inhale, exhale.*

*Madoc's face flashes in my mind, and I tighten my jaw. Memories of my aborted pregnancy crash into his image, and my teeth rub together. My mother's voice enters my ears, and I suck my tongue dry, taking all of it, all of them, and swallowing the hard lump to the back of my throat, down my pipe, and I feel it all leave my brain.*

*It's still inside me. Heavy.*

*But it's quiet now, buried in my stomach.*

*My father releases my head and runs a thumb across my cheek as he holds my chin.*

*"Now who are you?" he implores.*

*"Fallon Pierce."*

*"And where were you born?"*

*My voice is calm. "Boston, Massachusetts."*

*He takes a step back, giving me room. "And what do you want to do with your life?" he asks.*

*I finally look at him, whispering. "I want to build things."*

*He reaches to my side and picks a towel off the shelf, handing it me. I hold it to my chest, not really feeling the cold anymore. Not really feeling anything.*

*He leans in and kisses my forehead and then meets my eyes. "'Nothing that happens on the surface of the sea can alter the calm of its depths.'" He quotes Andrew Harvey. "No one can take away who you are, Fallon. Don't give anyone that power."*

I hadn't cried since that day that's suddenly on my mind. I'd come close, but two whole years and not one tear. My father kept me home for exactly one week to heal the injuries from the shards of glass from the windshield that had cut me up, but then he sent me back to boarding school to get on with my life.

And I had. That's something everyone needs to learn on their own. Life goes on, smiles will come again, and time heals some wounds and soothes the ones it can't.

I brought up my grades, made a few friends, and laughed a lot.

I simply couldn't forgive, though. Betrayal cuts deep, and that's what brought me back to town last June.

I just didn't expect Madoc to still affect me.

He wanted me. I knew it. I felt it. But why? What did I really ever do to deserve him?

He'd been faithful to me when we were sixteen. Of that, I was pretty certain. I couldn't hate him anymore for looking for a good time when he'd thought I'd willingly left him.

There are so many things I should tell him. Things that he had a right to know. And then I felt that I'd told him too much.

Madoc was better off without me. Our relationship started off in the wrong place to begin with. We had nowhere left to grow. He didn't know me or what interested me. We talked about nothing.

Once he'd had his fill of the sex, he would leave. Not to mention the baby. If he ever found out about the baby, he'd jump ship. No doubt. Madoc wasn't ready for anything that heavy. I wondered if he'd ever be.

I turned up "Far from Home" by Five Finger Death Punch and swallowed the guilt all the way back to Shelburne Falls as I drove home at my mother's request. She'd texted this morning to let me know I had stuff at the house. If I didn't come to collect what I'd left last summer, it was going in the trash.

I shook my head and ran a hand over my weary eyes.

Punching the gate code in, I inched Tate's G8 forward as the black iron bars creaked open.

It was Saturday, late morning, and the October sky was lightly sprinkled with clouds. It was chilly out, but I hadn't brought a jacket, opting for my black-and-gray-striped long-sleeved T-shirt and some jeans. My hair still hung loose from last night, but it'd been fluffed after my shower this morning. For some reason, though, I'd wanted Madoc's smell to stay in my hair along with the tiny bits of grass I kept finding. My long bangs fanned around my cheekbones, and I picked my glasses off the passenger seat as I parked in front of the Caruthers's house behind my mother's BMW.

My glasses had been intended for reading years ago, but I took to wearing them almost all of the time. It felt safe somehow.

Walking into the house, I traipsed through the foyer and down the hall next to the stairs leading to the back of the house where I was sure to find Addie in the kitchen.

The quiet house seemed so different now. Almost hollow as if it weren't filled with memories, stories, and a family. The bitter chill of the marble floors shot through my sneakers and up my calves, and the high ceilings didn't magically hold in warmth anymore.

Looking out the glass patio doors, I saw Addie sweeping up around the pool that already had the cover rolled over it for the coming winter.

When I looked farther out, though, I noticed that the Jacuzzi was covered as well. When I lived here, that continued to be used throughout the cold months as well as the lawn furniture and barbecue area. Madoc's dad loved grilled food, and he and Madoc would venture out to throw steaks on the barbecue in the dead of January.

Now the entire patio seemed barren. Dead leaves blew this way and that, and it didn't look like Addie was making any progress. It didn't even look like she was trying to.

This house had problems, but it also had a history of laughter and memories. Now everything just looked dead.

I opened the sliding glass door and walked out across the stone tiles.

"Addie?"

She didn't look at me, and her low, quiet voice wasn't welcoming like last time. "Fallon."

I took off my glasses and stuck them in my back pocket. "Addie, I'm so sorry."

She folded her lips between her teeth. "Are you?"

I didn't have to tell her what I was sorry about. Nothing escaped her notice in this house, and I knew she knew that the divorce mess was my fault. That Madoc being sent away was my fault.

"Yes, I am," I assured her. "I never meant for this to happen."

And that was the truth. I'd wanted to be the one to leave Madoc, and I'd wanted Jason and my mother to feel a pinch, but I didn't know my mother would fight the divorce so hard or that Madoc would be caught in the middle.

Truth is, I hadn't thought of Addie at all.

She exhaled through her nose, and her scowl stayed trained on her sweeping. "That bitch thinks she's going to take this house," she mumbled. "She's going to take the house, sell off everything in it, and let it sit."

I stepped closer. "She won't."

"It doesn't matter, I guess." Her bitter tone cut me off. "Jason is choosing to spend most of his time in the city or at Katherine's house, and Madoc hasn't been home in months."

I looked away, shame burning my face.

*I did this.*

My eyes were starting to sting, so I closed them and swallowed. *I'll fix it.* I have to. I should never have come back. Madoc was fine. They were all fine before me.

This house, once alive with laughter and parties, was empty now, and Addie's family that she'd loved and taken care of was separated and broken. She'd been almost entirely alone these past three months. Because of me.

I backed away, knowing she wouldn't want to hear another apology. Turning around, I started back for the patio doors.

"You still have things in your room," Addie called out, and I turned back around. "And you have some boxes in the basement."

*What?* I didn't have anything in the basement.

"Boxes?" I asked, confused.

"Boxes," she repeated, still not looking at me.


*Boxes?*

I headed into the house, but rather than go upstairs to pack up the clothes I'd left months ago, I went straight for the basement door off to the side of the kitchen.

It didn't make sense for me to have anything down there. My mother threw away everything from my room, and I hadn't come to live here with much to start with.

I walked down the brightly lit stairs, my feet almost silent on the carpeted staircase.

For a huge-ass house like this, it featured an equally huge basement with four rooms. One was decorated as an extra bedroom, and another was Mr. Caruthers's liquor storage. There was also a room dedicated to tubs of holiday decorations, and then the large open area that held a gaming center with standing video games, a pool table, air hockey, foosball, a gigantic flat screen, and just about every other entertainment a teenage boy like Madoc could enjoy with his friends. The room also held a refrigerator full of refreshments and couches for relaxing.

But the only part I ever enjoyed about coming down here was when Mr. Caruthers decided that I needed my own outlet for activity in the basement.

My half-pipe.

He thought it was a way for Madoc and me to bond, and since I wasn't making friends, it served to put me side by side with Madoc's. While they played, so could I.

It didn't work.

I simply stayed out of there when Madoc entertained, and I worked on my skills at other times. It wasn't him so much but his friends. I found Jared moody and everyone else dumb.

Looking around the large area, I noticed everything was spotlessly clean. The beige carpets looked new, and the wood smelled of furniture polish. Light poured in from the set of patio doors leading outside to the sunken backyard off the side of the house. The tan walls still burst with Notre Dame paraphernalia: flags, pennants, framed photos, and souvenirs.

An entire wall was splashed with family photos, mostly of Madoc growing up. Madoc opening Christmas presents when he was eight or nine. Madoc hanging from the goal post on a soccer field at ten or eleven. Madoc and Jared under the hood of his GTO as Madoc throws a goofy gang symbol with his hands.

And then one of him and me. Right in the middle of the wall, over the piano. We were out by the pool, and Addie had wanted a picture of us. We must've been about fourteen or fifteen. We had our backs to each other, leaning against each other with our arms crossed over our chests. I remember Addie kept trying to get Madoc's brotherly arm around my shoulder, but this was the only way we'd pose.

Studying the picture closely, I noticed that I was half-scowling at the camera. There was, however, a hint of a smile. I tried to look bored despite the butterflies in my stomach, I remembered. My body had started having a reaction to Madoc, and I'd hated it.

Madoc's expression was . . .

His head was turned toward the camera but down. He had a tiny smile on his lips that looked like it was bursting to get out.

*Such a little devil.*

I turned around and ran my hand over the old piano that Addie said Madoc still played. Though not anymore, since he was away at school.

The lid was down, and there was sheet music scattered on the top. The music rack had Dvořák on it, though. Madoc had always been partial to the Eastern European and Russian composers. I can't even remember the last time I heard him play, though. It was funny. He was such an exhibitionist when it didn't matter and not one when it did.

And that's when my foot brushed something. Peering down underneath the piano, I noticed the white cardboard boxes.

Kneeling down, I dragged one out only to notice that there were about ten more underneath.

Flipping the lid off, I froze so still that only my heartbeat moved my body.

*Oh, my God.*

*My stuff?*

I stared down into a box full of my Legos. All of the robots and cars with remotes and wires were thrown in here, scattered with loose pieces around the box.

I licked my dry lips and dug in, taking out a Turbo Quad I made when I was twelve and a Tracker that I'd just started on before I left. *This was my stuff from my room!*

I was frantic, smiling like an idiot, ready to laugh out loud. I dove under the piano, pulling out two more boxes.

Tossing off the lids, I gasped in surprise at all of my mock engineering blueprints and another box of Legos. I shuffled through the papers, memories flooding me of the times I'd sit in my room with my sketchpad and design futuristic skyscrapers and ships.

My fingers started tingling and a shaky laugh broke out, causing me to giggle like I hadn't in a very long time.

I couldn't believe this! *This was my stuff!*

I scurried back under the piano, slamming my head into the edge in the process.

"Ouch," I groaned, rubbing the top of my forehead and pulling another box out much slower this time.

I went through all of the boxes, finding everything I'd missed and things I didn't even remember that I'd had. Skateboards, posters, jewelry, books . . . nearly everything from my bedroom except the clothes.

Sitting cross-legged on the floor, I stared at all of the stuff around me, feeling strangely disconnected from the girl I used to be yet so glad to have found her again. All of these things represented a time when I'd stopped listening to others and started listening to myself. When I'd stopped trying to be what she wanted and just started to be.

These boxes were Fallon Pierce, and they weren't lost. I closed my eyes, clutching my sea otter stuffed animal I'd gotten from my dad at SeaWorld when I was seven.

"Madoc."

My eyes popped open, and I saw Addie at the bottom of the stairs.

She had her arms folded across her chest and let out a long sigh.

"Madoc?" I questioned. "He did this?"

"He lost it a little when you left." She pushed off the wall and walked toward me. "Stealing his dad's liquor, partying, girls . . . he bounced off the walls for a few months."

"Why?" I whispered.

She studied me and then gave a defeated half-smile before continuing. "Jason sure had his work cut out for him. Madoc and his friend Jared wreaked havoc like nobody's business the summer after sophomore year. One night he went into your room and saw that your mom had cleaned everything out to redecorate. Only she hadn't packed anything. She'd thrown it out."

Yeah, I knew that. But somehow the pain in my chest wasn't spreading. If she threw it out, then . . . I looked down, closing my eyes against the burn again.

*No. Please no.*

"Madoc went outside and dug everything back out of the trash." Addie's soft voice spilled around me and my chest started to shake. "He boxed it up and saved it for you."

My chin started trembling, and I shook my head. *No, no, no . . .*

"That's what makes Madoc a good kid, Fallon. He picks up the pieces."

I crumbled.

The tears spilled over my lids, and I gasped as my body shook. I couldn't open my eyes. The pain was too great.

I doubled over, clutching the sea otter, and put my head down, sobbing.

Up came the sadness and despair, and I wanted to take back

everything I'd said to him. Every time I doubted him. Everything I didn't tell him.

Madoc, who saw me.

Madoc, who remembered me.

Six hours later I was sitting in Tate's bedroom, my leg slung over the side of her cushioned chair near her French doors, and staring out at the tree outside. All of the fall colors swayed in the breeze, and the soft glow of the day's last light slowly disappeared from the branches, inch by inch.

I hadn't talked much since getting there, and she'd been good about not asking questions. I knew she was worried, because she avoided the topic of Madoc so well that he was like a planet sitting in the middle of the room. I wondered if he'd been angry to find me gone this morning.

I rubbed my hand over my eyes. I couldn't shake him.

And what's more? I didn't want to.

"Tate?" I called.

She peeked her head around the door of her closet, pulling out a black hoodie.

"If you . . . betrayed Jared," I stammered. "Like not cheated, but lost his trust somehow. How would you go about getting him back?"

Her lips flattened into a line as she thought about it. "With Jared? I'd show up naked." She nodded.

I snorted and shook my head, which was about as much of a laugh as I could summon right now.

"Or just show up," she continued. "Or talk to him, or touch him. Hell, I could just look at him." She shrugged, smirking, and threw on her hoodie.

I doubted I had that kind of power over Madoc. Whereas Jared seemed more animalistic, Madoc was a mind-fuck.

She sat down on the edge of her bed, slipping on her black Chucks. "Sorry," she offered. "I know I'm not much help, but Jared has just as much power over me as I do him. We've been through enough. There isn't much we wouldn't forgive each other for."

Half of what she said was true for Madoc and me as well, but I hadn't earned his forgiveness. What the hell was I supposed to do?

"For Madoc, though?" She smiled, knowing exactly what I'd been getting at. "He appreciates mischief. Maybe some sexy texting would be in order."

I couldn't help but laugh. "Sexting? Are you serious?"

"Hey, you asked."

Yeah, I guess I did. And she was probably right. It sounded like something Madoc would get off on.

But phone sex? Yeah, that's not going to happen. Totally not my thing.

I looked up, realizing Tate was still staring at me. When I didn't say anything, she lifted her eyebrows and took a deep breath.

"Okay, well . . . my dad's gone to the airport, just to remind you, so—"

"Yeah, Tate. I'm not having phone sex tonight. Thanks!"

She held up her hands to fend me off. "Just saying."

I nodded to the door, giving her the hint to take a hike. "Have fun and good luck at your race."

"Are you sure you don't want to come?"

I gave her a half-smile. "No, I need to think right now. Don't worry about me. Go on."

"All right." She gave in and stood up. "Jax is having a party next door after the race, so come over if you want."

Nodding, I grabbed my Kindle off my lap and pretended to start reading as she left. My fingers tapped on my thigh as if I were playing a piano, and I knew I probably wasn't going to get any reading done tonight.

I didn't want to read. I wanted to do something. There was a tiny snowball in my stomach that was turning and turning, building to something bigger the longer I sat.

*Sexting.*

Madoc deserved more than that.

Okay, he deserved that and more.

*"Sorry"* just seemed empty. I needed to say more, tell him more, but I didn't know how to start. How do you tell someone that you stayed away, never giving them closure, had a secret abortion and then in a post-traumatic stress blackout tried to hurt yourself, and then were responsible for them losing their home? What do you say?

What will stop him from running away from a train wreck like me?

Digging my phone out from between the cushion and the chair, I squeezed the shake out of my fingers as I typed.

**I don't know what to say.**

I hit Send and immediately shut my eyes, letting out a pathetic sigh. *"I don't know what to say"? Seriously, Fallon?*

Well, at least I said something, I guess. Even if it was moronic. Consider it a warm-up.

Five minutes passed and then ten. Nothing. Maybe he was in the shower. Maybe he left his phone in another room. Maybe he was already in bed. With someone. Ashtyn, maybe.

My stomach hollowed.

An hour passed. Still nothing.

I didn't read a single line of my book. The sky was black now. No noise from next door. Everyone must still have been at the race. Or did Tate say they were getting something to eat first?

I threw my Kindle down and got out of the chair, pacing the room.

Another twenty minutes passed.

I swallowed the lump in my throat and snatched my phone.

*Great.* I was texting him again after not getting a response. I was like those creepy, overbearing girls that scare the shit out of men.

Please, Madoc. Say something . . .

I leaned back against Tate's wall, bobbing my foot up and down and keeping my phone in my hand. Twenty minutes later and still nothing. I buried my face in my hands and took some deep breaths.

*Swallow it down.*

*Inhale, exhale.*

*Inhale, exhale.*

And then I dropped my hands, tired tears rimming my eyes.

He wasn't listening.

He didn't want to talk to me.

He'd given up.

I typed in one last message before bed.

I'm a shit.

My chin shook, but I calmly set the phone down on Tate's night-stand and switched off her lamp.

Crawling under the covers, I looked out her French doors and saw the moon's light casting a glow on the maple outside. I knew that tree was the inspiration for Jared's tattoo, but Tate would never really talk about their story. She said it was long and hard, but it was theirs.

I agreed. There were things I don't think I'd share with anyone that wasn't Madoc.

My phone chimed, and my heart skipped a beat as I shot up in bed and grabbed it off the nightstand.

I let out a relieved laugh, wiping a tear off my cheek.

I'm listening.

Every part of my body tingled, and I almost felt giddy.

I didn't know what to say, so I just typed the first thing that came to mind.

I miss u.

Why? he shot back.

My mouth was suddenly as dry as a desert.

He wasn't going to make this easy, I guess.

My fingers just went. Jumbled or poetic, it didn't matter. *Just tell him the truth.*

I miss hating you, I typed. It felt better than loving anyone ever had.

That was the truth. My mother, my dad, any friends I'd had, no one made me feel alive like him.

After a couple of minutes he hadn't texted back. Maybe he didn't understand what I'd meant. Or maybe he was just trying to think of what to say.

I'm fucked-up, I told him.

*Keep going, Fallon.*

I remembered all of the things he'd said to me in front of the mirror that night, so I told him what was in my heart.

I miss your eyes looking down at me, I said. I miss your lips in the morning.

I'm listening, he finally texted back, urging me on.

I bit my bottom lip to stifle my smile. Maybe Tate was right about sexting after all.

> I miss your hunger. I miss the way you touch me. It's real, and I want you here.

He only took about ten seconds to respond. What would I do to you if I was there right now?

The rush of blood through my heart warmed my body instantly. God, I wanted him here!

Nothing, I responded. It's what I would be doing to you . . .

I curled my legs in and set the phone in my lap, covering my very happy and embarrassed face with my hands. I was sure I was ten shades of red right now.

My phone chimed again, and I nearly dropped it twice trying to pick it up.

What the fuck?! Don't stop! Madoc texted, and I couldn't contain my laughter.

This felt good, and Madoc liked it. *I can do this.*

I wish you were naked in my bed right now, I taunted. I wish my head was under the sheets, tasting you, my tongue all around you.

What would you be wearing? he asked.

Madoc liked me in my pajamas. He'd said so once. I'd borrowed a fitted baseball T-shirt and short sleep shorts from Tate. Not really lingerie, but Madoc wouldn't be able to keep his hands off me either way.

> You can see it if you want. I'm only an hour and fifty-eight minutes away.

His response came back within seconds.

I'll be there in fifty-eight minutes.

I burst out laughing in the empty room. Of course, he'd risk his life speeding for any opportunity to get laid.

I shook my head, my face stretched with a smile. I'll try not to touch myself until you get here, I texted.

Goddamn it, Fallon!

I crashed back onto the bed, laughter and happiness shooting out of every pore.

## CHAPTER 22

# MADOC

I rubbed my hand over my mouth, blaring Trapt's "Headstrong" the entire way home. I'd gone round and round today, wondering if I should come back for the race. Wondering if Tate would've dragged Fallon along. Wondering, hoping, and then giving up.

For some reason, Fallon didn't want to stick around to see if we were going to be something, and I only had so much pride to spare. Maybe Jared was right and I needed to chase harder.

But I needed something—anything—from her to show me it was worth it. When she first texted, I didn't respond. I sat in my house, watching a pay-per-view fight with some of my teammates and waited.

If she didn't know what to say, then I'd let her figure it the hell out. When she started opening up more, I was in. She missed me, she wanted me there, and Jared was right. I couldn't let her go again. If she tried pushing me away or running, I was going to push her until she told me what her deal was. Relationship or not, I needed to know what the fuck was going on with her.

And then when she started flirting, I was already grabbing my car keys.

An hour and five minutes later, I was pulling up in front of Tate's house, the street already packed with cars from the party going on at Jared and Jax's house next door.

Parking across the street, I climbed out of the car only to notice Fallon running out of Tate's front door.

*Jesus.*

She wore short, little pajama shorts and a tight white-and-gray baseball tee, the thin strap of her little handbag hanging across her chest. She had sneakers on with no socks, showing me all of her beautiful legs from the ankles to the tops of her thighs.

*Fuck lingerie.*

In good-girl PJs with her hair hanging in beautiful waves, Fallon was the only thing I could see or think about.

My arms hummed to hold her, and when I saw her running down the porch steps and across the street, I had just enough time to reach out and catch her as she jumped into my arms. Wrapping her arms and legs around me, she crushed her mouth to mine, and I groaned as we fell back against my car.

"Damn, baby," I gasped out in between kisses. Her mouth on mine went hard, fast, and deep. Her tongue rubbed against mine and darted out to flick my top lip, and then dived back in again. My arms were wrapped around her waist, and she was practically crawling on me, trying to get closer with each kiss.

There was no kindling for this fire. A blaze was already painfully strong in my jeans, and my dark blue T-shirt burned my neck where she grasped and pulled it.

But I didn't care. My fingers dug into her back, eating up all of this. Her moans vibrating in my mouth, the way she clung to me . . .

I spun us around, so that her back was against my car door, and started to give it back. Her hands ran into my hair and down the sides of my face and then dived lower.

I pulled my face back, gasping with our noses pressed together. Her hands went into my shirt, and I broke out in chills when her fingertips dragged along my stomach.

Her lips bit at the air, trying to catch mine. She then pushed herself up, wrapped her arms back around my neck, and began raining soft, light kisses around my mouth, on my cheek, and down my neck.

My dick pressed against my jeans, and I fucking wished we were somewhere private, so I could get inside of her right now, right here.

"Madoc." Her whisper sounded like she was in pain.

"Shhh," I ordered, going in for her lips again.

But she pulled away. "No, I need to say this." She held my face and looked into my eyes. That's when I noticed she wasn't wearing her glasses.

Her beautiful green gaze searched my eyes with a little fear, and her face was flushed pink. *God, she was beautiful.*

"Madoc, I love you," she whispered. "I'm in love with you."

My fists tightened around her shirt, and I almost dropped her there.

*What?*

My heart seemed to thud deeper and deeper into my chest, descending into my stomach. Sweat broke out across my forehead, and my legs were nearly gone.

She stared at me, looking scared but definitely awake and alert. She knew what she was saying, and I ran the words over and over in my head.

*Madoc, I love you. I'm in love with you.*

I lowered my chin, narrowing my eyes. "Do you mean that?" I asked.

She nodded. "I've loved you forever. There's so much I need to tell you."

My arms tightened around her, and the biggest fucking smile I ever felt broke out across my face.

"Nothing else matters," I told her, sweeping up her lips for another kiss so hard we couldn't breathe.

"Hey, guys?"

I heard a shout come across the street, from the party I would assume. Without breaking the kiss, I stuck my middle finger out behind me toward Jared's house.

I heard a laugh. "As much as I'd like to watch you two have sex and all, I really don't want to have to clean up another round of *Teens Gone Wild* on the Internet!"

*Jax.*

Fallon buried her mouth in my neck, hugging me and laughing. "What's he talking about?" she asked.

Yeah, long story. Jax rocked it with computers, and he was definitely right. We needed to get off the street.

"Jared and Tate." I leaned in, kissing her and completely fucking turned on right now. "I'll explain another time. Let's get inside."

"No." She shook her head but continued to come in for quick kisses, stroking my chest and neck. "Take me home. To your bed. Lock me up in your room and feed me until the only thing I know how to do is moan your name."

I pushed her back into the car and drowned in her lips again, slamming my hand into the door in frustration. *Jesus Christ*, I wanted her so bad right now.

Several hoots and calls erupted behind me, and I knew we had an audience now. I heard Jax laughing and yelling at us while others simply screamed, "Whoo!"

*Idiots.*

"I love you," I whispered into her mouth. "Let's go home."

The entire drive to the house was fucking torture. Fallon wouldn't stop touching me, nibbling on my ear, running her hands up and down my thighs . . . I was harder than a steel pipe and ready to pull over and screw her on the side of the road.

"I'm sorry," she breathed in my ear. "Is it too much?"

"Hell, no." I slammed into sixth gear after we got through the Seven Hills gate. "I like this new you. But you're killing me right now."

She exhaled a hot breath in my ear, and I closed my eyes, tightening my jaw. I wasn't going to last long.

"Madoc, get me to bed," she begged.

I groaned, speeding into our driveway and breaking to a screeching halt in front of the house. Fallon was out the door before I was, and I rounded the car, grabbing her hand and dragging her toward the house.

Unlocking the door, I pulled her through, and we ran through the foyer and up the stairs.

"Madoc?" I heard Addie's voice come from around the corner. "Fallon?"

"Hi, Addie!" we both yelled, not even stopping as we charged up the stairs, two at a time.

I picked up a whimpered "Oh, dear" as we reached the second floor and had to laugh. *Poor Addie.*

Fallon reached my bedroom before me and swung the door open so hard it shook the wall when it hit. I slowed to a walk, crossing the threshold with my eyes glued to hers as she spun around to watch me. She backed up into the room, one timid, light step at a time as if in slow motion, kicking off her shoes and tossing her bag to the floor.

Without taking my gaze off her, I closed and locked the door behind me.

"I want to make a deal," I challenged, stalking slowly toward her.

Her fiery gaze heated me. "And what's that?" she asked, whipping her shirt over her head and letting it fall to the ground.

My eye caught the Valknut tattoo on the side of her torso. It wasn't big, but I'd never gotten the opportunity to study it. I'd have to remember to ask her what it meant.

"If you," I threatened, "so much as leave my bed without my permission in the next twelve hours, you have to get my name tattooed . . ." I smiled.

She arched a defiant eyebrow.

"On your ass," I finished.

A smirk played at the corners of her mouth, and I continued to advance on her slowly, drinking in her smooth skin and white lace bra.

"Deal?" I reached at the back of my neck and pulled my T-shirt over my head.

Skimming her fingers inside her shorts, she slid them down over her ass and let them fall to the ground. "I won't leave without a good-bye. I won't leave at all, Madoc," she promised.

"Do we have a deal?" I pressed, my voice more demanding.

"Yes."

Coming up to stand in front of her, I tensed when her fingers grazed my stomach. She undid my belt, whipping it out of the loops. I toed off my shoes and then reached behind her to unclasp her bra. Peeling it from her body, I let my mouth fall open a little at the sight of her full breasts and nipples, dark and hard.

But when she started to unbutton my pants, I grabbed her hand.

"Not yet," I whispered, snatching her bottom lip between my teeth. She tasted like vanilla and warmth and home. I couldn't imagine ever being hungry for anything else but her.

She whimpered as I dragged my teeth over her lip, but I let go and slipped my hands inside her panties, pushing them down her legs.

I felt like a kid on the Fourth of July. Fireworks were popping everywhere.

With her naked and me still in my jeans, I left her standing there and went to sit down in the cushioned chair in the corner.

Her eyes went wide, shifting left to right. "Um, what are you doing?"

"Sit on the bed."

She stood there staring at me for about ten seconds before finally dropping to the navy blue comforter and scooting backward to the middle. Pulling her knees up, she hugged them and teased me with playful eyes. Trying so hard to look innocent.

The hair on the back of my neck spiked. Her hair spilling around her, the curves of her waist, the muscle tone in her thighs . . . Fallon hid a lot under her boyish clothes, and I was the luckiest guy in the world to have been the only one to see her like this.

She lifted the corner of her mouth, challenging me. "What now?"

I leaned forward, my elbows on my knees. "When was the last time you were on a board?" I asked.

She blinked and asked with a shaky laugh, "You're asking me that now?"

She was right. I was killing the mood like a bucket of ice.

But I waited anyway.

"Well," she said, looking unsure. "I guess it's been two years. The last time I lived here."

"Why?"

She shrugged, more like she didn't want to tell me than she couldn't. "I don't know."

I stood up, taking a few steps toward her. "Did you lose interest in it?"

"No."

"Then why?" I stopped and crossed my arms over my chest.

Fallon loved skateboarding. She'd put in her earbuds and go off to Iroquois Mendoza Park for hours, alone or with friends, and just get lost.

Licking her lips, she said with a small voice, "I guess at first, I didn't want to enjoy anything. I didn't want to smile."

That sounded like guilt. But why would she feel guilty?

"Were you angry with me?" I asked. "For not coming after you?"

She nodded, her voice still small. "I was."

"But not now?"

At the time, I'd thought she'd wanted to leave. I never thought about going after her, because I thought I was the one she ran from.

Her eyes met mine. "No, I don't blame you for anything. We were so young." She looked away and added as an afterthought. "Too young."

I guess she was right. At times, I knew what we were doing was dangerous, but I was consumed with her. I didn't care. And whereas she slowed down and took her time growing up, I charged ahead. I didn't sleep with as many girls as I bragged about even though the opportunity was there, but I definitely couldn't say I'd saved myself for her, either.

I moved closer, stepping up to the end of the bed. "Why did you never try to come home?"

"I did."

# CHAPTER 23

# FALLON

So Madoc wanted to talk.

This was new.

I couldn't get off the bed without his permission, and I was totally naked and vulnerable while he conducted his Q&A.

I sighed, knowing I owed him this much. And more. "A few months after I left I snuck back," I added. "You were having a party, and you had someone with you."

As much as I'd gotten past hating him for that, the feeling of betrayal could never be forgotten. He had been sitting on the edge of the hot tub with his legs in the water while some girl blew him. He had been leaning back on one hand with his other in her hair, and his head had fallen back. He didn't see me looking through the patio doors.

His dad and Addie were home but undoubtedly asleep. I thought I'd worked it well, arriving in so late. He'd be in bed. I'd sneak in. We'd talk.

My timing couldn't have been more wrong. Or more right.

I ran out of the house, away from someone I was too young to love.

Madoc averted his pained eyes. "You shouldn't have saved yourself for me. I don't deserve it."

"I didn't," I whispered. "I saved myself for me. Part of it was that I didn't want anyone else but you, but the truth was I just didn't want anyone. Even you. I was in over my head. I needed to grow up."

His body was so still. He'd stopped advancing, and I wanted him to know that none of this mattered anymore. I'd lived with it and had plenty of time to get over everything. He was still adjusting.

I lay back on the bed, watching his eyes come back to me as I rolled onto my stomach and looked over my shoulder at him.

"Fuck the past. Remember?" I told him, keeping my eyes and tone serious. My pose might be to redirect his attention back on me, but I wanted him to know that while I understood his concerns, we were done talking.

His eyes softened, and he walked around the bed, leaning down over me on his hands.

He was so close, and I faltered when I felt a streak shoot from my chest down between my legs.

*Please touch me, Madoc.*

I gave him a sly smile and hooded my eyes, trying to be sexy. Kicking up my legs, I crossed my ankles and swung my feet back and forth.

He turned his head, running his eyes the whole length of my body in a way that made me feel as if a warm blanket covered every inch his gaze touched. Reaching out, he grazed the skin of my back with his fingertips, and I closed my eyes.

"How's school?" he asked, and I popped my eyes open again.

"Madoc! For Christ's sake!" I yelled.

I hated questions, and now was not the time!

He arched a scolding eyebrow at me. "Temper, Fallon," he warned.

I clenched my teeth, seething.

But then I was shocked out of my anger when he grabbed me by my thigh and hauled me to the edge of the bed, flipping me over onto my back.

*"Madoc!"*

Parting my legs, he hooked me under my knees and yanked me to meet him at the edge.

My heart pumped like a ten-pound weight pressed against my chest, and a sweat broke out over my neck.

*What the hell? Why was he handling me?*

"School," he urged like a warning.

"It's . . . it's . . . good," I stammered. "I'm studying Mechanical Engineering. You?"

I didn't laugh, because I was mad, but this should've been funny, I guess.

He ran his fingers between my legs, massaging my entrance. "Pre-Law," he responded in a light, nonchalant tone. "Surprise, surprise." He sounded like he was having a business conversation.

"Yeah," I breathed out, trying really hard to figure out what the hell my mind should be on right now. His questions or the sensation of his prodding fingers. "Pre-Law? How's that?" I asked.

"I like it, actually." His eyes weren't on mine. He was watching everything his hand was doing. "I think I'll be good at it. So what does the Valknut tattoo mean?"

He slipped a finger in, and my belly exploded with fireworks.

"Um . . . what?" I gasped.

*What was the question?*

His finger—or fingers, I thought it was one, but I felt so full—had to be buried down to the knuckle, because he was so deep when he started massaging my insides with small circles.

*Holy shit.* My eyes rolled to the back of my head.

"The Valknut symbol, Fallon," he reminded me.

I barely unclenched my teeth. "Can I tell you another time?"

*Please, please, please, pretty please?!*

His sly little smile peeked out as he watched his fingers moving inside me. *Triumphant bastard.*

"One more question." He raised his gaze to mine. "Do you trust me, Fallon?"

I stilled, knowing right away what my answer was. "You're the only person I trust."

Sitting up with my legs still hooked on his arms, I looked up at him and whispered, "And I'll make you trust me."

He was going to wake up in the morning with me still here.

He pulled me up to stand on the bed, and I wrapped him up in my arms, hugging him to me. His smooth jaw rubbed against my chest as his head lowered, trailing kisses over my collarbone and down my breasts.

I ran my fingers through his short blond hair and leaned into his mouth. Chills spread everywhere, and I shivered.

He took a nipple between his teeth and then covered it with his entire mouth, sucking hard. "Damn," I sighed, completely helpless.

I let my head fall back as I moaned. His hot mouth sucked and released, bit and let go, over and over again until I felt like there was a spark of electricity shooting from my heart straight to the heat between my legs.

Then, he turned his attention on the other one: kissing, nibbling, and damn near eating me alive.

Sucking in my bottom lip, I dug my nails into his shoulders while he feasted. The torture was so good, but it was building so much that I wanted to throw him down, climb on top, and ride him.

I jerked, my eyes popping open when I felt his fingers back between my legs.

"Damn, you're wet," he groaned into my neck.

Yeah, I could feel it.

I pushed against his chest and dropped to the bed, scooting back to the headboard in a slow crawl.

"Stop toying, Madoc," I challenged through hooded eyes. "Time to put up or shut up. Let's see what you got."

He broke out in a bright smile, stilling my heart. Laughing and watching me, he stalked around the bed unfastening his jeans.

"My little rival. You think I can't rise to the occasion in this game?" he shot back.

I couldn't hide the smile at the corner of my mouth. Leaning back on my hands, I bent my legs up, locking my knees together with my ankles apart.

I lifted my eyebrows with a look that said *prove it*.

But my face fell when he smiled again, this time more sinister.

*Oh shit!*

A yelp caught in my throat as he darted out his hands, grabbed my ankles, yanked me down, and then paused only a moment to gloat at my wide-eyed expression before flipping me over to my stomach.

Fast, shallow breaths poured in and out of me, and my insides clenched and throbbed with the friction of the blankets on my stomach.

I choked on air. "Mad—"

"Don't talk," he growled low in my ear, and that's when I realized I was trapped by a wall behind me.

He still had his jeans on. I could feel them rubbing against my ass.

His hand dipped back between my legs, and I closed my eyes as he smoothed them up and around the entrance, across my clit in circles but never entering me. I propped myself up on my elbows and started moving into his fingers.

The bed dipped, so I knew he must've brought a knee up to lean over me. A hot, wet tickle ran up my back, and I shivered at the feel of his tongue licking me.

A hard nibble descended on my side, and I clenched the blankets under me.

"Madoc." But he didn't stop. Coming down again and again, he sucked on the skin of my back, taking it between his teeth each time. It felt like glass splintering. One kiss and the tingles spread out in an even radius all over my body.

"You want to challenge me again?" He pressed himself into my ass, and I could feel his hardness trying to get free.

"Madoc, damn it!" I tried to sound angry, but it came out as a whimper-cry-beg instead. "I'm about to hump the damn bed! Please!"

Looking over my shoulder, I soaked in his sexy-as-hell smooth, tanned chest and six-pack that I wanted to lick. "I need you," I mouthed.

He must've seen the pleading in my eyes, because he reached over to his nightstand and plucked out a condom. Ripping it open with his teeth, he pulled his pants and boxer briefs down and kicked them off his feet. I held his eyes as he rolled it on. I held his eyes when he knelt on the bed and lowered himself on me.

But I lost him when he arched one of my legs up, my inner thigh lying flat on the bed, and nestled himself between my legs.

As he positioned both of his arms on the bed next to each of my shoulders, he leaned down over me, his hand under my chin, and tipped my head up to meet his lips.

*Oh.* He covered my entire mouth with his, and slipped inside of me, slick and fast.

I whimpered into his mouth.

"I love you," he groaned against my lips.

I reached behind me and clutched the back of his neck, closing my eyes and absorbing every back-and-forth movement of his body as it thrust into mine.

Grinding my teeth together, I sucked in air as he drove deeper and faster, his body sliding up and down my back.

His long, muscled forearms at my sides flexed and tensed, and each time he entered me, I started moaning at the pleasure of what he could do to me that I couldn't do to myself. I think people called it the G-spot, and he was really good at finding it. I started squirming against the bed, pushing up against him to increase the speed. The faster he went, the more I felt it.

His hot breath hissed in my ear. "No patience tonight, huh?"

"I'm sorry," I moaned, not lessening my speed one bit. "I'll make it up to you. This position is just . . ."

My belly started to swirl with butterflies like I was free-falling, and my insides tightened and released. I dropped my head to the bed and arched my ass up to meet him and held it there as he slammed into me.

"Oh," I moaned, feeling the burn, and I went wild, seeking him faster and harder.

Until he stopped.

What?

*WHAT?*

My eyes burned with fear and anger, and the pulse between my legs raced.

Before I even had a chance to turn around, though, he grabbed my hips, yanked me up on all fours and entered me again.

"Oh, God!" I cried out, steeling my arms and widening my legs as he slammed into me just as hard and fast as before.

"This position is even better," he remarked, holding onto my hips.

*His fucking cocky tone.*

And then I was gone. I tightened around his cock, throbbing and bursting as the orgasm scorched my insides, making my heart jump into my throat.

My forehead fell back to the bed, but Madoc didn't stop and didn't relent in his pace, even after my orgasm had passed.

And that was mind-blowing, too.

Continuing to feel him after I came was so good. He squeezed my hips, moving faster and faster. *Damn, I loved his power.*

He grunted a couple of times, breathing hard and finally drove as deep as possible two more times before spilling and slowing his pace until he was done.

Collapsing back to the bed, he finally let me fall, too.

My cheek rested on the bed, and my sweaty hair was stuck to my face. Or maybe his hair was stuck to my sweaty face.

Whatever.

# CHAPTER 24

---

# FALLON

I often wonder if the past looks better to people because they hate the present so much or if it looks better because it was better. Expressions like "the good ole days" implied that life used to be of a higher quality than it is now, but I think everything looks better in retrospect. After all, it's not like we get the chance to go back and relive it knowing what we know now and test that theory.

Except for me.

I did get to come back home. To a place I hated. A life I didn't want. And to a boy I despised.

And even given all of that, I'd still missed Madoc. I never stopped wanting him and loving him.

I had still been obsessed with hurting him even though in the pit of my stomach the ache of needing him still burned. I thought for sure I would come home to a revelation, like: *Why did I ever think I loved him*, or *What the hell was I thinking*?

But no. In this case I didn't remember our time together fondly because I wanted to. I remembered it fondly because it was that good.

I remembered the truth. Not some watered-down, sugarcoated version my mind whipped up after time dulled the pain.

*It really was that good.*

"Madoc," I warned in a playful voice.

He breathed a laugh in my ear. "You're so warm everywhere," he said, spooning me. "And still wet."

His arm was draped over my waist with his hand rubbing between my legs.

We'd fallen asleep last night after a much sweeter and calmer round of lovemaking, and I was exhausted. After barely getting sleep the night before, the long drive back to Shelburne Falls, discovering the boxes in the basement, and then coming back here last night, I needed rest and food.

But I still smiled, because I knew why he'd woken up early.

He was probably on high alert even though he didn't realize it. His subconscious probably thought I was going to skip out when he was asleep.

"I was dreaming about you." I yawned and then nestled my nose into the pillow. It had the scent of his cologne all over it, and I just wanted to pull the sheet over my head and crawl into his smell.

His fingers began to work their magic, stroking and circling around me, and I felt the throb of my arousal.

"Tell me about the dream," he urged.

Mmmmm . . . I had a better idea. Yeah, my head felt like a balloon, and I could barely open my eyes, but who cared?

Reaching over, I took one of the condoms Madoc dumped on the nightstand last night after the first time. I should've known then that he had plans in the middle of the night.

Turning over, I pushed him onto his back and climbed on top, straddling him.

Licking my lips, I ran a finger across his cheek. "I think I'll show you."

"Oh, my God. You remembered." I covered my mouth with my hands, accidentally letting the sheet fall to my waist as I sat up in bed. Pulling it back up, I eyed the box of Krispy Kremes like it was the living end. My stomach growled immediately.

He plopped down, lay on his side, and opened the box that sat between us. "No, not really," he admitted. "Addie still gets them every Sunday. She gets our regular assortment. Lemon-filled for you, chocolate-glazed for me, and just plain glazed for my dad."

And nothing for my mom, I remembered. She would never eat doughnuts.

He picked up his favorite and took a bite. The flaky icing on his lips moved as he chewed, and for some reason, my heart nearly exploded.

Diving in, I snatched up his unsuspecting lips, and had to hold back my laugh when he jerked in surprise. Licking off the icing, I couldn't believe how hungry I was. Madoc made me promise not to leave bed without permission for twelve hours, and now I thought he'd have to drag me away.

It wasn't food I wanted now.

I hovered over his mouth. "I like you."

He inched back, peering at me with suspicion. "I thought you loved me."

"Oh, I do. But we can love people we don't like. You know?" I dug in the box for my lemon-filled. "Like our parents, our siblings . . . but with you, I like you, too. I like being with you and talking to you."

He narrowed his eyes and stuffed a huge bite into his mouth.

"You just think I'm cool, because I have all of the seasons of *Vampire Diaries* on DVD."

*Oh, my God!*

I burst out laughing, covering my full mouth with my hand as I chuckled.

"You do not!" I blurted out, disbelieving. "You don't still watch it, do you?"

He scowled at me and snatched another doughnut from the box.

"It's your fault," he grumbled. "You just had to watch it every Thursday, and then I got hooked."

"Madoc." I swallowed the rest of my bite. "I haven't watched it in years."

"Oh, you should." He nodded. "Damon and Elena? Yeah. Then there was Alaric. That kind of sucked. And then the Originals came into town. They're pretty awesome. They have their own show now."

I started laughing again, and he cut his eyes to me, frowning.

"I'm serious," he implored.

"I can tell."

We sat there, eating and chatting for the next hour, and then Madoc reluctantly let me out of bed after I'd begged to use the bathroom.

I wanted to go for a run, but I'd had sex four times in the last nine hours. I was sweaty, sticky, and sore. I needed a hot shower badly.

I also needed some think time to figure out what I should do about my mom and how I was going to tell Madoc the rest. The baby, my mother trying to take his house . . . We were both feeling so good now, and I didn't want to ruin the high. I just had to tell him and get it over with, though. He'd be so angry with my mom, and perhaps a little angry with me for keeping it from him, but I trusted that he'd stand by me.

I opened his body wash, smelling its wonderful contents that sent the hormones buzzing wildly throughout my body.

As if on cue—I think he had a sense about when my body needed him—he opened the glass shower door and stepped in.

His eyes were dark—almost angry—as he scaled down my body.

"Hell, Fallon," he said in a low growl. Pulling me into him, he dipped his head to wet his hair, smoothing it back.

His mouth came down on mine, and I forgot all of my worries in the warmth of the shower and safety of his arms.

"Want to watch a movie?" I asked as he tossed me a towel. We'd finally emerged from the shower an hour later, and I thought going down to the in-house theater would be a good opportunity to talk to him. Alone, away from Addie's loving ears.

He'd wrapped a towel around his waist and had another one on his head as he dried his hair. "Well, I was thinking it might be fun to see if Lucas is around today. I need to see him."

I didn't say anything. He was right. It was my fault Madoc had left early last summer and was taken away from Lucas. We needed to see him right away.

"And then I was hoping you might stay here a couple of extra days," he continued. "I'm on Fall Break, so I don't have to be back until next weekend."

Disappointment weighted me to the same spot. "Northwestern doesn't have Fall Break."

He nodded, leaning on the bathroom counter looking hot as hell with his hair spiked up everywhere. "I know. I looked it up this morning. But if you can spare a couple of days, it might be worth it."

"Why?"

I'd love nothing more than to stay here and spend extra time with him, but my classes weren't for the faint of heart. Miss one day and you miss a lot. I'd already missed Friday.

"Your mom's trying to take the house. I want to go talk to Jax and see if he can help."

"How would he be able to help?" I walked toward him, and he swung his towel off of his neck and around my towel-clad body, pulling me in closer.

"He's good with computers," he explained. "He can find things on the Internet others can't. I just want to see if we can find anything on her."

He wasn't going to. My father's man had already been all over it, and other than frequenting male prostitutes, my mother's life consisted only of shopping, dining, and socializing. Madoc's dad had the info that he refused to use.

I didn't tell Madoc that, though. He knew my role in our parents' divorce, and I wasn't going to remind him.

"Jared, just give it a chance!"

Madoc and I both jerked our heads toward his bedroom door at the shouting outside.

"Woman, you are high!" Jared barked. "No way."

"Oh, you're such a pussy! It's just ballroom dancing," Tate yelled.

Madoc and I both looked at each other wide-eyed before running to his door and yanking it open together.

Jared and Tate had just rounded the corner and were heading down the hall in the opposite direction toward the other side of the house. To their room, presumably.

Jared turned around, walking backward. "Absolutely not."

Madoc slung an arm around my shoulder and called out. "What is she trying to get you to do now?"

Tate swung around, hands on her hips, while Jared stopped retreating.

"Ballroom dancing lessons," he gritted out. "I don't know where she got the idea."

Tate looked down. "I just thought it could be a new experience, Jared," she said with her back to him. "I can't expect Madoc to dance with me at *every* occasion, can I?"

I narrowed my eyes, studying her. *Every occasion?*

And then it hit me.

*A wedding.*

That's what she was thinking, only Jared's severe arched brow and Madoc's snort told me they didn't get it.

She was in love with Jared, and even I could see that he had every intention of marrying her someday. She'd want him to dance with her at their wedding, of course. And Jared didn't dance.

He might not need the skill for a few years, but she was just thinking ahead. Chewing on the side of her mouth, she looked angry, but she had too much pride to say why she really wanted him to learn.

"I've got an idea," I spoke up, holding the towel securely around me and peeking around the door frame.

"A race," I suggested. "She wins, and you have to take lessons until you can waltz like a pro. You win, and you don't have to."

He looked away with a bored expression. "I don't have to right now. What's really in it for me?"

Tate pinched up her lips, looking about ready to beat the shit out of him.

"All right, dickhead." She spun around and addressed her boyfriend. "You win, and I'll do that thing you've been wanting me to do."

His eyes perked up, flashing with mischief, and I'd imagine that's what Jared Trent looked like on Christmas morning.

"Do you have a deal?" Madoc asked.

Jared strolled up to Tate, pinching her chin between his fingers. "Next Saturday night. I'll call Zack and set it up." And he walked to their room, digging his phone out of his pocket on the way.

"What does he want you to do?" I could hear the smile in Madoc's voice. "Anal? I would've thought you two had been there by now."

Tate's hair swayed across her back as she shook her head. "It doesn't matter. He'll lose."

She sounded more confident than sure.

Madoc laughed. "Yeah, okay. The last time Jared lost a race was . . . hmm, never."

*He's right.*

I think I'd just had a really stupid idea, and Tate was in for it now.

# CHAPTER 25

# MADOC

After another hilarious argument, Jared and Tate finally left town to go back to Chicago and school. He was trying to convince her to leave her car in Shelburne Falls—since they'd be back in five days anyway—and she decided it was best they drive separately and not see each other all week. He had an outburst, and she mumbled something about sexual frustration weakening his normally sharp skills on the track next weekend.

I wasn't in a hurry to rush my time with Fallon this week, but I couldn't stop smiling at the idea of going to the Loop again. I'd missed my friends more that I'd admitted to myself.

Fallon decided to stay an extra day or two, so we dressed and jumped in my car. After seeing Jax, Fallon and I were going by Lucas's house.

"Jax!" I called out, opening the unlocked front door. "You awake?" I heard steady footfalls on the floor above and waited until he began descending the stairs.

He was shirtless as usual around the house and wore black

Adidas track pants with no shoes or socks. His hair was pulled back in its normal ponytail, but stray hairs stuck out of it as if he'd just woken up. And he was sporting a bruise on the side of his lip. He looked tired as hell, but in a good mood.

"Hey, man." I gave him our slap-fist-bump combo. "Put on a shirt, would you?"

It was kind of a joke. Kind of. I was hotter than him. No doubt. But I grabbed Fallon's hand, reminding her that she could look but not touch.

Jax had begun working out with Jared and me about a year ago, and while he was still young and growing, he could hold his own with both of us. He took care of himself the way other kids his age didn't. He had a thing about being healthy and while he dabbled in alcohol here and there, he never touched cigarettes or drugs.

In fact he had a huge problem with drugs. A guy offered him weed once, and he flipped out.

Fallon squeezed my hand, smirking at my jealous demand for him to put on a shirt.

He crossed his arms over his chest. "You're lucky I put on pants, dude. What's up?"

I motioned to the stairs. "Let's step into your office."

He turned, and we followed him upstairs to his lair. Or that's what I joked it was. Jared's mom, Katherine—and my soon-to-be-stepmom—had taken Jax out of foster care and brought him home with her so that her son could have his brother with him.

Unfortunately, Jax was the sun, moon, and stars to her, and she spoiled him rotten. Jared got the mom that put herself first and neglected him, and Jax got the mature mom who'd grown up and behaved responsibly. Jared got left alone, and Jax got home-cooked meals and a number one fan at his lacrosse games.

It was fine, though. He damn well deserved a break after the childhood he'd had, and Jared was happy that his family had finally come together.

Jax had been allowed to take Jared's bedroom when he moved to college and used the spare room as his "office." You walked in and felt like you were in an FBI surveillance van. It was dark and a little intimidating with switches, screens, and wires snaking up and down the walls. Six huge touch-screen monitors lined the wall, three in each row, and then there was a seventh propped on a tripod that Jax used to control all of them. There were three long tables lined with electronics that I wouldn't have the first clue about as well as a PC and a laptop.

When I asked him last year why he needed all of this, he'd simply said that he played a lot of video games.

*Yeah, this wasn't gaming. This was severe.*

But given Fallon's and my situation, I was grateful Jax was around. He might be able to issue paperwork that would have me extradited to the Sudan to stand trial for treason against their king—or whatever they had—but he was on my side, so that was a plus.

"Whoa." Fallon stopped short when we entered the room, and I ran into her back.

Steadying myself, I wrapped my arm around her gray T-shirt-clad waist and waited, letting her take it all in.

Everything was as I remembered, but it was still a lot to absorb. Every screen was active, a couple displaying line after line of code that was meaningless to me, while other screens had Web pages, documents, and IMs displayed. I had to blink several times, because my brain was on overload. How the hell did Jax look at all of this action every day?

"Jax . . ." Fallon started with concern thick in her voice.

Jax circled the room, switching off monitors and not looking at us.

"Ask me no questions, Fallon, and I'll tell you no lies," he said as if he'd read her mind.

Her eyes went round at me. "Okay," she drawled out in a whisper.

"Hey, man. I need a favor." I walked to one of his long tables where I spied a pen and paper. "Can you search this name? Patricia Caruthers." I continued writing her other surnames as well as her phone number. "She might also be found under Patricia Pierce and Patricia Fallon. Look for police records, credit card statements, friends in low places, her social calendar . . ."

I handed him the paper.

"Patricia Caruthers. That's your stepmom, right?" he asked, looking between Fallon and me.

"It's my mom." Fallon stepped in, glancing back at me before continuing. "Jax, I'm sorry we're getting you involved, but she's taking things too far with this divorce. We want to see if you can"—she shrugged apologetically—"get anything on her. To persuade her to back off, you know?"

His thoughtful eyes continued to shift between Fallon and me, but he finally nodded. "Give me a few hours."

After we'd picked up Lucas, we went to Chevelle's Diner for lunch and then headed to the skate park. I'd told Lucas where we were going at the restaurant as I walked him to the bathroom—and stood guard outside the door, because of creepers. He'd never been skateboarding. I also told him to keep his flippin' mouth shut. I wanted to surprise Fallon, and to be honest, I wasn't sure how she'd take the idea. So I decided to ambush her.

Better to ask for forgiveness than permission, right? That's my motto.

My phone kept buzzing in my pocket as I drove, and I felt for the power button through my pants, switching it off.

Fallon looked over at me, narrowing her eyes on my pants.

I grabbed her hand. "Stop checking me out."

She rolled her eyes.

My mom and dad had been calling and texting for the last hour. And I knew why. I didn't want Fallon worrying, though.

They knew we were together, and I knew how they knew.

I didn't blame Addie for telling them, though. She would never have volunteered the information. One of them must've talked to her and asked about my whereabouts. Addie couldn't lie, not that she should.

My mom was far away in New Orleans. I didn't worry about her showing up tonight.

My dad, on the other hand, might be surprising us.

And at this point, it was do or die. I wasn't giving up Fallon.

She rubbed small circles across my knuckle, and I peeked in the rearview mirror to see Lucas bobbing his head to his iPod. Darn kid had grown up so much. His hair was longer around his ears, and he'd grown at least two inches in the past four months.

Fallon's grip on my hand tightened, and I looked at her out of the corner of my eye, seeing that she'd noticed we'd turned into Iroquois Mendoza Park.

Her scowl tightened as the wheels turned in her head.

I bit back my smile and wiggled my hand loose, sticking it between her legs and cupping her to distract her.

"What are you thinking about?"

She grabbed my hand with both of hers. "Stop it!" she whisper-yelled, making swift, nervous glances over her shoulder to Lucas.

He still bobbed his head and stared out the window.

I started massaging her and rubbing circles. At least she wasn't thinking about possibly being mad at me about the skate park right now.

Keeping my eyes on the road, I slid my hand out and down her thigh, increasing the pressure.

Looking over at her, I mouthed, "I'm going to take you so hard tonight. Just watch."

She pinched up her lips and threw off my hand.

I turned my smile out the front windshield and jerked to a halt. "Awesome! We're here!" I shouted, yanking up the parking brake and turning off the ignition.

Lucas followed me out of the car right away, and we rounded to the trunk to dig out the skateboards. I'd snuck down to the basement this morning to round them up where they hid between the half-pipe and the wall.

I'd also noticed that the boxes underneath the piano were emptied and Fallon's stuff was all over the floor. She wasn't talking about it, and I was in no rush to explain myself, so we'd avoided the subject of her whole life tucked safely away these past two years.

"Fallon!" I called. "Quit jerking off and get out here!"

The door swung open. "Madoc!" she screeched. "He's a kid! Mind your language."

I arched a sarcastic eyebrow at Lucas.

He shook his head, mumbling, "Chicks."

I lifted the lid of the trunk, steadying it with one hand and peeking around it toward Fallon. "Come on. Pick your poison."

# CHAPTER 26

# FALLON

*Pick my poison?*

I'd rather have Lucas shoot rubber bands at my face.

Slamming the car door, I stuffed my hands into my pockets and stiffened my arms against the chill in the air.

"This is why you insisted on loose clothing," I accused.

When I'd started putting on jeans this morning, Madoc had told me to wear something loose-fitting and to shut up about it.

Such a charmer.

So I donned some loose, straight-leg black pants, a gray Obey T-shirt, and stuck my hair in a ponytail. Ready for whatever little adventure he had planned.

Every muscle in my body had tightened. Even though I used to be a proficient skater, I was out of practice. Whereas my body was still in shape, my confidence wasn't, and with skating, confidence and quick wit were the keys to the kingdom.

I tried to ignore Madoc as he waited, to let him know that I wasn't up for this, but my gaze couldn't resist shifting to the trunk.

I gasped without making a sound, my mouth hanging open. I pulled my hands out of my pockets and clutched the edge of the trunk, gaping at all of my skateboards.

*My boards!*

"Don't start crying," Madoc teased me. "I wouldn't save your Legos and not your boards."

I couldn't help it. Tears blurred my eyes as I looked at all five boards, each one having a special set of memories. My first board that was splintered on every centimeter of the edges and probably had blood on it. My second and third boards that I'd adorned with custom wheels and first learned how to do ollies, kick-flips, and heel-draggers. My fourth board that was my favorite to use in the bowl. And my fifth. Brand-new. Never been used.

My lungs were empty, but I didn't feel the ache.

Looking up at Madoc, I actually gulped through my smile. "I love you," I said in a shaky voice.

He winked in his oh-so-sexy way, telling me he'd take that as a thank-you.

"I'll use this one," Lucas called out, grabbing the never-been-used board.

"Oh, no." I snatched it from him. "This one's for you." I held out the ratty, torn-up one with the traction nearly worn away.

He stuck out his top lip, taking the board from me.

"You have to graduate," I explained. "Got it?"

He nodded and took the board while I grabbed the new one. Madoc slammed the trunk shut without taking one. I looked at him, raising my eyebrows.

"I'm not skating," he mumbled. "I like to watch."

I gripped the board at my side, grumbling, "Great."

"Lucas," Madoc called, and we both turned around. "Put these on."

Madoc tossed him a mesh bag with pads and a helmet, and I tried to contain my smile. Lucas pinched his eyebrows together like he was way too cool for protective gear, but I was impressed.

Madoc was good at this big brother thing.

Was he like this years ago? Or had he grown up after I'd left? I searched my memory, remembering times he'd drink my Snapples to piss me off, but then always come and watch TV with me, making me feel less alone.

And all of the times he ignored me at school, but then send me candy-grams and balloons so I wasn't left out when everyone else got classroom deliveries on holidays. He'd jot down some profanity or a gross poem, of course, but it still felt good to receive something.

Addie was right. Madoc picked up the pieces.

"Lucas." I set my board down on the sidewalk and ruffled his blond hair. "Have you ever skated before?"

"Not yet. But I want to do that!" He pointed down into the bowl as we stood near the edge. He already had his helmet and elbow pads on.

"You can get in there today," I assured him, taking his board and setting it down next to mine. "But it'll take a lot of practice before you're ready to go fast. Let me show you the first steps. Do you know which one is your front foot?"

The blood flowing through my arms felt hot, and my heart was pounding. Damn, I was glad Lucas was here. Madoc sat down, arms spread out and slung over the back of the bench as he watched us. Or me.

At least having Lucas here meant I wasn't the center of attention. Madoc should've just told me to come out here on my own. Get my feet wet again without an audience.

But he knew me. He knew I wasn't going to do anything without being pushed.

"Front foot?" Lucas looked confused as he lifted one foot and then set it down to lift the other, unsure.

I smiled, touching his arm to get his attention. "Okay, go and walk up those stairs over there." I pointed up the sidewalk.

"Why?"

"Just do it," I ordered with more authority but keeping my voice soft.

Lucas left his board on the ground and swung his arms back and forth as he walked up the path.

As soon as he raised a foot on the first step, I yelled. "Stop!"

He halted, keeping his left foot raised and wobbling as he looked back at me.

"That's your front foot," I told him. "Come back."

Madoc had gone back over to his car and left the doors open so we could hear music. Method Man's "All I Need" vibrated out, and my face tingled with amusement seeing Lucas bob his head like the teenage boy he wasn't. This song was older than Madoc and me, for crying out loud.

"Okay." I bent down and pointed to his feet. "Your front foot goes toward the top of the board, and your back one goes on the tail."

He did as he was told, and I watched as he climbed on, testing the give in the board by leaning left and right. My feet started humming for the feel of my own board.

I took a deep breath. "Now, when you're moving, turn your front foot forward and push off with your tail foot. When you put both feet back on, turn them sideways like this again."

He wasted no time. Before I'd even straightened back up, he was gone. He'd turned his front foot forward, at least as far as I could tell, since his black pants were so long his shoes were nearly covered. At least he looked like a skater.

Pushing off with his tail foot, he touched ground time and again, pushing faster and faster, increasing his speed.

His arms flailed, and I tensed.

"Whoa," he yelped, and I watched as he stumbled off his board and into the grass.

I let out the breath I was holding and looked back to Madoc.

He shrugged and shook his head. "He's going to fall, Fallon. Relax."

Madoc's outstretched arms were taut, and my eyes lingered way too long on the dips and curves of his biceps and triceps in his short-sleeved, heather gray T-shirt. The wide, toned expanse of his chest, I remembered, felt lean and rigid under my fingertips. Madoc was hard and soft in all of the right places, and my mouth actually watered at the thought of massaging him, so I could smooth my fingers along every inch of his skin.

With oil. Lots and lots of oil.

"Fallon."

I blinked, snapping my eyes back up to Madoc's face.

"Wipe the drool, baby," he commanded. "We're getting under the sheets later. Don't worry."

My sex clenched, lightning shot from my belly down to my legs, and I looked away, running my hands over my face.

And then he was laughing.

*Stupid asshole jerk.*

Shaking him out of my head—violently—I walked up the path to where Lucas was making his way back.

"You know what? You stayed on the board a lot longer than I did the first time." I put my arm around his shoulder. "And you did what you were supposed to do. When in danger, jump off."

"Don't be such a wuss," Madoc called out. "Show him how it's done."

I scowled at him through hooded lids and looked down to my board, curling my toes.

"What are you? Scared?" Lucas looked up at me, the honest question plain all over his face.

How could I encourage him to do something I wouldn't do? What kind of parent would I make?

Twisting my lips side to side and already feeling the sweat on my neck, I stepped onto the board, straightening my legs against the shake in my muscles. Leaning slowly back on my heels and then forward on the balls of my feet, I breathed shallowly as I swayed front and back, bending the board and remembering the feel of how to maneuver and guide myself.

People often think skateboarding is just about feet, but the truth is, it's a whole-body workout. Every muscle comes into play. You lean with your shoulders, steer with your heels and add or subtract pressure depending on how you want to jump, flip, or glide.

Turning my Van-clad foot forward, I kicked off with my other and bent my knees slightly, clenching my fists against the sudden rush in my chest.

*Shit.*

My eyes went wide, and I let out a laugh before covering my mouth.

Oh, my God. I hope they didn't hear that. I just got an adrenaline rush from kicking off?

Touching ground again, I kicked and kicked, my heart jumping in my chest as I tacked to the left, avoiding the stairs. Staying on the sidewalk, I continued kicking off and gliding on the sidewalk around the bowl, fireworks going off in my belly and brain.

*Fucking amazing. This is what it felt like.*

How did I ever give this up?

Digging into the ground, I pushed off hard and charged ahead straight for Lucas. Spreading out my arms, I dropped my back leg, bringing the front of the board up off the ground and skidding to a halt, circling Lucas until I stopped.

I squeezed every muscle in my body, wishing I could pinch up my face in a shitty-ass grin and jump up and down.

But that would be uncool.

Hopping off the board, my breaths fast and sharp against the afternoon cold, I got into Lucas's wide-eyed face.

"Do I look scared to you?" I teased.

His mouth was hanging open. "I want to learn that."

I stomped down on the tail of my board and caught the front end in my grasp. "Heel-draggers are way off. Let's do some tic-tacking."

Over the next couple of hours, Lucas and I exhausted ourselves with steering, bailing, ollies, and just plain practice. I showed him how to use his body, and how to fall with a smile. Because falling happens. A lot.

I promised him that we'd work on kick-flips next time, and then he spent some time practicing in the bowls while Madoc and I sat on the ledge to watch.

Laying my head on his shoulder, I closed my eyes and, for once, didn't want to be anywhere else.

"Thank you," I said in a raspy voice. "For today, I mean. I needed that." I think I had laughed, shouted, and cheered more in the last few hours than in the last couple of years put together. Even though I'd be feeling the pain tomorrow, I was light-headed with happiness. Madoc's smell enveloped me in the car on the ride home, I'd be cuddled next to him tonight, and every muscle felt loose from the release of stress.

He reached over and kneaded my thigh as he steered through the streets of town. We'd just dropped off Lucas in time for dinner and were heading home.

I sat back in my seat, my sleepy head lying sideways and looking up at him. "Don't be freaked out by this question," I started, "but did you have any relationships in high school? Like girlfriends?"

He snorted and flipped on the windshield wipers. "Women always have to ask questions they really don't want the answers to."

"But I do." My voice stayed light. I actually did want to know. We'd missed years, and I wanted to know everything about him.

"Yes," he admitted, nodding his head and not meeting my eyes. "A few."

Jealousy spread through my brain like a disease. Who were they? What did they look like? What did he do with them? What were their names, Social Security numbers, and addresses?

It's crazy how thoughts and suspicions can splinter your peace of mind.

"And?" I urged softly.

"And I never told anyone I loved them," he shot back. "Only you."

Then he turned to me, shutting me up with his serious, straight face.

The pulse in my neck throbbed, and it took a moment to realize my mouth was hanging open.

He tipped his chin at me. "So what does the Valknut tattoo mean?"

I inhaled an impatient breath and turned to look out the window. "Way to beat a dead horse," I half-joked.

"You're evading."

*Yeah, I am.* But what the hell could I do? How do you tell someone who you want a future with that you got rid of his child without his knowledge? Madoc would care. I just couldn't tell him exactly what the tattoo means. Not yet.

Why wasn't he asking about my Out of Order tattoo or the script down the side of my back?

I narrowed my eyes, focusing on the rain on my window. "The tattoo means a lot of things to different people. For me it's about re-birth." That was partly true. "It's about moving on. Surviving." And then I turned to him and shrugged. "It looked cool, okay?"

There. Hopefully that'd be the end of it. For now, anyway.

I'd tell him everything. Eventually. As soon as I could. For now, I just needed tonight with him.

And that's when I remembered one of the skills of a good talker.

*Distract him with a change of subject.*

Clearing my throat, I spoke up. "You never ask about the script on my back." And I watched his eyes dart down to my hands as I lifted my shirt up and over my head.

Madoc's round eyes were glued to my nearly naked chest clad only in a hot-pink, lacy bra.

"Eyes on the road," I reminded him in my sultriest voice.

He blinked and glanced back out the windshield. "Fallon, I'm driving. This is not cool."

A grin tickled the corners of my mouth watching him squeeze the life out of the wheel.

"See?" I turned and showed him the writing that ran vertically from the back of my shoulder down my blade to just below. " 'Nothing that happens on the surface of the sea can alter the calm of its depths.' It's my father's favorite quote."

I felt my body sway with the swerve of the car, and I had the good sense not to laugh. I liked his eyes on me, and I liked that I distracted him.

"And then . . ." I lifted up my butt, ignoring the excited lump in my throat as I quickly shimmied out of my pants, taking my shoes and socks off with them. "I have another one right here." I pointed to the shamrock on my hip.

"Fallon!" Madoc barked, his forearms flexed, showing the powerful cords in his arms as he jerked the steering wheel to get the car straight. "Damn it."

I smiled to myself and reclined the seat all the way back. Madoc's windows weren't tinted, and since we were still in town, anyone could see me in my bra.

"What's wrong?" I whispered, blinking innocently.

He barely unclenched his teeth. "We're not going to be home for another ten minutes. Are you seriously doing this to me right now?"

I gazed up at him with my hand behind my head and my eyes hooded. Dancing my tongue just outside of my lips, I caught the little silver ball between my teeth and watched the fire flash in his eyes.

My skin was probably flushed pink everywhere, but I didn't care. Nothing felt better than seeing his hands fumbling with the wheel as he tried to keep up on the road or the way his eyes glided down my body.

"Madoc?" I murmured, turning on my side and propping my head on my hand. "I want you to fuck me in your car."

His eyes flared, and his body went still as if the car was now driving itself. He gripped the wheel, yanking the stick shift into sixth gear, and sped out of town.

Before I knew it, the sky was dim, the rain poured hard, and we were parked on a silent gravel road for the next hour.

# CHAPTER 27

# MADOC

All through high school, I followed people. Followed my dad. Followed Jared. Followed the norm.

When you follow, you forget to grow. Days pass, years roll over you, and you're left with little to show for your life. My father was proof of that. He worked and hid, loving a woman he didn't have the courage to claim, and for what? So he could have a city full of people at his funeral and a hefty estate to leave his estranged son?

My father had nothing. Not yet, anyway.

I knew he loved me, and in that respect I was a lot luckier than Jared and Jax, but I didn't aspire to be like my dad. There were some good memories, but I honestly wasn't sure how I'd react if he were suddenly gone.

That's the thought that snapped me awake in my bed. Heat drifted down my neck and back, and I didn't have to touch my skin to know that I was sweating.

My father knew what he wanted, but he never took it. I didn't want those regrets.

I looked over, seeing Fallon curled into a ball and fast asleep at my side. She was dressed in a tank top and sleep shorts, and the blankets rested at her waist. With her hands tucked under her cheek and her hair draping over the pillow above her head, she looked so tiny and helpless.

My mouth turned up with a smile at the thought, because Fallon was anything but helpless.

I still liked enjoying this view of her, though. My heartbeat slowed, watching her steady breathing.

Grabbing my phone off the nightstand, I checked the time, seeing that it was only nine p.m. After skating this afternoon and our little detour, our bodies had been dragging. We crashed in my room, not even caring to eat the roast Addie had left in the oven for us.

My phone buzzed, and I held it above me, opening up the text from Jax.

**Can you come over? Alone?**

*Alone?* He must've found something on Fallon's mom, but why did I have to come alone?

**Be there in twenty.**

Turning on my side, I nudged Fallon awake. "Babe?" I whispered, kissing a trail from her cheek to her ear. "I'm going to run out for an hour. Be back soon."

She moaned, pursing her lips. "Okay," she sighed. "Can you bring me a Snapple when you get back?"

And then she was passed out again, and I was laughing.

———

I arrived at Jax's house about fifteen minutes later. The rain was still falling outside, but it was lighter, and I was happy to see light pouring out of his windows.

Katherine was home.

His "mom"—I wasn't sure what to call her—still spent a lot of time with my dad, but I heard she insisted on him staying at her house more so she could be home for Jax. I wondered how my dad felt about gaining two stepsons. He had a hard enough time with me.

The kitchen and living room lights glowed with warmth as I knocked on the front door and then immediately turned the handle.

I'd stopped waiting to be let in years ago, and we still lived in a town where you really didn't worry about keeping the doors locked at all times.

Waving at Katherine, who'd poked her head out of the kitchen, I sprinted up to Jax's "computer room" and walked in, closing the door behind me.

I jerked my chin at him as he cruised the monitor wall, touching different screens. "Hey, what have you got?" I asked.

"Hey, man. Sorry to drag you over here, but I thought you should see this in person."

Walking back over to his printer, he picked out a couple of papers, reading them over.

"What is it?" I asked, whipping off my button-down and wearing only my dark gray T-shirt.

"Well, I'm really not finding much on your stepmom." He shot me an apologetic look. "Sorry, but she's pretty one-dimensional. I accessed her social calendar, and personally, I find C-SPAN more entertaining."

My shoulders sank a little, and I sighed.

He let out a bitter laugh. "Aside from the dirty dippings into male prostitution—she has a standing reservation at the Four Seasons every Thursday night for that—she's actually pretty clean."

"So why am I here?"

His eyes fell, and he hesitated.

*Great.*

Sitting down in his office chair, he wheeled over to me. "I found something else, actually. I was going through all of her credit card statements, and this came up."

He handed me a paper and rolled away.

I stared down, my eyes scanning but not really reading. Words jumped out at me. Words like *clinic. Fallon Pierce.* And *Women's Health.* They came together as my eyes darted over the thin, white paper that started to crinkle in my hand.

Then my scanning slowed when I caught words like *pregnancy termination* and *balance due.*

My lungs were anchored to the floor. They wouldn't expand when I tried to breathe, and I narrowed my eyes as the words condensed in my head like moisture in the sky coming together to form a cloud.

One big, dark cloud.

I blinked and looked at the date of the bill. July 2. A couple of months after she disappeared two years ago.

My eyes shot down to the balance due. Six hundred and fifty dollars.

I gripped the paper, my eyes burning with anger . . . horror . . . fear. I didn't know what. I just knew I felt sick.

I closed my eyes. She had been pregnant. With my kid.

*Six hundred and fifty dollars.*

*Six. Hundred. Fifty. Dollars.*

"Madoc, Fallon's a friend." Jax spoke up. "But I just thought you might need to know about this. Was it your kid?"

The acid rolled in my stomach, and bile burned in my throat.

I swallowed, my voice sounding more like a threat, as I said, "I've gotta go."

"Where's Fallon?" I growled at Addie.

I'd stormed upstairs once I got home and found the bed empty. She didn't have Tate's car or her bike, so unless she left by foot, she had to still be here.

"Uh . . ." Addie's eyes rolled to the ceiling, thinking. "Basement, I think. That's the last time I saw her."

Her hands buried in dough, she nodded to the stove as I walked around to the basement door.

"You both haven't eaten dinner," she yelled behind me. "I'm packing it up! Okay?"

Ignoring her, I pummeled down the stairs, letting the door slam behind me.

The cement stairs were covered in carpet, so I was virtually silent charging down. The lights were on, but it was ghostly quiet.

I spotted Fallon right away.

She sat in the dip of her half-pipe, lying back against the incline with her legs bent up.

Dressed in a long, white cotton nightgown, her wet hair told me she'd just showered.

"I came down here so Addie wouldn't hear the yelling," she admitted before I said anything. Her hands rested on her stomach, and her eyes were glued to the ceiling.

"You know that I know."

The half of her face that I could see was relaxed and accepting, as if she'd expected a storm.

"Jax called when I was in the shower. He wanted to warn me. Said he was sorry, but he felt that you should know."

Every soft step up to the pipe was made with clenched muscles. I was fucking pissed. How dare she be this calm! She should be feeling what I'm feeling.

Or at least scared!

"You should've told me," I snapped, my deep voice coming from the pit of my stomach. "I deserved the truth, Fallon."

"I know." She sat up. "I was planning to tell you."

*Goddamn her.* She was still so calm, looking at me with sincere and unfailing eyes. Speaking with a golden voice. She was handling me, and that pissed me off even more.

I ran my hand through my hair. "A baby?! A fucking baby, Fallon?"

"When was I supposed to tell you?" Her voice was shaky, and tears watered her eyes. "Years ago when I thought you didn't want me? This past summer when I hated you? Or maybe the last two days when things between us were more perfect than anything has ever been?"

"I should've known about it!" I bellowed. "Jax knew before me! And you just got rid of it without me knowing anything about it. I should have known!"

She looked away, her throat moving up and down like she was swallowing.

Shaking her head, she kept her voice soft. "We weren't going to be sixteen-year-old parents, Madoc."

"How long did you wait?" I bared my teeth, sneering. "Did you even think about me before you did it? Or did you rush to a clinic as soon as you found out?"

Her pained eyes shot to me. "Rush?" she choked out. Tears spilled, and while she tried to hold them back, her face was contorted in agony. Red, wet with tears, and pained.

Getting up, she charged past me, and I grabbed her arm, pulling her to my side.

"No!" I shouted. "You stay here and fight. Own this!"

"I didn't rush!" she yelled, getting in my face. "I wanted the baby, and I wanted you! I wanted to see you. I wanted to tell you. I was breaking, and I needed you!"

Her head dropped, and her shoulders shook as she cried, and that's when it hit me.

Fallon loved me even then. She didn't want to leave, so why would I think she'd want to go through that without me?

Her hands fisted at her sides, and she stood there, shaking with silent tears but too strong to crumble completely.

"The Valknut," she gasped, looking up at me with desperate eyes. "Rebirth, pregnancy, and reincarnation. It was always with me, Madoc."

She closed her eyes, the quiet streams of tears cascading down her beautiful face.

The weight of what she went through alone slapped me in the face, and I remembered the signature on the bill I now had tucked in my pocket.

"Our parents," I realized.

She was silent for a few moments, and then sniffled. "Your dad knew nothing."

We stood there, so close yet so far away, and I was done. Done with everyone pulling our strings. Done with wondering and waiting.

Slipping my hand around the back of her neck, I pulled her in and wrapped my arms around her like a steel band nothing would ever break through.

I didn't know what to think right now.

Should I have been a sixteen-year-old father? Absolutely not.

But I wasn't happy about the abortion, either.

Putting Fallon through that? I wanted to kill people.

Taking me out of the equation completely and leaving me ignorant? Someone was going to pay.

I was done following. *Time to lead.*

I put Fallon to bed and headed for my father's safe. He kept three things in there—jewelry, cash, and a gun.

# CHAPTER 28

# FALLON

"Well, of course!"

My eyes popped open, hearing the snide voice, and I shot up in bed.

My mother stood at the open door of Madoc's room with one hand on her hip, and the other arm bent at her side, displaying glittering diamonds on her fingers.

I was still dressed in my nightgown, and I blinked away the sleep, trying to take in her appearance.

I swallowed down an exhausted grin at her ridiculous outfit. She wore fitted black pants, a sleeveless black-and-white animal print blouse—I hated animal print—and a black fedora.

Really? A fedora?

Every time I saw her, she was trying to look younger and younger. Or more like an Italian heiress. I wasn't sure.

"What are you doing here?" I was shocked at the gruffness in my tone. The episode last night with Madoc had worn me out, but I felt strong and alert—from the neck up, at least.

She smiled, her impeccable skin glowing in the morning sun that poured through the windows. "I live here, Fallon. You don't. Remember?"

Looking to the other side of the bed, I noticed Madoc wasn't there.

*Where was he?*

I narrowed my eyes on my mother as she walked to the foot of the bed. "Get out," I ordered.

She grabbed Madoc's T-shirt and started folding it. "Sleeping your way to the top, I see. I'm not surprised to find you back in his bed. Again."

I threw off the covers and reached for my glasses on the nightstand but then stopped.

*No.* I didn't need them to talk to her.

Dropping my hand, I stepped out of bed and lifted my chin. "If you don't get out, I'll remove you myself."

It wasn't a threat. I was looking for a reason to hit her.

"Jason's expecting me." She hooded her eyes, trying to look bored. "He's on his way. Did you know that? The sordidness of you and Madoc together is the one thing my husband and I can agree on."

I winced at the word "husband." It was funny. I never thought of them as married. Maybe because they never looked like it.

She stepped up to me, rubbing her cold hands up and down my bare arms. "Jason has ways of influencing his son. You'd better warm up to that fact as soon as possible, Fallon. For your own sake. Madoc isn't in this for the long haul."

"Leave," a deep voice startled us both.

My back straightened, and my eyes shot to the doorway where Madoc stood, glaring at my mother.

She'd turned as well at the sound of his deep command, and all of a sudden my arms and legs rushed with power. I felt stronger with him here.

Not that I relied on Madoc to fight my battles. It just felt good to not be alone.

"I am," she assured, and I heard the smile in her voice. "Your father will be here soon, so get dressed. Both of you."

She glanced between us and then walked toward the doorway as Madoc stepped in. His arms were crossed, and the muscles in his naked chest were flexed. Madoc wouldn't hit a woman, but right now he looked like he wanted to.

My mother stopped in the doorway and looked back at us.

"Madoc, you're going to be shipped back to Notre Dame. And, Fallon? You'll be coming with me today. Back to Chicago. I have the Triumph Charity Event to plan, and you're going back to school."

I couldn't help the laughter that sprang up. I pinched my eyebrows together in disbelief. "Are you from the planet Delusion? What makes you think you can tell me anything?"

"I'm taking you back to Chicago, and you're not seeing Madoc again." Her words were sharp, each syllable a threat. "There's no way I'm going to be associated with him or his father after the divorce. And they don't want you, anyway."

"Get out!" Madoc growled.

She shut her mouth and swallowed, momentarily stunned.

Arching an eyebrow, she continued, addressing Madoc. "Once your father arrives, he'll make you see sense. You won't see my daughter again, Madoc."

Madoc charged my mother, taking long, deep steps into her space until she was forced back into the hallway. I followed them, and he came to a slow stop, glowering down at her.

"Make that threat again," he challenged. "I will put you through a wall to get to her."

My eyes burned, and I smiled to myself.

He was at least six inches taller than my mother, and I didn't know if he'd really do it, but my blood rushed hot seeing him like this.

She pursed her lips in defiance before finally deciding to shut her fucking mouth and walk away.

*God, I loved him.*

"Madoc . . ." I ran up to him, and he turned just in time to catch me in a hug. I whispered in his ear. "You're so hot."

His body shook with laughter, and he wrapped his arms around my waist and pulled me up off the ground. I circled my arms around his neck and slammed the bedroom door after he'd walked us in.

"We've got problems," said matter-of-factly.

"We're eighteen. And my father is bluffing."

"But—"

"Trust me," he interrupted. "Do you love me?"

I nodded like a kid that wanted ice cream. "Yes."

"Like love me so much that you wouldn't even be able to kill me if I turned into a zombie?" he pressed with mischief on his face.

"Yes." I laughed.

He set me down and dug in his pants, pulling out a circular, black leather box. As he opened it up, I nearly slumped at the sight of what I saw.

A ring, beautifully detailed around the platinum band with a large round diamond in the center and several smaller round diamonds down each side, shimmered in the room's glow.

When my wide eyes looked up, Madoc was on one knee.

He smirked. "I have an idea."

"Man, are you sure you're ready to do this?" Jared leaned on the counter on Madoc's other side as we signed the papers for our marriage license.

"Don't be jealous," Madoc joked. "We can still be friends. Just not friends with benefits."

Jared rolled his eyes and walked back to the wall of chairs, sitting down with his elbows on his knees.

He didn't look worried. Definitely concerned, though. Maybe a little frantic, too.

I knew I certainly was. I was nauseous, nervous, petrified, worried, and tense.

And completely in love.

It had taken me all of two seconds to find my voice and whisper "yes" when Madoc asked me to marry him. And even though I had a hurricane of concerns and questions spinning in my stomach, I was completely sure and calm about one thing.

Madoc.

I didn't doubt him for a single moment, and I never hesitated when I asked myself if I was his.

I was, am, and will always be. This was it.

We'd left our house before Madoc's dad got home and drove straight into Chicago. I'd barely had any clothes with me, so we headed to my dorm first so I could clean up and grab Tate, and then we'd texted Jared to ditch class and meet us at the City Clerk's Office.

We needed witnesses and, of course, we wanted our friends there.

I definitely didn't look like a bride, though. Tate and I had the same style in clothes, which meant I was out of luck for dresses. It was probably for the best, though. I would've been uncomfortable.

I wore a flimsy, white blouse with a fancy tie collar and capped sleeves tucked into some nice skinny jeans, and some black ballet flats with a matching black Burberry military coat. It was fitted at the waist and flared out as it fell mid-thigh. Madoc complemented me in his usual expensive jeans and a black military style fall coat that fell just below his waist. He had slapped some paste into his hair to make it stick up and the way he looked at me now, flashing his bright smile, was already doing me in.

Tate and I had scrambled on hair and makeup, but Madoc wouldn't stop looking at me like he wanted to eat me, so I guess we did all right.

I interlaced my fingers, each hand clutching the other.

The big diamond ring felt like heaven on my finger, and that was saying something for a girl who didn't wear conventional jewelry.

He'd said it was a family heirloom, and that his father had given it to his mother for their engagement. When I hesitated, he'd laughed and explained that even though her marriage ended in divorce, the grandmother and great-grandmother who'd worn it before all had long, happy lives with their husbands.

Husband.

Questions flooded my head. Where would we live? How badly were our parents going to react? What about school? Would I be good to him? Good for him?

Looking down, I stared at the ring with its intricate detailing on the band, considering the history it represented and the man who gave it to me. He loved me. He was faithful. He was strong.

And our parents had to face the fact that we would never leave each other alone.

"You look happy." Tate stood at my side as Madoc finished up with the clerk.

I held my stomach and sighed. "I think I'm going to throw up, actually."

Madoc turned his head, eyeing me with raised eyebrows.

I rushed to add, "But it's like a wow-I'm-so-excited-I-think-I'm-going-to-be-sick feeling."

He leaned in and plopped a quick kiss on my lips. "Come on. Let's head to the courthouse."

He took my hand and grabbed the marriage license off the counter, but I dug my feet in, stopping him.

"Madoc?" My voice sounded as timid as I could make it. "I think . . . maybe . . . we should find a priest."

I scrunched my face in an apology.

"A priest?" he asked, his expression confused.

Madoc and I were both raised Catholic and attended parochial elementary schools. However, we'd both stopped practicing, so I could see how he was blindsided by my request.

I gulped. "I just think that my father may kill you unless a priest marries us." I tipped one corner of my lips up in a smile and clutched Madoc's hand, dragging him forward. "Come on."

Jared followed with Tate in his car, and Madoc and I led the way in his. Sovereign's Pub was on the north side of Chicago, between the Clerk's Office where we'd come from and Northwestern. We parked in the rear, and I led the way into the bar, knowing exactly where to go.

Sitting in a back room that could be closed off with red velvet curtains, I saw Father McCaffrey sitting at a round table with three buddies. Two of them priests like himself and one old-timer in a leather jacket.

"Father, hi," I greeted, my hand still in Madoc's.

He pulled his pint away from his lips and looked at me wide-eyed. "Fallon, dear. What are you doing here?"

He had a strong Irish accent even though he'd lived in this country for more than twenty years. I think he worked hard to maintain the accent. Not only did his parishioners love it, but I knew he helped my father with business and having the accent helped when dealing with Irish clients. And since he'd baptized me, I knew him well. He had graying dark-blond hair, light blue eyes, and a bit of a beer belly. Other than that he was in good shape. His freckles made him look younger than he was. Dressed in his black pants and dress shirt, he also wore an emerald green sweater vest that allowed his clerical collar to be visible.

"Father, this is Madoc Caruthers. My . . . fiancé." Madoc and I exchanged sideways glances and smiled.

In one respect it felt strange to say "fiancé" when I'd never even called Madoc my boyfriend.

"What?" Father McCaffrey's jaw hung open.

Right away my heart started to sink. He was going to put up a fight.

"Father, I know this is unusual—"

"Father." Madoc stepped forward, interrupting. "We'd like to get married. Can you handle that for us or not?"

*Way to sweet-talk him, dude.*

"When?" Father asked.

"Now." Madoc tipped his chin down like an adult speaking to a child. "Right here, right now."

Father's eyes about popped out. "Here?" he gasped, and I almost laughed.

I had actually thought I'd coerce Father McCaffrey back over to the church a few blocks away, but Madoc seemed to want to get down to business. Fine by me. If I had a choice between a staunchy Clerk's Office, a drafty church, or an old Irish pub smelling of furniture polish and Guinness, I'd rather be here. The wooden bar and tables and chairs all shined with the afternoon sun pouring in through the windows, and the green curtains made the place feel comfortable and homey.

"Father," I started, "when you're not in the church, you're at the bar, and we're ready."

"Fallon, shouldn't you be waiting for your father's blessing, dear?" The worry was clear all over his face.

"My father," I stated firmly, "trusts my judgment. You should as well, Father."

Madoc grabbed my hand, slid the ring off my finger, and set it down with the marriage license and the silver band he had picked out for himself this morning on the table.

"Marry us, please, or we'll have to go to the courthouse with or without the Church's blessing. That is something her father won't like."

Jared snorted behind us, and I looked back to see him and Tate trying to bite back smiles.

Glad they were enjoying this. Sweat broke out across my forehead.

Father McCaffrey sat there, and so did everyone at the table. They looked between Father and us, I looked between Father and Madoc, and Father looked between Madoc and me.

I wasn't sure whose move it was, but I didn't think it was ours.

Father finally stood up, and slipping his hand inside his vest, he pulled out a pen and leaned down, signing the paper.

I dipped my head, a huge smile stretching my face. Madoc turned to me, cupping my face, and leaned down to plant a soft kiss on my lips.

"Are you ready?" he whispered.

I breathed him in through my nose, inhaling his rich scent, and started taking off my coat. "Children will wait until after college," I stated low enough for only us to hear. "Agreed?"

He nodded, his forehead rubbing against mine. "Definitely. As long as we can have five later."

"Five?!"

Jared cleared his throat, bringing our attention back to the people around us, while Madoc laughed under his breath. I took a deep breath and swallowed.

Yeah, we were going to have to talk about that later.

Father brought us around to sign our parts under "Groom" and "Bride," and then Jared and Tate came around to sign as witnesses, also having to print their names at the bottom with Father Mc-Caffrey as the officiant.

"Everyone quiet now!" Father shouted to the fifteen or so people in the bar. They quieted down and turned to us, finally noticing what was going on behind them. The bar fell silent as the music was cut off, and Madoc turned to me, taking my hands in his as they hung down between us.

Father began the short service, but I barely heard him as I looked up at Madoc. His blue eyes that always held a bit of mischief. His angular jaw and high cheekbones that looked even more amazing when they were wet from a pool or shower. His broad shoulders that could encapsulate me with warmth.

But what I thought of most as Father bound us together was how little I was thinking about myself right now. Forever since I can remember, I'd thought about how much I hated my mother or missed my father. I thought about the disappointment and the anger, the wrongs and the loneliness.

I dwelled on the past, not realizing that it kept me from moving forward.

Now it was gone.

It wasn't forgotten, of course. It just didn't matter anymore.

This was my future, and as Madoc put the ring on my finger, I knew the best part of my past was right here with me.

I glanced at Tate, who watched with love in her eyes, and Jared, who had his arm around her, and the happy tears spilled down my cheeks.

Madoc smiled, grabbing me by the back of my neck and gently bringing my head into his chest. "Finish, Father," he ordered over my head. "She needs to be kissed."

The laughter in his voice was intoxicating. And I definitely needed to be kissed.

"I now pronounce you husband and wife."

Madoc wasted no time. Wrapping a quick arm around my waist, he hauled me off of my feet and kissed me hard, his lips shooting a lightning bolt of desire from my mouth straight down to my stomach. I held his face in my hands, and turning my head to the side, I kissed him back with full force.

Keeping me locked to him, he turned us and walked us out of the small space.

"Thank you." I grinned back at Father McCaffrey over Madoc's shoulder.

Madoc called to the bartender over my shoulder. "Do you have any music?"

"U2," the middle-aged guy answered.

Madoc scowled. "Is that it?"

"That's all a man needs." I heard the answer and started laughing in Madoc's ear.

He sighed. "Something slow then."

Lowering his hands, he cupped the bottom of my thighs and brought my legs up and around his waist. Next thing I knew chairs started grinding against the floor, and when I looked around, everyone in the bar was pushing back the table sets to make a dance floor.

U2's "All I Want Is You" started spilling softly out of the speakers, haunting at first as it drifted into our ears. Madoc started swaying from one foot to the other, moving us from side to side. I put my forehead to his, listening to him whisper the words to the song and fighting back the burn in my eyes. As the song built stronger and louder and we moved more, spinning slowly and every once in a while, I placed a kiss on his lips.

*All I want is you.*

# CHAPTER 29

# MADOC

As soon as we left Sovereign's, Fallon and I drove to the Waldorf Astoria for our honeymoon night. Tate thought we should all go out to dinner, but Jared got the hint.

The whole drive there, as the valet took the car, and during check-in I kept rubbing the inside of my pinky finger over the flat fit platinum wedding band. The discomfort of something new when I never wore jewelry—except for my piercing—contrasted to the hum I felt in my hand.

It was weird, but it was also powerful.

The ring reminded me that I was Fallon's. It reminded me that I was her protector, her lover, and her partner.

Eventually it occurred to me that the ring also meant I couldn't come and go as I like, I couldn't look at other women, and I was probably the only person in my high school graduating class that had a wife already, but I didn't care much about what others thought now.

I was cool with this. It was right for us.

By the time we reached the elevator, Fallon's hands were doing things that technically weren't allowed in public, and I was really fucking glad Jared and Tate had given us space.

Fallon had her hand under my coat, kneading my lower back. She was burying her nose in my chest as I walked with my arm around her. Her eyes were looking up at me saying everything that was in her head but couldn't leave her lips.

As soon as the elevator doors closed, I pushed her into the wall and leaned down into her face, her hot breath rushing against mine.

"Fallon Caruthers," I challenged, pushing hard against her body. "What do you think you're doing, huh?"

Her fingers started working the button of my shirt under my open jacket. "I'm sorry," she panted against my lips. "I'm just really ready for my husband right now."

And all at once her hands were inside my shirt, all over my bare chest, and my bottom lip was between her teeth. I grabbed her by the back of her thighs and hauled her up against the wall, diving into her mouth and tasting the raw heat that sent my cock jerking and hardening. I needed to get these fucking clothes off of her.

"And I'm not changing my name," she said between kisses.

I felt the laugh in my throat that I thought would be a really bad idea to let loose right now.

It was my wedding night. I wanted to get laid, after all.

"Yes, you will," I stated matter-of-factly as I put my hand between her legs and rubbed.

The elevator stopped, and I dropped her feet to the floor. Thank God no one was outside the doors, because we were flushed and breathless.

Dragging her by the arm, I dug the card key out of my coat pocket.

"Well, I'll hyphenate it then," Fallon mumbled behind me, and I took a second to remember she was talking about our last names.

"No, you won't." I slipped the key in, opened the door, and pulled her in. "Hyphenating your name is like saying 'I just don't want to admit defeat' when the truth is women who hyphenate their names have already lost. Men don't hyphenate their names." I pointed out, slamming the door behind me as I dug my slow heels into the plush carpet, stalking her. "Now. You are going to be Fallon Caruthers, because you love me, you want to make me happy, and you want everyone to know that you're mine."

She had about enough time to drop her jaw and for anger to flare in her eyes before I was on her. Taking the hair at the back of her head, I pulled it down to expose her neck, and I sunk my lips and teeth in, biting and kissing so hard and soft that she wouldn't know which end was up.

Truth was I was an easygoing guy. For the most part. But my wife would have my name, or else.

It wasn't about controlling her, and it wasn't about stealing her identity or whatever women liked to claim these days. It was about unity. We and our kids someday would have the same goddamn name, and that was it.

Hopefully she knew when some battles weren't worth fighting.

And that's when it hit me.

I pulled back and closed my eyes, running my hands through my hair.

*Kids.*

"Shit," I groaned. "I forgot condoms."

I heard her sympathetic exhale that sounded almost like a laugh. I looked up, scowling. This wasn't funny. I was harder than a rock right now.

"I'm sorry." She waved away the angry expression on my face. "We're fine, Madoc. I've been on birth control for a long time, actually. Ever since . . ."

Her eyes dropped.

The knot in my heart twisted tighter and tighter, and without hesitation, I scooped her up into my arms and carried her into the bedroom.

*Ever since the abortion*, she was going to say.

Since I'd found out about it, I'd had a hell of a time figuring out how I felt about it. I wished we'd had the kid, but I'm glad we didn't. Which didn't make sense, but it kind of did.

On the one hand, I hated that Fallon had to go through that. I hated that we weren't more careful. I hated that she was alone. I hated that someone else—someone I hate—made a decision about my kid without me.

On the other hand, I knew we were too young. I knew it probably would've changed our lives in a way that wouldn't have been beneficial. I knew that I wanted a house full of kids someday, but I didn't want them yet.

Final verdict: I'll be a good father. And I'm glad I get to wait to find out for sure.

Setting Fallon down next to the bed, I planted my lips on her, damn near chewing on her I was in so much need, and ripped off my coat and shirt. After I'd kicked off my shoes, I started working the button and zipper of her jeans.

"No," I growled low when she started undoing her shirt. "Leave it on. I undress you tonight."

Slipping my hands inside the back of her jeans, I couldn't help but run my hands up and down her smooth ass in her thong. As I pushed her pants down her legs and bent down to slide her shoes and jeans off, I breathed out a long breath, thankful she wasn't doing anything right now.

As much as I wouldn't change the nights we spent together years ago, I needed to redeem myself. A little more, at least. Going after her like a starving pubescent teen who can't hold his load wasn't how this night was going to go.

*Slow.*

She wore a tiny black thong, and her white blouse fell just below her hips. She looked down at me, heat and patience in her eyes, and just waited for me to make my move.

Unbuttoning her shirt, I felt the quick and shallow rise and fall of her chest under my hands. Sliding it down her arms, I kept it clenched in my fist and tightened as I felt a surge of blood rush to my cock.

She wore a matching black see-through bra, which I didn't expect. The white blouse didn't reveal it. Her breasts were perfectly visible through the sheer material, and I rubbed my hand over her hard nipple.

I touched her face, my thumb running along her bottom lip. "You're a dream."

She opened her mouth and took my thumb in, sucking on the length, drawing it out slowly. Every nerve in my body hummed like it had just fallen asleep.

Taking my hand back, I reached behind her back and unclasped her bra, pulling it forward and letting it drop to the floor. Then I took the blouse still in my hand and threw it behind her and slipped it up her arms again.

As I met her eyes, I saw the question there, but what can I say? I used to give her crap about her clothes and how much she'd hide, but it turns out I liked girls with mystery.

Pushing her down to the bed with a soft hand, I guided her to lay back and then slid her thong down her legs.

Coming to hover over her, seeing one of her breasts peeking out of the open shirt, I couldn't help my strained voice. "I want to see you in this shirt tonight, Fallon. In only this shirt. All night and every time I make you come."

Her eyebrows pinched together, but before she had a chance to say anything, I slipped a finger into her scorching heat, loving the little moan that came out of her and the way her head fell back.

Everywhere my finger touched was like a shot to my groin. She coated my middle finger so tight that it felt like it was in glove. I pushed in and out, completely turned on by how she pushed into my hand, grinding for more. Her moans turned to mewls, and I added another finger, barely feeling the strain in my other arm as I supported myself.

Her closed eyes and lips were tensed, and the sharp breaths coming out of her were the only sound in the room.

In my fingers went and out they came, wet and needy as I continued my rhythm and started circling her wet clit with my thumb. Her hips rolled faster and faster, sliding into my hand for more.

"Are you coming, Fallon?"

"Yeah," she whimpered, breathing hard. "More, faster." She sucked in a breath, crying out.

Sliding in faster and harder, I watched as she slammed up and down, falling into a rhythm with my hand. Every thrust and exhale was like a plea.

*More.*

*Faster.*

*More.*

*Harder.*

"Damn, baby. Look at you." I swallowed, knowing she was almost there. Knowing she couldn't go any faster.

Diving as deep as I could go, I sunk my fingers into her and held them there, massaging her insides in circles.

"Oh, God!" she cried, arching off the bed in waves as she came all over my hand. Throwing her head back two times, she drew in quick, ragged breaths as I held my fingers inside of her and rubbed my thumb over her clit again and again.

Everything about her was gorgeous. Hovering right over her, I whispered, "Fallon."

She blinked her eyes open, the aftershocks of the orgasm still straining her face and a light sheen of sweat on her forehead.

"You were my first everything. And my only love."

I wanted her to know that. Even through all the years, the separation, the pain, I wanted her to know that she was the only one I'd loved.

Sitting up, she held my face in her hands. "No one can stop us now." But it sounded more like a battle cry than a fact. It was like she was saying "Yeah, we're married, and you can't take that." But also "Go ahead and try."

I caught her lips and slipped my tongue into her mouth, kissing her fiercely with every muscle in my body tight.

Pulling away, I stood up and stripped out of the rest of my clothes. Her eyes shot down to my erection, and I couldn't tear my eyes from the shirt draped over her braless chest.

Coming down on her, I flattened her on the bed and didn't stop kissing her as I worked my cock into her entrance. Dipping inside— just barely—I slipped back out, bringing her wetness with me and swirled my top around her clit. The vibration of her groan hit my lips, and I entered her again—only halfway—and pulled out, rubbing the tip of my dick around her hard nub again.

"Madoc?" she whimpered, sounding pained. "I'm not a piano. Stop playing me."

I grinned and entered her again, taking each centimeter of her slowly. "Am I too heavy?" I asked, putting all of my weight on her.

When I had sex, I usually didn't favor missionary. Other positions felt better and allowed you a better view of the woman's body, but this time was different. I wanted to feel her everywhere.

She shook her head under my kiss. "No, I love it." Her hands scaled down my back and pulled my hips deeper into her. "Right there," she begged. "Just like that."

*Jesus.*

I put my forehead to hers and inhaled the breaths she was letting loose. Her chest—the parts that peeked out of the shirt—were moist with sweat, and the friction of her hot skin was sending me reeling. My dick was slick with her, sliding in and out faster with her urgent hands pulling me in harder.

Fuck, she was so damn needy, and it was turning me on. I wasn't going to last long. Grabbing her thighs, I rolled us over so that she was on top. Her shirt had fallen off one shoulder, and one breast lay bare. As much as I wanted to touch her, I just watched her move. Holding onto her hips only, I kept my eyes glued to her grinding on me, the corner of her bottom lip between her teeth, and her exposed skin glistening with sweat.

"Oh, God!" she cried out, riding me faster.

I groaned, shutting my eyes. "Come on, baby."

The tingles spreading throughout my body weren't going to hold off. I was too damn turned on, and she was too damn hot.

"Madoc." Her pained whisper shot right to my heart, and I arched up off the bed, pushing up into her as hard as I could.

"Ahhh." And she came apart, jerking and moaning, and I let go as well, releasing everything inside her and thrusting up again and again.

*Christ.* My eyebrows remained pinched and my eyes shut. My body was anything but relaxed right now.

I'd never come inside of a woman without a condom before.

Except Fallon. Years ago.

No wonder the consequences could be bad. There was always a price on something that felt that good.

Fallon collapsed on my chest, and for a while, we just stayed silent and tried to calm down.

But then she whispered into my neck. "Fallon Caruthers, then."

And I flipped her on her back, ready for round two.

We stayed tangled together in the hotel room for the next twenty-four hours, finally pulling ourselves out of each other's asses—no pun intended—to have a conversation.

"Well, I do have a little money. My father pays my tuition up front and puts extra funds in my account for spending money. It's not much but enough to set up an apartment."

I kept my lids shut but gave her my attention. "What about your tuition for next year? Won't you need the money for that?"

She didn't say anything for a few seconds but then answered. "We'll figure it out."

I had to chew the inside of my cheek to keep from smiling, but it didn't work. The rumble escaped my chest, and I let out a soft laugh.

"What?"

I sighed, still not looking at her. "Fallon, baby, we're fine. We will have no money problems if our parents cut us off," I finally told her.

"What do you mean?" Her tone was more abrupt.

"I mean we're fine." I shrugged. "Don't worry about it."

When she said nothing and didn't press, I opened one eye and peered at her staring at me over her laptop. She looked like she was about to start boiling.

I exhaled an annoyed breath and leaned on my side, propping myself up with my elbow. Grabbing her laptop I logged in to my account and then turned the laptop back to her, showing her the screen.

I didn't wait to see her expression before I lay back down and closed my eyes.

"Oh, my God," she exclaimed quietly. "Is this . . . your savings account?"

I grunted.

"All of this money is yours?" she pressed, sounding like she didn't believe me. "Your dad doesn't have access to it?"

"Most of the money in there has nothing to do with my father. My mom's family is wealthy in their own right. She gave me my inheritance when I graduated high school," I explained.

I rarely touched the money in my bank account. My father made sure all of my expenses were paid, and I had a credit card for things I didn't have cash for. He liked to see what I was up to, so the credit card statements came in handy to him when he wasn't around to see what I did with my days. It wasn't that he didn't trust me. He did. I just think looking at my purchases made him feel like a part of my life and let him feel like he was in control.

*Oh, look. Madoc got gas at 8 a.m. on a Saturday. Must be coming home from a party.*

*Oh, look. Madoc bought car parts. He must have a race coming up soon.*

*Oh, look. Madoc went to Subway. Glad he's eating.*

"Your mother gave an eighteen-year-old this much money?"

I snapped my eyes back open, coming back to the now.

Looking over at Fallon, I scowled with mock hurt. "Hey, I'm trustworthy. You know that." I laughed at her arched eyebrows and continued. "My father also gave me a third of my trust when I started college, so that's some of the money in there, too. I get another third when I graduate and another third when I turn thirty. But even if I don't get those two-thirds, obviously, we're going to be fine." I waved my hand at the laptop, referring to the balance in my account. "You'll go back to school next Monday, I'll withdraw from Notre Dame and transfer, and we'll get an apartment here in Chicago."

I locked my hands behind my head and waited for her to say something. It made me feel happy she actually risked giving up her security for me, but that would never have to happen.

She pursed her lips and narrowed her eyes. "You've had this worked out all day, haven't you?"

"Of course, I have." I flashed her a boyish smile. "You think I'd give myself a wife to take care of and not have a plan?"

Leaning up, I slipped my hand around her neck and brought her in. But as her eyes closed for the kiss she was no doubt expecting, I flicked her nose with my tongue instead and plopped back down, closing my eyes.

"Just don't try to divorce me and take half," I threatened.

"Ugh, that was gross," she whined, probably wiping my spit off her face.

I heard the laptop close and the bed move as she climbed on top of me, straddling my waist. I went to place my hands on her thighs, but she grabbed them and pinned them to the side of my head.

"Nope." I shook my head. "I'm exhausted. I won't do it. You can't make me."

But it was too late. Her weight on me and her heat on my stomach already had me rolling my hips into hers as her moist breath sent a silver shot down to my groin.

Shit.

I was fully hard now, and I needed some damn sleep. Didn't want sleep but needed it. Her mouth darted up to my neck, and she sunk her teeth in. I opened for her.

"Baby." I choked out a groan. "I never want to leave this room. Take my T-shirt off your body. Now."

Pounding on the door sounded from the other room, and we both jerked our heads toward the noise.

"Madoc Caruthers?" a stiff voice called.

Fallon turned her wide eyes to me, and I sat up, setting her to the side of the bed.

Walking toward the door, I shook my head in dawning realization. I should've had Jared register the room. I'd been smart enough not to use my credit card, but I never thought my father would take the time to call the hotels of Chicago looking for me.

"Yes?" I asked, opening the door and then immediately dropping my fucking jaw.

*The cops? What the hell?*

"We'd like to ask you a few questions," a lean black officer said with his hand resting on his baton. I didn't take that as a threat. Maybe I should? The other cop was a female. Middle-aged with red hair.

"What's this about?"

The lady cop tipped her chin at me. "Is Fallon Pierce with you?"

My heart started thumping. *What now?*

"Yes," I finally answered.

"Your stepsister, right?" the male cop confirmed.

I hooded my eyes and sighed. "For the moment, yes. Our parents are getting a divorce."

"What's going on?" Fallon asked, stepping up to my side. She was dressed in jeans and her white blouse from yesterday tucked in. All of the clothing that had been sitting in a ball on the floor for the past twenty-four hours. She also had her glasses on.

"Are you Fallon Pierce?"

Fallon crossed her arms. "Yes."

"Your mother reported you missing yesterday morning," Redhead explained. "She says she was threatened by Mr. Caruthers, claiming he said he was going to . . ." She looked at her notes and continued. "'Put her through a wall.' And then you were taken."

Both cops looked at me, and I wanted to laugh. Fallon turned to me with a smirk on her face, and as serious as cops visiting your door is, we started laughing.

The officers exchanged a look as my chest shook and Fallon covered her smile with her hand.

"Did you threaten Mrs. Caruthers, sir?"

Which Mrs. Caruthers? I felt like asking, but I resisted. No one would know about our marriage yet, and our parents had to find out from us and no one else if we were going to be taken seriously.

"Officers," I assured, "these are family issues. I would never have touched my stepmother. Fallon is here of her own free will, and there is no problem."

"Mr. Caruthers," the male cop started. "We know who your father is—"

But then all hell broke loose. A woman and her cameraman rushed up behind the police officers and stuck a microphone between them in my direction. I reared back, and Fallon grabbed my hand.

"Madoc Caruthers?" the woman shouted, stumbling into the cops. "Son of Jason Caruthers? Are you having an affair with your stepsister? Her mother claims you kidnapped her?"

My fucking heart lodged like a baseball in my throat, and I couldn't breathe.

*Motherfucker! Shit!*

I swallowed, looking down at Fallon.

"Now, that's enough!" one of the officers growled, both turning around and holding up their hands to shield us from the intrusion.

What the hell? My dad was a big deal, but not that big of a deal. Someone had to have tipped these people off.

The female cop kept her voice calm. "Let's get this under control. You're interfering with police business."

"Is he holding you against your will?" The reporter shook her brown bangs out of her eyes, looking intense and determined.

I leaned over to grab the door to close it, but Fallon barked.

"Stop," she ordered. "He's not *Mr. Caruthers.* And he's not holding me against my will, for Christ's sake! And we're not having some sordid relationship. He's my . . ."

*Oh, no.*

". . . husband!" she finished.

I closed my eyes, wincing, and let out a low groan.

*Shit. Fuck. Son of a bitch.*

I shoved Fallon back, grabbed the door, and slammed it shut, hearing the cops ordering the reporter and her cameraman away.

Locking the door, I slid down the wall next to it and crashed to my ass.

Knees bent, I rested my forearms on them and banged my head against the wall once.

"Awesome." I breathed in and out, barely noticing that Fallon stayed where I'd pushed her out of the way.

My fists clenched, and I was sure my face was beet red. I felt stupid. Why did I always underestimate Patricia?

"Oh, my God," she finally said, looking dazed. "That was creepy. My mother's insane."

"No, she's smart," I said flatly. "We just made the news and embarrassed my father."

Her head fell, and she walked over and sat down next to me.

"Madoc, I'm sorry. I panicked."

I put my arms around her. "It's okay. I guess we don't have to worry about making the rounds to the parents anymore."

Everyone—and I mean everyone—was going to know I was

married by the time they went to sleep tonight. There would be no end to the texts and calls for a while as my family and friends would all want to know what was going on.

"How did they know we were here?" she asked.

"I registered under my name." I sounded less embarrassed than I actually was. "Your mom wouldn't have had to work too hard to find us if she found out we weren't at school."

Her chest fell hard. "That's going to be on the eleven o'clock news."

"And it'll be on the Internet in about five minutes. Media outlets have to compete with the speed of Facebook, after all. They'll have that loaded up in no time."

I sat there, quiet and stunned, trying to figure out what to do next.

"Look at me," she urged.

I did and fell back into the comfort of her green eyes.

"We can't stay here," she stated. "Where should we go?"

Leaning my head back, I licked my lips, thinking.

Fallon and I did nothing wrong. We weren't running away just so we could have a mini-honeymoon. And we weren't starting our marriage fearing our parents' wrath. If we wanted to be respected as adults, then we had to face the music.

I stood up, pulling her after me. "Home," I said. "We're going home."

It was about ten o'clock by the time we rolled into the driveway at my house. The pitch-black sky exploded with stars, and the conifer trees Addie had had planted so that we could have green all year bent with the light wind.

The cops had come back to our room for a few remaining questions.

Yes, Fallon and I are married. Here's the signed license.

No, I did not kidnap her, of course. See? No bruises, and she's smiling.

Yes, I threatened my stepmom, and I'm using the "daddy" card on this one. You can't touch me, because I'm Madoc Caruthers.

Now, please go. We're honeymooning.

They left, we showered and got presentable, and we drove the hour it took to get to Shelburne Falls.

"Wait," I ordered when Fallon started to open her door.

Getting out and rounding the front, I let her out of the car, took her hand, and walked side by side with her to the front step.

I took her chilled face in my hands. "We're not raising our voices, and we're not apologizing."

She nodded and together we entered the house.

The foyer and all of the rooms off it were dark, and the house hummed with only the sounds of clocks ticking and heat pouring out of the vents. The smell of grilled steaks and leather hit me, and I immediately felt at home. It's what my house always smelled like.

I remembered that Tate once said she loved the smell of tires. It brought back memories for her, and it was familiar. When I smelled grilled meat, I always thought of summers out by the pool. My mom asking me if I wanted another Crush. My dad—on the occasions he was home—working the grill and talking to his friends. And me seeing the fireworks light up in the star-filled sky.

Despite the issues my family had—all families have issues—I was a happy kid. Things could've been better, but they were good enough, and I never wanted for anything. There was never a shortage of people to dote on me.

This house was my home, and with it came all of my good memories. Whenever I escaped, this is where I wanted to run first. Patricia Caruthers could take our name, take the money, but I'd be dead before she took this house. I had to find some way to beat her.

I didn't know if my dad was in bed, but I knew he was here. His Audi was in the driveway.

Hand in hand, Fallon and I walked down the hall and veered to the left, coming up to his office.

"Do you think our children hate us?" a woman's voice asked, and I halted.

I motioned for Fallon to stay quiet by putting my finger over my lips, and we both leaned into the cracked door, listening.

"I don't know," my father answered, sounding resigned. "I guess I wouldn't blame Madoc if he did. Does Jared love you?"

*Katherine Trent.* That's who he was talking to.

"I think so," she said softly. "And if he got married tomorrow, I'd be worried as hell, but I'd know he was following his heart. I mean, look at us, Jason. Who's to say they can't make it at eighteen when we failed long after that age? Are we experts?"

*Damn.* Invisible hands wrung out my stomach like a washcloth. My dad knew I was married.

I heard hard footsteps. "It's not about that. It's about priorities, Katherine. My son needs to finish college. He needs to experience life. He's been given the gifts of privilege and opportunity. Now he has a distraction."

I took Fallon's hand and held her eyes with mine.

There was some shuffling around the office, and then I heard the wheels of my father's desk chair shift as he let out a huge breath. He must've sat down. Narrowing my eyes, I tried to figure out if he was angry or upset. I couldn't tell. I heard a grunt and some more heavy breathing. It sounded like hyperventilating. But not.

"I messed up." His voice caught, and I heard the tears.

"Shh, Jason. Don't." Katherine started to cry as well.

*My father*, I thought. *My dad is crying.* My chest got heavy, and I looked down to see Fallon's thumb rubbing back and forth on my hand. When I looked up, her chin was quivering.

"My house is empty, Katherine." His voice was so sad. "I want him home."

"We weren't good parents," she choked out. "Our kids have paid for our lifestyle, and now it's our turn to pay for theirs. He's got a girl that he can't stay away from. They're not doing this to hurt you, Jason. They're in love." And I smiled at her words. "If you want your son back," she continued, "you need to open your arms wider."

I clasped Fallon's hand tighter and whispered, "I need a few minutes alone."

Her watery eyes sparkled, and she nodded her understanding. Walking past me, she headed for the kitchen.

Pushing the door open, I saw my father in his desk chair, leaning on his knees with his head in his hands. Katherine was kneeling in front of him, comforting him, I assumed.

"Ms. Trent?" I called, slipping my hands into the pockets of my jacket. "Can I talk to my dad alone, please?"

Both of their heads popped up, and Katherine stood.

She looked beautiful in a cream-colored forties-style house dress with red polka dots on it. Her chocolate dark brown hair—the same shade as Jared's—hung over her shoulders in loose curls, but pieces were brought up in two barrettes on each side of the top of her head.

My father, on the other hand, was a mess. Disheveled hair he'd probably been running his fingers through, a wrinkled white shirt, blue silk tie hanging loose, and he'd definitely been crying.

He sat there, unmoving, and actually looking a little afraid of me.

Katherine cleared her throat. "Of course."

I stepped out of the doorway as she walked past, but I reached out and grabbed her hand, stopping her. I kissed her cheek and gave her a grateful smile. "Thanks," I whispered.

Her eyes shined, and she nodded before leaving.

My father hadn't moved from his chair, and I did a sweep of the room, remembering that I was never allowed in here as a kid. My father wasn't hiding things. Not in here anyway. But he once said "his whole life" was in this room, and it wasn't a place for kids.

I think that was the first time I realized that I wasn't my dad's top priority. There were things he loved more than me.

But looking at him now . . . his weary eyes, his physical strain, and the silence that told me he didn't know what to say to me offered up a different conclusion.

Maybe my dad cared.

Taking a deep breath, I stepped toward him. "I never liked you, Dad." I spoke slowly, taking my time. "You worked too much, and you never showed up when you said would. You made my mother cry, and you thought money could fix everything. And the worst part is that you're not stupid. You knew the void you left in your family, but you did it anyway."

I narrowed my eyes, challenging him to say something. Anything to account for himself.

But his eyes had dropped to the desk with my first words, and they had stayed there.

So I continued, straightening my shoulders more. "I love Fallon. And I love this house. I want you in my life, but if you're going to throw your weight around like it matters, then you can go to hell." I paused, coming up in front of the desk. "We don't need you. But I do love you, Dad."

My jaw tightened, and I blinked away the sting in my eyes.

He raised his eyes, and it was a look I'd never seen before. They shimmered with tears, but they were hard. My father wanted to fight.

In his head he worried about my education, Fallon and me having jobs, dealing with marriage when we were still growing up, but that's what he didn't notice.

I'd stopped growing up when Fallon left.

And I started again when she came home.

You have to have something to love. Something to fight for to make living a goal instead of a job. Fallon wouldn't keep me from tomorrow. My father had done that.

I held his stare, ready for whatever he wanted to throw at me, but he should know better. If he didn't support us, we were doing it without him.

Finally standing up, he ran his hands through his hair and tightened his tie. I watched him as he went to his safe, dialed in the combination, and took out some papers. Returning to his desk, he signed the document and handed it to me over the desk.

I hesitated. It was probably a new will leaving me in the cold or some such bullshit.

"I'm keeping the other two-thirds of your trust and doling it out as was already planned," he explained. "But here's a wedding gift . . . if we can fight hard enough to keep it."

Confused, I unfolded the papers again, and a sliver of a smile escaped my lips.

"The house?" I asked, surprised.

He'd given me the deed to the house, but it wasn't in my name. Excitement and confusion rushed through my very clouded brain.

Did I want the house?

*Yes.*

Forever and ever and ever?

*Hell yes!*

I loved it here, and so did Fallon. If we could keep it in Caruthers hands, we would. But what did this mean for my father? I didn't necessarily want him gone.

Kind of.

No, not really.

"Patricia's trying to take the house. I'm sure you know." My father's eyes clouded in an expression I was more familiar with. "But I'll drag her through court for as long as I can. It may take a year, but I'll win. The house is in my name, but as my wife, she has rights to it until a court says she doesn't. I'll transfer the house to you officially when I take away that threat." He stood up straight, reaching out his hand to me. "But the house is yours for all intents and purposes. I know you and Fallon—and Addie—love it here, and I want you to have your home.

I took his hand, and the furious flow of blood through my veins relaxed. I wasn't sure if my father was really giving up, if he was just that tired of drama, or if he was bluffing.

But when I looked at him, I saw his relaxed eyes turn bleary, and before I knew it I was yanked in for a hug.

"Whoa," I grunted against the crush of his arms and almost laughed. I wasn't sure if this was a joke or if it was supposed to be funny, but rare and weird things are funny. To me.

But as I tried to catch my breath, I kind of realized that my dad wasn't letting go. His arms were as tight as steel around me, and I couldn't remember the last time he'd hugged me.

And I don't think it was ever this tight.

I found my arms slowly wrapping around him and returning the embrace.

"Katherine's right." He stepped back and squeezed my shoulders. "You can't stay away from her, can you?"

"If you could go back with Katherine and redo things—"

He nodded. "Then you and Jared would've been stepbrothers a long, long time ago," he finished, understanding.

"I won't live with those regrets. I'm doing this, Dad." I held my position. "We'll be fine."

Fearing the breakup of his marriages or contending with Katherine's alcoholism in the past were things my father had let get in his way. From him I learned that mistakes can be dealt with. Loss of time can't.

He slapped me on the back and let out a heavy breath. "So where's Fallon?"

## CHAPTER 30

# FALLON

Katherine had come into the kitchen shortly after me, and I wished I could shrink away.

Until she came up and hugged me.

I held my breath, completely confused.

*Yeah, hi.* I'm the girl that nearly threatened to expose your affair on TV, and I'm solely responsible for your boyfriend's divorce chaos right now. But sure, I'll take some hugs!

Once she let go, I sank into the barstool as she dug out all of the fixings for sundaes from the refrigerator.

There were lots of questions I wanted to ask her. She was, after all, having an affair with my mother's husband. I should despise her. Or at the very least dislike her. I definitely shouldn't respect a home-wrecker.

But for some reason—or many reasons—I felt like my mother was the sleazy one out of the group.

And one thing could not be denied about Katherine. A nearly eighteen-year affair was love.

She was very beautiful, too. And young. Still young enough to have more kids.

"I'm surprised you're so calm about this." I picked at my vanilla and caramel sundae.

She shrugged, still scooping a serving for Madoc. All chocolate. "I started young, too," she conceded. "But unlike me, you and Madoc have an excellent support system." Yeah, she was right. I still didn't know where my dad stood on this, and I planned on calling him first thing in the morning. But Madoc and I had means to live, and we had Addie at the very least. We were lucky.

"Aren't you afraid Jared will get inspired and propose to Tate?" I teased.

Her head fell back as she laughed softly. "No." She sounded sure.

"No?"

"I think you and Madoc have overcome . . . more mature issues, shall we say? I can understand how marriage feels like the natural next step. Jared and Tate on the other hand? They were in so much heartache for each other for so long that I think they just want to be left alone for a while. They need their calm."

Just then we heard Madoc's and his dad's voices coming down the hall, and Katherine and I turned to see them enter with smiles on their faces.

My stomach pinched with anticipation, but my shoulders relaxed a little. Seeing Jason head straight for me, I pushed my hair behind my ears, taking inventory of everything I was wearing. Jeans and one of my black fitted, long-sleeve T's, but I was still wearing my Burberry coat. My hair was still in loose curls from the "wedding," and it still looked good last time I checked, despite the twenty-four hours Madoc and I had spent in bed.

Jason's eyes were relaxed and welcoming, but he looked like he wasn't breathing. His expression was pleasant but guarded.

Tipping my chin up, he placed a quick, gentle kiss on my forehead and then took my hand, looking down at the ring.

"Looks good on you. Congratulations."

*Huh?*

That's it? That can't be it.

"Thank you," I mumbled, searching the floor for my jaw.

"If you both want some advice from a man who's about to have two divorces behind him . . ." Jason looked between Madoc and me. "Fight. Fight through everything. Don't leave the house angry or go to bed mad. Fight until it's settled. The end of fighting is the beginning of giving up."

And then he looked at me. "Don't let him off the hook. You understand?"

I swallowed and gave him a small nod.

"Mr. Caruthers?" I asked.

He raised his eyebrows at me. "Jason."

"Jason. I owe you an apology. This mess with the divorce—"

"Had to happen, Fallon," he finished, cutting me off. "It's fine. Well, it will be fine eventually," he offered.

With a nod to Katherine, they walked out the way they came in. "Katherine and I are going to her house for the night," he said. "We'll see you Friday night at the charity auction."

And they left.

Madoc plopped down on the stool at the bar. Pulling me in between his legs, he nuzzled my neck, sending shivers down my spine.

"Madoc?" I closed my eyes, leaning in to his spectacular kisses. "Baby, I am sorry, but I think I need to get back to school tomorrow."

He stopped. Like stopped so fast, I thought he was dead. Taking his head out from my neck, he flashed slightly pissed blue eyes at me.

"Why?" It sounded more like a dare than a question.

"Oh, I got an e-mail from a professor." I picked up my phone, gesturing with it. "He's fine with me missing a few classes, but I'm going to miss a guest lecturer tomorrow and a test on Friday. They're both really important."

I'd already missed three days of classes.

He finally heaved a sigh. "All right. I'll crash with Jared, so we don't have to be separated. You go to class, I'll work out getting transferred to Northwestern, and we'll start looking for apartments. We have to be in Chicago for that charity thing on Friday anyway. We'll leave early in the morning."

Hanging my arms over his shoulder, I joined my hands behind his neck. "Thank you."

Sinking into him and his man scent, I took his top lip between my lips, and he took my bottom lip between his. It's the kiss we always ended up in. All four lips, layered as one as we just stilled and breathed each other in.

Can I just say how much I loved to smell him? I loved that he wore cologne, and he always would. Or else.

"Come on, let's go shower," he whispered into my mouth.

I shook my head. "No, you go."

"No, I mean I want a shower with you."

I backed away, unbuttoning my coat. "I've got other plans. Go get your shower, and find me in ten minutes."

His forehead wrinkled. "Find you?"

I said nothing more. After about twenty seconds, he realized I was done talking and walked off upstairs grinning.

I smirked to myself. He thinks he's the only one capable of mischief.

Grabbing some printer paper from the fax machine in the kitchen, I scrawled a riddle to Madoc—knowing how he loooooooved riddles—and left it on the bottom of the bannister.

*Back in the days when we used to go to war,*
*I'd wait for the nights when you'd knock on my door.*
*Now you'll have to look for me in a room on this floor,*
*Where the vampires hunt and from your lips I was torn.*

Slipping off my coat, I dropped it in on the floor next to the stairs. Taking a few steps away, I started stripping off the rest of my clothes and dropping them at small intervals on the black-and-white tiled floor. My flats, my jeans, my shirt, and then I unclasped my bra and dropped it in on the plush, beige carpet leading into the hallway to the right.

Clad only in my red lace thong, I walked down the dimly lit hallway and entered the theater room, thankful that the chill on my body distracted from the drumming in my chest.

I hated this room.

And I loved this room.

Slowly turning the dial on the wall, I brightened the area only enough to cast a soft glow. As I looked around, I took account that nothing had changed. Not that I expected it to.

This room was used rarely, but it was built for a crowd. Several black leather recliners and two long black leather couches all sat facing a massive flat screen mounted to a wall that was adorned with three smaller screens on each side. Family photos and more sports paraphernalia dressed the coffee-colored walls, and with the cream-colored carpet, everything looked cozy and cavelike in here.

Madoc and I used to watch TV in here a lot, even though we rarely said anything nice to each other. And the only time Jason Caruthers came in here was for Super Bowl Sunday.

Walking up on soft feet, I ran my hand over the cool, smooth black leather of our couch. The one we watched the *Vampire Diaries* on. The one we ignored each other on, despite the thick cloud of tension between us. And the one we last slept on together before I was taken away.

My womb tightened, and a shock weaved down between my legs, making my jaw tingle with a smile.

This place should be intimidating to me. This was the place I'd been shocked awake by one screaming parent and another one so angry, he couldn't even speak. My mother had hauled me off the couch nearly naked, wearing only Madoc's shirt. Jason Caruthers had stood in the hallway, refusing to even make eye contact when I was dragged past him. Madoc was nowhere in sight, and within twenty minutes, I was dressed, packed, and driven away, unknowingly carrying a child inside of me.

This room should've been bad news to me, but it wasn't.

This couch had felt good on my skin, and I remember being so grateful Madoc had talked me out of finally leaving my room that night.

Climbing onto the sofa, I knelt up against the back and rested my forearms over the top. I wanted to see Madoc when he found me. When the door handle started to turn, I had to swallow down my smile and curl my toes to keep my excitement at bay.

As Madoc opened the door, his eyes shot straight to me, and I gave him a sexy, little smirk, hopefully coming off as playful and not the nympho I'd become. He wore black pajama pants that hung low, and his golden skin looked so warm and smooth that my mouth was watering. The little hills of his six-pack flexed, and I trailed my eyes up to his pecs and further, loving the way his kind-of wet hair stuck up like it'd been styled that way. When I got to his face, though, his ever present amusement was gone.

He swallowed and held up the riddle I'd left. "The theater room."

Why wasn't he looking at me? His eyes were shifting around.

"I'm . . . a . . ." I stammered. My heart was starting to pump too fast. *Shit!* Was he mad?

"I'm glad you figured it out," I said, cocking my head to the side, trying to entice him to come in.

"Yeah, well . . . the last line helped." He let out a heavy sigh. "Look, Fallon. I don't want to be in here. Can we just go to bed?"

*What? Why?*

"Madoc." I rushed to stop him. "I know that this is the last place we saw each other before I left, but we don't have to be afraid of it."

I got off the couch and stood up next to the arm, my hands folded in front of me. His steamy blue eyes fell down my body and then trailed timidly back up to my face.

He walked over to me, every hard step vibrating through my veins. Taking me by the back of my neck, he kissed me deep, slipping his tongue in immediately and making every part of me warm.

"Madoc," I gasped when he pulled me up off the ground. As he cupped my ass, I wrapped my legs around his waist.

I loved that he picked me up.

But I didn't like that he started walking us to the door.

"We leave in six hours," he threatened, "and that may or may not be enough time to taste every part of your body. But I want to get started right now. We're going to bed."

"Madoc, no!" I shot out my arms and caught the door frame, stopping him in his tracks. "No! I want to be in here."

He pushed a little, and I tightened my grasp on the door frame against the stretch in my arms. If he wanted to get me out of here, he only had to push a bit more. He was going easy on me.

"Well, I don't," he shot back. "Come on. We're not kids anymore. We're going to do it in a bed like grown-ups and not on a couch like horny teens."

"We are horny teens."

He scowled up at me. "Let go, or I tickle."

My chest tensed, and I almost closed my arms with the threat, but I didn't.

Squirming out of his grasp, I lowered myself to the ground and slammed my hands into his chest, pushing him backward. Reaching over, I grabbed the door and threw it shut.

Madoc's wide eyes locked on mine as I walked the few short steps over to him, backed him up against the back of the sofa, and started to maul him. My hand dug into his hair, my lips kissed him hard and fast on his mouth and then his neck, and my other hand shot down to his thick erection already pulsing in my hand.

"Fallon, Jesus," Madoc cursed.

But his head fell back as the pleasure overtook him, and he threaded his fingers into my hair as I trailed kisses down his chest and stomach.

Setting down on my knees, I freed him from his pants and, taking him in my hand, I circled my tongue around his tip, my tongue ring bumping with his piercing. He jerked, and his eyes popped open, looking down on me with fierce eyes and bared teeth.

"Fallon," he warned.

"I want to. Please?" I asked softly.

He squeezed his eyes shut and the grip in my hair loosened.

Coming down on him again, I drew him in long and slow, savoring the smell of body wash that made me so hungry. I swayed my tongue from side to side on the underside of him, so he could feel the ball on my tongue. His cock twitched in my mouth, and I got more eager with the taste of him and his silver. Bringing him in slow, I relaxed my throat, taking in all of him down to the base.

"Babe," he whispered, sucking in air through his teeth. "You better not have learned this on another guy."

I drew him out and sucked hard and fast on the tip about ten times before answering. "Tate and I got a book for research last month."

"Really." It wasn't a question. "That's hot."

If I knew Madoc, he was probably imagining Tate and me practicing on cucumbers.

She had wanted to do this for Jared, but neither of us had had any experience. Obviously, she wanted to blow his mind, so I suggested watching some porn. She gave me a huge "no," saying she wasn't watching seedy videos on the Internet. So we went online and bought a book.

I sucked him all of the way into my mouth again, slowly down to the base, and swirled my tongue around him.

Reaching behind him, I pulled his pants down just below his ass and held his hips for support as I moved faster up and down his length. My roots stung from where he was fisting my hair. He was fully hard—I hope, because I couldn't take anymore—as I savored the feel of every inch of his skin.

He groaned and inhaled sharp, fast breaths, and I loved the sight of Madoc worked up. With his face pinched and eyes shut, looking like he was in pain, I had a sudden urge to crawl up his body.

My head was pulled away, and Madoc looked violent.

"Stop," he gasped. "I want you. But not on this couch."

Licking my lips, I pinched my eyebrows together in confusion but didn't push it.

Who the hell cared right now? The couch, the chair, the floor . . .

Grabbing my hand, he pulled me over to one of the other leather couches, swung me around, and brought me down on top, straddling him in his sitting position. His erection rubbed between my legs, and then . . .

Whoa!

He slid both hands into the string of thong at my hip and ripped them clean off.

My panties were gone, and my core pulsed so damn hard that I had to bite my lip to keep from crying out.

I was uncontrollable. I dove into him, sliding my tongue across his lips and lifting up as he rubbed his tip into my entrance.

"Oh, Madoc," I panted.

Damn, that felt good.

I held his face in my hands and looked into his eyes, unable to stop grinding on him. "Why did you leave me in here alone that night?" I ventured. I assumed that's why he was uncomfortable with the other couch. Maybe that was why he hated this room.

"I didn't mean to." His eyes were apologetic. "I covered you up," he breathed out, shutting his eyes with the pleasure of my movement on him, "and went to get a shower. I'd planned on coming back down to wake you up, but by the time I got back, you were gone."

All this time I thought he'd had his fun and just went up to bed, leaving me.

"I hate this fucking room," he finished. His mouth closed but then opened again, looking like he wanted to tell me more but didn't.

I grabbed the remote and turned on the stereo. Lorde's "Team" came on, and I clutched the leather sofa behind him with both of my hands and lowered myself onto him slow enough to drive him crazy. "I'm going to make you love it again," I promised.

He filled me up, and I dropped my head back at the feel of him inside of me.

He let out a low growl and hooded his eyes. "I'd like to see you try."

# CHAPTER 31

# MADOC

"*There you are,*" *a voice says behind me, and I tense.*

*Turning around, I see my stepmother, Patricia, and I don't hide the frown at seeing her in her short white silk nightie.*

*Clutching the bottle of water, I slam the refrigerator door shut and try to keep my eyes averted. My head feels staticky from the liquor at the bonfire, but it doesn't dull the awkwardness of this situation.*

*Her long blond hair hangs loose, but it looks freshly styled as does her makeup, and her posture isn't modest. One hand on the kitchen island, another hand on her hip, she sways playfully and smiles.*

*"Where's my dad?" I snip.*

*"Asleep," she sighs. "In his room. Did you have a good night?"*

*Why was she being so nice lately?*

*"Yeah, up until now," I answer flatly.*

*I'd just gotten back from a race and a hell of a win against Liam. And I got to see Tatum Brandt race for Jared. Along with the bonfire afterward, it had been an entertaining night.*

*But I am tired and not in the mood for whatever poison Patricia wants to spew.*

*I walk around the island, heading out, when she steps in front of me.*

*"Madoc." She puts her hand on my chest, and I inch back. "You've gotten big with the working out. You look good." She nods her approval and gives me innocent eyes. "Did you know that your dad's having an affair?"*

*Jesus. What the hell?*

*She definitely isn't hiding much in that nightie, either. I can see inches of her cleavage and the tan, smooth-looking skin of her arms, legs, and shoulders. Patricia works out a lot and takes care of herself very well with my father's money. At forty, she looks much younger.*

*A ten-ton brick crashes in to my stomach when her lips inch in for my neck.*

*What. The. Fuck?*

*I push her hand away. "Are you for real?" I'm almost breathless with shock.*

*Walking past her, I stomp down the hallway and dive in to the theater room. The only place I want to be anymore. Slamming the door, I walk over and plop down on the couch—the one Fallon and I were last together on—and drop my head back, closing my eyes.*

*My heart is thundering in my chest, and my whole body is hot with anger. I can't believe it. My stepmother just came on to me.*

*With my head swimming, I pinch the bridge of my nose, trying to get my head straight from my alcohol-induced blur. The cool leather at the back of my neck calms my breathing.*

*I don't understand why, after all this time, I still end up sleeping in this room most nights.*

*Fallon left. She never really liked me, so why did I want to be reminded of her betrayal?*

*But still . . . this is the place where we spent the most time together, some-times in silence and one time not-so-silent.*

"*Look at me,*" *Patricia says, and I snap my eyes open.*

"*Get out!*" *I shout, my lips tight in seeing her standing in front of me. Why didn't I lock the fucking door?*

*I stand up and get in her face.* "*This is my room. Get out.*"

*Her eyes flash with excitement.* "*You're in a mood. I can see why Fallon feared you.*"

*I shake my head.* "*Fallon didn't fear me. I don't know what she told you, but—*"

"*She couldn't handle you, Madoc.*" *She looks up at me, drawing her bottom lip between her teeth.* "*She's in your past. You need to move on. She certainly has.*"

"*What do you mean?*"

"*She's dating someone at her boarding school,*" *Patricia says, and my heart rings in my ears.*

*I barely register Patricia's hands on my chest, rubbing me through my T-shirt.*

"*She doesn't even talk about you or ask about you, Madoc. I ask her to come home for visits. She won't. She doesn't deserve the man you've become.*" *My eyes close, thinking about all of the time I spend in here, all of the nights thinking about her, and I know it's a waste of time. I fucking know it. Sure, I dated, too. I hooked up—not as much as I bragged to Jared—but there had been girls. My heart never belonged to any of them, though.*

*Patricia's whisper wafts across my neck.* "*I know what you crave. What will please you. And I can keep secrets.*"

*She closes the distance, wrapping her arms around my neck, and smashes her lips to mine.*

*She moans, and all of a sudden I can't breathe.*

*No . . .*

*No.*

*No!*

*Grabbing her by the shoulders, I shove her away from me.*

*"Jesus Christ!" I yell. "What the fuck?"*

*Her skin is flushed, and she arches an eyebrow. "No?" she laughs. "I don't think you mean that, Madoc."*

*I want to hit her. I actually want to slam her into a wall and erase her from the planet. Most of all, I want her out of here.*

*"Out," I order.*

*Smirking, she walks to the couch and lays down on it. "Make me," she challenges. "But you'll have to touch me to do it."*

*I stare down at her, lying in the same place I'd last seen Fallon. Her hand rests above her head, and she looks hideous. Like something I never want to remember.*

*I straighten my expression and speak low. "Leave tomorrow, or I'll tell my dad about this."*

*I should tell him anyway.*

*But maybe I don't feel like protecting my father right now. Maybe I want him to suffer in this marriage. Maybe I hate him for bringing both of these bitches into our house.*

*Or maybe if I lose Patricia, I fear losing Fallon for good.*

*I don't know.*

*I walk out, leaving her on the couch and get out my phone.*

**Are you up?** *I text, but I'm already heading for my car without waiting for a reply.*

*My phone buzzes.* **I'm in bed. You have to come to me.**

*I shake my head, knowing that's not a problem. I need to blow off some steam. Jess Cullen, the cross-country captain, and I have a friends with benefits thing going, and I love her to pieces. Not love her, love her, but I respect her, and she's a good girl.*

*I punch in a reply.* **Be there in ten.**

**See you soon.** I left and never entered the theater room again. Not until tonight. Many times I even entertained the idea of hosting a bonfire for that fucking couch that'd now been ruined by that woman's sleaze. But after that night, she took a lengthy vacation, and I didn't see her until yesterday morning when she threatened to take Fallon away from me.

When I'd seen Fallon's note tonight, instead of getting excited like I'm sure she wanted me to, I'd groaned. I didn't want to be in there, and I for damn sure didn't want her in there.

Who knew how she'd react if I told her the truth? It certainly wasn't important, but I didn't want to risk something else fucking with our happiness again.

Carrying her up to bed that night, I leaned in and kissed her hair. Fallon, like me, had seen her parents living exactly how she didn't want. Lucky for us, our vicarious experience felt like we'd already made our parents' mistakes. We knew what we wanted now.

Even though I knew she was strong, it didn't stop me from wanting to protect her and give her everything.

No one and nothing would stop us.

During the next couple of days, Fallon and I started getting things sorted out in Chicago. She went to class, while I handled the paperwork of withdrawing from one school and transferring to another. At night, if she wasn't doing homework, we got online to look for apartments.

Fallon had been trying to contact her father to tell him about our marriage, but when she contacted one of his men, he'd said that Ciaran was "unreachable" at the moment.

Which meant he was being detained for questioning, probably. No one was "unreachable" in the twenty-first century, unless their cell phone had been confiscated.

"Daniel," she spoke to one of her father's men on the phone, "if I don't hear from my father by tomorrow, I'm going to the police myself. I, at least, need to know he's not dead."

It was Thursday night, and she was sitting on the couch in Jared's apartment, while Tate and I had just gotten back from a run. Fallon normally joined us, but she'd opted to stay in and make her calls.

Jared was still at ROTC training, and he'd been gracious enough to let Fallon and me have the extra space in the loft of his apartment this week.

"Shower?" I asked Fallon as I tore off my sweaty T-shirt.

She held up a finger for me to wait, still talking on the phone.

Tate was still breathing hard as she walked into the living room and grabbed her phone.

"Jared's mom called," she said more to herself.

After pushing some buttons, she held the phone to her ear, calling Katherine back, I would assume.

I walked into the kitchen, grabbing a Gatorade out of the fridge as they had their conversations. Jared walked in, slamming the door and just as sweaty as Tate and me.

"Toss me one of those," he said, gesturing to the Gatorade in my hand and using the bottom of his T-shirt to wipe the sweat off his face.

Throwing him mine, I snatched another one out of the refrigerator, and we were silent for a few minutes, drinking and catching our breaths.

"This shit's for the birds," he grumbled, yanking his shirt by the back of his neck and pulling it over his head.

*Yeah*, my throat itched with laughter.

Jared in the Army—or whatever branch he was choosing—was still weird to me.

Jared as part of a team. Jared following orders. Jared pressed and dressed in a uniform. Jared as a leader? For the good of mankind? I still shook my head at the idea.

"So get out," I told him. "There's lots of stuff you could do with your life. Stuff you'd be good at."

He looked at me like I had three eyes. "I'm not talking about ROTC. I'm talking about Tate. Look at her."

I tipped my head around him, watching her on the phone. It was October, and she was running in short shorts and a tank top. Probably to tease him.

I smiled. I liked Tate a lot. There was even a time when I wanted her. But she was like a sister now.

The kind of sister I wouldn't screw, I mean.

"What about her?" I shrugged.

He scowled. "She's driving me nuts, that's what. She wears stuff like that to turn me on, and it's working. I'm actually Googling 'ballroom dancing' to find out if it's really that bad." He looked at me, wincing. "I'm caving."

I threw my head back, laughing. "You look like you're about to cry," I choked out.

"Well, would you do it?" It sounded like an accusation.

I rolled my eyes. "How long have you known me, dude? There's not a lot I wouldn't do."

He blinked long and hard, knowing that that was true and then turned his head to watch Tate, probably daydreaming about all the things he was missing out on.

Fallon hung up and walked over, smiling as I put my arm around her.

"Everything okay?" I asked.

She nodded. "For now." And then she scrunched up her nose. "You need a shower."

I shot a look to Jared. "Can we have the bathroom first?"

His fist tightened around the Gatorade, and I felt sorry for him. He probably wanted to do the same with Tate, and he was hurting.

"All right," Tate called. "We need to pull together for this, so listen up."

All heads turned to her as she walked up to the bar in the kitchen.

She arched an eyebrow in Jared's direction but withheld eye contact, and I had to fold my lips between my teeth to stifle a laugh.

"Your dad." She looked at me. "And your mom." She finally looked at Jared. "Are going to your family's charity function tomorrow." She then looked between Fallon and me, talking about our parents' Triumph Charity for Disabled Children.

I absorbed what she said, surprised but not uncomfortable by the news.

My dad and Katherine were appearing as a couple at his and his wife's charity function.

That would be awkward for some people. Not me, though.

"So," she continued. "Katherine has invited us to attend, but I think it's more for moral support."

"Did she tell you that?" Jared asked, looking concerned.

"No, but I just got the impression. It's her first public appearance with your dad"—Tate looked to me—"and his wife and her friends will be there." Her eyes snapped to Fallon, an apology in them. "I'm sure there will be talk. We have a family table, so all of us will be seated together for dinner."

I jerked my chin at Tate. "Is Jax going?"

"She said he'd be there."

"Okay, then." I cleared my throat. "Let's do it."

"Fallon?" Tate picked up her bag off the barstool. "Meet you after your noon class tomorrow, and we'll go shopping?"

"Sounds good."

Tate looked up to me, ordering, "And you two get tuxes." She referred to Jared as well but didn't look at him.

She swung the strap of her bag over her head to rest at her hip and grabbed her jacket, walking to the door.

"Where are you going?" Jared snapped.

"Back to the dorm," she barked, rounding the wall leading to the door. Fallon and I couldn't see her, but Jared shot her a death glare.

"Unless you've changed your mind about dancing," she singsonged, taunting him.

He scowled but then his eyes widened, and he shot out of the chair. "Did you just flash me?"

We heard the door open and slam shut, and he left, chasing after her.

## CHAPTER 32

# FALLON

On the drive I held my hands in my lap, clenching my fists so hard that my nails were digging into my palm. My body was strung tight, and I could feel my pulse throbbing in my neck.

*Son of a bitch.* I did not want to see that woman tonight.

Or any night.

"What are you doing?" Madoc asked as he drove up to the valet at the Lennox House, the usual venue for the annual Triumph Charity Event.

Hitting Send, I stuffed my phone back into my bag. "Texting my dad to let him know where I'm at in case he's able to get in touch."

"You're worried about him."

I shook my head. "I'm worried about you." I smirked at Madoc, trying to hide my concern. "My dad still might kill you."

I caught the little smile on his lips before he climbed out of the car. Coming around to my side, he opened my door and then tossed his keys to the attendant.

"He's not going to kill me." He kissed me on the forehead and then turned to nod at Jared helping Tate out of his car behind us.

"You're so sure."

He snorted. "Of course. Everyone loves me."

*Yes. Yes, we do.*

Placing my hand on the inside of his elbow, we walked into the large ballroom, followed by Jared and Tate. Both Madoc and Jared wore black wool suits with crisp white shirts and black silk ties. Madoc had a deep purple handkerchief, and Jared had nothing. Their shoes shined, their hair was adorably messy, and they were hard not to look at.

Judging from the ladies turning heads when we walked in, I'm guessing they weren't ogling Tate and me.

Well, maybe. We looked pretty good, too. We'd both decided to stick with black, opting for cute little cocktail dresses.

She wore a sleeveless black dress with a sheer overlay that fell to mid-thigh and flared out just a little from the waist down. It shined with horizontal, black, silk striping and showed off her great legs and arms. Her sunshine hair was curled and then pulled over into a side ponytail at the bottom of her neck.

I'd also opted for a sleeveless dress but with more of a draping effect. The boatneck strap circled my neck and drew together down low in the back. It was bunched up at the left side of my waist and was held with a gold jewelry piece. My hair was styled with big curls, but I had thrown it over my shoulder, so I could feel Madoc's hand on my back.

And while Tate and I wore strappy black heels, we still fell inches below our men.

I inhaled the fragrance of flowers in the air. My mother loved events like this, even if she was only in it for the prestige.

"Wow, this is going to be fun." I heard Jared's sarcastic sigh behind me. "Where's my mom at? And my brother?"

No one said anything as we surveyed the enormous ballroom, looking for Jason, Katherine, and Jax.

The room was crowded already. Filled with the happy sounds of chatter, laughter, and music, the room was dressed in white draperies, white lights, and white flowers everywhere. The shiny windows around the room let the moonlight spill in, adding to the soft glow in the room. Not overly bright, but not too dark.

The stage, also decorated in white, featured a podium and a band playing some peppy covers. The dance floor was already fairly busy with three to four dozen couples dressed in their finest and smiling among their glittering jewels. Around the dance floor sat dozens of round tables adorned with white linens, candles, and the finest crystal.

"All right," Tate started. "We'll circulate—"

"Welcome!" A voice I knew too well confronted us, and my back stiffened.

Turning around, I arched an eyebrow at my mother who approached us with a glass of champagne in one hand and a very young escort in the other.

Someone that young and handsome—who looked like he followed orders—had to be an escort.

She wore a floor-length black evening gown with a black lace overlay and cap sleeves. Her blond hair was in a chic, tight updo, and her makeup was stunning. She looked about eight years younger than she was.

Coming around in front of us, she looked at us with mock concern. "It's funny. I don't remember sending any of you an invitation. But . . ." She peered behind me, probably ogling Jared, but I was too disgusted to find out. "You are all most welcome."

"You don't invite us to my family's functions, Patricia," Madoc spoke low and threatening. "And Fallon has more of a right to be here than you do. You're on your way out of the family, remember?"

"Oh, that's right." She tipped her chin at us, smiling. "I forgot about your marriage. Congratulations." Her eyes dropped to my hand, and her jeering expression made me want to punch her.

"I see you got the family ring," she observed, taking another sip of her champagne. "It'll be a comfort to you when you're alone at night, and he's off screwing someone else. He probably already is. Didn't take his father long after our marriage."

Madoc stepped forward, but I yanked him back. "No," I warned. "She's grasping at straws. Let her spew her words." And then I looked at my mom. "They're all she has, after all."

Her face tightened, and her eyebrow shot up. "You'll see. It may be one year or five, but you will see."

She spun around with her fancily dressed and enormously quiet boy toy and walked off.

"Wow." Tate laughed the kind of laugh where the only other option is to cry. I understood the feeling.

"Are you okay?" she asked next to me.

"I'm fine." I nodded and let go of Madoc's arm. I couldn't hold on to him like a security blanket all night. "I should've hit her."

"I would've," Tate deadpanned.

Jared and Madoc snorted at the same time, and Tate looked down, smiling to herself. I got the impression that there was a joke I wasn't getting.

She smirked at me, seeing my confusion. "Violence never solves anything, but"—she paused—"it can get people's attention. Sometimes— and I stress *sometimes*—violence is the only thing some people respect. Take Madoc for example. I broke his nose and kicked him in the balls. He finally understood me."

*Wait, what?*

"Excuse me." I looked between Madoc and Tate. Jared rolled his eyes when I looked to him for explanation.

"You didn't tell her about us, Mr. Can't-Keep-His-Hands-to-Himself?" Her expectant eyes on Madoc made him blush.

"Yeah, thanks, Tate." He looked away like he had a bad taste in his mouth. "I'll have to explain that now."

I swallowed, not sure I liked the sound of where this was going.

But Jared seemed to read my mind.

"No worries, Fallon," he comforted. "Madoc was only trying to get Tate and me together. He just thinks the end justifies the means is all."

*Yep, lawyer material*, I laughed to myself.

We finally found Katherine and Madoc's dad, and we spent the next hour either hanging close or on the dance floor. Katherine looked stunning in a deep red evening gown, much in the same style as mine, except hers fell to the floor. Her espresso brown hair hung down and looked beautiful next to the rich color of the dress. While we were certain she needed moral support—what with these people knowing she was Jason's mistress—it apparently was just fear on her part. Everything seemed fine, actually.

I realized that even though my mother's friends were the wives of Jason's colleagues, and they may be on my mother's side, they also knew what side their bread was buttered on. Their husbands followed Jason, and they followed their husbands.

"Did you text Jax?" Jared asked Madoc as we lingered around the bar. "He's not answering me."

Madoc took out his phone, looking through his messages. "Yeah, I texted twice. I've got nothing."

Jared shook his head, starting to look worried.

Madoc pulled me into his side. "I'm going to the men's room. Want to come?" he asked, waggling his eyebrows at me.

"Mmmmm." I put my finger to my chin, thinking. "Madoc Caruthers Caught Bending Stepsister over Bathroom Counter. Jason Caruthers Shamed in Front of All of Chicago," I read the mock headline, smiling.

He slapped me on the butt and walked away backward, mouthing, "You're so hot."

He turned around and disappeared down the hallway, while Jared took Tate out onto the dance floor. I smiled after them, thankful Madoc wasn't so inhibited about dancing. They kind of just did the hold-each-other-and-sway-from-side-to-side thing, but it was cute that he was trying.

I stood around the bar waiting for Madoc, but after about five minutes he still wasn't back. I tensed the muscles in my thighs, trying to ignore the proposal he'd made for me to join him.

Taking out my phone, I noticed that Jax still hadn't texted me back, either. It was strange for him to be out of touch. *Where was he?*

I made my way through the small groups of people and stepped softly, afraid of tripping in my heels. When I made it into the much quieter hallway, I dialed his number and held the phone to my ear.

"How badly do you want it?" I heard my mother's taunting voice coming from the men's room, and I looked over to the swinging door. She spoke in the soft, sultry kind of voice that only means one thing.

I walked over and opened it just enough to peer inside. She and Madoc were standing there, and I winced at the sight of her leaned against the wall with her dress pulled up high on her thighs. He just stood there. Watching her.

*Why the fuck was he watching her?*

He rubbed his hand over his forehead. "You really are something else, aren't you?"

"I have a room at the Four Seasons, Madoc. Think about how

good it would feel. One night with me, and you'll get what you want. I'll let go of the house. You wanted me that night, didn't you?"

*That night?* What happened between them? I could barely make out what they were saying, the thunder in my ears so loud that my eyes were watering.

"Yeah," he shot back, washing his hands. "I wanted you so much that I ran and screwed someone else right after I left you in the theater room."

*Oh, my God.* I clenched my fists, drawing breaths in and out faster and faster. My face in its anger couldn't get any more tightened. My feet were anchored to the fucking floor.

What the hell? I slammed my fist into the door, sending it swinging so hard that it hit the wall behind it. Both of them spun around to face me where I stayed rooted to the doorway.

"Fallon!" My mother made a big show of fixing herself. Putting her hand to her chest, she looked at me with sympathetic eyes.

"Fallon." Madoc held up his hand and shook his head as if he was trying to stop my thoughts in their tracks. "Baby, it's nothing, okay. Look at me."

"I told you, honey," my mother started. "Madoc doesn't care about you. He and I—"

"There is no you and me!" he bellowed, turning his head and killing her with his eyes.

"Tell her, then." She pushed off the wall, face even and voice calm. "Tell her about the theater room, you kissing me . . ."

"Shut up!" Madoc walked over to me, looking like he was in pain. "Fallon, look into my eyes."

*What?* I dropped my eyes to the ground, trying to make sense of this.

"Ask him." My mother's voice drifted from somewhere behind us. "I told you he can't be trusted, Fallon."

I closed my eyes, starting to feel my feet melt into the floor.

"Fallon, nothing ever happened!" someone said. "I never touched her. She kissed me . . ."

*I hated turning corners. Closed doors.*

I could still hear them talking, but I had no idea what they were saying. My feet were gone. My legs up to my knees had faded away, and I couldn't feel anything when I tried to tense my muscles.

*Your life doesn't interest me, Fallon.*

*You know what I used to call you? Pussy-on-the-Premises.*

I sucked in quick breaths, but they left me slowly as if my body might not have the strength to take in air again. In quick. Out slow. In quick. Out slow.

How could he do this? How could she?

*You're just a slut like your mother.* Madoc's words hadn't cut before, because I knew they weren't true. Why did I feel pain from them now?

*Did you really think he loved you? He used you!*

I squeezed my eyes closed even tighter and swallowed. *Swallow it down. Swallow it down.*

I heard my name. Madoc. He was saying my name.

"Fallon! Look at me!"

*Open your eyes! What do you see?*

My eyes snapped open, and I saw Madoc standing in front of me. His eyes were watery, and he was squeezing my shoulders.

*Who are you?* My father's smooth, Irish voice washed over me. *Who are you?*

I tightened my fists again and again, blinking as Madoc kissed my forehead.

*I don't try to kill your demons. I run with them.*

*That's what makes Madoc a good kid, Fallon. He picks up the pieces.*

I felt his hands on my face, his thumbs stroking circles on my cheeks.

*He picks up the pieces.*

*Make that threat again. I will put you through a wall to get to her.*

*Finish up, Father. She needs to be kissed.*

Madoc.

My heart swelled. He was mine. He was always mine.

*Madoc. My Madoc.*

I looked into his eyes, seeing the love, the worry, the fear . . .

And I held him in my gaze, filling my lungs with air.

*"Nothing that happens on the surface of the sea can alter the calm of its depths."*

"Fallon, please," Madoc begged. "Listen to me."

"No," I finally uttered, dropping my hands and tilting my chin up. "Stop talking," I said firmly.

I walked around him and slowly—very slowly—approached my mother with my hands folded in front of me.

I kept my expression flat and my tone low as I dove into her space, sucking the oxygen up around her. "Lawyer up," I threatened. "Madoc and I want the house, and it is very lonely in your corner, Mother." Leaning into her face, I barely unclenched my teeth. "Stand against me. And. You. Will. Lose."

I spun around before she even had time to react and sauntered out of the bathroom, grabbing Madoc's hand on the way.

"Fallon, let me explain. Nothing ever happened. She came onto me, and I—"

I halted in the hallway and turned to face him. "I don't even want to hear it. I don't need any reassurances where you're concerned."

Taking his face in my hands, I took his lips that captivated my entire body the moment they touched. Madoc had me body and soul, and no one could stop us. Least of all my beast of a mother.

I certainly didn't give her the reaming she deserved, but it wouldn't have done anyone any good. I would've wasted my breath.

The only things that woman respected were money and power, and I just threatened her with both.

Any more of my attention, and it would be at my cost.

Never. Again. Madoc and I have a life to live.

"I love you," I whispered into his lips.

He let his forehead fall to mine as he sighed, "Thank God. You had me scared."

I heard someone clear his throat, and I twisted my head, only to have my heart jump into my throat.

"Dad!" I gasped and pulled free of Madoc to nearly knock my father over with a hug.

"Hey, little girl," he said, grunting from the impact.

"Are you okay?" I asked, pulling back to get a good look at him.

His light brown hair was slicked back, and his face—usually clean shaven—was scruffy as hell with his usual patches of gray showing. He was wearing a black Armani suit, favoring the necktie like Jared and Madoc instead of the bowties everyone else wore.

"Fine." He nodded, rubbing my arms. "Sorry that I worried you."

I wanted to ask him questions, but I knew this wasn't the time or place, and he generally didn't tell me much, anyway. He trusted me, but I think he thought it was better that his daughter not know about his seedy business, as if I didn't pick up things on my own anyway.

"Sir, I'm Madoc." My husband reached his hand out. "In case you don't remember."

They had only met once, that I know of. But my father would definitely remember him. Especially after everything that had happened.

He hesitated only a moment and then took Madoc's hand. "I remember. And I know everything." His look was a warning. "This is the wrong place to talk about this, and there are things I want to say to both of you, but for now, I'll just say this." He narrowed his eyes on Madoc. "You are aware of the burden of this marriage, right?"

Madoc grinned down at me. "Fallon's not a burden, sir."

"I'm not talking about Fallon," my dad shot out. "I'm talking about me. You do not want me as a pissed-off father-in-law. It would be safer for you if my child stays happy. Got it?"

*Wow. Awkward.*

"She'll be happy," Madoc asserted, looking my father in the eye.

I smiled at both of them. "I'm already happy."

I could tell it was hard for my father. He'd barely had me growing up, always contending with my mother and his risky business. Neither let him be the dad he wanted to be, but those were his choices, and I wasn't going to feel sorry for him. I loved him. But I chose Madoc. And I would choose Madoc forever.

"Congratulations." My father kissed me on the cheek. "But please tell me you were married by a priest."

Madoc snorted, and I told my father all about it as we walked to the table.

By the time we got there, we saw that everyone else was seated. Jared and Tate together, an empty seat for Jax next to Jared, then Katherine and Jason, followed by three empty seats for Madoc, my mother and me.

But there's no way in hell she was sitting at this table, so I sat my father down, and Madoc and I took the two remaining seats.

I made introductions for my father to Tate, Jared, and Katherine. But Jason didn't wait for me when it was his turn.

"Ciaran." He nodded, placing a napkin in his lap.

"Jason," my father responded.

And that was about as much as they talked. Jason defended guys like my father, but he didn't necessarily want to be seen hobnobbing with them, either.

And he definitely feared for his son being attached to the Pierces.

I was loyal to my father, but I understood where Jason was coming from.

Waiters started coming out with trays of the first course, and everyone started relaxing more. Katherine and Jared were talking, probably still wondering where the hell Jax was, and Tate relayed to my father and me the story of how Madoc asked her to Homecoming senior year. With totally unromantic motives, I was assured.

If not, I may have had to stop their runs together.

The band hummed with a soft jazz tune, and since the appetizers were circulated while everyone socialized and danced, the seven-course meal started off by moving right into the soup. An excellent creamy white asparagus soup was served, and although it was good, I still couldn't believe people paid ten thousand a plate to get in here tonight. Well, not per plate exactly. Per meal. But that's high society charity, I guess.

"I hope everyone's enjoying the evening."

My mother came up behind us, and I warmed at the feel of Madoc's hand at my back.

"Ciaran, Katherine," she greeted. "Certainly not the crowd I anticipated this evening. You've got some nerve."

I couldn't see my mother. And I wasn't going to look at her, either.

But I saw Katherine's eyes widen and then drop. "That's enough," Jason intervened. "I notified you that I'd be bringing Katherine."

"Your whore is sitting in my seat."

Jared shot out of his chair, nearly knocking it over as it rocked on its legs. "If you don't stand up and control that bitch," he warned Madoc's dad, "then I'm taking my mother out of here."

Jason stood, trying to squelch the situation. "No one's leaving. Patricia. You're making a scene. Stop."

"Stop? But I'm already out." She crossed her arms, her small bag dangling from her wrist. "Why would I care about making a scene? In fact, I'm just getting started. I may lose this battle in court, but your slut will sink down into the mud in front of everyone. I haven't even started."

Just then, two cell phone ringers sounded, and everyone pulled their attention off Jason and Patricia.

Unsure whose phones were going off, everyone reached for theirs.

But then a few more ringers went off until we were all getting messages.

I heard Tate groan, "This can't be good," and I wondered what was going on.

Jason arched a brow at my mom before he paused their argument to check his phone as well.

"Oh, boy," Madoc let out, looking at his phone. "Is that Jax?"

He looked confused, so I hurriedly opened up my messages, and my goddamn eyes just about popped out of my head.

My father leaned over to see, and I tucked the phone to my chest in horror. Looking around the table, I saw everyone frozen, each with a different emotion plastered on their faces as they watched the video.

Jared. Angry.

Tate. Disgusted.

Katherine. Hurt.

Jason. Dismayed.

Patricia. Dread.

Madoc. Disturbed.

"Fallon," he breathed. "Is that Jax with your mom?"

I slowly brought my phone away from my chest and looked at it again. It was unmistakable. Jax sitting on a bed. His ponytail hanging down his back. My mother on top of him. The camera cut and got to the part with her climbing off of him and walking into the bathroom. He threw a white sheet around his waist and walked up to the camera.

Not a single person breathed at the table.

"Hi." He smiled at us. "I'm Jaxon Trent. And I'm seventeen."

And then he was gone. The video went black, and every heartbeat at the table was probably rushing as quickly as mine.

All eyes started shifting to my mom who stood there, still staring at the phone she held up with a shaking hand.

"Hi, everyone."

We all jumped. Jax walked up to the table and pulled out his chair.

He was dressed just like Jared, minus the tie. His hair was braided in three rows above each ear and brought back to his usual ponytail at the back of his head.

"What is this?" my mother whimpered. She looked about ready to cry or die.

"Sit down," he ordered, gripping the back of the chair. "Now."

Her eyes widened, and I could hear her heavy breathing. Was she thinking of running?

Jax held up his phone. "This video is ready to go out to everyone in this room. Sit. Down." His growl was deep, and like I'd never heard from him before.

My mother walked as if in a daze to the chair and sat very softly, not looking down but not looking at anyone, either.

"Jason. The papers?" Jax held out his hand.

Jason had one hand on the back of Katherine's chair. "That was you that texted me?"

"I told you to trust me," he said with a cocky tone.

Jason reached into the inside pocket of his jacket and withdrew what looked like legal papers.

"Sit down, everyone," Jax commanded. "You're drawing attention."

Only Madoc's dad and Jared were standing, but they didn't take their eyes off of him as they lowered themselves into their chairs.

I didn't know why any of us weren't saying anything. No one asked questions. No one voiced concerns. We just all shut up, watching Jax take control of the table.

"Jaxon?" Katherine piped up, panic wafting off of her like perfume. "How could you have done this?"

He looked at her with innocence. "I'm the victim here."

And then the corner of his mouth turned up, and he set the papers down in front of my mother with a pen that he retrieved from his jacket.

"Here's your revised divorce agreement," he said, leaning over my mother's shoulder. "A nice amount of cash, no house, and no alimony. Sign," he ordered.

"If you think—"

"Oh, no," he interrupted her. "Don't issue empty threats now. That's my mom for all intents and purposes." He pointed to Katherine. "And you're fucking with her happiness. That ends now."

I blinked, my eyes burning from watching the scene in awe.

Jax reminded me of my father in demeanor. Controlled and smooth. My dad always knew the score when he walked into a room, he was always prepared, and he didn't hesitate.

When my mother didn't budge, Jax held his phone out in front of her.

"You do not want this video leaving this table. Did you know that the state can press charges even if I don't?"

Her lips pursed in anger, and she looked from side to side as if there was a way out somewhere. But she knew better. She picked up the pen and signed where the tabs indicated.

"And here." Jax turned the page, pointing.

"And here," he said, flipping another page.

In all of two seconds, he'd snatched the pen back, folded the paperwork, and stood up.

He looked to Jason. "The check?"

I looked at Jason and almost laughed when he actually shook his head for about a second as if to figure out if that had really just happened.

Taking an envelope out of the inside of his jacket, he handed it to Jax.

Jax handed what I would assume was her settlement money to my mom and smiled his bright, white smile. "Congrats. You're divorced." And looking back at Jason. "Now, the house?"

Jason tossed him more papers to which Jax threw the folded bit across the table to us.

"Homeowners." He nodded. "Is everyone happy?"

Madoc and I opened up the packet, and I covered my mouth with my hand, seeing that it was the deed to the house.

In our names.

"Jax," I barely whispered, my throat too tight.

"What about the video?" My mother was more scared than I'd ever seen her. She was practically shaking as she looked up at him.

He leaned down into her face, speaking to her like she was a child. "Your only concern right now is never pissing me off again. You behave, and so will I."

He took the payoff check off the table, shoved it into her chest, and stood up. "Leave."

Clutching the envelope, she didn't even look back at me as she walked out of the ballroom. I felt Madoc squeeze my left hand, and my father took my right.

*My husband.*

*My home.*

And I looked around the table . . . *my family.*

My chest shook with silent hysterical laughter.

"This is so surreal." Jason wiped his hand over his face as the waiters started clearing the bowls. "I'm not sure how I should feel about all of this," he mumbled as he stood back up and held out his hand. "Jaxon, thank you. I don't know what to . . ."

Jax swung and clocked Madoc's dad right across the jaw, sending him reeling to the ground as everyone straightened in their chair and Katherine yelped.

Silverware clattered and all conversation in the room stopped. Everyone that hadn't realized what was happening at our table saw us now.

Jason lay on his back, head up off the ground and holding his jaw.

"Jaxon!" Katherine screeched, jumping out of her chair along with Jared and Madoc.

Jax stood by her side, looking down on Madoc's dad. "You should've married her years ago," he scolded.

He gave Katherine a peck on the cheek and turned, walking away.

Jared, Tate, Madoc, and I took no time leaving the table and running after him. Katherine was getting Jason seated back at the table, and the room was still filled with broken conversation.

"Jax, stop!" Jared yelled.

He pulled to a stop in the foyer, turning around to face us. But I wasn't going to let Jared yell at him.

"Jax, thank you." I stepped in. "You shouldn't have put yourself in that situation for us." I held the deed with both hands to my chest.

"Don't sweat it." He stuck his hands in his pockets, looking very much like the boy I knew and not the threatening presence he had proven himself to be.

I shook my head, tears welling. "I would never want you to . . ."

"It's fine, Fallon," he cut me off. "You're happy, Katherine is happy, and that makes me happy." He took a deep breath and slapped Madoc on the arm. "See you tomorrow night for the race."

I saw him jerk his chin at Jared, and he and Tate followed Jax out of the room.

Madoc wrapped his big arms around me, and I looked up him through blurry eyes.

"We're free," I whispered.

He took my ass in his hands and lifted me off the ground, slipping his tongue past my lips and kissing me so hard that I had to hold on to his neck.

"No one stops us," he breathed huskily into my mouth.

*No one.*

A throat cleared, and I snapped my eyes open as Madoc set me back on the ground.

My father stood there, probably wishing he hadn't just seen that.

"I'm heading out," he told me.

Madoc let me go and cleared his throat. "I'll go check on my dad."

I smiled to myself and watched him walk away, giving my father and me some space.

I took my father in a hug, instantly cozy and reveling in the smell of leather and Ralph Lauren.

"I'm going to Shelburne Falls for the weekend, but I'll be back Monday. Will you be in Chicago?"

"Yes," he answered. "I'll call you for lunch. Both of you," he added.

I gave him a grateful smile as he started to walk away but then stopped. "Fallon?" He turned back around. "Who is that kid exactly?" He gestured to Jax talking to Jared and Tate just outside the doors.

"Jaxon Trent. He's Madoc's friend."

"What do you know about him?" he asked, still watching Jax.

*Not much, unfortunately.*

"Um, well, he lives with his half brother's mother. Dad's in jail, and his real mom split a long time ago. He's in his last year of high school. Why?"

He spoke low as if thinking out loud. "He's a very impressive young man."

# CHAPTER 33

# MADOC

"So what is the Loop exactly?" Fallon pulled her baseball cap down over her eyes and lay her head back on the headrest.

"Tate didn't tell you?"

"I know it's a race," she yawned. "But is it a real track or what?"

"You didn't have to come tonight. I know you're beat." I leaned over and rubbed her leg.

"I'm okay." She tried to sound peppy, even with her eyes closed.

She certainly hadn't had it easy this week. Aside from the nonstop fun last night of dealing with her mother, her father, and then Jax showing up, she'd gotten married this week and between studying and me keeping her up half the night, her body was crashing. Hard.

We hadn't gotten to bed until three this morning, and then we woke up early to look at an apartment before driving back to Shelburne Falls. When we got here, we started reorganizing my bedroom to make space for her and her things here.

Even though we liked Chicago, we loved it here more. This is where we'd raise our kids.

Not that I'd talked to her about that yet, but she was getting knocked up as soon as college was over.

She'd agree, of course. No one could say no to me.

"We're here," I announced, pulling to the end of the driveway that came up on the Loop. The rounded-square track split to the left and right ahead of us, and I turned off to the right, pulling off the side and backing into a space in the grass.

My blood rushed through my body like running rapids, filling me with energy so fast I felt high.

Damn, it felt good to be back here.

I wouldn't admit it to anyone, but I was a little apprehensive about the new crop of drivers coming in this school year. While college kids like Jared, Tate, and I came back once in a while, this was mostly a high school scene.

But getting out of the car, I already saw at least ten people I knew, so I was home. Jared and Tate were already in place up on the track and had a crowd of people around them, including K.C., who must've come back from her school in Arizona for the weekend.

Looking around, I also spotted her boyfriend, Liam, and some of Jared's and my friends that had stayed close to home as well this year.

Jax hung back, sitting on the hood of his car with his headphones on and staring into the crowd. He never raced. Although he came to the events, I got the impression that it bored him, even though I suggested that actually racing was a hell of a lot more fun than watching. He said he was working on something new for the Loop, but he wouldn't tell us what. Knowing him, I was afraid to ask.

Fallon climbed out of my GTO, and I took her hand, pulling her up onto the track. We made our way through the thick crowd, ignoring calls and congratulations on our marriage. I knew they were all laughing behind my back.

Madoc got married? *Yeah, right.*

I took a page from my father. Don't give them attention, and they won't give us attention. Only those close to Fallon and me understood, and we were not explaining ourselves to others. I'm sure most of them thought I'd gotten her pregnant.

"Hey, man," I greeted Jared, who turned away from Sam, grinning. He had Disturbed's "Inside the Fire" blasting out of his car stereo, and it felt like old times.

Fallon went and talked to Tate, who stood leaning against her car, talking to K.C.

"You're smiling," I observed flatly, eyeing Jared. "That's weird."

He stuck his hands into the front pocket of his black hoodie and shrugged. "Why wouldn't I be smiling? Even if I lose—which is a huge *if*—Tate will stop with her antics, and I can stop sleeping alone. It's her birthday tomorrow and our anniversary. I've got plans."

I laughed to myself, shaking my head. "I really wanted to see you ballroom dance." I narrowed my eyes, thinking. "In fact . . ."

I twisted my head to see Tate, Fallon, and K.C. chatting. "Tate!" I called. "Come here."

She shot me an annoyed look and walked over, followed by the other two.

"I'm riding shotgun," I told her.

"Whyyyy?" she drawled out.

"Just in case you need advice. I want you to win."

I grinned at Jared, seeing his quirked eyebrow.

"I have raced before," Tate said as if I thought she was inexperienced. Her hair danced in the light wind and kept blowing into her face.

I wrapped my arm around Fallon's waist and brought her into my side. "You haven't raced Jared," I pointed out to Tate. "I'm coming with you. That's the end of it. Will you come?" I looked to Fallon.

"Oh, no." Jared jumped in. "You take my chick, I'm taking

yours." He hooked the collar of Fallon's T-shirt and pulled her over to his side. "But not for help. She's a hostage."

"No way!" Fallon burst out. "Like I want to be killed or seriously injured in an illegal racing ring, protected by shady law enforcement and a crowd of drunk teenagers."

"Yeah." I brushed it off. "She'd be scared."

Her green eyes stung like bullets. "Bite me," she barked, folding her arms over her chest. "You're going down."

"Fallon!" Tate fumed. "You're my friend!"

"No worries." I looked down at Tate and took out my iPod from my coat pocket. "We've got MC Hammer," I bragged to Jared and Fallon, motioning between Tate and me. "You can't touch this."

Tate immediately lost it. She doubled over, holding her stomach and laughing her ass off at my play on MC Hammer's song. "You are not putting that shit in my stereo!" she choked out through her laughter.

"Oh, yeah," I threatened.

But just then, we all straightened up. Zack the Racemaster came up between the two racers—or teams—and cleared his throat.

Putting his hands around his mouth to form a circle, he bellowed into the night air, "Let. The. Games. Begin!"

Fallon and I smiled at each other.

*And let them never end.*


A crack of thunder exploded through the midnight sky, and I opened my eyes as it bellowed over the house. As it slowly traveled away, I blinked against the flashes of lightning coming through the window.

Flipping my head to the side, I saw Fallon still sleeping peacefully in her green T-shirt and panties. She'd kicked her side of the blankets off, and that was one thing I'd noticed we had in common. We both overheated when we slept.

There were lots of quirks about her that I'd found out, and I hoped mine didn't annoy her too much.

Her neck glowed with a thin layer of sweat, and her lips opened and closed barely enough to even notice. A slice of her stomach peeked out, and her innocent face looked absolutely beautiful.

Just looking at her, I felt myself harden with want. We'd already attacked each other after the race. In fact, Jared and Tate and Fallon and I all came straight here after the race, skipping the bonfire altogether. They went to their room, and we came to ours.

She'd slug me if I woke her up for sex, though. Not that I would. She was exhausted.

Taking a deep breath, I threw off my blankets and got out of bed, pulling on my pajama pants and leaving as quickly as possible. The harder I got, the more I didn't want to be honorable.

So I left.

I went down to the basement, rubbing my thumb across my fingers the entire way. It'd been months since I played, and I felt the hum in my hands. The cool keys under my fingertips.

Playing wasn't an obsession or something that I needed to do. I just appreciated having the skill to play, though. Everyone should have a way of expressing themselves, letting the stress out—even if it was just sexual frustration for me right now.

Pulling out the bench, I sat down at my family's completely restored 1921 Steinway grand piano and sifted through the music, picking a Dvořák piece.

Placing my fingers on the keys, I started playing the same notes I'd been practicing off and on for years. I didn't change up my music a lot, preferring to master a piece before I moved on to something else, but as I got more comfortable with the music, I'd find myself adding my own flavor. Speeding up, slowing down, softer, harder . . . A single composition can have so many meanings depending on the person playing.

I liked the freedom to explore and take risks.

The same could be said for Fallon's skateboarding. She enjoyed it but only so much as she was left alone to own it.

Cool skin touched my bare shoulders, and I straightened, taking my hands off the keys.

"Addie said you came down here to play at night." Fallon set her chin on top of my head. "Why don't you just have the piano moved upstairs?"

I reached up and took her hands. "It's something I would rather do alone."

"Oh," she said quietly. "I'm sorry." And she pulled away.

"No, I don't mean that." I turned around and yanked her back to me, pulling her into my lap. "I mean without my father around. I like to play. I just don't want to be forced."

She leaned back against me, straddling my legs and facing the keys. "It was a sad tune."

"The best music is," I said into her ear. "I'm happy, though."

She ran a delicate hand over the keys, leaning her head back on my shoulder. "I think we should do the dancing lessons with Jared and Tate. It would be fun." She inched up, kissing my jaw. "I still can't believe he lost."

My chest shook. "He threw that race. You know that, right?"

"He did not," she maintained. "Tate was awesome. And . . ."

I sunk my teeth into her neck, and she groaned, cutting off her own thought before it even got out. I sucked on her neck, my whole body twisting with need at the smell of her. Wrapping my arm around her stomach, I shifted my legs further apart. Since her thighs were outside of mine, she stretched wide. Keeping my mouth on her neck and my arm around her, I slipped my other hand inside of the front of her sleep shorts.

"Always ready for me," I breathed out, feeling how wet she was between her legs. I moved my mouth up the side of her face and over to her ear. The heat on my fingers shot right to my dick, and I circled her clit, feeling it get harder between my fingers.

She reached behind her and grabbed the back of my head. "After we get back from hiking tomorrow," she started, breathing hard, "we should come home and try to get this piano moved up to the main floor again. Maybe get some of your friends over here to help."

Was she seriously trying to talk to me about this now? We were taking Lucas hiking tomorrow, and I didn't feel like thinking about anything else but her right at this moment.

When I didn't stop kissing her to answer, she pleaded, "Please?"

My hand around her waist slid up into her shirt. "On one condition." I snatched her lips in short, devouring kisses. "Your half-pipe comes upstairs, too."

She started rolling her hips back onto me, and I closed my eyes with the wave that washed over me.

"I don't think Jason and Katherine will appreciate that thing in the living room." She sounded so weak. It was turning me on.

"Awesome," I joked. "Because it's not their living room. This is our house, remember?"

"Yeah, but they still live here."

She was right, of course. Nothing had changed in the living arrangements. Katherine was moving in after Jax graduated next spring. It was our house in name, though, so I didn't care.

She was still rubbing herself slowly over my cock, and I slipped my fingers inside of her.

"All right." She gave in. "Half-pipe comes, too. Everyone will love that," she added sarcastically.

I took my hand out of her shorts and lifted her shirt. "This would be so much more fun for me if you were topless," I said, pulling it over her head with no resistance.

Reaching over and grabbing the insides of her thighs, I pulled her ass into me and nudged her upper body forward to lean over the keys.

Bending down, I swiped her hair to the side and dragged my tongue up her back, breaking every once in a while to sink my teeth in softly and kiss her.

God, I loved her. There was never anything or anyone I wanted more, and she was mine. When we were fourteen years old she came into my life on the heels of a cruel and self-serving woman, but I would do it all again. Every minute. Every ounce of pain. I would go through it all again to get to her.

"Madoc?" she whispered, tilting her face to the side. "What does 'Fallen' mean? The tattoo on your back?"

*Questions.*

"It doesn't say 'Fallen.'" I kissed a trail up her back, but she pushed herself up and turned her face to look at me, tears in her eyes.

"Fallon?" She pinched her eyebrows together in understanding.

I took her face in my hand, kissing the corner of her mouth. "I got it a couple of years ago," I told her. "I never forgot you. I never stopped loving you."

Her eyes closed, and she reached her hand behind her to caress my cheek.

Then, looking at me again, she gave me a small smile. "That's because we're unstoppable."

I dived in and kissed her hard. *Damn right.*

Don't miss the next engrossing romance
from Penelope Douglas,

# Falling Away

**Available in January from New American Library.**

---

*K. C. Carter has always followed the rules—until this year, when a mistake leaves her the talk of her college campus and her carefully arranged life comes crashing to a halt. Now she's stuck in her small hometown for the summer to complete her court-ordered community service, and to make matters worse, trouble is living right next door.*

*Jaxon Trent is the worst kind of temptation and exactly what K.C. was supposed to stay away from in high school. But he never forgot her. She was the one girl who wouldn't give him the time of day and the only one to ever say no. Fate has brought K.C. back into his life— except what he thought was a great twist of luck turns out to be too close for comfort. As they grow closer, he discovers that convincing K.C. to get out from her mother's shadow is hard, but revealing the darkest parts of his soul is nearly impossible. . . .*

inched around slowly, watching as his long body stepped off the stairs and walked toward me. The dark washed jeans hung off his hips, and I got a damn clear look at the muscles framing his abs in a V. He had a swimmer's body, but I wasn't sure if he was actually a swimmer. From the way the top of his jeans barely hung just above his hairline, I guessed he wasn't wearing boxers . . . or anything under the jeans.

He came up to stand in front of me, hovering down since he was a good seven inches taller. "What are you doing here?" he accused.

I scowled at the air around him, before shooting my eyes to the ground.

"K.C.!" He shoved his hand in my face, snapping his fingers a few times. "Why are you roaming around in the dark alone?"

I finally looked up and had to hide the way my face felt on fire at the sight of his blue eyes. For someone so dark and wild, his eyes were so out of place but never seemed wrong. They were the color of a tropical sea. The color of the sky right before storm clouds rolled in. Tate called them azure. I called them Hell.

Crossing my arms over my chest, I took a deep breath. "Liam's too drunk to drive, all right?" I bit out. "He passed out in the car."

He looked down the street to where Liam's car sat and narrowed his eyes before scowling back down at me. "So why can't you drive him home?" he asked.

"I can't drive a clutch."

He closed his eyes and shook his head. Running his hand through his hair, he stopped and fisted it midstroke. "Your boyfriend is a fucking idiot," he muttered, and then dropped his hand, looking exasperated.

I rolled my eyes, not wanting to get into it. He and Liam had never gotten along. Mostly Jax's fault.

I tipped my chin up and kept my tone flat. "I knew Tate was staying with Jared tonight, and I didn't want to wake up her dad to let me in the house to crash. I need her to help me get Liam home and to let me in her house. Is she up?" I asked.

He shook his head, and I wasn't sure if that meant no or "You've got to be kidding me."

Digging in his jeans pocket, he pulled out keys. "I'll drive you home."

"No," I rushed. "My mom thinks I'm staying at Tate's tonight."

His eyes narrowed on me, and I felt judged. Yeah, I was lying to my mother to spend the night with my boyfriend. And, yes, I was eighteen years old and still not allowed the freedom of an adult. I couldn't stand the way the little shit was looking at me now.

Okay, so he wasn't little. But he was still slightly younger, so I embraced the privilege to be condescending.

"Don't move," he ordered, and then turned around, walking back to his house.

After less than a minute, he walked out of the house and started across the lawn to Tate's, jerking his chin at me to follow. I assumed he had a key, so I jogged up to his side as he climbed the porch steps.

"What about Liam?" I couldn't leave my boyfriend sleeping in his car all night. What if something happened to him? Or he got sick? And Tate's dad would have a fit if I tried to bring him inside.

He unlocked the front door—I wasn't sure if he had Tate's or Jared's keys—and stepped inside the darkened foyer, then turned the key and pulled it out. Turning to me, he waved his hand in a big show, inviting me in.

"I'll get Jared to follow me in his car while I drive dickwad home in his, okay?" He hooded his eyes, looking bored.

"Don't hurt him," I warned, crossing the threshold and walking past him.

"I won't, but he deserves it."

I swung back around to face him, arching a brow. "Oh, you think you're so much better, Jax?" I smiled.

His mouth instantly tightened. "I'd make damn sure any girlfriend of mine knew how to drive a manual, and I wouldn't have gotten so drunk that I couldn't keep her safe."

Why was I always trying to cut him up? Jax wasn't a bad guy after all. His behavior at school was certainly better than his brother's had been in the past. Jax was respectful to teachers and friendly to everyone.

Almost everyone.

I took a deep breath and straightened my shoulders, ready to swallow a mouthful of pride. "Thank you. Thank you for driving Liam home," I offered, handing him the keys. "But what about your"—I gestured with my hand, trying to find the right word—"your . . . dates?"

"They'll wait." He smirked.

I rolled my eyes. *Oooookay.*

Reaching up, I worked my messy bun loose, pulling my mahogany hair down around my shoulders. But then I shot my eyes back up when I noticed Jax approaching me.

His voice was low and strong, without even a hint of humor. "Unless you want me to get rid of them, K.C.," he suggested, stepping closer, his chest nearly brushing mine.

I shook my head, blowing off his flirtation. It's the same way I reacted last fall the first time I met him, and every time after that that he made a suggestive remark. It was my safe, patented response, because I couldn't allow myself to react any other way.

But this time he wasn't smiling or being cocky. His suggestion was clear. If I told him to send the girls away, I'd take their place. And as he reached out with a slow, soft finger and grazed my collarbone, I let time stop as I entertained the idea.

Jax's hot breath on my neck, my hair a tangled mess around my body, my clothes ripped apart on the floor as he bit my lips and made me sweat.

*Oh, Jesus.* I sucked in a breath and looked away, narrowing my eyes to get my damn head under control. *What the hell?*

But then Jax laughed and dropped his hand. Not a sympathetic laugh. Not a laugh that said he was just kidding. No, it was a laugh that told me I was the joke. "Don't worry, K.C." He smiled, looking down on me like I was pathetic. "I'm well aware you're too precious for me, okay?"

*Excuse me?*

"You know what?" I shot out, my face cracking. "I can't believe I'm saying this, but you actually make Jared look like a gentleman."

And the little shit grinned. "I love my brother, but he and I are nothing alike."

*Yeah, I know.* My heart didn't pound around Jared. The hair on my arms didn't stand on end around him, either. I wasn't conscious of where he was and what he was doing every second that we were in the same room together. Jax and Jared were very different.

"Tattoos," I muttered.

"What?"

*Shit!* Did I just say that out loud?

"Um . . ." I choked out, staring wide-eyed in front of me, which just happened to be at his bare chest. "Tattoos. Jared has them. You don't. How come?" I asked, finally looking up.

His eyebrows inched together, but he didn't look angry. It was more . . . befuddled.

Jared's back, shoulder, arm, and part of his torso were covered with tattoos. Even Jared and Jax's best friend, Madoc, had one. You would think with those influences, Jax would have gotten at least one by now, but he hadn't. His long, sculpted torso was unmarked.

I waited as he stared at me and then licked his lips. "I have lots of tattoos," he whispered, so quiet. "Too many."

I don't know what I saw in his eyes, but I knew I'd never seen it before. It could have been sadness or loss, or maybe it was fear. All I knew was that it wasn't the usual Jax.

Backing away, he wouldn't meet my eyes as he turned and left the house. He closed the door, locked it, and walked down the porch steps quietly.

Moments later, I heard Jared's Boss and Liam's Camaro fire up and speed down the dark street.

And an hour later, I was still lying awake in Tate's bed, running my finger over the spot he'd touched on my collarbone and wondering about the Jaxon Trent that I never got to know.

*Two years later . . .*

Shelburne Falls was an average-sized town in northern Illinois. Not too small but barely big enough to have its own mall. To the naked eye, it was picturesque. Sweet in its no-two-homes-are-alike originality and welcoming in its can-I-help-you-carry-your groceries-to-the-car kind of way.

Secrets were kept behind closed doors, of course, and there were always too many prying eyes. But skies were blue, leaves rustling in the wind sounded like a natural symphony, and kids still played outside rather than staying inside zoned out on video games all of the time.

I loved it here.

But I also hated who I was here. When I had left for college two years ago, I made a promise to spend every day trying to be better than I was. I was going to be an attentive girlfriend, a trustworthy friend, and a perfect daughter.

I rarely came home, choosing to spend last summer counseling at a summer camp in Oregon and visiting my roommate, Nik, at her home in San Diego. My mother got to brag about my busy lifestyle, and my old friends really didn't seem to miss me, so it all worked out.

Shelburne Falls wasn't a bad place. It was perfect actually. But I was less than perfect here, and I didn't want to come home until I could show all of them that I was stronger, tougher, and smarter.

Yeah, that shit blew up in my face.

Not only did I breeze into town much sooner than I wanted, but it was on the heels of a court order. *Awesome impression, K.C.*

My phone rang, and I blinked, sucking in a breath as I came out of my thoughts. Adjusting the covers, I sat up in bed and slid the screen on my pink iPhone.

"Tate, hi." I smiled. "You're up early."

"Sorry. Didn't mean to wake you." Her cheerful voice was a relief.

"You didn't." I swung my legs out of bed and stood up, stretching. "I was just getting up."

Tate had been my best friend all through high school. She still was, I guess. During senior year, I may have pissed her off a little. Okay, for sure I pissed her off. A lot. Ever since then, she's kept about two feet of personal space between us when I'm around, and I don't blame her. I messed up, and I hadn't manned up to ask for her forgiveness.

She'd rolled with it, though. I guess she figured that I needed her more than she needed me to say I was sorry.

All in all, I was positive of two things. She loved me. But she didn't trust me.

She was chewing something as she spoke, and I heard a refrigerator shut in the background. "I just wanted to make sure you got settled in okay and that you're comfortable."

I pulled my white cami back down over my stomach as I walked to the French doors. "Tate, thank you so much to you and your dad for letting me crash here. I feel like a burden."

"Are you kidding?" she burst out, her voice high-pitched in surprise. "You're always welcome, and you'll stay for as long as you need."

After I'd gotten in to Shelburne Falls last night—by plane and then by cab—I'd made quick work of unpacking all of my clothes in Tate's room, showering, and inventorying the cabinets for any food I might need. Turns out, I needed nothing. The cabinets and the refrigerator were crammed full of fresh food, which was weird, considering Tate's dad had been in Japan since May and would be there until fall.

"Thanks," I offered, dropping my head. I felt guilty at her generosity. "My mom may warm up as the summer progresses," I appeased.

"What's her problem?" Her honest question threw me.

*Oh, where to start?*

I let out a bitter laugh as I opened up her white French doors to let the fragrant summer breeze in. "My police record doesn't match her lily-white living room. That's her problem, Tate."

My mother lived only a few blocks away, so it was funny that she actually thought she'd escape gossip by not letting me stay at home while I completed my community service. Those Rotary Club bitches were going to be on her case either way.

That wasn't funny. I shouldn't laugh.

"Your *'police record'*," Tate mimicked. "I never thought I'd see the day."

"Don't tease me, please."

"I'm not," she assured me. "I'm proud of you."

*Huh?*

"Not for breaking the law," she was quick to add. "But for standing up for yourself. Everyone knows I'd probably have a police record if not for Jared and Madoc tossing their weight around. You make mistakes like everyone else. Deal with it."

I stayed quiet, knowing she was trying to make me feel better. But then I shook my head as I inhaled the clean morning air. Everyone may make mistakes, but not everyone gets arrested.

I could do better. A lot better. And I would.

Straightening my back, I held the phone with one hand and inspected the fingernails of the other.

"So when will you be home?" I asked.

"Not for a few weeks. Madoc and Fallon left for a vacation yesterday to Mexico, and Jared's at Commando Camp until July first. I'm going to visit my father next week, but for now, I'm taking the opportunity while Jared is away to pretty up the apartment."

"Ah," I mused, staring absently through the trees to the house next door. "Here come the scented candles and throw pillows," I teased.

"Don't forget the frilly toilet seat covers and accent lamps."

We laughed, but I was forcing mine. I didn't like hearing about their lives, which I hadn't been a part of. Jared and Tate were going to college and living together in Chicago. He was in ROTC or something and was off on a monthlong training session in Florida. His best friend, Madoc—a fellow classmate of mine from high school—was married already and going to college in Chicago with Jared, Tate, and his wife, Fallon, whom I'd met once.

They were all some sort of little gang that I wasn't a part of anymore, and suddenly a weight settled on my heart. I missed my friends.

"Anyway," she continued, "everyone will be home before the Fourth of July. We're thinking of a camping trip, so do yourself a favor. Get ready. Be wild. Don't shower today. Wear a mismatched bra and panty set. Go get a hot bikini. Be. Wild. Got it?"

*Hot bikini. Camping. Tate, Fallon, Jared, and Madoc and their wild ways. Two couples and me the fifth wheel.*

*Riiiiight.*

I looked across at the darkened house next door, where Tate's boyfriend had once lived. His brother, Jax, used to live there, too, and I resisted the urge the ask Tate about him.

*Wild.*

I shook my head, tears pooling in my eyes and teeth cementing together.

*Tate. Jared. Fallon. Madoc.*

*All wild.*

*Jaxon Trent. Wild.*

The silent tears dropped, but I stayed quiet.

"K.C.?" Tate prompted when I said nothing. "The world has plans for you, whether you're ready or not. You can either be a driver or a passenger. Now, get yourself a hot bikini for the camping trip. Got it?"

I swallowed the Brillo Pad lodged in my throat and nodded. "Got it."

"Now, go open the top drawer of my dresser. I left two presents in there when I was home this past weekend."

My eyebrows pinched together as I walked. "You were just home?"

I wished I hadn't missed her. We hadn't seen each other in about a year and a half.

"Well, I wanted to make sure it was clean," she answered as I headed to the opposite wall to her dresser, "and that you had food. I'm sorry I couldn't stay to greet you, though."

Yanking open the drawer, I immediately froze. My breathing halted, and my eyes went round.

"Tate?" My voice squeaked like a mouse's.

"You like?" she taunted, the smirk on her face evident through the phone.

I reached in with a shaky hand and took out the purple "Jack Rabbit" vibrator still in its clear plastic packaging.

*Oh, my God.*

"It's huge!" I burst out, dropping both the phone and the vibrator. "Shit!"

Scrambling, I snatched the phone off the rug and hugged myself as I laughed. "You're crazy. You know that?"

The delighted sound of her laughter filled my ears, and I had gone from tears to laughter in no time.

There was a time when I was more experienced than Tate. Who knew she'd be buying me my first vibrator?

"I have one just like it," she told me. "It's getting me through Jared's absence. And the iPod has angry rock music," she pointed out.

*Oh, that's right.* I peered into the drawer again, seeing the iTouch already opened with earbuds wrapped around it. She must've already loaded music onto it.

"It will help you forget that asshole." She was talking about Liam, and I realized that I'd barely thought of my skeezer ex-boyfriend.

"Maybe it will help me forget K. C. Carter," I teased.

Bending down, I picked up the vibrator and kind of started to wonder what kind of batteries it took. "Thank you, Tate." I hoped my voice sounded genuine. "If nothing else, I already feel better."

"Use them both," she ordered. "Today. Also, use the word motherfucker at some point. You'll feel a lot better. Trust me."

And then she hung up without a good-bye.

I stared at the phone, confusion shredding my smile.

I've said motherfucker. Just never out loud.

PENELOPE DOUGLAS is the author of the *New York Times* bestsellers *Bully* and *Until You*. Born in Dubuque, Iowa, she earned a bachelor's degree in public administration and then a master's of education at Loyola University in New Orleans before becoming a teacher. She now writes full-time and lives in Las Vegas with her husband and their daughter.

---

CONNECT ONLINE

---

penelopedouglasauthor.com
facebook.com/penelopedouglasauthor
twitter.com/pendouglas